THE FIGHTING UNDERHILLS

The moon sailed behind another cloud. A rifle fired out in the darkness where Durham had run.

Bush felt his stomach rise toward his throat. An overwhelming fear took hold of him: Durham was shot! But then another rifle blasted and he recognized the report of it, for he knew well the rifles he'd made for his sons.

"Durham!" Bush yelled.

"I'm all right, Pap!" Durham called back, running into view again with the muzzle of his rifle smoking. "I think I killed him."

"That was my brother!" yelled the hostage guarded by Cordell, and he grabbed Cordell's rifle by the muzzle. Cordell held on. He staggered back three steps and fell, his rifle discharging and sending a ball hurtling into the sky.

Bush fired just as the moon disappeared again. Cordell's attacker screeched, let go of the rifle, and fell writhing in the dark.

The moon found another hole, sending through light that revealed the man was writhing no more . . .

TEXAS FREEDOM

CAMERON JUDD

St. Martin's Paperbacks

TEXAS FREEDOM

Copyright © 1998 by Cameron Judd.

ISBN: 0-312-96809-4

Printed in the United States of America

St. Martin's Paperbacks edition / December 1998

10 9 8 7 6 5 4 3 2 1

In memory of Roy Rogers

CHAPTER ONE

Femme Osage Creek, Missouri, the waning days of summer, 1837

With a resounding *thump* the ax handle struck its target, raising a great billow of dust that hung in the air a moment before dispersing in the wind. The ax handle sliced air again and again, administering the severest of beatings and choking the atmosphere with free-floating grit.

Lorraine Underhill paused, letting the air clear, and decided it just hadn't been worth it, all those long hours spent weaving this rug by hand from every scrap and tatter she could find. She'd never seen a rug so prone to draw dirt. She almost missed the days of dirt-floored cabins, when a domestic woman, out of necessity, lived at peace with the soil rather than waging a vain war against it.

She resumed her pounding, walloping the rug with vigor. When, almost ten minutes later, she'd convinced it to surrender the last of its dust, she paused to rest, leaning on the ax handle like a cane. A flicker of movement drew her attention toward the road, where a rider approached. Brushing a strand of graying hair from her brow, Lorry Underhill studied the newcomer. Her eyes widened with surprise as she recognized him, for this was the last fellow she would have expected to come calling. Man and beast passed slowly through the gate of the split-rail fence and stopped a few yards from her.

"Mizz Lorry, ma'am."

"Hello, Cantrell Smith."

"Good to see you, ma'am." Cantrell smiled tightly and

removed his hat, revealing a head nearly devoid of hair. Lorry had warned Cantrell many times that wearing a hat every waking hour would make him go bald faster. He should have listened.

She shielded her eyes from the sun with an uplifted hand. "Thought you was in Texas. With John."

"I was, ma'am." Cantrell scanned the yard and the fields beyond. "Is Mr. Bushrod home?"

"Hunting, with Durham. Be back by evening."

"Oh."

"You're bearing news." It was a statement, not a question.

Cantrell scratched his chin and looked uncomfortable. Lorry had always intimidated Cantrell, though she didn't try. Long decades on the Missouri frontier, raising children and burying others, had made her direct and forceful. Timid folks often found it hard to hold her gaze. "I do have news, yes."

"It's about John."

"Ma'am, I surely wish Mr. Bushrod was here. I'd rather tell both of you together."

"Cantrell Smith, you have news of my boy, good or bad, then you tell me now."

"Yes, ma'am." He turned his hat in his hands. "Could we maybe go inside? I'm parched from the ride and would 'preciate a sip from your drinking bucket."

"I'll have Sam put your horse in the stable. Cantrell . . . is John dead?"

"No, ma'am. I don't believe he is, anyway."

Lorry put her hands on her hips, drew in a deep breath, and let it out slowly, her eyes sweeping the broad land around her. "That's good, then. Come inside, Cantrell. I'll hear what you have to say."

Years spent in the wilderness had developed Bushrod Underhill a powerful intuition. Thus, as he and his son Durham rode back into their wide dirt yard with a field-dressed deer lashed over the back of a packhorse, he knew that rain would come before the next morning, and also that something noteworthy had transpired here in his absence.

Lorry came to the door as her husband dismounted, and looked at him silently.

"Put away the horses, Durham," Bush said to the thin, quiet young man with him. "Get one of your brothers to help you with the deer."

He walked up to his wife on the porch. "What's happened?"

"Cantrell Smith is in from Texas, Bush, with ill news of John and his family."

Bush stiffened. "Comanche?"

"It doesn't appear so," she said. "Come inside. I've got your supper waiting, and Cantrell can talk whenever you're ready to hear."

"I'll hear now. Supper can wait."

The rocking chair creaked softly beneath Bush's light but powerful frame. Though silver-haired, he was lean as a youth, with the looks and bearing of a man more than twenty years younger. Bush's craggy profile, limned against the light of the fire billowing smoke up the huge chimney, might have been chiseled from the stony side of a mountain. He said nothing during the ten minutes it had taken Cantrell Smith to relate his story, nor for several minutes thereafter. The entire household, gathered in the wide room of the big log house that Bushrod and his sons had built with their own hands, held its peace while Bush rocked in silence. They'd learned not to interrupt Bush's thoughts.

Finally the Missouri frontier veteran spoke. "Why do you believe it wasn't Comanche?"

"There'd been no sign of them in that area, none of the usual redskin indications at John's place. Or so they told me."

"So then why would an entire family just disappear?"

"That's the mystery, sir."

"Comanche or not, was there anything at the house showing there might have been a fight?"

"I couldn't tell you, Mr. Bushrod. I ain't been there since they went missing."

Bush bit back sharp words. He'd have thought that someone who would journey all the way from Texas to tell a man his son and his family had inexplicably vanished would have gathered all the relevant facts he could. But Cantrell, good-hearted young man that he was, and virtually a part of the Underhill family because of his lifelong friendship with their eldest son, John Underhill, had never been particularly shrewd or thorough. The time Cantrell had traveled ten miles to hunt, only to realize once he got there that he'd forgotten all his ammunition, had become a standing private joke among the Underhills. Bush was finding nothing to laugh at this time.

"I've feared something bad would come of John going to Texas," Lorry said. "It's dreadful, all that warring and fighting that's gone on there, John right in the heart of it."

"He's made quite a proud name for himself there, ma'am," Cantrell said. "He was one of the bravest to fight at San Jacinto, and Sam Houston himself lauds him as the finest of Texians. There'd been talk that John might get a post in the government."

"I heard about San Jacinto," Lorry said. "As much a massacre as a battle, they say."

"John took no part in the massacring," Cantrell replied. "He did his best to stop the worst of it, and it would have been bloodier if he hadn't. Still, it was the baddest kind of slaughter." He paused. "That's one of the reasons I left Texas. Every night when I close my eyes, I see them Mexicans being pounded to death with rifle butts, begging for their lives."

"No need to go into all that," Lorry said, glancing at her wide-eyed younger children.

"I'd have liked to seen that fight," Sam Underhill said. He was a sandy-haired, bright-eyed fellow in his early twenties, with his father's build, his mother's intensity and good looks, and a restless, caged-panther disposition all his own. He held the heart of every Missouri girl within fifty square miles, knew it, and relished the knowledge. "That's the way a battle ought to be . . . short and fierce, and with the right side winning."

"None should speak of what battles ought to be except

them who've fought them," Cantrell said very softly. Bush Underhill was surprised to hear something so deep and sensible spoken by a young man who'd always seemed as shallow as a drought-stricken pond.

Marian, fifth-born of the Underhill children and still single at the age of twenty, whispered, "Poor John," bowed her head and began to cry without sound. The younger ones watched her nervously, not fully understanding what was going on.

Bushrod went to the mantel. A pipe and tobacco pouch lay beside the framed silhouette of Sariah Underhill, the daughter Lorry already had when she married Bush. Sariah was herself married now, living far away in Virginia, much missed by Lorry and Bushrod, but happy and doing quite well for herself. Bush fetched down the pipe and tobacco, filled the bowl, lit up the packed leaf. Puffing, staring down at the crackling, burning logs in the fire, he said, "I'll be going to find John."

"Indeed," Lorry whispered.

Sam came to his feet. "I'll go with you, Pap."

Durham, in his softer voice, said, "Me, too."

Bush looked at both of them but answered neither, speaking to his wife instead. "I'm going over to see Cordell." Cordell, the second-born son, lived in a cabin of his own about a mile from the Underhill homeplace, on family property.

"You ain't just taking Cordell, are you, Pap?" Sam said loudly. "I can be of as much help to you as Cordell!"

"Son, sit down and fasten your mouth shut. There'll be a lot of thinking and talking between your mother and me before anything's decided on who goes. Until then, I'll hear no more about it."

Sam plopped back into his chair, glowering, then got up swiftly and headed outside, muttering inaudibly. His mother sadly watched him go, then picked up some sewing she'd laid aside earlier and went to work on it, her long fingers as nimble as a girl's.

"Is John dead?" asked Sally, one of the youngest children.

"He's not dead," Lorry said firmly. "Your father will find him."

Bush looked at Cantrell through the smoke of his pipe. "Will you come guide us, Cantrell?"

Cantrell suddenly found something terribly fascinating about his boottops. "My folks are getting old, Mr. Bushrod, and I figure, you know, maybe I ought to stay with them."

"I see." Bush knew Cantrell was making excuses. His parents were both hale, a long way from the grave. The horror of warfare and the disappearance of John, upon whom Cantrell had always seemed to depend for strength, had stripped his spirit.

"You got land down there, Cantrell?"

"I sold it. I'll give the money to my folks."

Bush nodded and puffed. It was probably just as well that Cantrell wouldn't go with them. He might make a good guide, but could be a liability if trouble came. Just as Sam lacked maturity, Cantrell Smith lacked backbone.

"Cantrell, I'll need you to write out what you can to guide us, and scribe a map and such." Bush knocked the ashes from his pipe into the fireplace. "Lorry, I'll be having that supper now. Then I'll go fetch Cordell. After that, Cantrell, we'll do some more talking, you, me, and Cordell."

Bush had always been early to bed, but this night the tall clock in the corner had chimed midnight before he finally crawled beneath the covers beside Lorry, who was not asleep, but sitting upright against feather pillows, awaiting him.

"Did you learn all you need to know from Cantrell?"

Bush settled into the hollowed mattress. "Believe so."

"Who'll be going with you?"

"Cordell, of course. And Sam, I think."

"You think Sam's got the common sense to go?"

"I think you can't temper metal without heat. So we'll put some heat on him and see if we can temper him. It's time he faced a challenge or two. Besides . . . he's the best shot of all the boys."

"You think there'll be shooting?"

"Why, no. I doubt it. But we have to be ready, you know, just in case." He paused. "I've got a mind to take Durham, too."

"I don't want Durham to go, Bush."

He'd expected this, and responded with words mentally rehearsed before he'd come to bed. "Durham's a good boy, a fine hunter. Got the makings of the kind of man who could take to the mountains alone for years and not miss the company of humans. Reminds me in them ways of old Boone." The reference was to Daniel Boone, who'd lived as a neighbor to the Underhills until his death in 1820. He and Bushrod had enjoyed many a long conversation and several short-range hunts during the famed old trailblazer's last years. "Durham's coolheaded, and might be a good balance for Sam."

"Not Durham, Bush. You mustn't take him."

Bush sighed slowly. Durham had always been Lorry's pet among all the sons, though she vehemently denied any favoritism.

"Very well, then. For your sake, Lorry, I'll leave him with you."

"When will you go?"

"We'll spend tomorrow preparing, and leave the next day."

"I fear for you in Texas."

"No need to. The revolution's over down there, Lorry. Texas is a big and growing place. The best frontier a man can find. Land, opportunity . . . you've heard me talk about it before. John was wise to go there."

"Wise . . . and now he's gone."

"We don't know he's gone. A lot of things could have happened."

"How many things could make a whole family vanish like ghosts? John wouldn't just take his family away somewhere with no one knowing."

Bush stared into the dark corner of the room, one of three bedrooms in the big house, and the smallest. The other two took up the entire second floor, actually just a single great chamber split down the middle by a wall, dividing sons from daughters. "Whatever's happened, Lorry, we'll set things right."

"When you find John, you bring him home. Him and all his family."

"Home? Back here?"

"Yes."

"Lorry, I can't do that. Not unless that's what they want. And they won't. Texas is the finest place you could find for a young family to be. You know that a man can go down there and get land for the cost of signing his name? There's a board of commissioners hands you a certificate, and you go out and find your land in the public domain, survey and register it, and you get your title. A hardworking man, married or single, can go to Texas and—"

"I know, Bush. You've told me often enough."

So he had. Bush had envied John when he set out for Texas, and Lorry knew it. Despite his years, Bush was still young in spirit and health. Age was a consideration that never came to mind when he thought about himself; he planned his future like he was a man of twenty.

He leaned over and kissed his wife. "I love you, Lorry. Lord knows I've never had so fine a treasure."

"Just find my son and his family for me, Bush, and keep all my boys safe, no matter what happens. Keep them safe, and keep them alive."

"I'll do my best."

"You promise me?"

How could she ask him that? He couldn't divine the future, or know what tragedies might have already transpired, as yet undiscovered. But neither could he deny Lorry anything she asked of him, and after a pause, he said, "I promise."

CHAPTER
TWO

Marie Underhill was Marie Paschall now, having married
Caleb Paschall in 1814. Time had treated her well, allowing
her to keep her looks as the years rolled by. She was an
elegant woman and still considered one of the greatest beau-
ties on the Femme Osage. But each time Bush saw his only
sister, for a few moments he would perceive not the woman,
wife, and mother she was now, but either the child she had
been in their days together as young white orphans raised
among the Chickamaugas, or as the shattered young beauty
of her young adulthood, when she'd been abused and scarred
by her ordeals as a captive of human vermin named Morgan.
Bush had spent many years of his youth searching for his lost
sister, and had regained her at last in an episode of death and
violence that still replayed itself often in his dreams.[1]

She welcomed him at the door of the beautiful stone house
her husband had built for her, and in which she had raised a
houseful of children who'd grown up alongside Bush's own
brood. He swept off his hat and entered, then stopped cold,
staring at something that lay on a small table just inside the
door.

Sighing, Bush picked it up and shook his head. What he
held was a book. The title was printed on the cover in large,
ornate type: *The Adventures of Bushrod Underhill, Frontier*

[1] *The Glory River*, Book 1 in the Underhill Series

Scout and Indian Fighter. Beneath was the author's name, F. Wickham Crabb.

"Marie, don't tell me you've been reading this bilge again!"

"Bush, I know you despise that book, and I know half of what's in it is either false or twisted . . . but I can't help but enjoy it."

Bush grunted and tossed the book back down. "Blasted book makes me look a puffed-up fool. Every time I lay eyes on it, shame hugs me, as Cephas Frank used to say, like my very own granny."

"Oh, Bushrod, the book isn't that bad! People are smart enough to tell when something's exaggerated. They expect it in books of that sort."

"Not that bad? My eyes, Marie! How can you say that? I should never have talked to that inkslinger," Bush said. "The least he could have done was to let me look over what he wrote before he printed it. The tall tales aren't the worst of it. It's the way he shows me to be an Indian fighter. I'd never have let him portray me as someone who found it a pleasure to shoot 'heathen savages,' as he's always calling them. Hang it, Marie, you and me were *raised* among what he considers 'heathen savages'! How could I hate them? One of the finest men I've ever known was old Tuckaseh—learned more good common sense from him than from any other man I've ever known! I never killed an Indian in all my life with any sense of pleasure. Old inkslinger Crabb uses my name to sell his book, and I get nothing for it but the embarrassment of all its lies and stretchers. I took every copy I had of the thing out to the smithy and took the fire and bellows to them."

Marie had heard this diatribe, almost word for word, several times before, and gave back an equally standard reply. "Well, like it or not, a book can't be unwritten, and you may as well learn to enjoy the attention it's brought you. Not to mention the business. You may not make money directly from the book, but you certainly have sold plenty of rifles because of it."

Bush couldn't dispute that point. Because of Crabb's lurid

volume, demand for the rifles he made in the stone-walled smithy behind his house had more than doubled, giving him a fine, steady income. Possessing an authentic Underhill rifle was the goal these days of more people than Bush could ever hope to satisfy.

"There's one thing in particular that makes it hard for me to see how you can bear to read that book at all, Marie," Bush said quietly. "The part involving you, and the Morgans, and all that you had to go through. I'm surprised you can bear to read it."

"It's odd, Bush . . . but somehow it helps."

"No! You mean that?"

"I do." She slapped on a tension-breaking smile. "But enough about that book. I could tell something was wrong the moment I saw you. Sit down and tell me about it."

Forgoing the fine overstuffed chairs Caleb Paschall had brought in from St. Louis, Bush settled himself on a three-legged stool in the corner of the front parlor. "It's John, down in Texas. He's disappeared, and his family, too. Cantrell Smith came back yesterday and told us about it."

"Disappeared?"

"Yes. Cantrell says he thinks John is still alive. In any case, it doesn't appear to be Comanches, which was my first worry."

"What will you do?"

"I'm going down to find out what happened to him, me and Cordell and Sam. Whatever's wrong, we'll set it right." Bush looked around. "Is Caleb home?"

"No. Gone to St. Louis again." Caleb Paschall, a successful dealer in horses and livestock, frequently visited St. Louis, the closest major center of shipping.

"I wish things had timed out a little different," Bush said. "We'd have gone with him, so we could pick up passage there on a downriver steamer."

"How will you find John once you reach Texas? It's a vast place."

"I've got John's letters to his mother, which tell a lot about where he settled, along with maps and such Cantrell Smith helped me draw up last night. John's house is within spitting distance of a little village called San Pablo, on the Brazos River. Besides, John's well-known in Texas since the revolution there, so that ought to make the search easier. I'm hoping we'll get there and find that Cantrell is just plain wrong, somehow, and John and his family are safe and sound.''

"I hate to harken back to that book again, Bushrod, but one thing I think you will find on the way is that John isn't the only one who's well-known. You're a very famous man the country over.''

"That's bilge, bilge.''

"No it's not. You spend all your time running with one little gang of hunting friends and horse traders, or tucked away from the world in your gunsmithy, so you don't realize how far your reputation has spread. I hear it from Caleb all the time, and he travels about more than any of us. I'm not exaggerating, Bush. Thanks to that book you hate so badly, your name is up there with those of Crockett and Boone the nation over. You're the nation's living image of the American frontiersman, now that that Boone has died and Crockett was killed.''

"Somebody's got Caleb fooled. I'm not famous. That book might have stirred some interest in my rifles here in the region, but you get away from these environs, and you'll find nobody's heard the name Bushrod Underhill. Why, I bet old inkslinger Crabb didn't sell a hundred copies of that sorry book!''

"Bushrod, don't you know? *The Adventures of Bushrod Underhill* is one of the biggest-selling books in the nation.''

"What?''

"It's true. I vow it's true.''

Bush gazed blankly at his sister. No, he hadn't known it. "How could that be?'' he scoffed. "I'd have heard about it!''

"No, you wouldn't. You keep to yourself too much, Bush. And when you do leave your stomping grounds, it's only to go out to some distant wilderness, not where you can find out what's going on in the world of human beings! You're a famous man, Bush, and you'll find out just how famous once you head for Texas.''

"It's nonsense. I'm *not* famous, no matter what notions Caleb has been feeding you. All that's going to happen is that I'll take my sons, quietly head down to Texas and find John and kin safe and sound, mind my own business and nobody else's, and come home again when it's through. Meantime, I'll at least have gotten to quietly explore Texas a bit and visit with John a little. Lorry wants me to bring him home with me, but I know he'll not want to leave.''

Bush obviously wanted no further discussion of himself, so Marie followed his shifting of the subject. "They say Texas is a wonderful land," she said. "Full of opportunities. But I find it frightening. Too much war, too much danger. Nothing is certain down there. Has Mexico given up its claim?''

"No. And the Comanches, of course, raid and kill. It's an uncertain place, but even so, I admit it draws me.''

She smiled. "It's like you, Bush, to see the adventure in everything. I for one wouldn't want to live in such a danger-ous place.''

"Keep in mind that Missouri itself was a dangerous place in its day. But for what it's worth, Lorry looks on Texas like you do. I've hinted some about resettling us there, but she'll have none of it. She likes our life here.''

"You'd leave Missouri for good?''

It was a delicate moment. For years after Marie's rescue from the abusive Morgans, she had been a weak and fractured creature who had clung to Bush like a child. Even now, after all these years and after marriage, and as strong as she seemed on the surface, she still leaned heavily on her brother. Some-times only he could see the lingering pains and fears she masked from others with a veil of dignity and beauty.

Quietly he said, "I might go, yes.''

Something much like a wince, but not quite, whispered across her face. "I'd hate to think of you going so far away.''

"Well, I don't know that I really will, but if I did . . . my eyes, Marie! Maybe you should come, too, you and Caleb!''

Bush grinned broadly. "Good, rich land down there. Wonderful for grazing. Caleb could do well for himself in such a place. It'd be prime, all us moving to a new place together like that!"

Marie didn't want to talk about it. "When will you leave?"

"Tomorrow morning."

"Bush, I hope John's all right."

"So do I."

"And Bush . . . don't let anything happen to you down there. Be careful. For me."

"I will. Don't you worry. We're going down prepared for anything, but expecting to find nothing. We'll discover there's a good reason John was gone for a spell, and that all is well. Why, it'll turn out to be no more than a pleasure trip for me and the boys. Bet you anything!"

The parting the next morning was emotional despite everyone's best efforts to maintain a happy temperament. Only Sam seemed unaffected. He actually looked put-upon as his mother gave him a tearful farewell hug. Marie had come to see them off; she stood to the side, weeping.

Durham Underhill remained deliberately uninvolved. Bush knew the young man was longing to go with him and wished he could invite him to do so . . . but he was unwilling to break his promise to Lorry.

The departees carried weapons, ammunition, food, supplies. It was hardly different from their scores of long hunts up the Missouri, but this time they headed the opposite way, for St. Louis, from where they would begin the long descent downriver to Arkansas, and overland to Texas.

Apart from occasional bursts of chatter from Sam, talk was sparse. Ten miles out from home, when Cordell moved his horse up beside Bushrod's, he spoke for the first time since leaving home.

"Somebody coming behind us, Pap."

"I know. How far back now?"

"Maybe a mile. Who do you think?"

"Durham."

"Great day! Ma will have a fit. Will you send him back?"

"I expect I'll have to."

"I doubt he'll go easy. Durham can be stubborn when he wants."

Sam, whose mind had been wandering far ahead, halfway to Texas already, suddenly picked up on the conversation. "What's that you're saying?"

"Durham's come after us. Probably left without his mother knowing it."

"Well! You'll send his tucked-in little tail back home, I reckon?"

"You taking over as head of this family, Sam? You making my decisions for me?"

"But Durham can't come with us, Pap!" Sam insisted. "He ain't got the grit. What if this turns out to be something dangerous? He'd run all the way back home like a beat pup!"

"Since you're speaking so frankly, Sam, I'll do the same. The truth is, I had to give a lot more thought to bringing you than I did about Durham. Durham not being here is your mother's choice, not mine. Durham's got more gravel than either you or she think. And furthermore, he don't cock-strut like you do, which says a lot for him. The strutting rooster is the one that gets himself plucked."

Sam glowered. "So that's how you think of me, Pap?"

"Sam, there's more to being a man than spouting brag-words and pining for trouble you may not be as ready for as you think."

Cordell said, "Want to ride back and meet him, Pap?"

"No. We'll wait here. If it's Durham, he'll join us soon enough."

They brought out pipes and tobacco and sat waiting, smoking, Cordell chewing on a twig between puffs. Sam, angry at his father, smoked furiously, raising great, stinking smoke clouds. Before long, a rider appeared behind them and stopped. As expected, it was Durham, who looked very surprised to find them waiting for him.

"Come on in, Durham," Bush called. "Let's go ahead and deal with this now."

Durham rode in and dismounted. He faced his father nervously but squarely. Bush shook his head. "I suppose I ought to warp your butt like you was a child, son. Your ma doesn't know you're here, I feel sure."

"She does know, Pap. I told her I wanted to come, and she said 'Go on, then.' So here I am."

"You expect me to believe that?"

"It's true."

"Look me in the eye and say it again."

Durham did.

Bush looked disgusted. "Like I figured. Lying like a government agent to an Indian chief."

"Very well, Pap. You don't believe me, you can go back and ask her yourself."

Bush was of average height, but stretched himself and seemed quite tall indeed, somehow seeming to tower over Durham even though Durham matched him inch for inch.

"You'll take no such tone with me."

"I'm sorry, Pap. But a man has to defend himself."

Bush glared at him, but the expression softened. "Yes. A man does." He paused. "I'm sorry."

Sam grunted softly and turned away. "He's *sorry*!" he muttered to no one in particular. "If it was me who'd sassed off at him, he'd have took a hickory pole and—"

"Shut up, Sam," Bush said. "This is not your affair. Durham, I'm sorry I thought you lied to me. I'm just surprised that Lorry would change her mind so fast, that's all."

"I was surprised, too."

"What made her give in?"

"I talked to her. I told her how much I wanted to help find my brother—"

"Crybabied to her, too, most likely," Sam muttered, drawing a quick, cutting glance from his father.

"—and anyhow," Durham continued, "she let me come. Broke down and wept, but she let me come. Rushed me on, matter of fact, so I'd be sure to catch up with you."

Bush patted Durham on the shoulder. "I'm glad she did."

As they made camp that night farther down the river, Sam

privately approached Durham. "Fine story you told. But you ain't fooling me. I know good and well Ma would never let you come. You snuck out on her."

"Know pretty much everything, don't you, Sam? Just as smart as God Almighty, you are."

"I don't know everything, but I do know Ma. And I know you. And I know a liar when I smell one."

"You ought to be glad I came along. Maybe I'll save your life somewhere along the way."

"You? Save *me*?" Sam laughed until his eyes watered.

CHAPTER THREE

St. Louis had thrived since the days of Spanish governorship, when it had been a capital. Bush enjoyed watching his sons take in the impressive city, with its long waterfront lined with boats of all varieties, where both passengers and cargo were loaded and unloaded.

Bush watched the steamboats, some like huge, floating, decorated wedding cakes, white and clean and gingerbreaded, beautiful works of floating architecture. As a man of some means, Bush could afford passage on any of these finer craft, and voyage down the river in carpeted, decorated staterooms, enjoying the best food and entertainment in the company of the elite of a booming nation. But he was at heart a frontiersman, and such ostentation held little appeal for him. Though Sam pleaded for them to take passage on one of the fancy boats, Bush had less exalted travel plans.

The craft upon which the Underhills would voyage, a rough-and-ready packet called *The Pittsburg*, was captained by a profane riverman named Keith Bascomb, and lacked almost all the ornamentation of the bigger steamers. Bush and sons placed their horses among the livestock on the boat, arranged their baggage at a protected spot on the same deck, and settled in to make their journey, at a dollar a man per five hundred miles, as common deck passengers.

Sam was appalled. To him it was a travesty to have to make his first steamer voyage amid the stench of manure.

Before long, however, Sam found something to brighten his attitude. Among the other deck passengers was a family named Tauby who were headed, like the Underhills, for Arkansas and thence overland to Texas. One of the Taubys was a young woman, blond and pretty, with brown eyes featuring surely the longest lashes ever to grace a perfect female countenance. She caught Sam's eye speedily, and they were not far down the river before he had worked his way to her, chatting and charming like a veteran womanizer, but with discretion, for her family looked on.

Bush also watched, from across the deck, and wondered how Sam had acquired such a way with the ladies. Bush had been a handsome buck himself in his day—still was, Lorry often told him, as did the glances of other women—but he'd certainly never operated with Sam's skill. Sam was the envy of his brothers, though they'd never say so. Cordell was big and husky, rugged rather than handsome, but was plagued with a perception of himself—more misguided than he knew—as unappealing to women. He tended to protect himself from anticipated rejection by making few romantic forays. Durham, smaller-framed than Cordell, more like his father, was good-looking but also shy.

Durham and Cordell stayed close to their father on the boat, keeping their eyes on the horses, guarding the baggage, and enjoying the open, breezy world of the river as *The Pittsburg* churned along.

Bush had always loved the Mississippi, and in his younger days he had hunted and trapped up and down the river, sometimes alone, usually with partners such as long-gone Cephas Frank and Becker Israel, the latter of whom had died during the quest to rescue Marie from the Morgans. Those days had been far different. No steamers then, just keelboats and flatboats and rafts. Though Bush appreciated the advances in transportation and trade that steamboats had brought, he missed the old days sometimes. There was a glamour and romance about them, hazed now in his mind in a kind of gilded glory of memory, that had almost vanished from the river. The steamboats were more beautiful, and efficient, but

Bush preferred the quieter days before they had come. Not many years would go by before the last of his beloved keelboats and flatboats faded. Already such crude craft had become the domain mostly of poor dirt farmers out of the Ohio country, or the occasional migrating family who was on the run from debt and couldn't afford even the cheapest of the packets.

Bush leaned back against some of the baggage and tilted his hat over his eyes. His nap was soon interrupted by commotion elsewhere on the deck. Tilting up his hat, Bush saw Cordell heading in the direction of the Tauby family. Loud, coarse voices were shouting threats, accusations, protestations. With displeasure Bush recognized one of the voices as Sam's.

Durham said, "Pap, I believe Sam's found himself some trouble with the brother of that pretty girl."

"My eyes!" Bush muttered, rising. He trailed after Cordell in the direction of the conflict.

Sam was facing a husky, red-haired fellow almost the size of Cordell, certainly big enough to toss Sam bodily off the boat if he chose, and from the look of things, the thought had probably come to mind. Bush wondered what Sam had said or done to rouse such ire.

Cordell was already intervening by the time Bush reached the scene. "Here, now," Cordell was saying, "let's calm down, try to settle this peaceful."

"Go away, Cordell!" Sam bellowed. "This ain't your affair!"

Cordell ignored his brother and spoke to the red-haired fellow. "I don't know what he said, but I hope you'll excuse him. Sometimes Sam speaks without thinking."

"He insulted my sister!" the other replied.

Cordell turned to Sam, whose face was flushed bright red. "What did you say to her?"

"Nothing! I just told her how pretty she was."

"That *ain't* how he said it," the red-haired fellow interjected.

Bush stepped up. "What's going on here?"

"Who are you?" the red-haired man responded.

"Name's Bushrod Underhill. That fellow you're mad at it, and this one here"—he gestured at Cordell—"are my sons."

"You'd best teach your sons some manners around the ladies, then, Mister—" He stopped suddenly. "Underhill? Did you say *Bushrod* Underhill?"

"That's right." *My eyes!* Bush thought. *Maybe Marie was right about my fame. This stranger knows me!*

"I've heard of you, sir," the fellow said, his manner suddenly very different. "I read that book about you. What a great book it is, too!"

"Obliged, but I hope you don't believe every word you read, for there's more lies told in ink than is ever spoke aloud. Now, as for my son there—"

"You being who you are, sir, I'm sorry I've had words with him. But I don't appreciate what he said to my sister."

"He's sorry. Ain't you, Sam?"

"But Pap, I swear, I didn't say—"

"You're *sorry*. For whatever you said or even what he might have thought you said. Ain't that right?"

Sam's face twitched, then with a force of will he petulantly blurted, "Fine, then . . . I'm *sorry*."

"Good, son. Now get on back to where Durham is yonder."

As Sam, muttering furiously, stalked away, a hand touched Bush's shoulder. He turned quickly. A pepper-haired, middle-aged man looked back at him. "Sir, did I understand correctly who you are?"

Dutifully, Bush said, "I'm Bushrod Underhill, from off the Femme Osage in Missouri."

"Well! My name's George Tauby," the man said, putting out a hand for a shake. "I'm pleased to meet so famous a man. Jacob there, my son, has your book, and I read it. Quite a story!"

Bush shook Tauby's hand. "Thank you. But it ain't my book. A man named Crabb wrote it and put in some big stretchers. I was just telling Jacob here that I'm sorry for anything my Sam might have done wrong. Sam's a good boy, but with too much child left in him. I feel sure that he had no bad intent, just maybe some bad judgment.''

Tauby waved it off and drew in close for a whisper. "Jake there has a temper as fiery as his hair, and likely he misunderstood something. He's deaf in his left ear and don't always hear things right.''

Bush grinned. "Peace, then?''

"Of course. And in fact, I consider this a good thing in that it allowed me to meet you.'' Tauby pointed over at the young woman at the center of the controversy. "That's my daughter Jane. There's my wife, Mary, and other children standing yonder.''

Bush tipped his hat to the women, and to Jane Tauby said, "Miss, I am sorry about all this.''

"Sam did nothing wrong,'' Jane said. "It was Jake getting upset over nothing, that's all.''

"Hush, dear. Nobody's upset now,'' Tauby said. "Mr. Underhill, I've always wished to have the chance to make your acquaintance. I was briefly a neighbor of yours some years ago, though our paths never crossed. I lived no more than ten miles away from you for a year. I heard much about you, and saw many of the rifles you've made. Excellent weapons, sir. I often considered buying one for myself, but never got to it. No finer rifle is to be found, many tell me, than an Underhill rifle.''

"I'm flattered, sir. Sorry I didn't meet you until now.'' They shook hands again.

Tauby said, "Tell me, sir. You wouldn't be heading for Texas, as I am, would you?''

"I am.''

"Leaving Missouri behind, eh?''

"Not for good. Just some matters I need to see to down there before I return.''

"Oh. Well, *I'll* not be returning. I'm a Texian from here on out. I have a brother there already, doing very well for himself. He went down years before the revolution to take up land under an empresario named Trippler, though in the end, by hook or by crook, he wound up in the Austin colony.

Which is probably good, since I hear this Trippler has become a very controversial figure.''

Bush and Tauby talked for some time, engaging in general, friendly conversation about Texas. Bush found he liked Tauby, and envied him as he talked about his plans for land acquisition and settlement.

''Texas will become the center of the cattle trade on this continent, I'm convinced,'' Tauby said. ''I intend to gain as big a share of it as I can.''

''Good luck to you.''

''Have you kin in Texas already, Mr. Underhill?''

''A son, name of John. I'm going to Texas to look him up, as a matter of fact.'' Bush saw no reason to go into any further detail.

When finally he and Tauby parted, Bush talked privately to Durham. ''I hope this little trouble with Sam isn't a hint of things to come. You're younger than Sam is, but older at the same time. I worry sometimes what will become of that boy. One of these days that careless manner and temper of his will get him into a lot bigger mess than this. I'd surely hate to see him cut down before he had a chance to grow up and gain a little bit of sense.''

Before the day was through, Bush had made a grudging, unhappy concession to his sister. Marie had been right. He *was* far more famous than he'd known.

Because of the incident between Sam and the Tauby girl, word spread among the passengers about the identity of the quiet, silver-haired man among them. Bush found himself visited by an almost steady line of smiling admirers, including the captain of the vessel, many of them asking him to sign his name for them on scraps of paper. It astonished him that anyone would value the mere signature of any man, much less himself, but he was obliging, and signed again and again, all the while answering questions, trying to correct misunderstandings resulting from the Crabb book. He explained to a few people the reason for his journey to Texas, and received another surprise: John Underhill's name was quite well-

known, too, particularly among those passengers knowledge-
able about Texas. The word ''hero'' was tossed about quite
freely, applied to both Bush and John, and many best wishes
were extended for a successful, happy fulfillment of Bush's
search. People seemed honestly concerned for John Underhill's welfare, and if nothing else about all this attention sat
well with Bush, at least that part did. Most people, he decided,
were really quite nice folks.

Sam, over his bad humor by now, thought all this attention
very wonderful. ''Maybe someday I'll do something that will
make somebody write a book about *me,*'' he said. ''Then
folks will be coming to me to sign my name for them.''

''Son, if that should happen, I'll gladly leave you to it. All
I want is to be left alone. And to find John, safe and sound.''

CHAPTER FOUR

They had made their voyage so far with few difficulties—no bad weather, no unforeseen sandbars or other natural obstacles, no mechanical problems with the rather rickety boat—but Bush knew as he stood on the deck, looking at a gray and windswept sky, that their good fortune was about to end. The livestock on the deck paced restlessly, and in the forests on either side of the wide river, fowl screeched and flew from tree to bending tree as branches whipped in the rising breeze.

They were near the mouth of the Arkansas River, the anticipated end of the river voyage for the Underhills, but it appeared they wouldn't make it before the storm struck. As the afternoon darkened to nearly the blackness of night, and lightning began to zigzag through the western sky, Bush braced himself for a tempest the like of which he hadn't seen in a long time. It took him back, in memory, to another stormy day on this river, when he'd nearly lost his life in a knife-fight atop the roof of an out-of-control flatboat. Ironically, the storm itself, along with an unexpected sawyer and sandbar into which the flatboat had grinded, had swept him off and saved his life, though the river did its best to drown him first.

"Going to be a bad one," Cordell said, standing beside his father.

"Indeed, son."

Sam wasn't present, being off with the Taubys. He'd made

his peace with them—even developed a rapport with former antagonist Jacob Tauby—and had resumed his flirtations with Jane Tauby. But Bush was sure Sam would be far more cautious with his courting style from now on.

"Look at that!" Durham said in a tone of disgust—and maybe some jealousy, too, Bush thought. Durham was eyeing Sam, who stood close to the object of his affection, talking and gesturing animatedly. "He's probably telling her how there's nothing to worry about, how he's not afraid of storms or hail or lightning itself, how he'll take care of her. Probably telling her fifty big lies about all the adventures he's wishing he'd really had."

"Sam gets your goat mighty easy, Durham," Bush said, grinning.

The storm hit hard and swiftly. Heavy sheets of rain tore free of the clouds and deluged the river, slamming against the steamboat, hammering the countryside off across the water. The birds, taking to hiding places, fell into silence. The river seemed to boil where the huge raindrops hit it, and from where he stood, Bush heard the captain cursing, directing his crewmen, and no doubt worrying more than he'd want his passengers to know.

Terrifying as the storm was, Bush enjoyed watching it. He'd always enjoyed the wildness of storms, had stood out in the midst of many of them for the sheer joy of it, the danger of lightning strikes be hanged. And this storm was a beauty.

Searing lightning turned the dark afternoon a brilliant white time and again, making the horses nicker and stamp and cast about in their confines on the deck, while the cattle bunched together and watched the river sidewise with their big, dumb eyes, full of fear. Somewhere among the passengers, Bush heard children crying, and a woman praying in a nervous voice.

The Pittsburg rolled on, moving swiftly now as the current heightened and the river rose.

"It'll have to end soon," Durham said, huddling into a small human package. "No storm this fierce can go on for long."

But it did go on. An hour passed with unrelenting rain and
the lightning growing heavier. The thunder was like cannon
fire, as if the world all around were at war.

As the rain swept in hard, almost horizontally, when the
wind picked up, it began to soak Bush and his sons and slam
against their baggage. "Farther in, boys!" Bush said, and
they grabbed their possessions and hustled in for better shel-
ter.

Cordell, a lover of storms like his father, worked his way
around to the other side of the vessel for a better vantage
point to watch the spectacle. Soon, amid the floating trees and
other river trash, his eye caught sight of a flatboat racing
swiftly along, caught in the current and, it seemed to him, out
of the control of the men who desperately sought to guide it.
It was in mid-river, riding slightly ahead of *The Pittsburg,*
but seemingly edging ever closer to the faster-moving steamboat's line of travel.

With increasing alarm, Cordell watched the flatboat drifting
closer, closer . . .

"Oh, no. Oh, no."

Cordell pulled back from the railing and headed back to
where his father and brothers still huddled amid the baggage.
"Pap! There's a flatboat out there, moving right into the
course of—"

His words were cut off by a huge, rending crash that jolted
the boat like an explosion. The sound of splintering wood and
human screams carried through the howling storm. Among
the livestock there was sudden bedlam.

"What the devil!" Bush said, coming to his feet.

A voice yelled, "We've hit it! We've hit it!"

The steamboat veered to one side, too fast, tilting slightly
for a few moments, then resettling.

Bush and Cordell raced along the deck, heading up to see
what had happened, though Cordell already knew full well,
and was mentally berating himself for having come back to
his family rather than warning the captain—though he
couldn't imagine why the captain and crew had failed to see
the flatboat themselves. Maybe they had, but had been unable

to turn the big sidewheeler packet quickly enough.

A wild general commotion engulfed the packet, tumult up in the pilot house, cries and screams from the passengers. "Oh, Lordy, we're going to die!" the praying woman yelled.

Bush leaned across the railing, and by the flash of a lightning sear saw the wreckage of the shattered flatboat in the water. Human forms bobbed around it, arms flailing, reaching for floating wreckage to keep them afloat in the turbulent water. Crewmen scrambled for ropes as passengers yelled encouragement.

"What can we do, Pap?" Cordell asked.

"Nothing, son. Try to stay out of the way. It appears they're already doing all they can for them. What in the devil would have made anyone try to steer a flatboat in the midst of a storm like this?"

"Pap, look!"

Bush looked in the direction his son was pointing, and in numb horror watched as a man who had been clinging to a piece of the shattered flatboat lost his grip and slid beneath the fast-moving water, vanishing. They waited breathlessly for him to reappear, but he did not.

"There's one gone," Cordell said in a tight voice.

Meanwhile, the ropes thrown over the rail were coming within reach of some of the victims, who were trying to swim or kick their way toward them—a manifestly difficult feat under the circumstances. One man at last was able to grab the end of a rope, and clung to it tightly, yelling and moaning and praying, while the crewmen began to pull him in.

Lightning burned across the sky, terribly close, illuminating the river, revealing at least a half-dozen other figures still trapped in the water.

"Pap, another rope there!" Cordell said, pointing to a coil of hemp that lay behind them. He went for it. With Bush clinging to the end, Cordell heaved the coil over into the water. It splashed down near a woman who was about to lose hold of a floating log and suffer the same fate as the unfortunate man who had already gone under.

"Grab hold, ma'am!" Bush shouted. "Hang on and we'll pull you in!"

She struggled to reach the rope, almost got it, then was pulled away by the current. Frustrated, Bush pulled the rope in and flung it once more, this time landing it almost upon her. She grabbed it with one hand but seemed afraid to unwrap her other arm from the log that held her afloat.

"Take hold with both hands!" Bush called. "Take hold and don't let go!"

She obeyed. Bush and Cordell pooled their strength and began to pull her in. It was difficult, the woman being large and sodden with water besides, but they strained and heaved, and slowly she began to rise. Another man joined them—George Tauby—and the work became easier. Up she came, swinging in the air, screeching and terrified.

"Hang on . . . all you have to do is hang on!" a passenger yelled at her.

They got her to the level of the deck. Cordell let go of the rope and grabbed her, pulling her up against the railing. "Hook your foot there . . . good! That's right! Now, up and over the rail . . ."

They pulled her across the railing and onto the deck, where she collapsed in the rain, sobbing and trembling. Bush knelt beside her. "You're safe now. You're safe." She didn't seem to hear him.

Bush turned his attention back to the river, tossing the rope to a man below.

Within ten minutes, all had been rescued who could be and the others were gone. The storm at last began to abate, rain declining, and a strange, eerie, late afternoon light began probing from beneath the lower edges of the drained clouds, bathing the river in a surreal glow.

The woman Bush and his companions had rescued was sitting up now, crying and clinging to another of the rescued ones, a big-framed man. Bush examined them. A rather odd pair, they were dressed, like all the others who had been pulled in, in heavy black clothing that covered them from head to toe. Quakerish in appearance, he thought. The man was quoting Scripture in the woman's ear.

The captain appeared, coming to the rescued and speaking softly and placatingly. No cursing now, Bush noted. The captain's face was gaunt with horror.

"How many?" the captain asked a crewman.

"We pulled aboard six," came the answer. "But there were others who didn't survive."

Bush said, "We saw one man go under. Can't vouch for any others."

The captain said, "Bring them to my quarters. We'll get them dried out, something hot in them . . . and then maybe we can find out why in devil's hell anyone would have been running a flatboat in the midst of a storm like this one!"

Two hours later, George Tauby paid a visit to the Underhills. He'd managed to pick up some facts about the flatboat victims.

"They're a band of religious folk," he said. "Call themselves Purificationists. Apparently they came out of a colony of their own kind in Kentucky. On a 'mission' to Texas, they say."

"They're missionaries, preaching folk?"

"I suppose."

"What's a Purificationist?" Durham asked.

"I don't know," Tauby replied. "They seem to be something like the Shaker sect, though not the same thing. Some sort of Protestant group. They'd brought that flatboat all the way down the Ohio and this far down the Mississippi. You'd think that after that much time on the water, they'd have known not to have such a flimsy craft out in the midst of a storm."

"So you'd think," Bush said. "How many did they lose?"

"Four. They've took down the names of all who were pulled in, and identifications for those who were drowned. None of the bodies have turned up yet—they'll probably find them days from now, washed up downriver. The captain's in quite a state. Blames himself, I suppose, though he's careful not to admit any fault.''

''I don't envy the captain,'' Bush said. ''It would be dreadful to have such a weight upon you.''

''How is the woman we pulled in faring?'' Cordell asked.

''Fine. None of them are bad hurt,'' Tauby replied. ''Let me think . . . four men and two females survived, I believe. Yes, that's right. The big woman, and a girl about my Jane's age—those were the only females of the six. All of them dressed the same—those heavy black clothes. Part of their religion, I guess.''

''You say they're Protestant?'' Durham asked. ''I thought you had to be Catholic to settle in Texas. My brother John had to declare himself Catholic to get his land grant.''

''That was in the days before the revolution, under Mexican rule,'' Tauby said. ''There's plenty who made themselves paper Catholics to get their land grants. I suppose I'd have done it myself, if it was required. Not fully honest, I admit, but a man does what he must to get what he needs. My family has always been Methodist, but my brother went Catholic long enough to make the vow. None of that matters now; Texas is wide open to anyone.''

Sam asked, ''That young woman who was pulled in, Mr. Tauby . . . what's she look like?''

Bush rolled his eyes. ''My eyes, boy! Do you ever think of anything but the young ladies?''

''Only when I got to.''

Tauby laughed. ''I was the same way at your age, young fellow. But I can't answer you. The whole gaggle of them looked like drowned mice when I saw them, and those clothes of theirs do nothing for anyone's looks. But why do you care? Are you already weary of my Jane? Why, I was already trying to get used to the idea of calling you son-in-law.'' He winked at Bush.

Sam reddened and looked away. He hated a lot of things, and what he hated worst of all was being laughed at.

CHAPTER FIVE

The accident had damaged the boat's paddlewheel, so they laid up to shore that night. By morning light, the captain and crew examined the wheel. An announcement followed that the boat would be unable to travel farther without repairs, but as they had nearly reached the mouth of the Arkansas, those who had planned to disembark at that point should do so now, and proceed on by land. An adjustment of fare would be made for those who so chose.

The Underhills were among those accepting the offer, though they were slightly later in departing than some of the others. The Taubys would have left at the same time, but Tauby's wife, who had gotten cold and wet during the storm, had developed a quick fever and congestion of the lungs, an ailment to which she had been prone for years, according to her husband. Tauby thus elected to remain in the vicinity until his wife was better, and the Underhills said farewell. Sam was particularly loath to part from Jane Tauby, though he tried to hide it.

"Perhaps we'll meet again in Texas," Tauby said to Bush when the final handshake came. "I'd hoped we could travel there together. By the way, I hope you weren't anticipating a quiet and unbothered journey into Texas."

"As a matter of fact, I was."

"You'll probably not get it. A good score of passengers have already set off ahead of you, and some were saying they planned to spread word that Bushrod Underhill himself is coming into Texas."

"I doubt anyone would care."

Tauby laughed. "It's an attribute of greatness and fame, I suppose, that it doesn't always recognize itself. I'd say you'll find yourself welcomed all along the way, just like the late Colonel Crockett was when he came into Texas along pretty much this same route."

Even after all the attention he'd stirred on the steamer, Bush couldn't really believe anyone would much care that he was coming into Texas. But he played along rather than argue. "Well, maybe having folks know I'm coming in will help me find John quicker," Bush said. "Mr. Tauby, best wishes to you in Texas, and I'm sorry we can't travel with you." There was more politeness than truth in that statement. Bush was eager to break away from others and concentrate entirely on his own quest. From here out he wanted nothing to distract himself or his sons from the mission at hand . . . and for Sam, if no other, the continued company of Jane Tauby would have been a distraction indeed.

The Underhills began their inland journey without fanfare. Though they traveled with no other party, they were hardly alone, finding abundant sign of other travelers just ahead, and others following close after. After a day's travel, they made camp beside an Arkansas creek, and saw many fires flickering both ahead and behind. Texas was the greatest of lures these days, with newcomers arriving by the herd, and more always on their heels.

Bush finished his supper and eyed Sam as he filled his pipe. "You've been unusually quiet this day, son," he said.

"Nothing worth saying," Sam replied.

"He's pining for his deary," Cordell said.

"You shut up!" Sam barked.

"Well, it's true! You had yourself a fine romance going with pretty little Janey, and now you're away from her. Can't hardly bear it, can you!"

"I told you to shut up!"

"Let it go, Cordell," Bush said. "It's been nice to have

Sam quiet for once. No need to get him stirred up to jabber again.''

Sam rose, muttering angrily, and stalked away into the darkness. The others shared amused glances.

"I don't know why I like to torment him so," Cordell said.

"I can tell you," Durham replied. "It's because of his deuced attitude. He asks for it. And besides, it's just fun to watch him stomp off.''

Half an hour later, Sam returned, and not alone. Bush rose, surprised to be receiving a visitor at such a time and place, and surprised further to discover Sam's companion was the Purificationist man he'd seen comforting the rescued woman on the deck of the steamer.

Greetings were exchanged—the fellow was named Peter Gruenwald—and Sam pulled his father aside to privately explain how he'd managed to meet up with him.

"I was out there in the dark, just quiet and thinking, and all at once he came striding close by, headed toward our camp. We saw each other at the same moment and it like to have scared us both to death. Anyhow, he's come here because his camp has no food. I suppose they lost it all in the accident. He saw our fire and hoped we'd be willing to share.''

"I'm surprised that bunch has come so far this fast," Bush said. "I'd have thought they'd linger at the river, at least until their dead were found. And you mean to tell me they set off across country without food?''

"That's right. Guess they're in a hurry for some reason.''

Bush went to Gruenwald and talked a bit, making friendly chat, then said, "Bring in your people. We'll share what we have. I hope you don't mind plain trail fare.''

"Any food at all would be a godsend," Gruenwald replied. He had a stiff, rather cool manner even in his gratitude. "We'll not be wasteful of your hospitality. Enough to keep body and soul together is all we seek.''

Bush sent Durham and Cordell off with Gruenwald to fetch the rest of the Purificationist party. Cordell said, "Pap, we may not have enough food to last us if we have to share it with six folks."

"Son, a man shares what he has. That's a rule you don't break." He paused. "It's not the food I'm worried about. I'm more worried that we might have picked ourselves up some folks who'll want to be our travel companions all the way into Texas. I ain't looking for company. We've got our own row to hoe, and I don't want to be stuck hoeing somebody else's, too."

They built up the fire a little more, dug out more food, and waited for their guests to arrive.

Bush had met many odd people in his day, but these folks struck him as maybe the oddest of all.

They were a quiet bunch, somber. Obviously hungry, they ate voraciously, but kept Gruenwald's promise not to over-consume from the limited food supply. Bush in fact had to encourage them to eat more than they did, seeing that they were cutting themselves far too short. And though he really didn't wish for long-term company in his camp this evening, he did the polite thing and invited the Purificationists to join their camp with his for the night. They quickly accepted the offer.

Peter Gruenwald seemed to be the leader. The other two men of the group, William Niles and Charles Parring, maintained a stoic silence they broke only when directly asked a question, and even then they usually referred the question over to Gruenwald. The two females, Sheba Grover—the heavyset woman Bush, Cordell, and George Tauby had pulled out of the river—and the much younger and very pretty Chasida Gruenwald, Peter's daughter, were even quieter. The latter held the full attention of the Underhill sons nonetheless, particularly Sam and Durham. Though Bush thought these people strange, he liked one thing: they didn't seem to know who he was. Most likely lurid, violent books such as *The Adventures of Bushrod Underhill* were not common reading for radical religious types.

Peter Gruenwald revealed that Sheba Grover was his sister.

There was, however, no Mr. Grover present, nor a Mrs. Gruenwald. Bush asked if they had been among those lost in the accident. Gruenwald shook his head.

"Mrs. Gruenwald died many years ago, before my conversion, just as my sister lost her own husband before her own conversion," he said. "There will not be another Mrs. Gruenwald. Nor will Sheba ever marry again."

Bush replied, "I can understand. Were I to lose my own Lorry, I can't imagine finding another in her stead."

"That's not the issue in my case," Gruenwald said with a sudden puff of righteous pride. "It is part of our belief that man and woman, in this dispensation, should not marry or be given in marriage."

"No marriage?"

"That's correct."

"Well, surely you don't favor unfettered fornication."

"We favor no carnal relationships between the sexes at all."

"That's a Shaker notion, ain't it?" Cordell asked. He'd read some about the sect, which had originated in England the prior century as an offshoot of the Quakers, but which had come to prominence mostly in Kentucky, whence the Purificationists also sprang.

"The Shakers hold to many truths, such as this one, but fall short on others," Gruenwald replied. "Their failures are what led the prophet who founded us to break off from their sect to form a more perfected, purified body of believers."

The two younger Gruenwalds stirred a bit as their father talked; Bush eyed them sidewise and thought he detected in their expressions some displeasure. This was particularly true of Kirk Gruenwald, who had about him a certain hard-to-define restless quality that made Bush think of his own Sam.

"How do you plan for your group to grow, if there's no marriage and children?" Bush asked.

"We'll grow by the addition of converts," Gruenwald answered proudly. "If we are of the Lord, as we believe, then He will bless us with new believers to keep the truth alive."

"So you're bound for Texas to seek converts?"

Gruenwald glanced at the other men, and answered, "We accept converts wherever we find them."

A cryptic reply, it seemed to Bush, and perhaps this thought showed, for Gruenwald added, "We have other business as well that takes us to Texas. Private concerns."

Conversation lulled to an uncomfortable silence, so Bush pulled out his tobacco and made an offer to the men. Gruenwald shook his head. "We do not partake of the weed."

"Oh. Part of your belief?"

"Yes. No offense, sir, but we consider tobacco to be a dangerous and sinful vice."

Bush quietly put away his pipe. Cordell, who had been packing up a pipeful of his own, did the same. Sam rolled his eyes. Bush hoped the Purificationists didn't notice.

"I note, sir, that you carry no weapons," Bush said. "I presume you lost them in the river. I'm a maker of rifles myself, and I have a spare one with me that you can have to find meat and protect yourself along the way."

"We did lose supplies to the river, particularly our food, but weapons we never had to begin with," Gruenwald replied.

"You've traveled all the way from the Ohio River without arms?"

"We are people of peace, Mr. Underhill. We have no need of weapons."

"But without rifles, how can you hunt?"

"We don't hunt. Normally we take all our sustenance from the produce of the soil. That is God's plan." The look of surprise and confusion on the faces of each Underhill—for all the Purificationists had just downed helpings of jerked venison stewed in broth—prompted Gruenwald to add, "We will eat meat when nothing else is to be had, as was the case tonight. But it isn't our normal practice." Gruenwald smiled slightly. "You find us odd, I think."

"Well . . . all this is new to me."

"The world is ever a stranger to the people of God, and so the people of God ever seem strange to the world."

Marveling at this eccentric band, and wondering if there

was anything a man could do or say or offer that wouldn't violate one of their precepts, Bush asked, "How many folks back in your Kentucky colony?"

"We number about fifteenscore."

"I see. Growing?"

Gruenwald didn't seem to like the question. "No, no . . . I must confess to you that it is not."

Bush wasn't surprised. He doubted many folks were eager to convert to a sect that banned marriage, meat, and gun-carrying, and forced its membership to dress in such a drab and shabby fashion besides.

"The truth is, Mr. Underhill, our colony has declined some in the past few years. We suffered a . . . crisis, as it were. A problem with our founding prophet. Besides that, it's difficult to persuade our younger members to remain with us. The young fall so easily prey to the temptations of the world." He looked meaningfully at his son Kirk, who turned his eyes elsewhere.

Again, Bush wasn't surprised. It would be dreadful for a young man to be trapped in such a stifling sect. Pondering this, he unthinkingly reached for his pipe again, stopped himself, then thought, *What the deuce!* He was under no obligation to pretend to be one of them, and this was his camp, after all, not theirs. So he filled the pipe and blatantly lit it. Cordell, looking grateful, brought out his own pipe again and followed suit.

Puffing, Bush said, "Mr. Gruenwald, sir, I believe in respecting the beliefs of everyone, but I must tell you that this lack of weapons concerns me. Peaceful folk you may be, but it's Texas you're going into, and the Comanches and none too few white folks as well are of a very different attitude than yourself."

"We trust in the Lord to care for us," Gruenwald replied. "And we yield entirely to His will. If He chooses harm to come upon us, as it did on some of our own at the river, then so be it. 'Though He slay me, yet will I trust Him.' Death holds no fear for us."

Bush thought back on Sheba Grover, trembling and weeping on the sodden deck of the steamer. She'd certainly seemed fearful enough.

Kirk Gruenwald stood suddenly. "Begging your pardon, but I'm going to stretch my legs . . . pardon me, my *limbs*."

"Don't wander far. It seems a demonish night to me," the elder Gruenwald said. Glancing at Bush's pipe, he added, more softly, "The smoke of Satan's weed often draws his imps."

Fine with me, Bush thought. *If a few imps come along, maybe they can feed you the next meal, instead of me having to do it.*

CHAPTER
SIX

After a few more minutes of such conversation, Sam Under-hill had heard all he could stand. Rising, he said, "Believe I'll take a walk, too. Maybe watch out for Kirk out yonder in case any imps come along." He walked quickly away, avoiding the reproving glance his sarcastic comment evoked from Bush.

The night was pitch-dark, and Sam discovered before long that he was unlikely to find Kirk Gruenwald by sight. This disappointed him. Like Bush, Sam had detected things in Kirk's manner and expressions that indicated he might hold some viewpoints notably different from his father's—and this, naturally enough, made him intriguing to Sam Underhill, the rebel.

He poked about some in the dark, calling quietly for Kirk, then gave up. Well, at least he could have a smoke out of the reproachful view of Gruenwald.

Bushrod Underhill often annoyed Sam, but there was one thing about his father Sam greatly admired. Bush was very inventive, particularly in contriving devices to make the life of a frontiersman a bit easier. Bush, for example, had invented a fire-making device back in his younger days that used a plunger inside a piece of cane to compress air so swiftly and powerfully that it generated enough heat to light a wad of kindling. Five years ago, he'd gone one step further, devel-oping a kind of match that far outperformed the common sulfur-tipped sticks that had to be dipped in phosphorus to light. Unknown yet to the Underhills, an almost identical match had been made independently by an English druggist named Walker, the year before, and it was he who would receive credit in history for the invention, though Bush had beat him to it by four years. But Bush had little interest in marketing his inventions; to him, creation was a hobby pursued for its own sake, and his own convenience.

Sam filled his pipe and stuck it between his teeth, then produced one of the Underhill matches, along with a small piece of sand-coated paper. Folding the paper around the tip of the match, he pulled the match quickly out, with strong friction. Nothing happened. He repeated the act, and the match flared brightly. Lifting it to his pipe, he fired the tobacco.

"How in the hell did you do that?"

The voice, Kirk Gruenwald's, startled Sam. Obviously Kirk had been close by, watching him. It buffeted Sam's woodsman's pride a bit to think he could have been so close to another person without detecting it.

"Lord! You know how to startle a fellow!"

Kirk's form, vaguely visible now that Sam knew where to look, moved in closer. "Sorry about that. But how did you make that fire just then?"

"It's a match my father came up with. But tell me something, Kirk. Did I just hear you cuss? Doesn't your religion frown on that? It surely frowns on about everything else."

"It's not my religion. It's my father's."

"I ain't surprised to hear you say that. From the very beginning I knew there was something about you that ain't like the others."

"Hallelujah! Glad to hear it shows—even with these deuced clothes they make me wear. Hey, that match is prime. What's on the tip of it?"

"I don't know. Something with sugar and other such stuff . . . . you'd have to ask my father. He worked it all up in his gunsmithy a few years back."

"I've heard of your father, you know. I read that book

about him. He's led one hell of a life, he has! I couldn't let anybody know I knew him, though. I'm not supposed to read books like that. None of them probably have any notion they're in the camp of a famous man."

"That book doesn't tell everything quite straight. Pap's fussed about it for years. I don't know why, though. I'd be tickled silly to have people make over me like they do over Pap."

"Hey, can I have a smoke on your pipe when you're done?"

Sam grinned. "Here. Take it now." He handed over the pipe. "I believe I like you, Kirk."

"What's there not to like, except for the company I keep?"

Kirk smoked like a veteran, which Sam found amusing. "I believe maybe you ain't really the same fellow who walked out of the camp a few minutes ago. Maybe you're one of them Satan imps who took his form and was drawed here by that tobacco."

Kirk, sounding disgusted, said, "Have you ever heard such nonsense as all that?"

"To tell you the truth, no."

"God knows I have. I hear it day in, day out. It wears on my mind until I want to scream at them. But I just hold quiet until the feeling passes."

"If you don't believe what they do, why are you with them?"

"Got nowhere else to be. And there's my sister to look out for. And, after all, he is my father, crazed as he is. I suppose a fellow owes it to his father to stick by him."

"Your sister's mighty pretty. No offense, but I could take a shine to somebody like her if she wasn't part of a group that don't even believe men and women should marry. No point in shaking a tree that don't give apples."

"My sister isn't really one of them. Not all the way, anyhow. Certainly not like Aunt Sheba and the other women back at the colony are. Chasida tells herself she believes in it all, but she has her doubts about some of it. The marrying part in particular. Every now and then she talks to me about it, private."

"A girl like that is too fine not to marry. Reckon she'd ever be interested in a fellow like me?"

"Don't waste your time. Chasida will never do nothing our father wouldn't like. She's a hell of a lot more loyal to him than I am. One of these days, though, I'm going to get her away from him. When she and me are just a little older. We'll bid good-bye to the Purificationists and become real people, wearing real clothes, living real lives."

Sam chuckled. "Listening to you talk, it's hard to figure they'd have picked you for a Texas missionary. You don't seem to speak too well of the great cause."

"This isn't the kind of mission you're thinking of."

"What do you mean?"

"We're not going to Texas to get converts. We're going looking for somebody. Kind of a score to settle."

"A score?"

"There was this man, you see, the so-called prophet who started up this church of ours, and he . . . well, I ought not say. I ain't supposed to talk much about it to gentiles." Kirk took a last draw on the pipe, knocked it empty, and handed it back to Sam. "Thank you for the smoke. I needed it bad."

"Keep the pipe, I've got another. You got tobacco?"

"No."

"Here." Sam handed him his pouch. "I've got another of those, too. And a snuffbox I made out of the skull of a cat-amount. I'll show it to you if I get the chance."

"There won't be a chance. You'll be moving on in the morning, I assume."

"Yes. Won't you?"

"No. Tomorrow's Thursday. Every Thursday we pray and fast all the becussed day long."

"Fast? You mean, no food?"

"Not supposed to be. I generally manage to sneak a bite or two."

"I feel sorry for you, Kirk. I really do hope you and your

sister can get away from that bunch. Hey, what's a gentile, anyway?''

"Somebody who ain't a Purificationist. A normal human being. A sane person. The kind of person I'm going to be, and sooner instead of later, I hope.'' Kirk looked toward the flickering light of the Underhill camp and sighed. "Well, I'd best get on in. You got any food you can slip to me to help me make it through the fast tomorrow?''

"I'll get you something, don't worry. Come on. We'll go back in together.''

The Underhills bid good-bye to the Purificationist band the next morning and left their camp without breakfast. "It just don't seem right to eat while a bunch of folks who are getting ready to do without food the rest of the day stare at you, even if it is their own choosing,'' Bush explained when they were away. "We'll go on a distance and pause to eat once we're well away from them.''

Sam laughed. "Kirk will fare a little better than the rest of them today.''

"How so?'' asked Cordell.

"I left him a bit of food on the sneak. Kirk ain't what he appears to be. I found that out last night when we went out and had a smoke together. He's a good, regular fellow. Wouldn't mind getting to know him better if I had the chance. Get him away from that group of babblers and he'd be just fine.''

"That Purificationist boy actually smoked a pipe?''

"Yep. Cussed, too. Told all about how he's got no use for that religion and how he'll bust loose soon as he can. He stays with them now mostly because of his sister. He's going to bring her and himself away from them once they're both old enough that their Pap has less claim on them.''

Bush said, "That young man did strike me as a restless sort. I'd be much the same, asked to believe the kinds of things they believe. I'm surprised they find it permissible to breathe.''

"And breaking wind, I'm sure, is completely out of the question," Cordell said.

They all laughed. "No doubt," Bush said.

"What else did he tell you about them, Sam?" Durham asked.

"Not much. Something about how they ain't going to Texas to make converts, but are looking for the man who started up their church. He ain't supposed to talk about it to 'gentiles,' he says. That's us—'gentiles.' "

"Gruenwald said something about that, I believe," Bush said. "I didn't quite follow it, and it don't matter. We've shared our food with them, and now their business is their own, not ours."

They stopped shortly after and had breakfast. Durham was silent, looking back the way they had come.

"No point in thinking about her," Sam said. "Like I told Kirk, nothing gained by shaking a tree that won't give apples."

"What are you talking about?"

"Chasida Gruenwald! You're thinking about her. But she don't believe in marrying, so there's nothing to hope for where she's concerned. That's what I mean about shaking the tree."

"How do you know what I'm thinking? I might have been thinking about John and his family, and how we're going to go about finding them."

"Right. I'll bet that's what you were thinking about. Truth is, you're trying to picture what that Quaker-looking gal would look like in a wedding dress . . . and then out of it, come evening. Ha!"

"Reckon their wedding dresses are black, too?" Cordell asked.

"Why, they don't have them! No marriage, remember?"

"You're right. I'd forgot. Sam's right, Durham. No point in shaking that particular tree."

Durham snapped back, but Bush reminded him that Sam had been the target of some similar teasing on the steamer and had every right to some turnabout. "But let me tell you,

boys, we're going to have to forget every kind of distraction
from here on out. No more females, no more Taubys or Purificationists or anybody else. We've got a task before us and
I want us to give it our full attention. We've had an interruption or two so far, but from now on, it's just us, and the
business at hand.''

The influx of newcomers to Texas had been good for those
in Arkansas. All along their route, which followed the Arkansas River, they encountered hostels and stands and boarding facilities of all kinds, most of them makeshift and rough,
hardly more than barns, yet seemingly doing good business.

In one community the Underhills rode to a two-storied
building irregularly made of unhewn logs and chinked with
mud, but which had a roof that looked stout enough to hold
off the coming rain, and a big stable built behind.

"You fellows wait here with the horses, and I'll go see if
I can't get us some real beds for the night," Bush said.

The proprietor was seated in a corner, in a rocker, en-
grossed in a battered copy of the 1836 *Crockett Almanac,* a
garish volume that presented the late congressman and Alamo
hero in his mythic bigger-than-life persona, a persona Crockett himself had done more than a little to perpetuate before
his untimely demise.

"Well, hello, sir," the man said, looking up and laying
aside the almanac. "Was so caught in my reading I didn't
even hear you come in.''

"Davy Crockett, eh?" Bush said. "Quite a man he was.
Knew his family for a time in my younger days.''

The man rose, eyes wide. "You knew the Crocketts? Lord
a'mercy, sir, do you know what an honor you've had give
you, just to know the man?''

"Can't say I knew the man. I met his father and mother
and some of his brothers and sisters, and maybe him, too,
when I'd fresh growed to manhood. If he was one of the ones
I happened to meet, I never knew it. Even if I had, at the
time, it wouldn't have meant anything. He was still a boy,

and nobody yet knew who David Crockett was going to turn out to be.''

"No, but he did turn out fine, didn't he! I'm honored to say I laid eyes on him my own self, when he passed through here on his way to Texas . . . but listen to me, chattering on, when like as not you've come to ask after a room."

"I have. Me and my three sons out there. One room with a couple of beds would do the job."

"I'm sorry that I have no room with two beds . . . but I can give you a room with one bed, and make you up floor pallets."

"That'll do, if the price is right."

The price was, and Bush turned to go back out to tell his sons he'd found their lodging for the night. As he did so, he said, "Write that room down under the name of Underhill. Bushrod Underhill."

He heard the innkeeper's pen fall to the floor. "Bushrod Underhill?" The innkeeper darted around and cut Bush off from the door, staring at him as if Bush were some human god. "You mean to tell me, sir, that I've been talking to Bushrod Underhill himself, the boy hero of the Cumberland, the fellow who brought down ten Indians in a fair fight at the age of seven?"

That blasted book again! When Bush got back to Missouri, he'd have to apologize to Marie for doubting what she'd said about his fame. "There wasn't ten of them, and I was older than seven."

The innkeeper grabbed Bush's hand and pumped it hard. "Sir, I'm honored, honored, honored, honored! Some travelers through here earlier said that Bushrod Underhill was on his way into Texas, that they'd been with him themselves on a steamer, and that he—*you*—singlehandedly rescued a whole gang of Quakers from the river when their flatboat hit the steamer. But I didn't believe it! My, sir, my! Why, this is as good—*better*, even—than laying eyes on Crockett!"

Bush was taken aback by all this excited simpering. "Mister, I don't deserve even to be mentioned in the same sentence as Mr. Crockett, after the heroism he showed. And I didn't rescue those folks alone, and they weren't Quakers.''

"Oh, you do yourself disservice, sir, but it's a mark of the great to count themselves with the lowly. If Colonel Crockett walked through that door right now, he'd be as pleased as I am to meet you.''

Bush wondered if the man was actually so smitten with celebrity, or just a habitual flatterer. "If Davy Crockett walked through that door, I'd make you a new one out that back wall. I've no desire to meet a ghost.''

The innkeeper raised one brow. "There are those who say Colonel Crockett is yet among the living.''

"That old legend about Davy being captured by the Mexicans and hauled off to work a mine somewhere? I've heard that one. Them kinds of stories get started every time somebody famous dies, and folks don't want to let go of them.''

"Oh, it's more than just a rumor, or so people swear. There's a lot of odd talk about that coming out of Texas. A lot of talk.''

"Well, if talk was food, we'd all be fat men. I don't put much store in wild tales.''

"Colonel Crockett's situation be what it may or may not be, I'm pleased you've chose to come to my establishment,'' the innkeeper said. "And for you and your sons, Mr. Underhill, there is no charge.''

"Thank you, sir, but I pay my own way.''

"Oh, but I'd be proud to—''

"And I pay in advance,'' Bush said, and plopped money into the innkeeper's hand. "If you'll excuse me, sir, I'll go back out to fetch in my sons.''

"Certainly. But Mr. Underhill . . . I hope you'll put your mark on my almanac here. I would have you sign the book that you wrote, but I'm afraid it was stole from me by one of my lodgers.''

Bush gave a small inner sigh. "I didn't write that book. It was the work of an ink-slinging stretcher-teller I never should have talked to. But I'll sign your almanac, if you want. Lord knows I've been signing my name on every other kind of thing lately.'' The innkeeper scurried about for a pen and ink, and Bush wrote his name across the cover. "There. Suit you well enough?"

"It'll be hanging on that wall yonder as soon as I can get a frame for it."

Bush started out the door, but stopped and turned back to the innkeeper, thinking back on what he'd said about hearing talk coming out of Texas. "Sir, in all these rumors coming out of Texas, you wouldn't have heard one regarding my son John, would you?"

"John Underhill . . . he's your son?"

"Yes, he is."

"I should have realized it! Greatness gives birth to greatness! John Underhill is a hero, sir. His bravery at San Jacinto is a legend. Like as not they'll be writing books about him someday, just like they do about you. Why, if he were here, I'd be asking him to put his name on this almanac, too. And I would then treasure it all the more dearly, sir, because—"

"Yes, yes. But about John . . ."

"I'm afraid I've heard nothing about him lately, Mr. Underhill."

"I see. I'm asking because I've been told he's disappeared. Him and his family, and nobody knows why. That's what's brought me and my boys all the way down from Missouri. We're trying to find him."

"I wish I had information for you. I do hope you'll find him safe and sound."

"I hope so, too. Oh, and by the way, Mister . . ."

"Dedham. Jack Dedham, at your service."

"Mr. Dedham, where might a man find himself some good victuals in this town?"

"Down that street, and to your right, you'll find a tavern. More of a tippling house than anything else, sorry to say, but they do serve good meat when they have it. Just watch out for the patrons. Sometimes a few of them can be a bit ill-behaved."

Bush thanked Dedham and walked out. Dedham watched him go with a look of admiration in his eye. Holding up the signed copy of the *Crockett Almanac,* he smiled broadly. "Bushrod Underhill, right here in my own place! And here's the written proof, in his own hand! My, my! Wait until I tell Eunice!"

CHAPTER
SEVEN

Dedham's words had done the tavern a disservice, in Bush's opinion. Dedham's description of it as a tippling house and his warning about its patrons had led him to expect a raucous, drunken riff-raff inside. Instead the tavern was nearly empty, and the few drinkers within were quiet and not intoxicated.

Someone had slaughtered a hog the day before, so the Underhills dined well. Pork and bread and stewed vegetables, washed down with cold water by Bush and Durham, and beer by Sam and Cordell, made for a satisfying meal. Afterward they enjoyed a dessert of sugar cake topped with molasses, and coffee.

Bush was just opening his mouth to expound upon Dedham's mischaracterization of the place when a hoot and holler echoed down the street outside, followed by a shot so loud that each Underhill came to his feet. More hooting and yelling, drawing closer.

"A fight?" Durham asked.

"I don't know," Bush said. "Sounds more like a bunch of drunk rowdies coming into town."

The accuracy of this guess was verified when five husky, trail-dirty, drunken men pushed and staggered through the door and headed for the bar.

"Time to leave, boys," Bush said. He had little patience with drunks. At one time in his life he'd briefly taken too much to the bottle himself; now he seldom touched a drop. He rose, pushing back his chair.

"Pap . . ." Cordell nodded toward the nearest drunk, who was already arguing with the tavernkeeper over something or another.

It took Bush a moment to catch what Cordell had spotted. When he did, it was as if someone had slapped a cold hand on the back of his neck.

"There's another there, wearing the same," Cordell said, indicating another of the drunks. "And that one, too."

Sam and Durham caught on now, and stared, comprehending.

Bush shook his head, muttering, "And all I wanted was a quiet journey, with no attention, minding nobody's affairs but my own! Oh, well."

He strode toward the closest drunk. "Beg your pardon, friend. I'd like a word."

The man wheeled and faced him, bleary eyes studying him, stinking breath gusting against Bush's face. "Who the hell are you?"

"My name's Bushrod Underhill. I want to know where you got that coat you wear."

The man looked down at the black coat, slightly undersized on his barrel-chested form, then up at Bush again. "I got it at the getting place. Now be off with you." He put a big hand on Bush's shoulder and gave him a light shove.

Bush stepped a foot closer to him, ignoring the stench of fetid breath. "I recognize that coat. And the coats on your partners there . . . and that hat the yonder one has on. They belong to some folks I know. Religious folk from out of Kentucky. Run into them up the trail, did you? Found them praying and unwilling to fight you back, did you, and so you took what you wanted?"

The drunk's expression grew a little stonier, but he grabbed a companion and made an effort to joke Bush away. "Hey, Rance . . . this feller says we took these black coats from some religious folks. Why do you reckon he'd say that?"

"He accusing us of thieving?" He turned to Bush. "That what you trying to say, *amigo*?"

"He ain't answering, Rance. I think you got him scared of you. Maybe he ought to just turn and go away while he can, don't you think? Maybe learn to keep his damn nose in his own business?"

"That's right. He don't want trouble with us! We're peaceable men. Hell, look at us! We're Quakers!" He laughed raggedly and tugged at the lapel of his coat, which Bush recognized as having belonged to William Niles of Gruenwald's group. The coat on the first man he'd accosted looked like that of Gruenwald himself.

"What did you do to the people who wore these clothes?" Bush demanded, while behind him, Cordell appeared, shoulders thrown back, big body stretched to full height, lightning in his eyes. Durham and Sam, though less imposing physically, drifted up like shadows and lent their silent backing as well.

The mood shifted. The drunks were losing their joviality. Grins became glares.

"Well . . . look at this!" one of the drunks said. "Got us a bunch of toughs here! Who was it this one said he was, Rance? Davy Crockett?"

"No, no. He said he was Bushrod Underhill. It's *you* who's Davy Crockett. Me, I'm Daniel Boone."

Bush caught himself thinking that it was actually rather nice to meet someone who didn't believe he was who he was. But this foolish back-and-forth needed to end. "I'll ask once: you going to tell me what become of the folks you took those clothes from, and when you're going to give them clothes back?"

Rance leaned over and put his face two inches from Bushrod's. "Go away. You're starting to get on my nerves."

"Fair warning. It's fixing to get a lot worse than that," Bush replied.

And it did.

*   *   *

The fight in the hardscrabble little tavern was one Arkansans would talk about for years, particularly when it turned out that the participant who claimed to be Bushrod Underhill really *was* Bushrod Underhill. Versions of the fight, given with widely varying degrees of detail and accuracy, would linger in books of popular history and folklore for generations to come. When one F. Wickham Crabb would put down his own version of the fight a decade later in his top-selling sequel to the original Bushrod Underhill book, he'd have Bushrod fighting alone, besting a dozen fearsome Mexicans with only his fists, and them all armed with pistols and sabers.

Though the actual fight was less epic than its later folkloric descriptions, it was still quite a row. It had been a long time since Bush had participated in an all-out free-for-all fistfight, but he found he hadn't lost much for lack of practice. Smaller than his foes though he was, he was also faster, not to mention sober while they were drunk. His fists did much damage, swiftly.

Cordell had taken part in a fight or two, as had Sam, but for Durham this was a new experience. He presented himself well, taking down one of the drunks with a series of fast, well-aimed blows, culminating with a triumphant stripping from the man of the stolen black coat he wore.

The Underhills' upper hand went undisputed. In the end the drunks confessed. Yes, they had attacked and robbed a band of strange, praying people in black clothing. Only one had resisted, a young man who had cussed them thoroughly as he fought them. The other men of the group had simply stood by and allowed the young scrapper to do their fighting for them. Hard as he'd fought, he hadn't been able to over-come five men alone, and they'd left him senseless on the ground. They beat the men, though not as severely, just for the fun of punishing such obvious cowards who would allow one brave youth to take a pounding while they did no more than stand and watch and moan out prayers. But the defeated drunks swore to Bushrod that they hadn't touched the fe-males. They might be scoundrels, but not *that* kind of scoundrels.

The Underhills left the tavern, recovered Purificationist garments in hand, while the drunks lay battered on the floor, too thoroughly whipped even to want to follow. The tavernkeeper, and others who'd been drawn to the place by the rumor of Bushrod Underhill's presence, were already talking about how grand it was that such a famous frontier fighter had actually done battle right in their midst.

On the street, Bush was startled to receive a cheer from some of those who'd been drawn by the commotion.

"That's the way to go at 'em, Bushrod!"

"Hurrah for Underhill! Skinned 'em alive!"

Bush recognized a face or two as former fellow travelers from *The Pittsburg.* He nodded greeting but was careful not to encourage the cheers. He didn't fight his battles for show or public praise, and all this attention was as uncomfortable to him as funeral clothes.

But Sam whipped off his hat and waved it in the air, drawing another cheer from the onlookers. A man rushed over and pumped Bushrod's hand. "Mr. Underhill, sir, you're every bit the man your book said you were. You'll be glad to know that a bunch of us have been spreading word everywhere we go that Bushrod Underhill himself is coming through, bound for Texas along the same route that Colonel Crockett himself took! The news of your coming is spreading before you even as you travel!"

"That's wonderful," Bush said glumly. "Truly wonderful."

"Confirm something for us, sir. There is, is there not, a symbolic significance in the fact that you are following Crockett's own course?"

"I'm just trying to get to Texas, that's all."

The man chuckled and winked. "Ah, playing it cagey, I see. I suspect we'll know more of your intentions soon. Politics, sir? Is that your goal?"

"You ain't some kind of ink-slinging newspaper sort, are you?" Bush asked warily.

"Oh, no, no. Just a private citizen, repeating speculations I'm hearing."

"Is that all folks got time to do? Sit and throw out speculations about a man who just wants to be left alone? No offense, sir, but I've got no intentions about anything, and can't for the life of me imagine why anybody would care, anyhow. Now good evening, and let me pass."

Trudging back toward Dedham's hostel, Bush asked, "What do you reckon that was all about? Why's everybody so interested in me all at once? Can a mere book of lies and stretchers really spark up so much attention?"

"Obviously so," Cordell said. "Sounds to me like them fellows believe you're going to Texas to get into politics or something, like Crockett probably would have done had he lived."

"Why would anybody think I've got political ambition?"

"I don't know. Maybe because of John. John's been talked about for politics. Maybe folks figure his pap would do the same. And since we've chanced to follow Crockett's route to Texas, people are reading something into that. Think about it, Pap. You come from Tennessee, like Crockett did, you've made a name for yourself as a frontiersman and hunter, like he did, and there's a book floating all around the country, bolstering you up to fame just like Crockett's autobiography did for him. Folks like their rumors, and they like their heroes. Now that Crockett's dead and gone, they're looking for you to take his place."

"You really believe so?"

"I do. That's human nature at work, Pap. It makes its own kind of sense if you add it up."

"Well, I don't know about me taking Crockett's place in some way. As a matter of fact, from what Dedham at the boarding house said, Davy might not have left any empty shoes to fill. Apparently some people honestly believe he's still alive."

"Ha! Texas must be fertile ground for wild tales, then," Durham said. "Everybody knows Crockett's dead."

"People can be made to believe anything, Durham. I mean, look at all these rumors already flying around me, when all I'm doing is traveling across Arkansas toward Texas to make sure my son's safe. But I'm tired of talking about it. Let's get up to our room and ready ourselves for a most tiring and inconvenient journey."

"Where are we going?"

"Back to find our Quaker-looking friends and make sure they ain't been hurt worse than them bruisers in the tavern let on."

"We're going back all that way . . . tonight?"

"No choice. They ain't family or really even friends, but as old Tuckaseh once told me, a man can't choose his duties, only accept them. Nobody else is likely to be seeing to those folks' welfare."

"Pap, what if Chasida Gruenwald is hurt?" This from Durham.

"That's one of the 'what-ifs' we have to find out about." Bush sighed. "I tell you, boys, it ought to be a simple thing just to go from one place to another. But there's always somebody like Gruenwald and his bunch who come along like babes in the woods, and you got to look out for them. Gets downright troublesome every now and then. What kind of bunch are these so-called Purificationists, anyhow? Letting folks come in and beat them, and not even lifting a finger to resist?"

"They said the young one fought. That would be Kirk."

"And I say good for him, Sam. I just hope we don't find him dead. Let's hurry. We've got a long, dark ride ahead."

CHAPTER
EIGHT

What they found at the end of their ride was alarming at first sight, but after they examined the situation and realized that no one had been seriously hurt, the whole scenario suddenly seemed more sad and pitiful than anything else. Also infuriating, and not only because of the injustice of simple people being attacked by a bunch of rowdies. Bush understood the notion of pacifism held by some, could grasp the abstracts of it . . . but he didn't accept it. He'd been raised by a French-born "woods runner" among Cherokees and Creeks, and though the fierce views of retaliation and vengeance they had ingrained had been tempered by the passing years, the moderating and iconoclastic influence of his old Cherokee mentor, Tuckaseh, and the teachings of church and society, Bush still viewed the world Indian-style, in terms of balance. When one man attacked another, that balance was unsettled, and nothing was at rest until the balance was evened again. The idea of standing idle, doing nothing to stop another from being harmed, was beyond Bush's grasp.

But apparently that was what had happened. Kirk Gruenwald had been pounded senseless by five drunks while his own father and two other healthy men stood by, just letting it go on.

Now Peter Gruenwald sat off to himself beneath a tree, head hanging. He hardly looked up when Bush and his sons came riding in by the earliest light of dawn. The other men stood together, talking quietly, while big Sheba Grover, plopped down on a mound of moss with Chasida Gruenwald at her side, comforting her, looked just as she had on the deck of *The Pittsburg* after her rescue, the only difference being that this time she wasn't wet.

Kirk Gruenwald, meanwhile, was pacing back and forth, his face bruised and swollen, his expression as fierce as a lower Mississippi hurricane. Bush was relieved to see that Kirk was moving about and obviously not badly hurt—and was startled to see that he was openly smoking Sam's old pipe. He was startled again when Kirk saw them riding in, came their way, and said, "Do you know what happened here, Mr. Underhill? Do you know what a big bunch of damned drunks did to us yesterday?"

Bush glanced at Sam, who flicked up his brows. Something in the dynamics of this little religious band had changed significantly since they'd last seen them. Kirk was no longer even trying to hide his sins and heresies from the others.

Dismounting, Bush said, "We do know what happened. We met up with the same bunch in a little town up ahead. Had a bit of a row of our own with them."

"Good! Beat hell out of them, I hope."

"Well, suffice it to say we got back the clothes they took from you."

Charles Parring and William Niles approached. Peter Gruenwald still sat slumped beneath his tree, not even watching. Parring glanced at the bundle of familiar black clothing Durham had over his arm. "Thank you, sir," he said. "We didn't anticipate seeing those garments again."

"Take them. How did all this happen?"

"Well, as our rash and apostate young Brother Kirk said—" And that was the sudden end, for several minutes, of normal conversation.

"Don't 'Brother Kirk' me!" Kirk exploded, cutting Parring off. "Don't call me 'apostate' because I had the courage to fight! I've had my fill of this damned nonsense! I fought those men alone. Alone! Not a soul willing to help me, not you, not Brother Niles—not even my own *father*! All of you just

stood by, wringing your hands, whining and moaning, letting
me be beaten half to death . . .''

Peter Gruenwald, over at his tree, slumped even lower,
tears coming.

Kirk was like a barrel of anger that had suddenly shattered,
everything flowing out in a rush, unstoppable. His sister
looked on with wide eyes as she listened to her brother's
tirade. ''All my life I've lived among this bunch of fanatics,
being told that I was never even to think about or glance at
a girl, never to fight to protect myself from those who made
fun of us, never even to read any book other than those few
deemed fit . . . and never once have I been given the chance
to make the choice for myself. Well, I'm making it now! No
more! I'm through with this!'' He yanked off the plainly
made square black hat he'd been wearing and slammed it to
the ground. ''I don't believe in the 'prophecies' of High Elder
Pepperdine anymore, Father! The truth is, I haven't believed
since I was old enough to think two sensible thoughts for
myself! And I'll not pretend a moment longer to be what I'm
not! I'm a gentile, Father! Did you hear me? A gentile!''

Peter Gruenwald raised his head and spoke for the first time
since the Underhills' arrival, but all he said was a feeble,
''Oh, son, don't give up your belief!''

''Why shouldn't I, Father? You tell me! Why should I believe that a man like Elder Pepperdine spoke words right from
the Lord, when all of us know him for a liar and fraud who
wanted no more than the money and possessions of the folks
he claimed were his flock? Why should I believe in a religion
taught by a man who told his people never to marry, but
fornicated with half the women in his group and said it was
the 'Lord's will'?''

''Brother Kirk! I admonish you—stop this blasphemy!''
This from Charles Parring, in a piping voice.

''Blasphemy? Truth is blasphemy? What have you come
to, Brother Parring? Your own *sister* was one he took advantage of! And Sister Grover, too, my own aunt! Don't stand
there looking so shocked because I dare to say such things!
We all know every word is true!''

Parring blanched and backed away. Sheba Grover buried her face in her hands and bawled. Chasida Gruenwald, who had been comforting Sheba with an arm across her meaty shoulder, self-consciously drew it off and away, as if she'd just learned that the woman she'd been touching was a secret leper.

Kirk paced back and forth, seeming unable for a moment to find further vent for his ire. Slowly he calmed, just a little. "I know what you think of me, talking this way. God knows I've held it in for a long time for the sake of all your feelings, and my father's. But this . . . this sitting back while wicked men come in and do what they want, mistreating innocent folks, no one fighting them, no one but me lifting a hand . . ." Kirk stopped, suddenly seeming weary. He walked slowly away, while all eyes followed him, and sank down on his haunches, back turned. He stared off into a nearby grove of woods, for now empty of words, but still charged with a rage perceptible even in his silence.

Bush looked back at Niles and Parring, both very pallid men at the moment. "I mean no insult to your ways of thinking, but I must agree with the boy," he said quietly.

Parring shook his head. "Faith is difficult . . . we often have to do what others find foolish. We are often misunderstood."

"I'll not stand in judgment of what's foolish or not foolish, but I will say this unwillingness of yours to fight is dangerous. Not resisting the kind of trash who did this to you is something I can't conceive of . . . you're fortunate no one was killed. It could have been a worse bunch than a band of rowdy drunks who came upon you."

Niles tilted his head back, seemed to inflate, and went on the defensive. "Had more of us acted the foolish way young Brother Kirk acted, yes, indeed, someone might have been killed. A soft answer turns away wrath, not a violent response."

"We'll never see eye to eye, sir, and I have no desire to debate you. We came back here to see that all of you were still alive, and to return your clothes. Now we've done that. We'll be going on.''

Kirk sprang up and turned. "Take me with you. And Chasida.''

Bush, stunned by the request, hardly reacted. But for the first time, Peter Gruenwald showed some evidence of life. He rose, wavering like a drunken man, and said, "No . . . no . . . you mustn't take them. They're my children!''

Durham stepped up and said, "I believe we *ought* to take them with us, Pap.''

"So do I." This from Sam.

Peter Gruenwald came to Bush, grasped his shoulders. "Sir . . . you can't take them with you! They're my children . . . my only children!''

Bush said, "I have no desire to take anybody with me except my own sons!" It all suddenly became too exasperating. He pushed Gruenwald's hands off him. "Hang it all! You people bring your own problems on yourself by your own choices. You run flatboats down the river in a storm and right into the path of a steamer! You head out to Texas on foot, having made no provision to replace the food you lost, and have to come borrowing off neighbors. You refuse to carry guns, refuse to defend yourselves . . . I've whupped your attackers, brought back your clothes, offered you a weapon that you've turned down, given up a full night's sleep in a real bed just to come back and make sure you hadn't been murdered. I've done more than my share for you, and now I wash my hands of you." To his sons he said, "Come on, boys. Let's go.''

Durham, eyes on Chasida, said, "Pap . . . we have to help her. And Kirk. We have to get them away before these fools bring worse troubles upon them.''

"Ain't our affair, son. Let's go.''

"Pap, Durham's right," Sam said. "If they stay with that man"—he gestured at Peter Gruenwald—"he might get them killed.''

Bush paused, then glanced at Cordell, hoping for something different from him. But Cordell said, "The boys might have a point."

Peter Gruenwald groaned and staggered away, weeping.

"What's wrong with him, anyway?" Bush asked. "Why is he in such a state? Did they beat him bad?"

"No. No. They did little harm to us. It's guilt that's hurting him," Niles answered readily. "Great feelings of guilt . . . over the very things you've said. It was Brother Gruenwald who insisted we keep traveling down the river during the storm, and guided the boat into the path of the steamer. It was he who urged us on even though we had no food and our dead ones had not even been found yet. It was he who chose for us to camp here, where those wicked men attacked us. He blames himself. And now his own son is condemning him, cursing his religion, blaspheming, wanting to leave him and take his only daughter as well. He's a broken and ruined man . . . and he'll be leading us no more."

"What? Are you talking of some sort of a religious mutiny?"

"He's already cast off his authority over us. Brother Gruenwald no longer thinks himself worthy. He wants me to take his place in leading this effort of ours."

"And just what is that effort, sir? For what cause have me and my boys gone to such pains?"

Niles looked at Parring, a silent, quick conference, then back at Bush again. "You've done many good things for us. You've earned the right to understand who we are and what we're doing."

Even though he'd asked, Bush suddenly wasn't really sure he wanted to know. These were not his people, their situation not his own. He had a missing son, a missing daughter-in-law, missing grandchildren to find in Texas. He wanted to turn and ride away. But a look at his sons told him that he could not do so. They were ready to hear them out.

Bush nodded at Parring. "We'll hear your explanation, sir, if you want to tell us."

*　　*　　*

Parring was well spoken and precise in his speech, lacking the rather cloying pomposity that had marked Gruenwald's spokesmanship.

"We've told you, and others, that we're going to Texas on a mission, and by that most people believe we are going to seek converts," Parring said. "That really isn't accurate. We're not looking for converts this time, but a scoundrel."

"This High Elder Pepperdine that Kirk mentioned?"

"Yes. High Elder Pepperdine is the founding prophet of our faith. But he fell into evil, taking advantage of the faith and trust of our own people, and robbed them of all they owned."

"The very founder of your group did this?"

"I'm afraid so, yes. Very shocking to us all. It unnerved the faith of many people . . . caused us to lose many who had joined us. They went apostate because of Elder Pepperdine's sin."

"Apostate?" Bush repeated, remembering that the same word had been tossed about during Kirk's diatribe.

"It means when folks turn their back on their beliefs, Pap," Cordell explained.

"I see. I ain't surprised people would drop away because of this Pepperdine. What surprises me, in fact, is that there's any who *didn't*."

"Truth doesn't cease being true simply because the man who speaks it falls away," Parring said, and it sounded very practiced, a formula answer. "Elder Pepperdine, though a true prophet of God at one time, simply fell victim to common temptation. That didn't undo his earlier, holy work."

"How did he steal from you?"

"It's a central tenet of Purificationism that possessions belong not to the private man, but the corporate, purified, and holy community of saints. Thus when we joined the band, we turned over our worldly wealth, money, jewels, any sort of valuables. Any land possessed by a convert was sold and the money given over to the common treasury."

"A big step," Bush said.

"A step of great faith, is how I would put it," Parring

replied. "It is no light thing to join the community of truth."

"No cheap thing, that's certain. But let me guess what happened. This Elder Pepperdine, once he saw the value of all this gathered wealth, couldn't resist it, snatched it, and fled off somewhere . . . to Texas. Right?"

"Yes, sir. But we believe we know where he is now. There is a religious body that's formed in one of the small towns in the Austin colony. From what we've heard of it and its founder, we believe this is another work of Elder Pepperdine."

"Using a different name, I'm sure."

"Indeed."

"It's rather odd, sir. Your little traveling band of missionaries is actually a group of manhunters."

"In a way, yes."

Cordell cleared his throat. "What's your plan for this Pepperdine once you find him?"

Kirk Gruenwald had been sitting by, silent, during Parring's talk. Cordell's question sparked him to life again. "That's the prime question right there! One I've asked myself, and my fellow travelers, more than once. And there's no answer. Apparently they believe that they can waltz up to Pepperdine, spit a few Scriptures at him and shake their fingers under his nose, maybe holler 'Shame! Shame! Shame!'— and he'll up and repent and give back all he took, glory hallelujah and pass the biscuits! It's nonsense, like the rest of it."

Parring glared at the upstart. "We believe that the power of God will intervene to help us with our fallen brother and founder."

"You believe a lot of things," Kirk muttered. "Most of them foolish on their face."

Bush said, "Again, I ain't trying to judge your faith, but it does seem to me the force of law would be helpful to you in such a situation. Have you gathered evidence to back your charges against Pepperdine?"

"We seek to avoid worldly courts and affairs of law, sir," Niles said. "We don't believe in such things."

"My eyes, folks! It seems to me that you don't believe in anything useful! No guns, no fighting, no marriage, no courts, no law . . . I'd advise you to rethink some of your notions. Gather some solid evidence against this Pepperdine and get some help from the law, just this once. Think of it like that meat you ate when there was nothing else, even though it was against your usual way."

"They ought to be willing to do anything to Pepperdine," Kirk said. "He's worse than just a thief. He misused the women, too."

"So I gathered."

"He's a wicked man, dangerous, and this society of fools wants to walk right in and challenge him without so much as a single gun in hand."

"God will protect us," Niles said.

"Was I protected from those drunks who almost beat hell out of me?"

"You're alive, are you not? Had you acted more faithfully, you'd not have been beaten as badly as you were."

Kirk addressed Bush directly. "This kind of blind foolishness is why I want to get away from them . . . especially to get Chasida away. They'll get her killed, get us all killed."

"Pap, we can't let that happen," Durham said intensely.

"We've got to take them, Pap," Sam chimed in.

Chasida Gruenwald raised her hands. "Wait!" she said loudly, startling everyone. She'd been so quiet, the Underhills had unconsciously begun to perceive her almost as a mute; hearing her speak surprised them. "Does it not matter what *I* want to do?"

Kirk spoke sternly. "What matters is your safety. I'm your brother. It's my job to look out for you, Chasida. Father is certainly doing no decent job of it."

"Kirk, I know there are many things about our order that you question or even disbelieve in, and you know I've had questions of my own, but one thing we teach that I believe in with all my heart is that there is no difference in the eyes of the Lord between man and woman. It is *not* your job to look out for me, or to make my decisions. That's *my* place!"

Kirk, flushing, opened his mouth to argue, but seemingly found nothing to say.

Chasida turned to Parring. "I'll continue with you. I began this mission and will see it through to the end. If my brother wants to leave us, he may do so without me. I'm staying on to help my father. He's in a sad way right now, and needs me."

All eyes turned to Kirk Gruenwald, who glanced about unhappily, swore beneath his breath, and said, "Hell, then I have to stay, too. I can't go off and leave behind my own sister."

Bush saw and seized opportunity in one swoop. Here was a chance to end an association he'd never chosen to begin in the first place. "Well, that's all settled, then. You've got back what the drunks took from you, nobody's hurt, and everybody's in agreement. And all of us can get back to minding our own business." He made the latter statement with a meaningful look at Durham and Sam, then thrust out his hand and shook Parring's, Niles's, and Kirk Gruenwald's. He nodded to the women and lifted his hand cordially to Peter Gruenwald, who remained away from the others, still weeping. "Best of fortune to you all. I hope you find this Pepperdine and get back what you lost. Good day to all." He turned to his sons. "Let's get on our way. Quickly."

CHAPTER NINE

"I don't like it," Durham grumbled as they rode slowly, wearily along, groggy from lack of sleep. "We shouldn't have left her behind. What if she gets hurt, or worse?"

"Durham's right, Pap," Sam said. "We ought not to have left her. Or Kirk, either."

Bush yanked his tired horse to a halt and wheeled it to face his sons. "Fellows, did you happen to notice that she didn't *want* to come with us? You think I should have took her away from her own pap, against her will? It was never our choice to begin with! And let me say something more, and only once: we didn't begin this journey to Texas as a pure lark. Nor did we come to take on the problems of every stray gang of strangers we run across. We came to look for your brother and his family. Now, we've already done more for those poor deluded folks than most would ever think of doing. We owe them not a thing more."

"But I'm afraid something bad will happen to Chasida Gruenwald," Durham said. "I mean . . . it would be bad for anything to happen to *any* of them, but worst of all for an innocent young lady."

"An innocent, *pretty* young lady," Sam added.

"And right there, we get to the root of it!" Bush said. "If that gal was homely, you'd not be giving her two thoughts right now."

"That was Sam talking, not me!" Durham said fiercely.

"Don't go taking things he says as if I said them, Pap! You may think it's just because she's pretty, but there's more to it than that, at least for me! There's something about her that's different and good and . . ." He trailed off, reddening, embarrassed that he'd revealed such intensity of emotion before his kin.

Bush said, "I'm sorry I said what I said, then. Accept my apology, Durham. But the fact remains that she chose not to join us, and there's nothing we could do to force her."

Durham looked away, still red-faced.

For many miles, Durham and Sam rode side by side, well back from Bush and Cordell. Despite Bush's little sermon, their unhappiness was palpable, Durham's in particular. Each time Bush glanced back, he saw their sour faces, felt silent accusation in their blank stares.

At last Bush spoke softly to Cordell, riding beside him. "Well, did I do wrong?"

"What do you mean?"

"Are Sam and Durham right? Should I have brought them with us?"

"If they'd both wanted to come, I'd say yes. But with her refusing, and Kirk then opting to stay with her, there's no more to be said about it."

"You're right, I know, but still, I hate to see Sam and Durham perceiving me as deserting my duty."

"They're just besotted with the girl, Pap. With Sam it's probably the usual lust. With Durham, maybe something more. He seems to have quite a spark of true feeling for her, and him not even really knowing her."

"Durham's always had a stronger depth of feeling than a lot of young fellows. I believe that's why your mother has always taken such a special shine to him, even though I know she loves you boys all the same." Bush yawned broadly. "Lordy! I'm tired, Cordell. I can't stay awake all night and not feel it the way I did when I was your age. Since none of us so much as got to lay down last night, maybe we ought to catch us some sleep in them beds we already paid for before we go on."

"I won't argue. I'm tuckered out."

"Those Purificationists are mighty odd, eh, son?"

"Strangest bunch I ever laid eyes on."

"Amen to that, Brother Cordell."

Dedham the innkeeper went all ajitter when Bushrod and his sons entered the front door.

"Oh, Mr. Underhill, I'm so glad to see you! I was worried about what had become of you." He came out from behind his counter. "I heard about the . . . uh, trouble across the street, the men you had to deal with. I hope all of you are unhurt."

"We're fine," Bush said. "Sorry to have sullied the reputation of your community with such a scrap."

"Ah, sir, if anything, you've enhanced it!" Dedham exulted. "Bushrod Underhill himself, and his boys, scrapping and fighting like panthers right here in our very community! Oh, this is the stuff of legends. It's just what this little crossroads needs! Why, we may grow into a town because of this!"

Bush thought that the silliest thing he'd ever heard, and come to think of it, Dedham maybe the silliest man he'd ever met. "Mr. Dedham, I'm flattered you think me so grand that I can plant a town just by busting the heads of a few drunks. Now, if you'll excuse us, we're going to head upstairs and catch a little rest. We had to spend the night elsewhere, returning some things to some folks who'd lost them, and are clean wore out. Oh . . . and if you would, sir, I'd appreciate you making sure nobody disturbs us."

Dedham looked proud to have the assignment. Designated guardian of the great Bushrod Underhill! "Sir, I assure you not a word of your presence here will pass my lips. And you may stay in that room as long as you want, free of charge, until you're rested. As a matter of fact, since you missed out on a night's lodging last night, why not stay on through tonight in last night's stead?"

"Thank you, sir," Bush said. "We'll roll out early in the morning, though. We're eager to reach Texas."

"Ah, yes! To search for your son John . . . about which, I'm glad to tell you, I've received some news since we last spoke."

All at once Bush wasn't tired at all. "What?"

"Well, sir, after your scrap last night, and after you left for wherever you went, there was plenty of talk about what had happened out on the street. And I heard two men talking to one another, strangers both of them, obviously men passing through from Texas, and one says, 'Well, I don't believe it. John Underhill would never do such a thing. He'd never co-operate with someone like Trippler.' And the other says, 'I don't know—if Colonel Crockett would support such a man, why wouldn't John Underhill?' And the other replies, 'I'll never believe a man who fought like John Underhill did at San Jacinto would ever conspire to hurt Texas at the hands of a man like Trippler, even if Colonel Crockett really is on Trippler's side. John Underhill would never betray the republic, no sir.' "

"I don't understand all that. What were they talking about?"

"You know about as much as I do, Mr. Underhill. I'm simply passing along what I heard."

"You didn't talk to them yourself?"

"I try to mind my own business, Mr. Underhill."

Bush hadn't been a swearing man in years, but Dedham tempted him to backslide. He was exactly like Cantrell Smith, gathering just enough information to raise questions and fears, but not enough for answers. Bush forced himself not to show his frustration as he asked, "So all you know is that two strangers were talking in a way to imply that John is thought to have done some kind of a bad thing with somebody named Trippler, and folks are arguing over whether it's really true?"

"That's what I'd put together from it, sir."

"Mr. Dedham, I do wish you'd found out more, at the very least what John was supposed to have done. Trippler . . . where've I heard that name before?" Then he recalled. Tauby had mentioned Trippler's name back on the packet steamer.

Some empresario from whom his brother in Texas had once planned to get land.

Dedham said, "The only Trippler I know of in Texas is William Gordon Trippler, who set up a small colony of Americans when Mexico still held the land."

"This talk you heard implies that John's had some dealings with him, or is thought to have."

"Yes. Unfortunately I don't know much more about Trippler than I've already told you."

Well, Bush thought, *at least it's the start of a possible lead to John.* "Thank you for your information."

"Glad to provide it, sir."

"Did the men you overheard leave town yet?"

"I'm afraid so, sir. They passed on through last night."

Bush slumped his shoulders and gave up. He was too tired to go chasing rumors just now, anyway. And there was probably nothing to it anyway, considering that the men talked of Davy Crockett as still alive. Not much credibility in that.

Dedham said, "One other thing, sir . . . I think you'll enjoy seeing this."

"What?"

"Just something a traveler dropped on the street and that I picked up. Amazing! Especially considering that I was having you sign Mr. Crockett's almanac only yesterday. If I'd known *this* was coming, I'd have waited and had you sign it instead. I only wish you'd told me you were publishing an almanac!"

As Bush stood perplexed, Dedham scurried back around his counter and came back with a thin paper volume. He handed it to Bush.

Bush gazed down at an astonishing and appalling sight: a picture of a grizzle-bearded frontiersman choking a bear with a rope made from two rattlesnakes tied together. The snakes were minus their rattles, though, those having been bitten off by the frontiersman, and still hanging from his gritted teeth. The bear was choking so terribly that its eyeballs were popping from their sockets like marbles on strings. Above the garish picture were the words *Bushrod Underhill's Almanac*,

with the coming year's date, 1838, printed to the side. Below
the picture, in smaller type than the nameplate, "Bushrod
Snakes the Eyeballs from a Bear."

"What the devil is this!"

"Well, sir, you would know better than anyone, I'd think!
Obviously it's your new almanac!"

"You found this on the street?"

"I did. The truth is"—Dedham leaned forward and spoke
conspiratorially—"I saw it fall from the owner's saddlebag,
and went over to get it and return it to him. When I saw what
it was, I thought, *His loss, my gain.*"

Bush opened the volume. More pictures, all of them along
the same tawdry, harsh lines as the cover illustration, filled
it, depicting a man he guessed was supposed to be himself,
involved in such impossible feats as riding upright on bare
feet on the back of an oversized alligator, throwing a rope
around the neck of a giant sea serpent, and killing a small
army of Indians with a club improvised from the wooden leg
of a man who stood by, cowering, balanced on the one foot
he had left. Along with the pictures were printed, in small,
hard-to-read typeface, crudely worded tall tales that matched
the illustrations. "Bushrod Skins a Gator." "Bushrod at the
Slave Auction." "Bushrod and Tom Purly in a Fight to the
Death." With a story about Bushrod's infancy was a scrib-
bling of the biggest, ugliest baby Bush had ever seen. The
child was dining on a bit of chopped-up humanity simmering
in a kettle, beneath a big line of type reading, "Baby Bushrod's Boiled Injun Stew." Bush grimaced, disgusted, and
looked further. Scattered throughout the pages between the
illustrations and stories were the typical calendars, moon-
phase diagrams, zodiac charts, and so on, just enough of them
to allow the publication to pass itself off as an almanac. As
Bush looked closely, he suspected the standard almanac material had been stolen right out of one of the Crockett almanacs.

Wonderful, Bush thought. *It looks like ink-slinging Crabb's
book of falsehoods has given birth to a bastard child.*

"If I didn't tell you this almanac was coming, it's because
I didn't know," Bush said. "I know nothing about it, and

whoever printed it, did it without my permission.''

"Do tell!" Dedham exclaimed. "So this is as much a surprise to you as to me?"

"That's the size of it."

Dedham didn't seem to know what to make of that. "I suppose it must be an honor that someone did such a thing, anyway."

"Oh, surely," Bush said, still frowning. "This is surely the very thing I needed, yes sir."

Dedham, utterly missing the irony in the words, nodded with vigor. "It is, sir, especially if you have in mind to make a place for yourself in the public life of Texas. Why, this could do for you the very thing the Crockett almanac did for the colonel! Having his name before the public eye in such a way bolsters the career of any man who enters politics."

"I ain't interested in politics." He held up the almanac. "May I keep this, sir?"

Dedham lost his grin. Clearly he didn't want to give up his precious find . . . but this was Bush Underhill himself doing the asking, so he reluctantly nodded. Bush thanked him and put the almanac under his arm, not feeling too bad about depriving Dedham of it. The innkeeper would only show it to everyone who came in, just furthering the kind of nonsense Bush had no desire to see spun around his life and person.

"Good day to you, Mr. Dedham. And remember—don't let anyone disturb us. We're some mighty tired folk."

CHAPTER
TEN

Once in the room, Bush plopped down on the bed and looked at the almanac some more.

"What do you make of it, Pap?" Cordell asked.

"This is worse than what that lying Crabb did to me. More lies, and pictures besides!" He flipped a page. "This ain't about Bushrod Underhill. It's about a . . . I don't know what it is. Surely don't seem to be human. Look at this." He held up a page, showing a picture of the fictionalized Bushrod tearing a panther into pieces with his bare hands. Indeed, the wild-eyed man in the picture looked even less human than the panther. "They make me look like something out of one of them old Cherokee monster stories I heard from Tuckaseh while I was a sprout."

"Pap, I had no notion you were so famous until we made this journey," Durham said.

"Bad will come of this, boys. I'm a private man. I don't want folks seeing me as some kind of make-believe Nimrod Wildfire character."

"I think it's prime, Pap!" Sam exclaimed. "I can't figure why you don't enjoy it. I would!"

"Yep, you're the kind who would."

"I think I know what's happening, Pap," Cordell said. "People are starting to think of you the way they thought of Crockett. Maybe you're beginning to take his place as the people's hero. And if I had to guess, I'd say that John contributed to this.''

''Contributed how?''

''Because folks see him as such a hero in Texas. He's made the Underhill name even better known. So somebody's figured they'll make some money for themselves, playing it up. They've took what Crabb started in his book, and carried it a step further. It ain't right it's been done without your permission, but you can see how somebody could be tempted to try to cash in on your name. John Underhill, the hero of San Jacinto, has him a pap who spits lightning and chokes bears to death with snakes!''

Bush glared at one of the uglier illustrations. ''You reckon somebody really thinks I look like that?''

''It ain't really you, Pap, no more than the Crockett in the Crockett almanacs was the real Davy Crockett.''

Durham took the almanac and studied it. ''Pap! This here was printed at Little Rock.''

''That right? Well! We'll be passing through there. Maybe we'll just take a bit of time to look up whoever did this. Have a little prayer meeting with them.''

''I'd like to shake their hand,'' Sam said.

''So you think it's a good thing somebody's making your old father out to be some kind of wild mountain screamer?''

''I think the young ladies will consider it fine to know the son of a hero. Why, this could be almost as good as being one of Davy's own boys!''

Bush grunted with disgust. ''I should have left you home, boy. You ain't got the sense God gave a horseshoe.'' He rolled over, and within a minute was sound asleep.

They slept hard, and awakened the next morning later than they'd planned.

Durham woke up ill, sick to his stomach. Three times he lurched outside to vomit, and Bushrod feared for the welfare of the expedition. They had no time for this!

Time or not, they had to deal with it, and unless they wanted to abandon Durham altogether, to wait on it.

Bushrod made arrangements for extra time in the lodgings, and throughout the day looked out the window of the room and examined the street, wondering if the Purificationists would come in on their heels. If they did, he missed them.

By evening, whatever had ailed Durham no longer did. He apologized for having caused a whole day's delay, but by now Bushrod was over being irritable about it. He and his sons returned to the tavern where they'd fought two nights before, and were ushered to a table and brought food at no charge. The tavernkeeper was thrilled to have his famous patron back again.

Sam had brought the almanac with him, to Bush's displeasure. When the tavernkeeper saw it, his eyes grew large, and he begged Sam for a glance. As he flipped through it, he said, "Where might I obtain a supply of those to sell?"

"If you favor doing kindness to the reputation of a man who has done you no wrong, please don't even try to sell those," Bush said.

"It's not your own publication?"

"Lord, no. It's an insult, the turning of a living man into a joke on paper. How can somebody take another's name, make up stories about him without permission, and make money he don't even share with the one whose name he's selling?"

"Beg your pardon, sir, but it can make a man's name famous. Folks love that sort of book."

Bush grunted unhappily.

"Really, sir," the tavernkeeper persisted. "Just such books helped make Crockett what he was."

"What he *is*," said a man at the nearby bar, who leaned over a drink with a dispassionate air.

The tavernkeeper chuckled and said, "Crockett's dead, my friend. You ever heard of the Alamo?"

The man turned. He was a balding, broad-faced fellow. He looked Bush up and down. "So you're Underhill."

"I am."

The man scanned him once more. "Hmm. You don't look as big as they say you are."

"Which pack of lies have you read, the book or the almanac?"

"Neither. I've just heard the tales people tell."

"Well, take those tales like you'd take the one about Crockett surviving: be very slow to believe."

"I am. Make it a habit. But I do believe the one about Crockett. Too many people telling it for it not to be true. Even your son John, who ain't quick to buy into things, was beginning to wonder if there was something to it."

Bush came to his feet. "You know John?"

"A little. Why?"

"Because I hear he's gone missing. It's why I'm going to Texas."

"If he's missing, I don't know about it. I been out of Texas for a spell, though."

Remembering the conversation Dedham had overheard and passed on, Bush asked, "You know anything of a man named Trippler?"

"William Trippler?" The man leaned over and spat on the floor contemptuously. "Everybody's heard of Trippler. And everybody's got an opinion as to whether the man's a great leader or a betraying Judas. But there's no argument as far as I'm concerned. I believe the man would love to see Texas back in the hands of the Mexicans."

"How so?"

"He's trying to build an empire for himself. They say he's sneaking about, conniving with Mexico, trying to gain them some sort of foothold to retake Texas, his price being a wealth of power for himself once it's done."

"You know all this for a fact?"

"No . . . nobody knows anything for a fact where William Gordon Trippler is concerned. Why are you asking, sir? You think he has something to do with your son?"

"I've heard the names tied together, that's all. A fellow told me he overheard two men, fresh out of Texas, arguing over whether John would throw his support to this Trippler, whatever he's up to."

"I can answer that one. He'd not do it. Not if Trippler is

up to what I think he is.'' He paused. ''Interesting you should
have brought Trippler up, sir. These Crockett tales tie in with
him, too. The story is it's Trippler who's nursing Crockett
back to health.''

''And you believe this?''

''Like I say, when you hear something from so many
places, it's hard to keep doubting it, unlikely as it sounds.''

When Bush and his sons had finished their meal, they returned to the boarding house. Bush wished they were well on
down the trail instead of still lingering here, especially now
that he had a few rumors about John to pursue. But it wasn't
so bad. They'd enjoy one more night on good beds, then set
out early come morning.

Their immediate goal was Little Rock—Bush was still debating with himself about whether to find the printer of the
unauthorized almanac, or just let it go—and from there they'd
head to the Red River, follow it for some miles, then cross it
and plunge into Texas.

They slept well and set out at first light of what promised
to be an excellent, clear day. Many miles fell away behind
them; their camps were pleasant and restful. The Purificationists, if traveling this way, didn't cross their path, which suited
Bush, especially now that Durham and Sam seemed to be
forgetting about the lovely Chasida. They saw the light of
other campfires at night, but visited none of them and received no visits.

Despite the pleasant weather and travel, Bush was increasingly concerned. He had a nagging feeling that John was in
trouble, and he worried about a possible connection to this
mysterious Trippler fellow. He struggled, however, not to
take his feelings too seriously just yet. His long-dead adoptive
father, a misplaced intellectual named Jean-Yves Freneau, had
always taught him that a man needed knowledge, not just
rumors and feelings, before he formed his opinions. Texas
was a turbulent place these days, and under any rock a man
could find two scorpions and three rumors. The hints that
John might be tied in with Trippler were probably as poorly

founded as this absurd tale of Crockett still being alive.

When the Underhills reached Little Rock, Bush found that his admirers from the steamer had done just as they'd promised. His arrival was anticipated. A gang of boys, waiting at the edge of town, pummeled him with questions and commentary.

"They say Bushrod Underhill himself is coming this way, and we're waiting for him! Did you know he killed a bear with nothing but a sharp stick, and killed four wild Indians with his bare hands before he was fifteen years old? You ain't seen him along the way, have you, mister? The pictures we've seen show him more than six feet tall, with a beard thicker than the hair of a buffalo. You seen anyone like that?"

Bush stared sadly at the boys, noting that two of them had almanacs in hand, and one a copy of the book that had sparked all this nonsense to begin with. They were obviously expecting Bushrod Underhill to look just as he was depicted in the almanac. "Why do you figure Bushrod Underhill would be coming this way?"

One of the bigger boys answered, "Some folks are saying he's headed into Texas to rescue Davy Crockett from the Mexicans!"

Great day! Bush thought. *Already the tall tales are growing.* "The version I hear is that Crockett's already rescued and is laying up to heal," Bush said.

The boys shook their heads, confident their rumor was the more accurate. "When Bush Underhill gets here, we're going to have him sign his name in these books," one said.

"That almanac there, son—do you know who printed it?"

"Yes, sir. It was a traveling man, coming through with a press. Going into Texas to set up a newspaper. He stopped in Little Rock for two weeks and set his press up in a tent, and printed these up to sell. And he's sold a fair sight of them, too! He told my pa that he got these stories from Bushrod Underhill himself."

"Did he, now? I'd like to meet a man who knows old Underhill as well as that. Can you tell me where to find him?"

"Oh, he's gone on, sir. Packed up his press and kept on moving."

"Selling them almanacs as he goes, no doubt."

"I'm sure he is, sir. He's going to get plumb rich on them, I'll betcha."

"Well, good day to you, boys. And by the way . . . don't believe every word you read. There's folks out there who like to spread big lies. If you meet Bushrod Underhill, you might want to ask him just how much of what's in that book, and them almanacs, is the truth."

They rode on, and did not linger in Little Rock any longer than it required to refresh their supplies, which were much diminished since they'd shared their camp with the Purificationists.

"You should've told those boys who you were, Pap," Sam said. "They'd have bugged their eyes like that bear on the front of the almanac."

"No, they wouldn't have believed me, and would have been disappointed even if I convinced them. I ain't what they think Bushrod Underhill is supposed to be. That's the way it is with folks. They get a notion set in their heads until the notion holds more force than the truth. And that's true of more than just children, too. As a matter of fact, the older folk are usually worse."

CHAPTER
ELEVEN

A few miles south of the Red River

Bush was feeling a bit gun-shy of humanity by the time he rode into the little community of Moreau. Past Little Rock he'd run across others who excitedly mentioned the spreading rumor that Bushrod Underhill was coming to Texas, not realizing they were speaking to Underhill himself. And he was following almost exactly the same route that Davy Crockett had taken back in late '35! they'd said. There was surely some significance in that. Something was up with old Bushrod, no doubt about it.

Bush perceived in perplexity that disparate rumors were being tossed together, and where they fit, melded into a single new and even more foundationless concept. He noted in amazement how human minds, armed with only the most meager and distorted facts, could find connections where none existed, or create them from whole cloth.

"There might be a good side to all this attention," Cordell philosophized. "The more the story spreads that you're in Texas, the more likely John is to hear it. We may be found by him before he's found by us."

They rode down the darkening, twilight street of Moreau, just another typical community of small houses and log-walled business establishments. Bush was relieved to see the place so wonderfully deserted, no band of excited citizen sentinels poised for the arrival of the hero Underhill. Maybe he was at last beginning to outpace the news of his coming that had so far preceded him.

"Think we can find a boarding house?" Cordell asked.

"Don't know. Mighty small settlement. Maybe we can find somebody who puts up travelers."

They found lodging an hour later in a big cabin with extra rooms built like cribs on the back so that the owners of the place could make some extra money off the continuing flow of incoming new Texians. The owners were a man and wife named Feely. The man had a bushy beard hanging halfway to his belly and a mustache he kept primped and combed with the meticulousness of a city woman tending her hair. Though the accommodations were shabby and drafty, Bush liked one thing: Feely seemed unimpressed that he had Bushrod Underhill on his premises. Just another lodger to him, apparently.

In idle conversation with his host, Bush learned there was one other lodger already in one of the rear rooms. A young man, traveling out of Texas back to the United States. Some sort of traveling printer, he thought.

That got Bush's attention, and after he and his sons had stashed their wares in their room, Bush said, "I believe I'll go call on this other fellow. If he's a traveling printer, maybe we've found the very scoundrel who is putting out that almanac."

Bush's knock on the door was answered by a fast, phlegmatic cough from the other side. "Just a minute!" a weak, choked-sounding voice said. Bush waited while someone bumped a chair about and fumbled with the door latch, then the door swung open to reveal a somewhat pallid, disheveled man of about thirty-five, wearing rumpled clothing. His hair, beginning to thin, was red and cowlicked, framing a freckled face that stared back at Bush through bloodshot eyes.

"Yes?"

"Hello, there, friend. Sorry to be bothering you this evening, but I'm told you're a traveling printer."

"A what? Printer? No, sir. I'm afraid you've been told wrong on that point. I'm a writer, but not a printer." He turned his face away and coughed terribly, growing very red.

A writer. Bush had his complaints with that breed, considering the unwanted fame F. Wickham Crabb had brought him, but if this man was merely a writer, then he probably wasn't the anonymous culprit behind the Underhill almanac. "Well, I suppose I've been misinformed . . . young man, are you well?"

The fellow was still coughing, bending over at the waist, hacking like he was trying to bring up the lowest portions of his innards. He turned and staggered back toward a chair, still bent double.

Bush, alarmed, followed him inside. "Mister, I believe you might need to see a physician."

The writer sat down weakly, eyes and nose running, face as bright as crimson. "I've already . . . seen plenty of them." He coughed more, but gradually brought it under control. When the fit was over, he sat back, tilting his head over the rear of the chair, breathing raggedly and looking like a very exhausted man.

"Is there anything I can do for you?" Bush asked. "Bring you some water or something?"

"Water would be . . . excellent." He waved toward a little table in the corner of the room, upon which stood a pitcher of water and a glass. Bush went to it, filled it, and brought it to the young man, who drank with a shaky hand. When he was finished, he smiled wanly, and Bush set the glass on the floor beside his chair. "Sorry about all that. It's quite embarrassing."

"Consumption?"

"I hope not. Lord knows. The doctors tell me it appears to be some sort of reaction of my lungs to something in the air. I don't know what it is, but there's places I go that make me into little better than an invalid. Texas being one of them, I've found."

"You're leaving?"

"I'm forced to." He hacked a couple more times. "I'd hoped to stay, but I swear, I believe it will be the death of me if I do." Another cough, but not so severe. "Other places affect me the same way. Louisiana. Arkansas. Parts of Georgia and Alabama, too.''

"You sound like quite the traveler."

"I am. It's travel that I write about, mostly."

"Sounds interesting. Good way to make a living, getting to see all the land, the different kinds of folks. I've done some traveling in my own time." Bushrod came forward and extended his hand. "I'm Bushrod Underhill."

The lifting of the young writer's brows told Bush that his name was no stranger to this man, either. "Sir, I'm honored. I'd heard you were coming into Texas."

"Seems like everybody's heard it. It's astonished me. Can't see why anybody would care."

"Please, Mr. Underhill, have a seat." He waved Bush to the other chair in the room. "You're astonished, you say? I'm surprised. You're a famous man, thanks to Wickham's book."

"Wickham? You on a first-name basis with that scoundrel?"

The other laughed, face reddening again, and a few more coughs jolting loose. "Pardon me. Every time I laugh, the coughs get started again. Yes, I do know Wickham Crabb. I worked with him briefly in North Carolina a few years ago. And yes, he is a scoundrel! I know that for a fact. He owes me nearly a hundred dollars that I expect never to see. If you should ever meet him again, Mr. Underhill, please tell him that Leon Shubel is still waiting for his money."

"I surely will, Mr. Shubel. And he ought to be able to pay it, considering how much money he's made off my name."

"It's none of my business, Mr. Underhill, but did Wickham make any arrangement for you to receive a share of the profit his book makes?"

"None. But hang it, who'd have thought such a book would make any money at all? Who'd have figured anybody would care about the life of a man like me?"

"Because your life is so interesting. I've read Wickham's book, and though I know him well enough to realize he probably made up some of what he wrote, there's still quite a story there. You've led a fascinating life. Your adventures remind me of the same sort that made famous men out of—''

''I know. Boone and Crockett.'' Bush shook his head. ''I still can't figure it. If I'd known what would come of it, I'd never have talked to Wickham.''

''Have you seen the almanacs that are flooding into Texas?''

''The ones that purport to be about me? I have. In fact, that's what brought me to your door. When our landlord told me you were a traveling printer, I thought maybe you were the culprit.''

''I'm glad to plead innocent on that one, Mr. Underhill. I have no idea who's behind those, but I can tell you I've been seeing new copies for the last several days. They're receiving a wide distribution, right along with the rumors about you entering Texas.''

''At least the rumors of me entering Texas are true. Them almanacs are solid lies.''

''Sir . . . would you do an ailing writer a favor?''

''What's that?''

''I came to Texas hoping to gather enough material to write the definitive guide and exposition for the would-be Texian. Now my health forces me away, and I'm left to make do with what material I've been able to gather. It would do much for my work if I could include an interview with the great frontiersman Bushrod Underhill, father of the Texian hero John Underhill.''

Bush normally would have turned down any such request without pause, but there was something about Shubel that he liked, and the fact that Shubel had just mentioned John in a familiar way made Bush realize that if he gave Shubel what information he wanted, perhaps he'd get some in return. ''I suppose no harm will be done . . . unless you're the same kind of writer as your old friend Wickham Crabb.''

''I assure you, I'm not.''

''Then we'll talk. But tell me one thing first. What do you

know of the whereabouts and situation of John Underhill right now?''

Shubel smiled. ''I'd anticipated you might ask that . . . and, in fact, I'd anticipated further that John Underhill's situation might be one of the things that has brought you to Texas.''

''It's the very thing that's brought me, though I know nothing definite about what's become of him. Only that he and his family have vanished.''

''And so they have, from what I've been hearing lately,'' Shubel said. ''Why, or to where, I don't know. Suffice it to say the rumors are worrisome.''

''Tell me what you've heard.''

''Contradictory things, Mr. Underhill. But with a common thread through them. One story is that John has gone off with the former empresario named William Gordon Trippler, and is preparing to make some sort of political alliance with him. Trippler is believed to be in the midst of some sort of political scheme, very controversial and poorly defined, and John Underhill is said by some to be throwing his support to the movement. I rather doubt it, in that most seem to believe that Trippler would actually betray Texas to the Mexicans. If so, John Underhill would never go along with it. I know that because I had the privilege of interviewing the man before he disappeared.''

''You spoke to John?''

''Yes, and he had nothing good to say of the rumors that were spreading about Trippler and his scheme. I'm certain he'd never go along with Trippler on anything . . . unless he were forced to do so. Which leads me to the second rumor: that Trippler has actually kidnapped John and his family, either to try to force John Underhill to give him his public support, or for the sake of ransom.''

''Ransom? To be paid by who?''

''Perhaps by the Texian government—not that Texas has a red cent to pay any debt, legitimate or otherwise, just now. About all Texas has to offer is land—which may be what Trippler wants.'' Shubel coughed again. ''The other possible and more likely source of ransom would be . . . *you*, sir.''

"That's a new one on me. I've received no notice of John being kidnapped, nor any demand for ransom."

"Then how did you know to come to Texas to find him?"

"An old friend of John's, who'd come to Texas with him, returned and told us he'd gone missing. But he had no more facts than that. Not even the name of Trippler, or any of these rumors. This fellow was always on the simple side in some ways, though, so I suppose I can't complain much about him."

Shubel looked seriously at Bushrod. "Let me warn you, Mr. Underhill . . . you should be careful. Even if John's disappearance isn't a kidnapping, even if there is no request for a ransom, the notion that you might be carrying a ransom could be very dangerous to you."

Bush smiled. "If I chose to worry about ideas as unlikely as that, I'd be jumping at every jackrabbit shadow."

"It may not be as farfetched as you think, sir. Texas right now is a land filled with tales and rumors and uncertainties. You hear the wildest kind of stories, but the odd thing is that more of them seem to turn out true than you'd expect. People become prone to believe what they hear. There's plenty swearing right now, for example, that Davy Crockett is still alive."

"I've heard the very tale. Had a man swear to me it had to be true just because so many are saying it. But it's always that way in opening country, or so I've found," Bush observed. "Stories get started, spread, take on a life of their own."

"Indeed. And another thing about 'opening country,' to use your phrase: it always draws people looking for a legitimate chance to make an honest living, but also plenty who have things to run from. Plenty of desperadoes would be quite interested in the notion that Bushrod Underhill was coming into Texas laden with wealth to ransom his son and grandchildren."

"I'll be careful," Bush said. But in fact he gave Shubel's warning little credence. His gut told him that a kidnapping was unlikely. John would die before he'd let his family be taken.

"I want to hear everything John told you when you talked to him," Bush said.

Shubel smiled. "And I thought it was me who was going to interview *you*. Very well, though. Let me dig out my notes. But I can tell you there won't be anything likely to help you. Your son talked about the war, about his ideas of the future of Texas . . . very general stuff, nothing that's going to help you now."

But Bush wanted to hear it, and did. Shubel found and read through his notes. As he'd said, there was nothing in them that could shed light on the mystery of John's disappearance, but still Bush savored hearing his son's thoughts and personal history, even in such an indirect way.

After many minutes, Shubel was at last free to get to the interview at hand. He talked to Bushrod for well over an hour, interspersing his interview with occasional coughing fits. Bush took advantage of the chance to clear up F. Wickham Crabb's falsehoods, and to lambaste whoever was responsible for the hideous almanac. Shubel nodded and scribbled rapidly, particularly seeming to enjoy Bush's diatribes against Crabb. When it was done, Shubel thanked Bush profusely. "Whatever I'm able to write of this failed Texas expedition of mine will be far, far better than it would have if I hadn't spoken to you. You're a great man, and gracious, Mr. Underhill."

"I don't know if I'm great, and I learned to be gracious from watching my Cherokee mother when I was naught but a child. I hope your writing goes well for you, sir, and that you'll give a fair accounting of anything I say. No stretchers like Crabb put in."

"I will be fully accurate, sir. I promise. And as for you, I hope you'll take care, and keep in mind what I said about the rumors of you carrying ransom money. You could be endangered."

"I'll watch my back. And you, sir, watch out for that cough. It sounds near consumptive to me." Bush touched his hat. "Well, good evening."

Shubel watched him from the door as he walked back toward his own room. A new fit of coughing hit him, and Bushrod glanced back as he heard it. Shubel backed into his room and closed the door, the sound of the coughs now muffled.

Bush made a face. Worst cough he'd ever heard. He still had some doubts about the wisdom of talking to yet another scribbler, but maybe it wouldn't matter. It seemed likely that Leon Shubel would cough himself to death long before he could ever get any book into print.

CHAPTER TWELVE

Late the next afternoon

Bush might have cussed himself for not seeing it coming. He'd let the trail and his mounting worries about John distract him too much, and before he noticed his horse had thrown a shoe.

Fortunately there was a blacksmithing farrier in the little community ahead. Bush scouted him down and found him as cheerfully helpful as most frontier folk, and that even without knowing who Bushrod was, for Bush didn't tell. Fame just didn't sit comfortably with him. He wondered how Crockett had come to love attention so much when he himself found it made him miserable. Crockett's soul must have been constituted more along the lines of Sam's than Bush's.

"That shoe needs replacing, Mr. Smith," the farrier said after a quick examination. "You got time for me to make you one?"

"I suppose I got to take time," Bush said, thumbing through a ragged little scrap of a publication that apparently was supposed to pass for a newspaper. He'd found it on the floor of the smithy. Cordell, meanwhile, was outside having a smoke and keeping an eye on the other horses. Sam and Durham were gone, taking a walk down toward the heart of the community, Sam's eye in particular on a place that looked invitingly like a saloon.

The farrier, muscled and broad and bearded, pursued his trade in the spirit of its oldest sense, serving not only as a shoer of horses but a doctor of beasts as well. "I don't much care for the gait of this beast," he said. "I watched it as you led it in. More wrong than just that shoe, I'm afraid."

"Nothing wrong," Bush countered. "That horse has always had its own kind of step. You're not the first to question it."

"I could take a closer look once I'm finished with the shoe."

"No need. Believe me, the horse has always walked just as you saw today." Bush turned a page of the little newspaper. "Well. Someone's got something to say about William Trippler. You heard of him?"

The farrier suddenly didn't seem so cheerful. He leaned over and spat emphatically, rolled his tobacco cud to the other side of his mouth, and said, "I've heard of him. Hell, yes."

"What do you think of him?"

"Not much. Everything I'm hearing of him makes my stomach do a slow turn."

"Heard any talk about him having Colonel Crockett, nursing him back to health?"

"Oh, I've heard that, yes. And not only that, but I hear as well that he's got his hands on John Underhill. Captured and held for ransom."

Bush had brought up the matter of Trippler not because it was in the newspaper—it wasn't—but because he saw in this anonymous setting a chance to put his ear to the ground and see what rumbled there, without the distraction that his true identity seemed to bring.

"You think there's any truth to it?"

"I don't believe that Crockett's alive. About John Underhill . . . I don't know."

"I heard a different rumor about Underhill. I heard he was with Trippler of his own free will. Throwing his support to his movement."

"Ha! Don't believe such a tale, my friend. John Underhill would never betray Texas."

"So you truly believe he was kidnapped?"

"I do." The farrier rolled his cud and spat once more.

"And you know what else I hear? I hear that his own pap is already in Texas, come down from Missouri bearing a bunch of gold, to free his son."

Bush felt chilled. Maybe that cough-wracked note-taker the night before had been right to warn him about the ransom rumor.

The farrier hammered for a while, shaping the shoe, concentrating on his work and filling the smithy with noise that ended all conversation for a minute or so. He held up the shoe with tongs, examining it with squinted eye, and said, "I wouldn't want to be Bushrod Underhill, coming into Texas with that much gold in hand. Mighty dangerous. Mighty dangerous."

Bush laid the little newspaper aside. "I believe I'll step outside and have a smoke with my son, sir." He rose and exited the smithy.

Cordell was refilling his pipe. "Where's Sam and Durham?" Bush asked.

"Walking up yonder way. They'll be back soon."

"Give me some of your tobacco, Cordell. And then let's have us a talk about a story that's going around. I just heard it for the second time in two days, and I'm beginning to wonder if it ought to make us take a different approach to our task."

"Aw, hell!" Sam said. "No saloon at all—just a store."

"What if it had been a saloon? If Pap caught you drinking anything, he'd kick your fundaments up about your ears."

"I ain't afraid of Pap."

Durham laughed.

"What? You think I worry what he thinks about anything?"

"I think you worry about what he *does* about things."

"I'm a grown man now, Durham. You are, too, for all practical purposes. I don't worry about Pap and you shouldn't, either. It's time we stood up to him."

"How do you figure we should go about doing that?"

"Just quit letting him boss us about so much. Stand up to

him like we did with that Purification-whatever-they-were bunch.''

"Didn't do much good that I saw. Chasida Gruenwald didn't come with us, you might notice.''

"Yeah, but that's only because she decided not to on her own. If she'd been willing, and we'd kept standing up to Pap, he'd have give in and let her come, and her brother, too.''

The brothers trudged along a few paces more, silent, until Durham said, "I wish she was with us. That's the prettiest girl I believe I've ever seen. Not trying to put down that girl you liked on the steamboat, Sam, but I believe Chasida's even prettier.''

"I can't deny it. I believe she got under your skin a little, brother.''

"I'd like to have had the chance to know her better, that's true. I wonder how she's doing now?''

"I don't know. It's hard to hope for the best, considering her pap and the others. Kirk's the only one in the group with enough salt to stand up for himself. If they should run across another bunch of roughs like them who took their coats, then—''

Sam's talk was cut off suddenly as he pitched forward, tripped up by a stick he'd walked right across without noticing. He slammed into the ground, catching himself on his hands, but his left hand, unfortunately, plunged deep into a fresh pile of horse manure.

Rough male laughter sounded from the porch of the store building to Durham's and Sam's right.

Sam rose, swearing and furious, shaking the soiled hand violently, flinging little flecks of manure in all directions.

"Hey, be careful!" Durham protested, backing away.

Muttering more curses, Sam looked over toward the store and the two men standing there, grinning at his misfortune. They were dirty, roughly dressed. Farmers, from the look of them.

One of them called to Sam in a false Irish accent: "Top of the evening to you, stranger! I see you've done met my good friend Paddy!''

The other man roared with laughter.

Sam went livid and swore yet again, very loudly, then made reference to his tormentor in most unflattering terms. The man, however, merely looked at him quizzically, and said something to his partner, who laughed again.

"You got something to say about me, you can say it to my face!" Sam bellowed, heading toward the store with fists coiled.

"Here now, my friend, don't be angry!" the man said cordially. "I admit we had a laugh at your expense, but there was no bad intent in it. Only yesterday I suffered the very same thing myself, and believe me, get laughed at I did!"

Sam mounted the porch and shoved his face up close to the man's. "Maybe you take to being laughed at, you rump-ugly jackass, but you don't laugh at Sam Underhill!"

"Begging your pardon on that point, Mr. Sam Underhill, but we already did laugh at you. But as I said, no harm meant, and as I can see, none done. Except maybe to that hand." He flashed a grin at his companion.

Sam reached over and swiped the hand off on the man's sleeve. The fellow's smile remained, and he did not resist, but something had subtly changed in the lighting of his eyes when he looked back up into Sam's face. "Now, why did you have to go and do that?" he asked.

Durham had followed Sam to the porch and now grasped his shoulder, pulling him back. "Let it be, Sam. Let it be. It's like he said, no harm done."

"Get your damn hand off me, Durham."

"I won't do it. We're not getting into a row just because you got your pride hurt. Now back off and let's say good evening to these good fellows, and get back to Pap and Cordell."

"You want to go back to Pap, you go back. I don't crawl away from nobody."

The other man was examining his manured sleeve. What Sam had done hardly mattered since the man reeked of sweat and dirt and manure anyway, but he seemed quite obsessed with the dark stain Sam had placed on him. Sam, observing this, wiped his hand again on the other sleeve.

"There you go. Now you match. Have a good laugh at *that,* if you got to laugh at something." He turned on his heel to go.

Sam had let his hair grow long and thick in the back, so the man found himself a good fistful to hold on to when he reached out and yanked Sam back. "Wait a minute, sweet darling. You and me ain't finished here."

"No, we ain't," Sam said. Ignoring the pain and the loss of not just a few hairs, he yanked his head free of the man's grasp, turned, and landed a solid punch on the fellow's jaw. The man shuddered, grunted, collapsed to his rump.

"You don't mess with an Underhill," Sam said to him. "I'm the son of the man who can jerk a knot into the tail of a comet, and I'm twice the man he is."

The partner of the fellow Sam had struck said, "You talking about Bushrod Underhill?"

"The very same." Sam thrust his chin out proudly. Durham thought he looked absurd.

The man Sam had struck came up, rubbing his jaw. He pointed at Sam's nose. "You ever come into my presence again, my fine young dear, and I'll pull that pug nose of yours off and use it to plug your bung."

"You want to talk big, then talk. You want to fight, then fight. Not the next time we meet, but now."

Durham jerked Sam away, hard. "That's it, Sam. You're going to get yourself knifed or shot if you keep this up."

"I'll not crawl from this jackass!"

"You'd best swallow that anger and come with me. Pap's already questioned whether he should have brought you. You get into a big row here, and Pap will send your hide home to Missouri."

Sam, still seething, kept his eye on his opponent for ten or so seconds more, but finally turned and walked away with his brother.

"Hey!" the man yelled. Sam turned. "You really an Underhill?"

"I am, indeed."

"So it's true that Bushrod Underhill really is in Texas?"

"It's true."

The pair on the porch looked at one another. "Give your pap my best, then. I read that almanac about him."

"Looked at the pictures is more likely. I doubt you can read your own name."

"For the sake of your pap, I'll overlook you saying that. I can read my name, cipher, recite, everything! I can even spell your name out: T-U-R-D . . ."

Sam made as if to run back at the fellow, but Durham restrained him. "Let's leave, now. No more of this."

Sam called back to the man, "Maybe you and me will meet again!"

"You'd best hope we don't."

Striding back toward the farrier's smithy, Sam said, "I could have whupped him, Durham."

"You probably could have. And maybe got a broken arm or nose. And then you'd be unfit to look for John, and Pap would skin you and tan you for leather. You'd best start remembering what's brought us to Texas to begin with, brother."

"Shut up, Durham. You prattle on like some old snuff-chewing granny." He paused. "No need for you to say anything about this to Pap."

"Why? You said you don't care what he thinks. You said we need to stand up to him more."

"You ain't going to say anything to him, are you?"

Durham paused, then grinned. "Of course I ain't. Pap would probably get mad and blame me as much as you. You know how he can be."

"Hey, Durham, let me ask you something, just between you and me. Did Ma really send you out to join us after we'd left, or did you just sneak off and lie to Pap?"

Durham glanced sidewise. "Let me ask you two questions, Sam. First, do you really think Ma would ever have give me permission to do what we're doing? And second, if I had lied about it, you think I'd admit it to you?"

Sam grinned. "I don't know if there's much point in me even answering them questions."

"You're right. Look . . . there's Pap and Cordell outside the farrier's place. Let's cut dirt. Likely Pap's going to fuss at us for wandering off."

CHAPTER THIRTEEN

The Underhills traveled no more than two miles before preparing to camp for the night, but a passing man took a great interest in them, introduced himself as one William Budd, and engaged them in conversation. It soon came to light that he was a first cousin of the farrier who had fixed Bush's horseshoe, leading to an invitation for them all to break camp, travel on a bit farther, and pass the night at his farm.

"We've got a small house, but stout, and there's a barn as well, so there'll be beds enough for all. It looks like rain may come before morning, so I hope you'll accept my offer," Budd said.

Bush, using the pseudonym of Jim Smith, expressed appreciation and gladly accepted the offer. He loved rain, always had, but wasn't fond of trying to sleep in it.

The evening at the Budd residence turned out entertainingly for all Underhills but Sam. Budd, their host, had but one child, a daughter, Dell, a hefty young woman with unfortunately plain features. These detractions, however, had not rendered her shy, and she turned upon Sam an intense and unwanted attention that had the other Underhills struggling not to laugh at his discomfort. Dell Budd hovered about Sam as if he'd just proposed marriage and she'd accepted.

Bushrod, who had wondered why Budd had shown such interest in them, soon found the answer. Budd had heard that the famous Bushrod Underhill and three of his sons were traveling into Texas, and had wondered if the "Smith" family might actually be the Underhills. Bush saw no reason to lie, and admitted the truth.

"I'd appreciate you not advertising it too much," Bush said. "I'm a quiet man by nature and don't care for a lot of attention. It's the reason I was using a false name to begin with."

Sam's predicament worsened now that his admirer knew he was one of a famous clan. Dell grew almost embarrassingly amorous, until at length even Sam's brothers ceased to be entertained and began to feel sorry for him.

"I believe I'll turn in," Sam declared when he'd stood all he could. "I'll head to the barn and make my bed there." He rose to go. " 'Evening to you all."

"Sleep well, young man," Budd said. "By the by, you'll not be alone in the barn."

Sam glanced at the fat daughter and looked worried, appalling things racing through his mind. "Not alone?"

"No . . . my two nephews are working for me these days, and they sleep out there."

"Oh. I see." Sam's relief was evident. "Well, I couldn't complain about that, me being the interloper. Good night."

Sam left the house with all haste, beating a welcome escape across the battered yard and hoping to high heaven that Dell Budd attempted no nocturnal visit. That others would be in the barn actually seemed good news to him since it would make any romantic sneak attacks on Dell's part more unlikely.

Sam entered the barn and noted the flickering glow of a lamp above in the loft. "Hello!" he called up to the unseen men above. "I'm a guest of the family, come to sleep in the barn for the night."

"Up with you, then," a friendly voice called down. "It's a big loft."

Sam put his hands on the rungs and climbed. He reached the top fast and deftly leaped up, heading for the two men who were coming to their feet and extending hands to greet him.

As eyes met, they all froze, staring at one another. "You!" one of the two loft-dwellers bellowed as smiles faded and hands that had stretched out for shaking balled themselves into fists instead.

Bushrod's host, meanwhile, was doing his best to argue Bushrod into lingering with him the next day for a day-long hunt when the sound of loud wails wafted through the night outside the walls of the house.

"What the devil is that?" Bushrod asked, coming to his feet.

"Sounds like somebody getting the holy fire beat out of him," Cordell said.

Hosts and guests alike headed out the door and toward the barn, from where the caterwauling came.

Durham jerked to a stop for a moment when he heard a shout in a voice that sounded familiar but wasn't Sam's. He tried to recall where he'd heard it, then realized it was the voice of one of the pair whom Sam had wrangled with earlier at the store. Those two were the very nephews of the man who now hosted them? Who could have guessed it?

The fight, though two against one, was most unexpectedly one-sided in Sam's favor. He had his father's fighting style, quick and businesslike, doing what was needed to get the job finished without bluster. Sam's fighting manner was the one thing about him that didn't lend itself toward bluster and fancy show. The pair who had attacked him were bloodied and retreating by the time those from the house reached them. They called on someone, anyone, to pull their foe away from them. Cordell and Durham each took hold of their brother and pulled him away and down the ladder.

The atmosphere between the Underhills and Budds was transformed. William Budd was furious and obviously held Sam to blame for whatever had happened. The pair in the loft quickly accused Sam of starting the fight, and when Durham and Sam revealed the day's earlier encounter and how it had led to this fight, the defeated ones simply denied it all.

Budd was so furious that he was shaking. "Is this the way

of the Underhills, sir? Do you always attack those who host you? And you, young man"—he wheeled upon Sam—"don't think your flirtations with my daughter weren't noticed!"

"My flirtations? *My* flirtations? The devil you say—"

"I'll have the law on you! All of you! I'll see you locked up for this, you brawler!" The latter threat was directed at Sam.

"Get Brutus on him!" Budd's fat daughter bellowed, getting so caught up in the fire of the moment that she actually turned on her beloved Sam. "Brutus will teach him!"

"Who's Brutus?" Durham asked.

"We'll not linger to find out," Bushrod said. "I believe we've wore out our welcome, boys. Let's move on."

"You'd best cover twenty miles before you even think of stopping!" Budd hollered at Sam. "Any closer than that, and Brutus will have your backside! I'm going to send him after you, no lie!"

"Who's Brutus?" Durham asked again.

"You just wait and see!" William Budd replied.

The Underhills, as eager now to be gone as the Budd family was to see them go, gathered their possessions, saddled their weary horses, and rode on into the night as clouds gathered above. No dry beds or warm lofts tonight. They'd sleep in the rain after all.

"I should have left you home, Sam," Bush avowed again as they traveled away. "Is there nowhere you can go without finding trouble for yourself and those of us plagued with having to live with you?"

"They started it, not me," Sam said, which was true enough of the row in the loft, but perhaps not true of the day's earlier encounter. But Durham was kind to his brother and kept his mouth shut.

"We ain't really going to travel twenty miles before we camp, are we?" Cordell asked.

"Of course not," Bush said. "They'll forget about us soon enough. We'll go out a couple of miles, camp as best we can, and move on come morning."

"Who is this Brutus they kept threatening to send after Sam?" Durham asked.

"I don't know," Bush replied. "Most likely he's a dog."

They found out the next morning that Brutus was no dog at all.

When dawn broke, they found Sam's bedroll empty. Thinking at first that he'd simply risen early and gone off to relieve himself, they made a fire and cooked breakfast and laughed about the fat Budd girl and waited for Sam to return. He didn't, so they set out looking.

The sign Bush found indicated that Sam had indeed gotten up in answer to a call of nature, but not recently. Sometime in the night he'd risen and wandered too far away. There were signs of a struggle, and a crudely lettered note pinned to the ground: "You should have listened. Brutus has him now. J. Budd."

"Pap, you don't think they've murdered Sam, do you?" Cordell asked.

"I hope not, son. I hope not." Bush studied the note, worried, unsure what to do. "Brutus . . . who in the world could it be?"

"And where'd they take Sam?" Durham asked. "And why didn't he holler or something if they came after him in the dark?"

The Underhills broke their camp and followed the sign. At length they came upon a small cabin occupied by a tall man who rolled his eyes toward the sky when asked if he knew anyone named Brutus who would haul a man off by night.

"That would be Brutus Budd," he answered. "He's a relative of William Budd's, who lives yonder way, and Elijah Budd, who has a blacksmith and farrier place some miles away, and all the other Budds hereabouts. I tell you, sir, no disrespect intended, but nigh every one of them Budds is only about half sane, if that. Elijah's the clearest-headed of them all, I guess, but Brutus Budd . . . he's the very worst of them."

"Sir, I'm afraid he's gotten my son. He wouldn't be the kind to murder a man, I hope."

"Murder? Not likely. What's probably happened is that he's got your son locked up in his jail."

"Jail? He's a ranger or officer or some such?"

" 'Some such' is as close as you'll get. The fact is, Brutus Budd ain't nothing. He has no more right to jail a man than you or me. But he took the notion some time ago that he was the law in these parts, threw him up a cabin with no windows and a stout roof you can't break out of, and declared it his jail. And sure enough, he'll 'arrest' folks and lock them away. Every now and again he'll lock somebody up just because he don't like the way they look, or talk, or smell or something, but most of the time he serves a purpose, I suppose. Most of those he locks up have done something to deserve it. May I ask what your boy might have done?"

"He got into a fight with some nephews of William Budd."

"William? Yep, he's almost as pop-skulled as Brutus. He probably turned Brutus on to your boy. William Budd's a nice fellow unless you make him mad, and if you do, it's look out, Moses."

"Where do we find this jail?"

The man gave directions. "But it's no use trying to get him out. Brutus acts as his own court and judge, you see, and he'll have given your boy a sentence. And come hell or high water, he ain't going to let him out until that sentence is served."

"That's piddle and nonsense," Bush said. "I'll get him out, by gall! Nobody's locking up one of mine who has no legal right to do it."

"I wouldn't threaten Brutus, sir. Just some advice for you. Brutus would stand up to oppose the very second coming of Jesus if you tried to force him not to. But get a little liquor in him, and he passes out faster than an Indian. That's your best bet for getting your boy sprung free."

"Thanks for that information," Bush said, and he tossed the man a coin that was received with gratitude.

They rode on.

CHAPTER
FOURTEEN

The worst of it was, the wild-looking man with the loose-barreled old flintlock rifle had taken Sam Underhill's pipe and tobacco.

Sam sat in darkness, leaned up against the thick, impenetrable wall of the hut into which he'd been roughly shoved several hours earlier. Even after all this time it was difficult to believe the surreal situation wasn't just some overly vivid dream.

Sam had risen in the night back at the camp, gone off a distance to make some water and have a smoke. That's when they'd gotten him, the wild-looking man and the other, silent fellow who'd hung back, watching. Maybe the man had thought Sam wouldn't recognize him in the darkness if he made no noise, but he'd known who it was. William Budd, making good his threat to turn old Brutus loose on him. Old Brutus . . . no dog at all, but a madman who apparently fancied himself an agent of the law.

Sam ruefully hoped old Brutus was enjoying that pipe and tobacco. Somebody might as well. And when Brutus was through smoking it, Sam could think of something quite original that madman could do with the pipe.

Sam stood again and paced back and forth in the makeshift prison, cursing softly, occasionally slamming his shoulder against the upright rooted log wall. This achieved no purpose but knocking loose a little of the mud chinking and making the cold wind blow through even colder—but he had to do *something*.

"No point in that, son," said the only other occupant of the hut. "You'll just bruise your shoulder up."

"I ain't in the mood to talk," Sam said. His fellow prisoner, already inside when Sam was thrown in, had already talked Sam's ear sore.

"May as well rest easy. Brutus will let you out when your time's up."

"And who decides how much time that is?"

"Brutus does. He's judge, jury, and jailer all wrapped up in one."

"He's a madman, is what he is."

"That's the truth. But he's harmless. Actually does some good. A lot of folks come through this new country thinking there's no law can reach them, and generally they're right. But Brutus makes for a good substitute. He'll lock up anybody he thinks has done something they shouldn't."

"Someday somebody's going to shoot the fool."

"I expect so. Until then, we just got to put up with him. Sit down. He'll let you out in a day or so."

"You been in here before, huh?"

"Three or four times."

"He'd have never took me if I'd been armed."

"I'm glad you weren't. You might have shot Brutus, and then no telling what kind of trouble you'd have been in."

"I was near my camp when he come upon me in the dark. I should have yelled for my pap and brothers. But he swore he'd shoot me if I made a peep." Sam rammed the wall again, then rubbed his aching shoulder. "I should have took the chance. I don't know if that rickety old rifle of his would have even fired."

"Don't be thinking that. Brutus is a dead aim with that old blunderbuss."

Sam sat down. "It's William Budd I'm maddest at. He's the one that sparked all this, just because I whupped his nephews after they attacked me."

"Will Budd is trouble, that's for sure. Nice man until you

rile him, then he turns almost as crazy as Brutus."

"Is everybody in Texas this loco?"

"Not everybody. Enough, though."

Sam fidgeted and stretched. "Well, I reckon I'll take your advice. I'll be out of here as soon as my pap and brothers track me down. What's your name, anyhow? You never said."

"I'm Jack Bean." The fellow, seated against the adjacent wall, leaned over and shook Sam's hand. "You?"

"Sam Underhill. My father's Bushrod Underhill. Maybe you've heard of him."

Given previous reactions to the Underhill name, Sam expected Jack Bean to respond similarly. But in the nearly pitch-black room, illuminated only by what thin shaft of moonlight penetrated the spaces between the walls where chinking had fallen out, Sam saw Bean merely nod. "Yes, I've heard of your father. A few folks passing through a day or so back said Bush Underhill was coming through."

"Pap's a famous man. I don't believe he knew he was so famous until we came to Texas."

"There's an almanac I seen . . ."

Sam, warming to Jack Bean a little, smiled. "Pap don't much like that almanac. He just wants folks to leave him be."

"I'd say your father is a fine man. He'd have to be to have a son like John."

"You know John?"

"Don't really know him, but I've seen him. Twice."

"Lately?"

"No, not for a spell." Jack Bean squinted in the dark. "Hard to see much in here, but I think I can see some similarity to John in your build, shape of your head and all."

"Where'd you see John?"

"The first time was at a public meeting after the San Jacinto fight. He got up and gave quite a fine talk. The second time was when I was called in to fix some wagons for . . ."

He stopped as the door rattled and shook, then swung open. The bushy-haired form of the madman jailer filled the door, limned against a sky at last beginning to grow light.

"Jack Bean," Brutus said, leveling the old flintlock, "time for you to go thy way and sin no more."

Jack Bean stood, grinning. "Obliged, Brutus. You going to let my friend go, too?"

"His time ain't up yet."

"Come on, Brutus. He's sorry for what he done."

"I am, indeed," Sam said, beginning to rise. A scowl from his jailer made him sink back down again.

"You'll go free when you've served out your time. Not a moment before. This is *law* you're up against, son! Law!"

Jack Bean said to Sam, "Brutus was in jail himself back in Louisiana. Had him a stern jailer, and he patterns himself after him. Ain't that right, Brutus?"

"Out of here, Jack Bean! Now!" The madman waved the rifle.

"Wait!" Sam said. "Tell me where it was you last saw John."

But there was no time for Jack Bean to answer. Brutus lunged forward, grabbed him by the shirt, and yanked him roughly outside, closing the door and barring it tight.

Sam hung his head, frustrated and angry, and hoping his father and brothers would show up soon to end this madness.

Bushrod Underhill lay on his belly, Durham on one side and Cordell on the other, and through the blowing grass studied the two little structures in the shallow hollow below. One was a typical Texas log hut, the other a heavier-walled structure made of upright, rooted logs, like some Indian dwellings Bush had seen in his youth. It hadn't been hard to find this place; Sam had done a good job of deliberately leaving sign behind him.

"You reckon he's in one of them houses?" Cordell asked.

"Maybe. No sign of life just now, though."

No sooner had Bush said that than the door of the more typical-looking hut opened and a strange human creature emerged. Raggedly dressed, with long bushy hair and beard, he strode out bearing a long flintlock rifle. Rooting himself before his rude dwelling, he cocked his head back and let out a long rooster crow, followed by a belch so loud that the Underhills could hear it all the way up on the rise.

"What in the world is that thing?" Durham asked.

"Looks like something you'd see locked up in one of them big-city places where they keep simpletons and madmen," Cordell said. "Reckon that's Brutus?"

"Well, whatever or whoever it is, I suppose I'd best go meet it," Bush said. "Maybe he's got Sam in there with him."

"Careful, Pap. He sure is keeping that rifle handy."

"So I noticed. Watch out for me, fellows. I ain't at all sure how this is going to go." Bush prepared to rise. "Let's hope this is another Bushrod Underhill enthusiast."

Bush pushed himself to his feet, left his rifle with Cordell, took a deep breath, slapped on a broad grin, and began walking down the rise toward the strange figure below, lifting his hand in a friendly hello.

By the time Bushrod was face-to-face with Brutus, he wasn't sure he would get out of the situation alive. The crazed-looking man had lifted his weapon and dropped to a rifleman's crouch the moment he'd seen Bush coming down the slope. Though Bushrod Underhill, gunsmith, had never seen a worse-looking rifle, badly made and battered, he wasn't about to assume the thing wouldn't fire. With heart pounding, hands spread to the side to show he was unarmed, and a grin still plastered across his face, Bush descended slowly, calling his howdy in the most cordial tone he could.

The rifleman squinted one eye and sighted down the long barrel, watching him silently.

"Going to be a pretty day, I believe!" Bush said jovially.

"Who you be?"

"My name's Underhill. Bushrod Underhill." Bush waited for the usual reaction and didn't receive it. For the first time since coming to Texas, he'd apparently met someone who didn't know the name of the frontier's latest literarily lauded hero.

"Drop your weapons," Brutus commanded.

"I got none to drop."

"Turn around slow so I can see there ain't no pistol hid behind you."

Bush made a slow pivot with hands still extended to the side, glancing up the slope toward his sons so that at least he could be looking at folks he loved when this maniac shot him in the back. But Brutus didn't fire, and when Bush faced him again, he came to his feet and lowered the rifle.

"Why you here?"

"Well, I'm looking for my son. I thought maybe he was here."

"Maybe he is, maybe he ain't."

"His name's Sam. Early twenties . . . got took by some-body last night near our camp. He'd been in a row with some fellows in a barn loft, and a man named James Budd was ready to turn the law on him . . . Are you the law here, sir?"

Brutus threw his grizzled head back and stuck out his chin. "I am."

"Well, good. Good. Every new country needs law, I al-ways say. Uh, might it be you who took my son a prisoner?"

"Yes, sir, it was."

Bush glanced at the other log building. "Is that your jail there?"

"Yep."

"Might he be in there?"

"Yep."

"He's not hurt or nothing, I hope."

"Nope."

"Good. Glad to hear it. Well, I suppose you've taught him a good lesson. He'll know to watch himself from now on, not get in any more fights."

"Yep."

"When do you reckon he'll be getting out?"

"Don't know yet. Ain't decided."

"I see. Might I maybe offer to, say, pay his fine for him and get him out now?"

"Ain't no fine."

"Oh. Uh, might you consider changing his sentence so he

could pay a fine and go free? I promise you I'll take him a long way from here if he can.''

The rifle came back up. "That's a bribe, pilgrim."

"No, no, I'm not talking about a bribe. A fine. Good and legal and all."

"I told you there ain't no fine."

Bush, eyeing the rifle, stuck his hands up a little higher. "Easy with that rifle, sir. I'm not going to cause you any trouble."

"I ought to lock you up."

"Why?"

"The bribe! The bribe!"

Bush began to feel quite antsy, and worried again that he'd be shot. "Maybe I ought to just go away."

"Uh-uh. Nope. I believe I will lock you up."

"Sir, you needn't do that."

Brutus clicked back the hammer of the flintlock.

Moments later, Bushrod was blinking in the semidarkness of the improvised jail. Sam, still seated against the wall, looked at him and slowly shook his head as the bar slid into place on the door outside.

"Got you, too, huh?"

"Got me, too, son."

CHAPTER
FIFTEEN

"Would you look at that!" Durham declared as he watched his father being hustled into the second log structure below. "What in the devil is going on here?"

"I don't know," Cordell replied. "Reckon we're going to have to shoot that loco fellow to get them out?"

"No need for that."

At the sound of the voice, Cordell and Durham jerked their heads and looked behind them, surprised that someone had managed to approach them unheard. A thin, tattered-looking fellow with a disarming grin stood there, nodding a hello.

"Who are you?" Cordell asked.

"I'm Jack Bean. I got turned out from that so-called jail down there at sunrise. Brutus got your pap, I see. That was your pap, warn't it?"

"It was," Cordell said. "You ain't here to cause us more trouble, are you?"

"Oh, no. It's just that I seen you fellows come up here and figured out who you was. The young man who was locked up with me talked about his folks coming to spring him loose. Thought I might give you some advice."

"What advice?"

"There's only one way I know to make Brutus cut somebody's jail time short. You give him whiskey, and he'll be nice as a kitten. Otherwise he's got no more give-back about him than a flying bullet."

"We got no whiskey."

"I do. My place is over that hill yonder, and I'll be glad to spare you a little, very cheap."

Cordell and Durham looked at one another. Short of entering an all-out fight, it seemed the only other likely option.

"You stay here," Cordell said to his brother. "I'll be back soon."

Less than an hour later, Cordell was standing in the same spot his father had shortly before, grinning the same kind of grin, and extending a little jug toward Brutus.

"Go ahead, take it!" Cordell said. "It's good whiskey, just right for paying off a debt to the law."

Brutus eyed the jug and shifted his rifle to his other hand. "Set it down at your feet, and back off."

Cordell complied, casting a quick glance toward the jail building, feeling the eyes of his father and brother on him as they watched the little drama from between the upright logs.

Brutus advanced, eyes shifting between Cordell and the jug, knelt, and took it up. He hung his rifle over the crook of his left arm, uncorked the jug, sniffed, and nodded.

"Get on with you," he said, turning back toward his house.

Cordell nodded, turned, and began walking back up the rise. When he heard the door of Brutus's house close, he darted straight over to the other building, lifted the bar, and swung open the door.

"Pap, Sam, I suggest that we all move just as fast as we can move."

They ran up the hill like the devil was at their heels, but Brutus never emerged from his house. Once over the rise, Durham slapped his father and brothers on the shoulders, grinning broadly, then joined them as they ran on to where the horses were. Jack Bean was still with them, having returned with Cordell to bring over the whiskey.

"Who's this?" Bush asked Durham as they loped along.

"It's Jack Bean," Durham said. "It's because of him that we were able to get you out of there. He sold us the whiskey."

"Obliged, Mr. Bean," Bush said.

"Glad to help, sir. I'm an admirer of yourn, Mr. Under-hill."

They reached the horses. "Pap," Sam said, "Jack told me while we were locked up together that he's seen John."

Bush froze a moment, then looked at Bean. "Where?"

"Like I was telling your son right before Brutus jerked me out of there, I seen him once at a public meeting after San Jacinto. The next time, I saw him at a place where I was fixing up some busted wagons."

"Where's that?"

"In Trippler's fort, where I believe him and his family are being held as prisoners."

They went directly to Bean's house, a dwelling almost as lonely and rough as that of the madman they'd just escaped. Seated inside beside a big fire that Bean built up on his flat stone hearth, they coughed in billowing smoke spewed back into the room by the inefficient chimney and listened as Jack Bean told both what he knew, and what he suspected beyond that.

"Trippler is a man I don't want to be around," Bean said, sipping from a whiskey jug similar to the one now in the possession of a jail-obsessed madman about a mile away. "He came to Texas as one of the empresarios, bringing in folks, mostly Americans, back under the Mexican rule. My brother was one of them, God rest his soul. He drank himself to death, he did." Bean took another swallow. "Anyway, ever since the revolution, Trippler's been a man folks don't know what to think about. They say he's got a scheme of some sort, something to do with politics and such. I don't know what it is, if anything, but I can tell you this: if there is a scheme, it'll involve Trippler doing all he can to make a king of himself. He's that way. Napoleon Trippler, some call him. Wants power, wealth. Everybody wants that, I reckon, but he's . . . different. I believe him to be sort of like old Brutus. Not right in the head. But Brutus is pretty much harmless. Not Trippler."

"Why would he have kidnapped John?" Cordell asked.

"Because of who John Underhill is. His influence. Folks

listen when John Underhill speaks. If Trippler had somebody like him as a spokesman, telling folks to support his schemes, he might be able to succeed with his plans."

"I've heard a rumor," Bushrod said, "that Trippler might be seeking some kind of alliance with Mexico again."

"I've heard the same."

"How'd you come to see John at Trippler's fort?"

"I'm a wagon maker by trade, whenever I bother to practice a trade, that is." He sipped again. "Trippler had some wagons that got damaged. I was in the vicinity and somehow he got word I could fix up a wagon right good. He sent some of his men to fetch me. My skin crawled every minute I was in that place, I'll tell you. I don't like Trippler, not at all."

"What kind of place is this fort?"

"I swear to you, sir, it'll make you think of the Alamo mission down at Bexar. But if anything, it's a hell of a lot better fortified. It's like the Alamo was once, an old mission with walls. Not as big a place overall. It's in the heart of Trippler's old emprasario grant on the Brazos, maybe ten mile or so from your John's own place."

"John's house is on land that was part of Trippler's empresario colony?"

"No. Just a short ways outside the line, though."

"Where did you see John at Trippler's?"

"Standing on a balcony in the building where Trippler lives. And Trippler right beside him, talking earnest in his ear. They stepped out only for a moment, and looked down to watch me working with the wagons. Then Trippler took him by the arm and pulled him back inside. I only saw John Underhill a moment or two, but it was him. I know it was."

Bush stared into the fire. "I'd heard the tale that John might have been kidnapped, but I discounted it. I'd never think anybody could take John against his will."

"Anybody could take anybody if they get their hands on their family first."

Bush thought about it, and nodded. "I should've realized that myself. But it's just that I saw little reason to believe that rumor, considering the other impossible rumor that always went along with it.''

"You're talking about the one that says Crockett is alive, and that Trippler has him?"

"That's right.''

"It ain't no rumor, sir," Jack Bean said earnestly. "It's the truth. For I seen Crockett there, too, with my own eyes.''

"What?"

"It's the truth. I went looking for an outhouse while I was working, and got turned around someway or another and stumbled into one of the buildings. A fellow come out of the door and told me in a mighty harsh way to get out of there on pain of being gutshot. Through the door behind him I seen Crockett there, laid out on a bed, looking weak and sickly as can be. I'd seen Crockett before, you see, back in Tennessee, where I lived before coming to Texas.''

"Why would Trippler want Crockett?"

"Same reason he wanted John. For his influence. The rumor has it that he aims to get Crockett well again, and have him come out in public for this scheme of his. I suppose he figures that if he has Davy Crockett and John Underhill both speaking out for his plan, folks will listen." Another sip, and a swipe of the mouth across his sleeve. "Me, I don't believe that. I don't think folks will ever listen to Trippler. He's too much a madman. I've heard other talk, you see. A lot of folks don't like these rumors that Trippler's been dallying with the Mexicans. And he's bringing in enough gun-toters to make a small army, and that makes folks nervous. Some of them gunmen are Mexicans, too. In taverns and such I hear people saying that they ought to just roust up a citizen army and storm Trippler's fort before he has a chance to do any harm to the republic.''

Cordell stood, face flushed. "Pap, we got to get John and his family out of there.''

"I know, son. And we will. Once I can figure out how to go about it.''

"Mr. Underhill," Bean asked, "is it true you've come bearing gold to ransom your son?"

"You've heard that, too, have you?"

"Yes, sir. You see, there's a lot of people who can't believe that John Underhill would ever support Trippler, no matter what, and Trippler knows it. So they figure he's holding your son, and Crockett, too, for ransom. Trippler does love wealth and land, no doubt of that. He's been buying up land certificates right and left."

"I don't know about Crockett, but I can tell you I've received no ransom demand for John. I didn't even have reason to believe he was kidnapped . . . until now."

"How long ago did you see John at Trippler's?" Sam asked.

Jack Bean scratched his arm, thinking. "Month or so. And once I got out of there, I hightailed it back here as quick as I could. I don't want even to be near Trippler's place, and I swear, while I was there, I wondered if I'd ever be allowed out again, considering what I'd seen. Matter of fact, I still can't swear that I would have been allowed. I seen an open gate and took out through it while I had my chance. Never even waited for my pay."

Bushrod filled his pipe. "Mr. Bean, would you consider going with us? You know the lay of the land around Trippler's fort."

Jack Bean looked sad and shook his head. "Mr. Underhill, I'm honored you'd ask, but I ain't a brave man. I don't want no more to do with Trippler."

"I understand, sir."

"So what do we do now, Pap?" Cordell asked.

"We go on to John's house, fast as we can. And once we're there, we'll figure out how to get him and his family out of that place."

"I hope you have the best of success, Mr. Underhill," Jack Bean said. "I doubt Trippler's got a sinner's chance in hell of pulling off any kind of scheme that would betray the public—it's a madman's notion, in my view—but there's still danger to your kin while they're in that place. No telling what might happen or who might get hurt if people rise against Trippler."

CHAPTER
SIXTEEN

The Brazos country, some days later

They crouched in a ravine, silent, rifles in hand and ears pricked. All felt an odd unwillingness to look at the others in the tension of the moment.

"Listen!" Durham said in a sharp whisper.

"I hear," Bushrod responded, lifting his head to peer through the grass and brush on the ravine's edge. "Good . . . it's Cordell."

Cordell, crouched and tense in his hurry, came through the brush and dropped into the ravine with the others.

"They're out there," he said. "Seven of them, all armed."

"They see you?"

"No. If they had, you probably wouldn't be seeing me now. They have a mean look about them. I have a mighty bad feeling about this, Pap."

"So do I. I tend to get bad feelings about folks who trail me on the sneak for two days, rifles bristling out all over them, especially when there's rumors flying all over that we're carrying ransom gold."

"How far to John's house?" Durham asked.

Bush dug beneath his coat and pulled out a crumpled piece of paper. Unfolding it, he displayed the map he'd scrawled out under Cantrell Smith's guidance back in Missouri. He studied it closely, shook his head, and folded it again. "Don't look likely to me. Too far, and they'd surely jump us before we got there. We can't chance it."

"There's seven of them, Pap. We'll never be able to shake them, and there's only four of us."

"I know the odds, Cordell. I've been playing them through my mind over and over."

"I say we can handle them," Sam said. "Bring them on! These are Underhills they're dealing with!"

"For Lord's sake, boy, don't you go starting to believe them almanac legends. Maybe Bushrod Underhill can ring the moon in one of those stories, but this is the real world. We don't stand much chance with the odds like they are."

"What if we could convince them we don't have any gold, Pap?" Durham said. "They'd back off, then, nothing to gain from us."

"We'd never get the chance even to try as things stand right now. If we got close enough to try to jaw with them, they'd just shoot us down." Bush rubbed his chin. "There's only one thing to do that I can see. When the odds are against you, you change the odds."

"What do you mean?"

"See that knoll yonder? I believe we can make use of it."

"We're going to fight them from up there?"

"Not how you're thinking. We're going to use that knoll to even the odds a bit." Bush looked seriously at his sons. "Young men, I believe the time has come that might lead to some doings you'll not ever forget. The kind of doings that make a fellow have to think twice, and ready himself."

"You're saying we may have to kill some men," Cordell said.

"That's right. We'll do our best to avoid it, try to convince them away, but I doubt their breed is the reasonable kind. Boys, if the moment comes when we have to start shooting, there can be no hesitating or doubting. Because if you hesitate, or you doubt, then it's you who dies, and not your enemy. Do you understand me?"

"I understand," Cordell said readily, echoed by Sam. Durham, his face pale beneath his tan, blinked a couple of times, then nodded.

"Durham, you're certain you can do this?" Bush asked.

"I'll do what I must, Pap."

Sam pulled a pistol from his belt and shook it in the air. "I'm ready right now. Bring them on!"

The face Bushrod turned on Sam struck the bluster out of his manner at once. "Sam, there's only one kind of man more dangerous in a life-or-death fight than one who hesitates, and that's one who's too eager. I've seen you fight with your fists, and I know you're good at it. You think, you work things right, you set your mind on what you're trying to do, and you do it. But a gun battle is different. A rifle ball flying your way is a bloody lot different than a set of knuckles."

Sam's expression grew somber; he seemed to deflate, and said nothing.

"You'll keep your head in this fight, if it comes to one, Sam. You'll think straight, think cool, think fast, but most of all, think clear." Bush looked at the others. "That goes the same for all of us."

Solemnly they all nodded, and once again it was difficult for them to look one another in the eye.

Bushrod nodded. "Very well. And now, sons, listen close. Here's what I have in mind."

The sun was westering, casting a reddish glow across the Brazos countryside. Cordell, positioned to make sure that anyone on the flatlands below could easily see him, labored atop the knoll, digging with a small camp shovel Bushrod had brought along strapped to his saddle. Sam stood with him, also in view, holding his rifle and making a show of pacing back and forth like a sentinel. They were silhoutted against the sky, knowing they were watched, and it gave them an odd, skin-prickling feeling.

Bushrod and Durham, meanwhile, lay hidden amid the boulders at the rim of the knoll's top, scanning the landscape.

"Can you see them?" Sam asked softly.

"Not much now that the light's fading, but they're still out there," Bushrod replied. "The main point is that they can see you, and tell what you're doing."

"Makes me nervous," Cordell said. "It's a long range, but a well-placed shot could—"

"Don't talk about it," Sam cut in.

"They won't shoot," Bushrod said. "They wouldn't see any cause for it. Right now, I'd wager they're smelling themselves a chance for easy pickings, with no fight. They're following men carrying gold, and now those same men are digging a hole as if to bury something . . ."

"But it don't make sense, Pap. They're bound to wonder why we'd be burying gold that we've brought to pay ransom with."

"No doubt they are. But it don't have to make sense to them, just lure them. That's the key. Their curiosity is going to get the best of them, and when we leave this hill, they're going to come up here and see what we've been up to. But they'll surely leave some with their horses, which means they'll be divided, and that should better the odds for us with whoever's left down below."

"This is risky, Pap. You sure there's no other way to get shut of them?"

"I'm hoping we can convince them we have nothing for them. If they won't take to convincing, there'll be no getting shut of them short of shooting any or all of them dead. For if we don't shake them off now, they'll just keep following us. And the closer we get to John's house and Trippler's fort, the more they're going to feel compelled to make a move before their chance for gold slips out of their hands."

"Reckon I've dug long enough, Pap?" Cordell said, eyes on the empty hole below him.

"I'd say so. Sam, bend down and lift up that saddlebag, and make as if you're putting it in the hole. But do it natural . . . we don't want them to catch on that we're putting on a show."

Sam complied, lifting the bag to within view of the dark flatlands below for a moment, then bending to lower it toward the hole. In fact he laid it to the side.

"Fill it up, Cordell," Bush said.

Cordell made quick work of filling the hole, then tamped

it down. He and Sam then lifted rocks and placed them atop it as if trying to hide the scar left by the digging.

"That should do it," Bush said. "Now, let's head down the side here and ride yonder way. Once we get beyond that little swell where they can't see us, we'll double back around."

"And then things will really get lively," Cordell said ironically.

Bushrod spat and nodded. "Then things will really get lively."

An hour later, after several minutes of secretive watching and refining of plans, Bushrod put his arm around the shoulders of each son in turn, then said, "The time's come, fellows, to put you to the kind of test you haven't had before. And God knows I don't know I'm in the right to do it." He turned to Durham. "I've got to know, Durham, if you're truly here with your mother's blessing, or if you came to join us without it."

Durham blinked hard. Sam had already asked him the same question, and he'd evaded it. But this was his father asking, and that, like the circumstances, made things manifestly different. "I sneaked away, Pap."

Bushrod didn't look angry, but his eyes grew soft and moist. "You lied to me, son."

"I know."

"I'd ask you why . . . but I know why."

"It's because I want to be part of helping John. He's your son, but my brother. I had to do it, Pap."

Bush studied him a long time, then looked for a time longer yet through the darkness at the vague forms of the would-be robbers who'd been trailing them. A divided band they were now, four of them back guarding the horses while the other three labored up on the knoll, moving rock and digging in the hole Cordell had made, seeking gold that wasn't there. It wouldn't be long now before they knew the truth.

"Pap," Cordell said softly, "if we're to act, we have to do it now."

Bushrod nodded, then faced Durham. "If aught should

happen to you, Durham, I'll never gain the forgiveness of your mother."

"And if you don't let me do my part here, Pap, you'll never gain the forgiveness of me."

Bushrod thought it over, and smiled slowly. "You're a man, that I have to say for you. You shouldn't have lied to me, shouldn't have left against your mother's wishes . . . but you're here now, and we have to play the hand we're dealt."

"I'll lead the way, if you want," Cordell said.

"You and me together will, son. This is my plan, and if there's to be trouble come from it, I ought to be the one to bear the brunt of it. Now, boys, if anything should happen to me, you don't get yourselves killed over it. You get on away from here, and you go on and find John."

"Yes, Pap," Cordell said.

"Nothing's going to happen to you, Pap," said Durham. "Nothing's going to happen to any of us."

"That's right, son," Bush replied. "We're going to do this right, and carefully, and nothing's going to happen." He turned and looked out through the darkness. "You boys . . . you *men*—are you ready?"

"We're ready," Cordell said.

"Then let's go."

CHAPTER
SEVENTEEN

The moon appeared sporadically, scudding in and out of holes in the clouds, at one moment casting a dim netherlight across the flatlands, other times vanishing to bathe it in darkness. In the lighter moments the advancing Underhills froze and sank into the blowing grasses and hid behind the autumn-dry brush, watching the four men who stood guard over the horses, men so far unaware of what was creeping up on them. When the moon was hidden, the Underhills moved, rifles ready, pistols in their belts.

Men labored on the knoll above and to their south and left, and those watching the horses were focusing their full attention on them. The Underhills moved close, closer, so close now they could hear the breathing of the horses and the hiss of one man's pipe as he drew smoke through a reed stem.

Bushrod and Cordell had moved in side by side, followed a few yards back by Sam and Durham. Now Bush advanced slightly ahead of Cordell, moved to a position to the side of the man smoking the pipe, and stood, leveling his rifle.

"Hold still, friend," he said softly. "Not a move, not a twitch, not even a puff on that sotweed."

The man jerked his head; the moon emerged from the clouds and revealed his face. He was middle-aged, roughly bearded, one eye dead and glassy and squinted, the other wide with quick fear. He stared at Bush's face, then at the muzzle of the rifle aimed at his midsection.

Cordell rose just as the other men became aware of what was happening. "Hold still, all of you!" Cordell barked in a hushed voice. "Not a twitch!" Then Sam and Durham were at his side, each aiming his rifle at a different man.

A silent, tense standoff followed, and Bush dared to believe his scheme was going to work. With these men as hostages, they would silently await the return of those on the knoll, disarm them on threat of the deaths of their companions, and then . . . after that Bush's plan was a little more murky.

"Lay down that rifle, slow," Bush said to the man he was aiming at. "All of you do the same. And them pistols you've got under them coats . . . out with them, and hold them by the muzzle."

"I believe they're skunked, Pap," Cordell said. And it was just then that the tension broke and things began to go awry.

The man guarded by Durham was positioned so that he was slightly hidden by one of the horses. He laid down his rifle, as ordered, and reached for his pistol, but brought it out ready to fire. Clicking back the lock, he snapped off a shot at Durham at almost point-blank range. The pistol boomed and flashed and Durham staggered back.

"Durham!" Bush yelled.

"I'm fine, Pap!" Durham called back. "He missed me."

But the man was running. After his shot he scooped up the rifle he'd laid down and veered off into the darkness.

"Let him go!" Bush called to Durham, but Durham was already in pursuit, and didn't hear.

A shout rang down from the knoll—"What the hell!"— and the moon sailed behind another cloud. A rifle fired out in the darkness where Durham had run.

Bush felt his stomach rise toward his throat. An overwhelming fear took hold of him: Durham was shot! But then another rifle blasted and he recognized the report of it, for he knew well the rifles he'd made for his sons.

"Durham!" Bush yelled, flicking his eye toward the knoll, where another quick flash of intermittent moonlight revealed figures scrambling down.

"I'm all right, Pap!" Durham called back, running into

view again with the muzzle of his rifle smoking. "Pap, I think I killed him."

"That was my brother!" yelled the hostage guarded by Cordell. And quick as a darting fly he reached over and grabbed Cordell's rifle by the muzzle and tried to yank it free. Cordell held on, but the man advanced on him, pushing the muzzle up so that Cordell couldn't shoot him, and back so that Cordell was unbalanced. He staggered back three steps and fell, his rifle discharging and sending a ball hurtling into the sky.

Bush fired just as the moon disappeared again. Cordell's attacker screeched, let go of the rifle, and fell writhing in the dark. The moon found another hole, sending through light that revealed the man was writhing no more.

Sam was busily trying to guard two men now—the one he'd originally leveled upon, and Bushrod's original hostage—and the latter apparently realized all at once that Sam's rifle was the only one still loaded. Bushrod was hurriedly reloading, Cordell doing the same. Durham, overwhelmed in the confusion, seemed frozen, then turned and realized that the men who had been atop the knoll were now moving this way.

"Load your rifle, Durham!" Bush yelled, and just then the man he'd originally been guarding threw down his pipe, groped for the rifle he'd dropped, failed to reach it, and darted off into the darkness.

Sam shot him just as he went out of sight, and they heard his death yell as he pitched facedown into the dirt.

Of the four men the Underhills had taken, only one remained alive. He was young, and scared, and dropped to his knees, wrapping his arms around his head and screeching in a high voice, over and over.

Bushrod finished reloading and moved toward the pitiful fellow, planning to secure him as protection against aggression by the men now running toward them through the dark. Because of the young man's obvious terror, he didn't anticipate any resistance, and thus was surprised when the fellow suddenly came to his feet with a knife he'd pulled from his boot, and slashed it at Bushrod. Bush felt a sting as it slashed a cut through his trousers and into his thigh. He pulled back, leveled his rifle, and fired just as the young man lunged at him again. The knife dropped and the fellow crumpled right over the muzzle of Bush's rifle, pulling it from his hands.

One of those who'd come off the knoll fired. The ball sang past Cordell's ear, making him duck.

Bush knelt and pulled his rifle from beneath the corpse of the young man.

"Loose their horses, Sam!" Bush yelled. It was unneccessary; Sam was already freeing the terrified horses. Two of them ran away at once, and the others stamped and snorted, looking sidewise into the melee and backing off to bolt.

"Don't let them get away, Sam!" Bush yelled, changing his mind as he realized they could use the horses to escape those bearing down on them. It was too late. Sam was able to grab the reins of only one horse. The others bolted away into the night. Then a shot obviously intended for Sam struck the single horse he'd secured, and it made a terrible noise and crumpled, almost falling atop him.

Bush yanked his pistol and fired it in the direction of their attackers, who were now taking to cover like snipers.

"Run!" Bush yelled. His sons obeyed at once. The Underhills ran north, away from the scene, as rifles fired behind them and bullets sang above and smacked into the ground behind their racing feet.

They ran a long way, then dropped into a ravine, where they lay panting and silent for almost a minute. There was no indication that they had been pursued, but Bush wasn't going to take that for granted.

"That ain't exactly how I planned it should go," he admitted once he had his breath, speaking in a whisper.

"Well, we did even the odds," Cordell said.

"More than evened them," Sam whispered. "There's only three of them left."

"I killed a man," Durham said, sounding stunned. "I killed a man."

"You did what you had to, son."

"How's that cut, Pap?" Sam asked.

"Not bad. It'll heal. Just startled me more than anything else." He paused. "I hated to shoot that fellow, him being so young."

"You had no choice," said Cordell.

"What now?" Sam asked. "Think they'll go away and let us be?"

"I wouldn't count on it," Bush said. "We've killed four of them. It's blood now. I doubt they'll let it go."

"Maybe we can get to our horses and get away from them before they round up their own," Durham suggested, his voice shaky.

"I've got so turned around I don't even know which way the horses are," Sam said. They'd left their horses hidden in a thicket well off from the scene of the fight.

"I can get us to them," Bush said. "But I'd like to know if we're being hunted before we try for them."

"I can't believe I killed a man," Durham said. "I feel kind of sick, Pap."

"Hold down your gorge, son. There'll be time for that kind of thing after we know we're really out of this situation."

Time passed and they neither saw nor heard evidence of the gunmen out on the flats. At length Bush signaled them to move, and under cover of night they traveled across the landscape, winding around and following the course of a small stream until at last they were in view of the knoll again. The moon came out and Bush noted that the bodies of the dead were no longer present.

"It's a good sign," he said. "They've collected their dead. That makes me think they've gone on."

The notion was quickly proven false. They had just begun to move on again when a shot rang and Cordell gave a yell. "Cord! You hit?" This from Sam.

"No—just scared me half to death. Damn! I'd convinced myself they was gone!"

Another shot rang out and the Underhills ran. The moon and clouds were cooperative, dropping the land into darkness again. Bush led his sons off and around, veering toward the same knoll upon which they had pretended to bury the gold they did not have.

"It's the best bet for us," Bush said, breathless, as he ran. "We can stand them off there."

The shooting had stopped for the moment, their pursuers, unseen behind them, no doubt reloading. The Underhills reached the knoll and climbed, muscles aching, hearts hammering at top speed.

Once they were atop the knoll, the moon sailed out again. The Underhills dropped behind a little ridge of rock, then peered over the edge. Faintly they could see the three men who wanted them dead, scrambling for cover of their own.

"Determined, ain't they?" Cordell gasped out. He was bigger than the others; the run and climb had been hard on him.

"They don't seem worried about the odds, either," Sam observed. "Four of us and three of them, but still they come on like mad dogs."

"That's because they *are* mad," Bush said. "We've killed some of their own. They're after vengeance now as much as gold."

For a time, it was substantially over. The men hidden below didn't show themselves much, one or more of them rising on occasion to send a fast, poorly aimed shot up toward the Underhills. Sam fired back a time or two, until his father told him to stop. "You're just wasting bullets."

"So what happens now?" Durham asked.

"We wait," Bush said. "And say a prayer or two that they get tired of it and move on before morning."

The night passed slowly, weariness creeping up on the Underhills. Cordell dozed off twice, but shook himself awake again.

"Go ahead and sleep, fellows," Bush said. "If anything commences again, you'll know it quick enough. I'll keep watch."

Cordell, however, was the only one who accepted the invitation. Sam and Durham were tense as overtuned fiddles, and Durham every now and then reached up quickly to wipe at his face. Bush knew he was thinking about the man he'd killed. It was a Rubicon in any man's life, killing another human being, no matter the circumstances. Bush had crossed that same line early in life, killing two Creeks in a canebrake when he was no more than a boy.[1] Even after all these years he still remembered every detail.

When at last the sun rose, weak and watery, over the edge of the Texas horizon, Bush examined the land below. They were gone. He'd thought in the night that he'd sensed movement, and had dared to hope. Now he stood, relieved.

"Perhaps now we'll see no more of them," he said.

Exhausted, the Underhills descended the knoll. Even Cordell seemed utterly drained despite his few hours of restless sleep. Silent, feeling relief that their enemies were gone, yet with no sense of victory or happiness over what had happened, they moved on foot toward the relatively distant thicket where they'd left their horses before the fight began.

A quarter mile farther, Bush stopped abruptly. "Look there."

The ground was scratched up and mounded nearby. The Underhills strode over and examined it.

"What is it, Pap?" Durham asked.

Bush knelt and began scraping away dirt. Mere inches down, his hand struck something fleshy and pliant. Brushing soil with his fingers, he uncovered the face of a dead man.

"It's what I figured. They've buried their dead."

Durham looked aghast at the pallid face of the corpse. "I think he was the one I shot, Pap." Quickly he turned away.

Bush scraped dirt back into place, re-covering the grave. "Ain't much of a burying job. The beasts will have these corpses dug up before you know it. I suppose it was the best they could do in the situation they was in, though." He stood, slapping dirt off his hands. "I'm surprised such a band of scoundrels didn't just leave them lying on the ground."

[1] See *The Glory River,* Book 1 in the Underhill Series

The Underhills continued on, seeing ahead the thicket where they expected to find their horses.

And once there, they stopped, and stared in surprise at what they found instead.

CHAPTER EIGHTEEN

It was actually a case of what they *didn't* find. The horses were gone. Even Bush, who reacted coolly to almost any turn of events, was stunned.

"Who do you reckon, Pap?" Cordell asked.

Bush didn't immediately answer. He paced about, examining the earth, finding tracks of horses and men. He shook his head in frustration.

"No way to know who took them. It could be somebody who happened along and found them. Could be the very men we fought. Matter of fact, it probably was, close as this place is to that excuse for a grave back yonder. We know they passed this way."

Durham whistled between his teeth as he considered that. "So we run their horses off, and they come and find ours."

"Could be."

"Pap, they have all our supplies, too," Sam said.

"I know. Which means we have to follow them."

Durham blanched. "Another fight?"

"Who can say? We have to do whatever we must. Those are our horses, our supplies."

Cordell cocked a brow at Durham. "Thinking maybe you should have stayed home with Ma after all?"

Durham glared at him. "I came because I believed it was my duty. I got no regrets."

"That's the spirit, son," Bush said. He breathed deeply.

"Don't know when I've ever felt so tired. I was looking forward to riding instead of walking."

"What'll we do if we can't find them?"

"We will find them."

The trail, fortunately, was quite clear and fresh. Whoever had taken the horses had done so no more than a couple of hours before, which lent credence, in Bush's estimation, to the likelihood that the horse thieves were the remnant of the same band they had fought at the knoll.

The farther the group traveled, the clearer the tracks became and the more their weariness decreased, replaced by the energy of nervous anticipation. They checked and rechecked their rifles and pistols.

An hour later, they found them. Because of the lay of the land, they almost were seen in turn. They'd rounded a shallow hill onto a decline, and below, there they were. Three of them, seated together, eating, all of them rough-looking Anglos. The horses were nearby. On the ground before the seated men lay the saddlebags and the pack from the packhorse, the contents taken out and scattered here and there.

"Makes my blood boil, seeing them having pilfered our things like that," Bush said, crouched with his sons behind some brush they'd taken to as quickly as they saw the horse thieves. "I suppose they'd hoped to find gold among our gear." He paused, then whispered toward the thieves, "Sorry to disappoint you, gentlemen."

One of the men stood, slipping on a shirt that Cordell recognized as his. The fellow was small and the shirt nearly swallowed him, but he seemed satisfied with it.

"How should we go about this, Pap?" Durham asked. "They'll be moving on as soon as they finish their food."

"*Their* food? That's some of our victuals they're eating, Pap," Sam pointed out.

Cordell said, "They're keeping their guns close . . . see? Maybe anticipating that somebody might come upon them."

"I doubt they'd be sitting in such an open place if they

had that on their minds," Bush countered. "I don't think they anticipated us following them."

"So maybe the best approach is the direct one," Sam suggested.

"You're learning to think like a warrior, son." Bush glanced about at the others. "You fellows ready to dance another cotillion with our sweethearts?"

"Well, I know I want my shirt back," Cordell said.

The reaction of the three horse thieves showed that Bush's assessment was correct: obviously these men hadn't expected to be tracked.

The Underhills emerged as one before them, rifles raised and leveled. One man froze with a bit of dried cornpone about to enter his mouth. The second spat out what he'd been chewing and swore loudly, coming to his feet, and the third, who'd already bolted down his meal, simply stared, wide-eyed.

"Good victuals, gentlemen? Hope they set well on your bellies. Now, scoot them feet out and push them rifles away, slow. Uh-uh, no, not like that . . . slow. Yes sir, that's right. No, don't move them hands. Put them up, slow. Good, good. That's the way to stay alive, yes sir."

The one who'd spat out his food had a belligerent air about him. "You Underhill? Bushrod Underhill?"

"One and the same."

"Hell, you don't look like no great shakes. I'd heard you was tall as a pine tree."

"I've seen a few pine trees shorter than me," Bush said. "Gentlemen, that's our horses you took. Our gear you scattered, and our food you been stuffing your mouths with."

"You accusing us of thieving? We found them horses!"

"Well, pardon me! Hope I didn't offend. But if you found them, then we've found them again in turn, and will now take them off your hands. And now, all three of you back away, slow. Three steps, no more, no less."

"He's going to shoot us!" one of them whispered sharply.

"Shut up!" barked the belligerent one.

The thieves backed away as ordered, hands raised.

"Good job," Bush said. "Now, with your left hands, I want you to reach down and remove them pistols from their braces, with two fingers, and toss them yonder way."

The three complied, the belligerent one never breaking his gaze from Bush's face.

"All righty. Good. Now, back up five steps more and lay down on your bellies, arms straight out before you. I want you to kiss that ground so deep you'll leave the mark of your face on it."

Bush had anticipated that the belligerent one would be the most likely source of trouble. He had a mean but stupid look about him, the look of a man who takes risks he shouldn't and thinks himself savvy and daring for it. Instead of backing off as ordered, he dived forward instead, scrambling for his rifle two or three yards away.

Bush was about to shoot him, but Cordell fired first. His weariness affected his aim, however, and the ball found not the target intended but one of the other thieves. The victim yelped and grabbed his wounded shoulder, dropping to his knees. The first man, meanwhile, got his hands on his rifle and was swinging it up when Bush shot him through the temple. He died with his rifle still in his grip.

Sam dropped to one knee and drew a bead on the heart of the third thief. "You want to die, too?"

"No! No!" the man yelled, thrusting his hands even higher.

"You shot me!" the accidentally wounded man said, watching blood seep through his fingers as he gripped his shoulder. "You *shot* me! And I hadn't done nothing!"

"My mistake," Cordell said, calmly reloading.

"I wouldn't say you'd done nothing, my friend," Sam said. "You did steal our horses, not to mention trail us for miles with the intent of taking gold we don't even have."

"I'm going to die . . ."

"You won't die of a simple shoulder wound, I don't believe," Bush said. "But you may feel the very pains of hell in it for some days to come. Wouldn't want to be you, no sir."

The man continued to stare at his bleeding wound, beginning now to play in the blood like a scared but fascinated
child.

"You there, Mr. Good Behavior," Bush said to the third
thief. "You can put your hands down now. Set on your rump
and you, me, and Mr. Shoulder Wound will have us a spell
of mutual pontification."

The man dropped to the ground and stared without blinking, eyes darting between Bush and his sons, over and over
again. Bush walked over to the dead man and nudged him
with his toe, just to make sure. "He's as dead as a man can
aspire to be," he said. "But if you two will avoid such foolish
mistakes as he made, we can get along just fine. Might even
let you go without shooting you."

"Sir, I'll tell you anything you want to hear, do anything
you want me to do, if you'll spare me," the third thief said.

"Tell me why you and your companions trailed us for so
long."

"Gold, Mr. Underhill. We'd heard that Bushrod Underhill
was coming in, bearing ransom gold to buy the freedom of
his son and family."

"So we had it figured. And you were ready to relieve us
of that gold, no matter if it meant the deaths of John Underhill, his wife, his children?"

The man moved his lips, but nothing came out.

"Where did you hear the story we carried gold?"

"From Jim . . . from him." The man gestured at the dead
man. "Where he heard it, I don't know. Jim always heard
things."

"His hearing days are through. And what he heard was
wrong. There never was no gold, no ransom ever demanded."

The man again couldn't find anything to say.

"Who did dear Jim there say that ransom was to be paid
to?"

"Trippler. It's him who has your son, him who they said
demanded the ransom."

"Why'd you believe such tales?"

"Jim believed them . . . I was just going along, that's all. I didn't want to bother you and your sons, sir. I spoke against trying to rob you."

"I'll bet you did. I'll bet you're up to be made a saint next week in the Catholic Church, huh? You should have been a little more persuasive. Seven of you to start with, and now only you and Bloody Shoulder over there left, all because of gold that don't even exist."

The bleeding man joined the exchange. "Mr. Underhill, it wasn't hard to believe you'd be carrying gold to Trippler. Asking ransom would be the kind of thing Trippler would do."

"You know Trippler?"

"Damn, this bleeding . . ."

"Answer my question."

"We know Trippler, hell, yes. Rode for him until some days ago."

"Rode for him? Hired gunmen?"

"Trippler called us his guards."

"So why'd you leave his hire?"

"Some mighty good reasons. First off, we figured that if Trippler's waiting for gold ransom, we might as well have that gold as him. Second, we weren't fools. Trippler's headed for a fall. He's a madman, and those foolish enough to stay under his hire are going to go down with him. So we got out."

"Did you ever lay eyes on John Underhill at Trippler's fort?"

"Seen him, yes. And his wife and children. That's how we knew it was true that he'd been kidnapped . . . why it was easy to believe the rumor you were carrying ransom gold."

"So Trippler's own gunmen don't know for sure what Trippler's up to."

"Trippler pays them to be there, to obey him. He don't explain all his schemes to them. You going to let me bleed to death, Mr. Underhill?"

"Maybe. Or if you want, we can shoot you through the head and end it a lot quicker. Tell me this first, though: does Trippler know that me and my sons have come to Texas?"

"I don't know what he knows. As I hear it, he ain't even in Texas just now. Nor is John Underhill."

Bush frowned. "Where are they?"

"Mexico, as I hear it. Couldn't prove it. God, my shoulder's hurting . . . this bleeding won't stop. I'm not feeling any too good."

"Sam, slap a rag against his wound there, see if you can make that bleeding quit."

Sam complied; the man howled as the rag pressed against the tender, fresh wound.

"You're lucky, mister," Sam said. "Looks like that ball went in one side and clean out the other. Nobody will have to dig in you."

"Why would Trippler take John to Mexico?" Bush asked.

"I don't know. Whatever the reason, you can figure it has to do with power and money. That's all Trippler cares about. Hell, they say he even killed his own brother so he could take his fortune."

"Why did you say Trippler was headed for a fall?"

"Because he's a madman. The people are against him, believing he's going to betray Texas. And maybe he is, I don't know. Even his so-called soldiers don't have any loyalty to him. Before long, the people are going to rise against Trippler, and when they do, not even the walls of that old mission will protect him. He'll go down, and most likely those around him will, too."

"Like John and his family."

"Ransom or no ransom, you need to get them out of that damned fort if you care about them. Trippler's days are numbered, and everybody knows it, except maybe Trippler himself. He's a madman, without question." The man winced. "I'm hurting bad. Bad."

The other man, who had fallen silent when his wounded partner entered the conversation, spoke again. "What are you going to do to us?"

"Strip you of your shoes, your trousers. Turn you loose afoot. And if ever I see you again, shoot you. That's what."

"We'll die out here if you leave us like that!"

"You won't die. You'll just get some mighty sore feet and a cold backside. Count yourself lucky we don't hang you. You'd have killed us every one if it had come down to it, and you know it."

"I think we ought to hang them, Pap," Sam said.

"No. Maybe that's the kind they are, but it ain't the kind I am. Strip them down, fellows. We're getting ready to move on."

"You'd best get your son and his folk away from Trippler," the wounded man warned again. "If you care a thing about them, you'd better find a way to get them out of that fort."

"How well guarded is it?"

The man laughed, but grimaced with pain and shut it off quick. "You think you can storm Trippler's fort, you're a fool. He's got gunmen all over. You'll never get them out of there unless Trippler allows it."

"We'll get them out," Bush said. "And Trippler will have no say at all about it when we do."

CHAPTER NINETEEN

The girl was an obvious mix of Mexican and Anglo. She stood in the door of a rundown saloon, watching the Underhills ride slowly down the single, wide dirt street of San Pablo. Sam and Durham noticed her at the same moment, their eyes drawn to her beautiful face, their hands reaching to their hat brims, touching them, nodding in a salute that was, as well, a tribute to loveliness trapped in a most unlovely setting.

When they'd ridden past, Sam said, "Did you see how she smiled at me?"

"What makes you think she was smiling at *you*?" Durham asked.

"Because they always smile at me. I suppose you wouldn't know much about that kind of thing."

"I know that some people get swell-headed without reason. You've always thought yourself the very gift of heaven to the female population."

"A man has to bear the burden life gives him," Sam replied. "I bear mine, you bear yours."

"What are you talking about? What burden do I bear?"

"Well . . . need I spell it out? One of us gets smiled at. The other just gets jealous."

"I ought to knock you out of that saddle!" Durham barked. "You're constipated with conceit, you know it? Backed up with it!"

"Better than what you're constipated with. You know, come to think of it, you do look sort of sickly just now. Are you?"

"I'm fine."

"No you ain't. Dark rings beneath your eyes, kind of pale-looking about the jaws . . . Oh. I know what it is. You're dwelling on that little shooting festival we just finished up with."

"And what if I am? You are, too."

"The hell! I already put that behind me."

"Sam, you killed a man. I killed one, too. *Killed* them!"

"What of it? They'd have sure not been slow to kill us."

"I know, but all the same . . ."

"It's just what I told Pap," Sam said. "Durham's too skittish for this. That's what I told him. He says, no, no, Durham's got gravel in his craw. Told me he was more worried about how I'd do in a pinch than how you'd do. Well, I guess that little question is settled. You're all racked up with your feelings, and I'm just floating along like always, letting the pretty girls smile at me!"

"You're two inches away from bawling like a baby, Sam, and you and I both know it. All this bluff and swagger you put on is as false as it can be."

Sam glared at Durham. "That's mighty close to fighting words. You trying to tell me I'm a coward?"

"You're no coward. Neither am I. We both did what we had to do in that fight. But I see no reason I have to feel good about having killed a man."

Up ahead, beside his father, Cordell said, "Listen to them, Pap. Going at it as usual."

Bushrod grunted, not particularly desiring to talk just now. He had a heaviness of heart and a sense of apprehension that he couldn't fully account for, and it kept his eyes shifting warily and his heart pounding a little faster than usual.

The little San Pablo community lay within an easy ride of John's house, according to the information Cantrell Smith had given. Bush would have thought that being this close to his destination would give him a sense of relief. Instead he felt vaguely unsettled, filled with foreboding. Something about this town, maybe. The atmosphere. The smell. The grimy look of the buildings. The obvious squalor. And something else, too, that he couldn't put his finger on. A sense that in any shadow, any alley, danger might be waiting for him and his sons. Maybe, he thought, he was having a belated reaction, like Durham, to the violent encounter on the flatlands. He hoped that was all it was.

He started slightly at the sound of a man cursing loudly and a horse whinnying in terror. All the Underhills turned to look into a wide alley between a saloon and a blacksmithy, where a young man was trying to settle a skittish horse he'd just freed from a hitching rail. He had it by the reins, but it was pulling and trying to buck away, spooked maybe by a rat or snake that might have passed across the alley . . . spooked maybe by its own young handler, who was swearing at it fiercely, jerking the reins, doing everything he shouldn't if he really wanted to calm the beast.

Bush halted his mount and watched the tense little performance a few moments. The horse grew more and more agitated, pulling harder away from the man, until finally the fellow had had enough and laid a hard slap right across the horse's snout.

"That's too rough with that horse there!" Bush yelled. He'd never been able to watch someone abuse an animal without butting his nose in.

Just then the horse pulled free from its handler and ran out of the alley, veering around and past the Underhills, loping toward the plains outside of town.

The young man, cursing even more bitterly now, came storming out of the alley, turning a fearsome scowl upon Bushrod. "What'd you holler at me just now?"

Bushrod didn't answer. Cordell glanced at his father and saw something that troubled him: Bushrod was gazing at the young man with an expression of either astonishment or fear. Cordell had never seen his father look afraid of anyone before, much less some half-drunk horse-beater in a shabby excuse for a Texas town.

"Pap?" Cordell said tentatively. Sam and Durham, meanwhile, were well behind and engaged in an argument of their own, not even noticing their father and brother.

"What are you staring at?" the young man said. "What's wrong with you? You about to pass out or something? You drunk?"

Bush jerked his head around and snapped the reins, riding away. The young man cursed after him, looked smug to see that he'd intimidated someone. Cordell paused long enough to tell the fellow he'd best watch how he treated his horse, turned and called to Sam and Durham to quit arguing and come on. Then he galloped up to join his father, who was riding stiffly upright, his eyes staring straight ahead.

"Pap, are you all right?"

Bushrod grunted.

"Did you know that young man?"

"No, no. I thought that . . . no. It couldn't be, though. It wouldn't be possible."

"What are you talking about?"

"Nothing. Forget about it."

"Pap, are you sure that—"

"I said forget about it." Bush speeded his mount and rode on ahead, leaving Cordell behind.

The sniping between Sam and Durham took a momentary respite as they left San Pablo, but renewed a mile out of town. Sam, who'd been able to get under Durham's skin ever since Durham was scarcely past infancy, and who always seemed to find being under Durham's skin an entertaining state of existence, worked hard on him, trying to push him over an emotional edge.

Cordell, distracted by Bush's strange manner, paid little attention to the arguing for a while, but caught on to it as it grew more intense. He turned to tell Sam to shut up, just in time to see Durham descend from his saddle, stagger off a few paces, and vomit forcefully onto the ground.

"Durham? What's wrong?" Cordell said, wheeling his horse and riding back toward Durham, who was still hunched over. When Durham didn't answer, Cordell turned to Sam. "What's wrong with him?"

"I don't know! All I was doing was talking some about that man he killed, and how his face looked when Pap moved the dirt off that shallow little grave. All at once he went pale and jumped down there, and up comes the spew." Sam shook his head and added innocently, "Who'd have thought he'd be so weak-stomached?"

"I've heard some of what you've been saying, Sam. Sounded to me like you were trying to get some reaction like this. What is it, Sam? You so torn up inside that you have to try to stir up your brother?"

"I ain't 'torn up' inside or out! It's Durham who gets all weepy just because he had to kill a man who deserved it."

Bush rode back and joined his sons. "What's wrong here?"

"Durham heaved up his belly," Sam said. "I believe he's not able to deal with . . . you know. What we had to do out there with them thieves."

"And you are, I reckon?"

"Well, I'm still in my saddle, and my victuals are still in my belly. I tried to warn you about Durham, Pap. I knew he wouldn't be able to handle it if trouble came."

"I seem to recall he handled himself just fine when it counted."

"He did no better than me!"

"You both did well. But you're both of a different turn of temper. Durham is the kind not to take pleasure in killing, and I say, God bless him for it." Bush poked his finger at Sam. "If I hear you give one more bit of trouble to your brother over any of this, I'll lay you over my knee just like I did when you were a little thing. And don't think I'm bluffing. You act like some bragging boy, you'll get treated like the same."

"I don't have to listen to this!" Sam declared, face going red. "Hell, Pap, I'm a man now! I've proved myself by how I handled that battle, and how I'm handling myself now it's done!"

"I couldn't tell you the number of times I've seen the bravest of men do just what Durham did after battle," Bush said. "The man to admire isn't the one who acts as if killing is nothing. The man to admire is the one who knows that a human life is a thing of value, even when it belongs to no more than some no-count thief, and not to be took away lightly."

Sam gazed coldly at his father. "How close are we to John's?"

"I expect to see it when we pass across that rise," Bush said.

"All right. Then I know where it is, so I can find it later. For now, I'm going back to that little town."

"Don't let him go, Pap," Cordell urged. "He'll just find himself trouble there."

"No," Bush said. "Sam wants to go, let him go. He thinks himself such a man now that he's drawn blood, we'll just let him go his own way." He lifted his head a little and looked down his nose at Sam. "That what you wanted to hear from me?"

"Didn't matter what I heard from you, Pap. No disrespect intended, but from now on I ain't necessarily going to be asking your permission every time I need to break wind. You keep talking about making a man out of me. Well, you've done it. And a man don't spend his time holding his pap's hand." Sam wheeled his horse. "Be seeing you later, at John's."

"Pap, don't let him go!" Cordell said again. "He'll just cause us problems."

"I'm tired of putting up with his smart mouth," Bush said. "Let him go find his own trouble, and deal with it himself. He says he's a man, after all." He looked down at Durham, who was standing now, looking a bit shame-faced because of his heaving. "You feeling any better, son?"

"I'm fine, Pap." He looked after Sam, whose horse was heading back San Pablo way at a good trot. "Maybe Sam's right about me. Maybe I ain't stout enough to abide this kind of thing."

"You're stout as an oak, boy. Don't ever let Sam tell you different, and most of all, don't ever let yourself tell you different. Now let's get on over the hill and see what kind of home John's made for himself here."

"Maybe John will be there when we arrive, free and safe again," Cordell said.

"I hope so," Bush replied. He paused a moment to watch Sam continuing on, sighed, and rode toward the hill.

The first sight of John's house was anticlimactic. They crossed the hill and there it was, a typical Texas spread consisting of low, log-walled ranch house, a few outbuildings, pens, a barn. A small stream ran through the center of the property, which was blessed with plenty of stout trees.

But it was an empty place. A mere glance revealed it. Bush's feeling of depression deepened as he looked at the silent, lifeless spread, trying to picture his grandchildren playing in the shade of the trees, John striding across toward the barn from the house, his wife scrubbing out laundry in the little stream.

"Pap, I see no hogs, no cattle."

"Maybe they were stole," Durham said. "After John disappeared."

"Or maybe some good neighbor is seeing to them while John can't," Bush said. "Frankly, it don't matter to me much just now. All I care about is finding John."

They rode down the incline toward the ranch. The front door of the house was slightly ajar; a wild cur dog ran out when they drew near, startling the horses.

"Want to ask you something, Pap," Cordell said, dismounting and watching the dog flee into the blowing grass. "Back in town, that young man who was mistreating the horse. I believe you must have known him."

"I thought I did, when I first saw his face," Bush said. "Somebody from a long time ago, and it startled me. But I knew it couldn't be, for this fellow would be much, much older by now."

"Just a resemblance, then."

"Couldn't have been a closer one."

They took their horses to the barn, stabled and fed them. Durham and Cordell rubbed them down.

Bushrod, glad for the chance to be alone, explored the spread. Sadly, the more he looked, the more evidence he found that the place had been looted. Someone had taken advantage of the absence of John and his family to remove furniture, dishes, even some of the window curtains and panes.

He wandered to the rear of the spread, where the creek curved through a grove of pecan trees. He knelt, watching the water flow, bringing out his pipe and tobacco for a smoke. He'd just fired up one of his specially created matches when he sensed something change in the atmosphere, a movement of light.

Bush rose and turned, expecting to see Cordell or Durham What he saw instead made him freeze for a moment, then reach for the pistol thrust under his belt.

CHAPTER
TWENTY

Sam Underhill shifted his weight from one foot to the other, took another glance up and down the dark street, and sighed in disappointment. He'd convinced himself that he'd find that half-Mexican girl waiting for him, smiling that alluring smile and batting those lovely deep brown eyes. But she was nowhere around. He'd looked the little town over three times now and found no sign of her.

Ah, well. Maybe he should simply mount up again and ride back to join his family at John's spread. He probably shouldn't have come there anyway, away from the others; the violence they'd gone through on the way there was proof enough that it wasn't particularly safe to be an Underhill just now, with those rumors of ransom floating about. He was astonished, in fact, that his father had not put up a fuss when he declared he was coming back to town alone. He could account for it only by the fact that his father had seemed strangely distracted at that point, with something weighing on his mind and maybe clouding his judgment.

The more Sam considered it, the more it seemed he should go back. Maybe he should even apologize to Durham for the way he'd harangued him. Not fair, really, how he'd done that. Sam would never admit it, but every time he thought about the man he'd killed, he felt just as sick at heart, and stomach, as Durham had. He just managed to hide it better.

But Sam was unwilling to yield to these admittedly rational

impulses. Pride was in the way. He'd never apologized to Durham—or much anyone else—for anything, and there was no reason to start now. And given that his father had inexplicably let him wander off alone like this, it would be rather a waste not to take advantage of the opportunity.

He'd stay for a spell. Might as well enjoy a drink, maybe a game of cards, a bit of distraction and relaxation, while he had the chance. He could enjoy himself a few hours, head in late with a smile on his face, and let them think he'd had a jolly time with that lovely girl. They didn't have to know he'd failed to find her.

Just as he was about to turn, a hand clapped down on his shoulder, making him jump and turn, reaching for his pistol. A smiling red face looked back at him through bloodshot eyes.

"No call to be startled, young man!" the stranger said cordially. He sounded Irish. "The name's O'Brien. Just wanted to make your 'quaintance, and see if you might have enough money to pay for half a bottle. I'm a bit short on the coin just now, you see, having only half what I need. If you're willing to share the cost, I'm willing to share the bottle."

Sam examined the man, a stocky, dirty, unappealing fellow. A far cry from the pretty young woman he'd hoped to find. But a companion nonetheless, someone to drink with. Maybe the girl would turn up in the meantime.

"I can take you up on that bargain," Sam said, sticking out his hand. "The name's Underhill. Sam Underhill." He realized right away that he should have made up an alias for safety's sake. Too late now.

The man's eyes widened. "Underhill? Not, by chance, of the same family as the famed Bushrod?"

"No," Sam lied. "Same last name, but no relation."

"Well, that's quite the coincidence, because everyone is saying that Bushrod Underhill and his sons are coming to this lovely little garden spot. Something to do with a missing son, who lives not far away."

"Do tell! Well, I wouldn't mind meeting such a famous

man as that. They say them Underhills are a true hellacious bunch.''

Sam followed O'Brien to the saloon, where they pooled money to purchase a jug of cheap whiskey which they bore to a table in the rear, opened, and began to imbibe. The stuff was powerful, liquid fire, and Sam, who drank much less than he'd admit to the fast-guzzling O'Brien, had to fight back a few winces as the heat poured down his throat.

An hour later, Sam was feeling quite fine, his body warm and comfortable, his spirits high. The girl was quite forgotten now, as was his sense of caution about having come to this town alone.

"I have a confession," he told O'Brien in the course of a rambling, aimless conversation. "I am indeed the son of Bushrod Underhill."

"No! Why didn't you tell me to begin with?"

"Didn't know what kind of fellow you were. When you've got a famous name, there's folks who'll sometimes try to cause you trouble for it."

The saloon door opened, ironically, at just that moment, and admitted a familiar-looking young man with a broad, proud grin. And well he should be grinning, because clinging to his arm was the Anglo-Mexican girl. It took Sam a moment to recall where he'd seen the fellow before. This was the young man who'd been mistreating that horse on the street earlier, the one his father had called down. He'd not paid much heed to the fellow at the time because he'd been sniping back and forth with Durham.

Sam couldn't help but stare at the couple. His face grew somber, and jealousy overwhelmed him. The young man swept his broad grin across the saloon populace, then lost it when he spotted Sam. He stared coldly, said something to the girl, and she moved over to a nearby table and sat down. She just then noticed Sam herself, and smiled at him as she had on the street. Her escort noticed, and the glare he turned on Sam grew even colder.

"That fellow seems to know you, Mr. Underhill," O'Brien said. He sounded nervous. Sam was suddenly nervous, too;

the young man was coming toward him, looking quite antag-
onistic. Sam wished he hadn't drunk quite so much. If there
was to be trouble, he didn't feel fit to deal with it now.

The newcomer walked up to Sam's table and stopped about
two yards away. He glared silently a few moments, then said,
"I seen you earlier."

"Did you?" Sam asked, playing innocent. "That's surprising, seeing as how I only got into town in the late afternoon."

"I seen you, all right, and them others with you. That older
one, he your pa?"

"I think you got me mixed up with somebody else," Sam
replied. "I came into town alone."

"The hell you say. I remember you—you were with three
others, one of them an older fellow with a damned smart
mouth on him and a nose he couldn't keep in his own business."

Sam was ready to play his bluff as far as he could, but
O'Brien blew it to pieces right away. "You'd best not try to
stir trouble with my friend," he said, rising. "Do you know
who this is?"

Sam thought, *Oh, no*.

"Why don't you tell me, Paddy?"

"The name's not Paddy, but who I am doesn't matter a
whit. The point is that this is Sam Underhill, son of the famed
Bushrod, and if the son is half the man his father is, you'd
best be turning your tail before he twists it off."

"I ain't looking for any trouble," Sam said.

His antagonist stared at him now in a new way, more intense, eyes full of surprise and something that looked to Sam
like hatred that had just boiled up into a full steam. "Underhill! You're the son of Bushrod Underhill?"

Sam saw that meekness was going to get him nowhere with
this one. He rose to full height, trying to stay steady despite
the whiskey swimming through his veins. "I am."

The expressions that played over the young man's face
were hard to fathom. He seemed to lose the ability to speak.
Sam thought maybe he was afraid, but that didn't quite seem

to be it. But something had certainly come over the young man. Sam let his hand slip closer to the butt of the flintlock pistol stuck under his belt.

The young man glared at him a moment more, breathing hard, then wheeled and walked back toward the door. He motioned for the girl to join him, but she shook her head. He froze, then went to her, leaning over and speaking in an intense whisper, his face close to hers. She pushed him away. He stared at her, balled his fist, and for a moment Sam thought he was going to have to intervene to save the girl a beating. But the young man looked back at him once more, a long, angry stare, turned on his heel, and departed the saloon alone.

Sam sank back into his chair, O'Brien doing the same.

"I believe you frightened the very soul out of that young fellow," O'Brien said.

"I reckon," replied Sam, reaching for his glass to take another drink. Blast it! His hand shook as he lifted the glass to his lips, and he hoped O'Brien didn't see.

"He seemed to want trouble from you at the start," O'Brien said.

"I know. My father had some words with him today, and I reckon he held it against me."

"I'd love the opportunity to meet so great a man as Bushrod Underhill," O'Brien said. "I'd shake his hand and—My, my. I think you have another visitor."

The girl was approaching the table. Sam watched her coming on and, despite his earlier ambitions, wished she wasn't. That fellow was already angry enough with him. He'd be furious if he thought Sam was stealing his girl.

But Sam had been raised to be a gentleman. He stood and nodded at her. Without awaiting an invitation, she pulled back an extra chair and sat down at the table, smiling at him. He sat again, and O'Brien, winking at him, said, "I'll be moving on now." He winked again and was gone. Sam wished fervently that he'd stayed.

"You are the son of Bushrod Underhill? *The* Bushrod Underhill?" Her voice was soft, and despite her obvious partial

Mexican heritage, it was touched by only the slightest Mexican accent.

"I am."

"Your father is a famous man. A great hero, people say."

"I reckon."

"And you, his son, must be famous, too, no?" She reached across and touched his hand. "I like famous men. And handsome ones." A forward girl, this one. Sam liked that kind, usually, but just now he was too drunk and too mystified by what had transpired to react in his usual fashion.

"I'm not famous," he said.

"No? But you are handsome. Very handsome."

"Look, uh . . ."

"Luisa."

"Luisa . . . I'm very glad to meet you. But I'm afraid I can't stay. Got to be going on . . . some business outside of town."

"Take me with you. I can be your business, too, can't I?"

"Not tonight."

She made a pouting face, but playfully, and Sam could see she wasn't going to give up easily.

"Listen, Luisa, I believe you're already with somebody, anyhow."

She looked around the room. "I don't see him. Do you?" She stroked Sam's hand. "What's your first name?"

"Sam . . . but you should know, I'm a married man."

"You wear no ring."

"I lost it."

"I think you're playing with me."

"Luisa, that fellow you were with. Who is he?"

"His name is Morgan. He's no one, just one of Trippler's band, sneaked away from the fort to find himself some pleasure for an evening. But I think it's you who'll find the pleasure."

"Morgan . . . I don't know anyone named Morgan."

"Forget him. I have."

"No offense, Luisa, but I think you should forget me, too."

"You'll not leave?"

"I have to go." Sam stood, wishing he wasn't drunk.

She lost her toying manner, and frowned at him. Standing, she said, "Maybe you aren't the man you look to be. Maybe you don't even like ladies."

"It's not that. You're a beautiful young woman. It's just that I must go."

"Then go! I hate you!" She turned and walked away, pushing her way out the door.

Sam heard mumbles from the men around him, saw whispering and shaking of heads, faint, mocking smiles, as if he were a fool.

Maybe he was a fool. Maybe he'd just thrown away the pride that he usually coddled. But just now it didn't matter. He wanted to get away from San Pablo as quickly as he could, and join his kin at John's spread.

Ignoring those who watched him with mocking eyes, he left the saloon and headed for the alley where he'd left his horse.

He'd scarcely left the town behind before he began to sense that he was followed. Sam's heart began to race, and fear even greater than that he'd known in the height of the battle with the would-be thieves out on the plains began to rise in him despite his best attempts to squelch it. That had been a battle of strategy, fought under the guidance of his father and the company of his brothers, fought with the Underhills as the aggressors. Fought sober.

This time Sam was alone, the hunted rather than the hunter. And he was far from sober.

He urged his horse to speed up, hoping he might outpace the one who followed him. *Morgan* . . . not the name of anyone of his acquaintance, though certainly a name of infamy in the annals of the Underhill family. The wicked men who'd held his aunt Marie in the foulest and most vulgar of bondages for several years of her maidenhood had been named Morgan. His father had rescued her from them violently, killing all but one of the Morgan brothers.

A frightening possibility came to mind. Might there be a

connection between the young Morgan who was pursuing him and the Morgan family who had been such enemies of his father? It seemed unlikely on the surface, but it would account for how oddly and intensely the young Morgan had reacted to learning that Sam was the son of Bushrod Underhill. If there were any remaining kin of the Morgans whom Bushrod had decimated earlier in the century, they surely hated the name Underhill. *And surely taught their offspring to hate it as well.*

Sam spurred his horse a little faster, more eager than ever to reach John's spread and the company of his father and brothers. He should never have gone to San Pablo alone.

Hoofbeats behind him, closer than he'd anticipated . . . motion in the darkness.

I can't run, he thought. *I'm an Underhill, and I can't be a coward. I've brought this trouble on myself, and I can't lead it straight to the doorstep of my family.*

Sam turned his mount to the right, leaving the beaten road and entering a copse of trees. Dismounting, he drew out his pistol, crouched, and waited. Fear, to his good fortune, had gone a long way toward sobering him up, but his head still buzzed and he regretted every drop of whiskey he'd swallowed.

He saw the rider minutes later, and prepared to step out of the copse and face him down. This problem had to be dealt with now, not held until later.

What had Luisa said? That Morgan was one of Trippler's gunmen? For a moment Sam hesitated. Would facing off with Morgan only create greater problems if the Underhills were forced into a showdown with Trippler, the very man who apparently was behind John's disappearance?

There was no time to think the matter through any further. Sam saw him now on the road, pulling his horse to a halt and looking around, maybe realizing that Sam was no longer moving down the road ahead of him.

Sam stepped out of the copse, leveling his pistol. "Out of the saddle," he commanded.

Morgan spoke. "So you've laid me an ambush, have you?"

"Out of the saddle."

"Don't believe I will."

"Then I'll shoot you out of it."

"That'd be your way. A damned, murdering Underhill, just like your father before you. Did you know your father is a murderer? Did you know he murdered my own uncles, one by one, and would have murdered my own father if he'd had the chance?"

So it was true. This young man could be none other than the son of Rafe Morgan, the only one of the Morgan brothers whose survival had been an unanswered question after the brothers had faced off violently with Bushrod Underhill more than twenty years before.

"Out of that saddle! Now!"

Sam never saw the pistol come into Morgan's hand. It boomed loudly, flashing bright in the night. Sam yelled, felt a jolt of sharp pain, and fell back on the road, his own pistol discharging in his hand and sending the ball hurtling straight up into the sky.

CHAPTER
TWENTY-ONE

At about the same time Sam Underhill and O'Brien were buying the jug of cheap whiskey, Bushrod Underhill, along with Durham and Cordell, sat down in the main room of John's empty house to begin a conversation with an unexpected visitor who was more lucky to be alive than perhaps he knew.

"I'm sorry I almost shot you, Mr. Dunning," Bushrod said to the man, a lean, tall, rather looming fellow with a broad gray mustache and generic, unimposing features that made him look unsophisticated, until one studied the keen, intelligent eyes and listened to his resonant, confident voice. "It's the way I tend to react when I think myself alone and find a stranger bearing down on me."

"My fault, sir, and therefore it's I who must apologize," Dunning said. "I should have made you aware of my presence in a less surprising way."

Cordell and Durham sat looking at Dunning with confused expressions. Seeing this, Bushrod explained: "I was by the stream behind the house, pretty much lost in thought, when Mr. Dunning approached me from behind. I turned and drew my pistol on him. But thank God I didn't shoot. He's been waiting for us here, figuring we would naturally come to John's home first. He has information about him."

"Real information?" Cordell said. "Not just the same

patchwork rumors we've been hearing right and left up until now?"

"Solid, factual information," Dunning said. "The kind of information I specialize in obtaining. The kind that President Houston hired me to obtain."

"Mr. Dunning is an agent of the Texas government," Bushrod said. "He was hired, secretly, by Sam Houston himself to study this Trippler and his schemes. The leadership of the republic is mighty concerned about what the man's up to."

"An agent? Like a Texas Ranger?" Durham asked. Durham held a special curiosity about the unique law enforcement agency called the Texas Rangers, which though officially formed only months before, was an outgrowth of more informal bands of rangers who had protected the Texas plains and settlements for years.

"Not a Ranger, though the Rangers have plenty of their own worries about what Trippler is up to," Dunning replied. "I'm part of no official organization and answer to no one but President Houston. If something were to happen to me, there would be no general knowledge of it, no acknowledgment from the Texian government, and no investigation unless it were launched by Houston himself."

"In other words, you're Houston's private spy," Cordell said.

"A very apt way to put it."

"How do we know you are what you say you are?"

"I've already shown your father my credentials."

"I believe he's authentic," Bush said. "He carries papers signed by Houston himself."

"If you report only to Houston, why are you sitting down to talk to us?"

"I enjoy a certain discretion in how I go about my work. I'm free to speak with whom I please, either openly or under some appropriate guise or another. In your case, I speak openly, because the things I've learned closely involve your family. Specifically, your brother John, who is in great and grave danger even now."

"That's why he was waiting for us here," Bushrod said. "He'd heard the same rumors as everyone else, that we were coming into Texas either to ransom John or to break him free of Trippler or even to join him *with* Trippler. He was smart enough to realize we'd come here, to John's house, first."

"I've waited for you gentlemen for two days," Dunning said. "I was almost starting to think you'd taken a different approach than I anticipated, when finally, today, you showed up."

"What do you know about John?" Cordell asked.

"It's best I begin at the beginning," Dunning said, pulling a pipe and tobacco from his pocket. "Let's look at the person of William Gordon Trippler. Former empresario. Builder of a small army of private gunmen. Murderer. Man of mystery, deception . . . and madness, in the most literal sense. But also a man of power, wealth, and influence, who has a talent for keeping all three, except, perhaps, the wealth. He has much less of that than he once did, and that's what makes him so dangerous. He must put his plan into motion soon, or else he'll not be able to afford to keep his private army paid, and will lose them. And it's that army, along with certain rumors he manages to perpetuate, that are keeping him from being swept away by those who mistrust him."

"I'm confused," Durham said. "I don't understand what you're talking about."

Bush offered Dunning a match, showed him how to light it, and Dunning lit his pipe. He shook the match out and stared at it. "Remarkable. Absolutely remarkable." Then to Durham he said, "Forgive me for my lack of clarity, and let me try to explain what isn't easily explained.

"William Gordon Trippler entered Texas shortly after it was opened, under its former regime, to American settlement. He played matters legally, obtaining all the necessary permissions, establishing himself as a legal empresario, and beginning a colony along the Brazos. A smaller colony by far than Austin's, but relatively successful. He set up headquarters in an old stone-walled mission, not many miles from San Pablo, which you passed through on your way here. All was well and good, though Trippler gained himself a justified reputation as an eccentric, rather troublesome man who possessed an extraordinary lust for power.

"When the revolution came, Trippler played it prudent, giving lip service to the Texian cause, but managing to stay mostly out of the conflict, something he achieved by a conveniently timed, lengthy journey into the United States, ostensibly to see to the welfare of a brother, whom he declared was dying and calling for him. His claim went unchallenged, until rumors begin to rise that the brother, George, whom Trippler claimed to be visiting, wasn't in the United States at all, in fact not even alive. George Trippler had come to Texas almost a year before, apparently fleeing out of Kentucky with wealth he'd gained in some illicit way from some strange religious sect. He'd founded the sect himself, using at the time the false name of—"

"Pepperdine!" Durham interjected.

"Indeed. How did you know?"

"Because we chanced to meet some of the very members of what must be that same sect, come to Texas, looking for an 'Elder Pepperdine' they said had cheated their group out of almost all it had."

"Remarkable!" Dunning said, frowning in a way that brought his rather bushy brows together atop his thin nose in one unbroken line. "This is news to me. Where did these people go looking?"

"We don't know, exactly," Durham said. "Not at Trippler's fort, though, as far as we know. We traveled the same route through Arkansas, but after that we saw no more of them."

"They'll never find the man they're looking for. George Trippler—'Elder Pepperdine'—is dead. William Gordon Trippler murdered him, murdered his own brother, for the sake of the wealth he'd taken from his own followers. By now he's spent most of it on his private army."

"So Trippler is almost out of money?" Bushrod asked.

"Indeed. But I have reason to believe he may be on the verge of obtaining more from another source. Mexico."

"Ah!" Bushrod exclaimed. "So it's true that Trippler has been dealing with Mexico."

"Yes, though I must admit that even I don't know the full details. Suffice it to say that Trippler has made several secret visits into Mexico recently. He's there now, in fact. And this time, he took John Underhill with him."

"John's not at the fort?"

"Not at the moment. But his family is."

"You're not saying that John is willingly helping this man?" Cordell cut in.

"Not willingly. Not at all. He's being threatened with harm to his family if he doesn't cooperate. Trippler keeps them under close guard, using them to force John Underhill to do his bidding. John, you see, is a man of great influence in Texas, and Trippler seems convinced that John's endorsement and support can actually make his scheme succeed. Trippler believes he can use John Underhill and Colonel Crockett to work the public sentiment around to his favor, and wind up virtually a king of his own little empire—a small price for the Mexican government to pay in return for obtaining an entry into Texas through his colony."

"It sounds like a desperate plan to me."

"And so it is, Mr. Underhill. But Trippler is a desperate man. He's nearly out of money, trying to hold on to and expand his base of power despite a public that is beginning to rise against him. The fact that Trippler is conferring with Mexico has reached the mills of rumor in Texas, and believe me, Trippler can't be happy about it. Those rumors are the thing most likely to bring him down, and he knows it."

"You mentioned the name Crockett," Bushrod said. "We've heard stories that Crockett is alive, and under Trippler's care. That's surely not true?"

"It's a question I can't answer, as much as I wish I could. It was one of the few matters I was unable to clarify through investigation. But I can tell you this: *someone* is in that compound, under medical care. Someone who several seemingly reliable informants have told me appears to be Crockett himself, alive and in the flesh."

"Do you believe it?"

"I don't know what to believe. But the rumor helps Trippler. If people believe that such a hero as Crockett is alive in Trippler's fort, it tends to keep matters dragging along, tends to delay any uprising against him. The Crockett question is just enough to cloud the issues and buy Trippler time."

"And the John Underhill question works for him in the same way."

"Yes. In fact, John Underhill may well be even more important to him than Crockett—assuming, which I don't, that it really is Crockett he has tucked away in there. John Underhill is healthy, able to speak out in public, to lend an active voice in support of Trippler."

Bushrod shook his head. "But most people don't seem to believe that John is with Trippler of his own free will. They believe he was kidnapped. Some even had the notion that I and my sons had come to Texas bearing gold to ransom John and his family."

"This is true, but remember, John Underhill has not yet made any public appearance or issued any statement on Trippler's behalf. I suspect Trippler has been unable to break his will so far. But eventually—and very soon, I'm sure—John will be forced to publicly endorse Trippler in some fashion. Either that, or Trippler will kill his wife and children. No man can stand up long against that kind of threat. Especially when the threat comes from a man who has already proven willing to murder his own brother."

"How do you know so much about Trippler?"

"It's my job to know."

"Have you been inside Trippler's fort?"

"I have. Briefly. But I was forced to exit quickly."

"Did you see John there?"

"I did, but I was unable to communicate with him. Trippler keeps him at hand almost every moment, with guards close. As for John Underhill's family, I didn't see them at all. But they are there, held apart from John and under constant threat. Believe me, Mr. Underhill, few men have had to endure the kind of pressure that your son John is under right now."

"But it's nonsense! Even if John somehow helped Trippler pull off some sort of betrayal to Mexico, in the end John would reveal that he was forced. He'd expose Trippler."

"Indeed. Which is why Trippler will not keep John Underhill and his family alive for one moment past their time of usefulness to him."

"This is all too unbelievable," Cordell said. "How can Trippler think such a house-of-cards scheme can really stand up?"

"Very simple, as I told you. William Gordon Trippler is a madman. I can tell you that his father died insane, and his grandfather before him. Trippler has notions about himself and his future that are absolutely Napoleonic. And until recently he has had enough wealth to buy loyalty and protection. Thus what should be no more than a pitiful madman's fantasy is in fact a very dangerous, active situation."

"But if he's running low on money . . ."

"Then he'll soon be unable to pay his men, who will then desert him promptly. And in his heart he knows this—one more reason to believe he'll make whatever move he's going to make sooner rather than later, and to cooperate with Mexico any way he can."

Bushrod lowered his head. The sense of depression and foreboding that had fallen upon him when he reached John's home had lifted somewhat after he met Dunning and discovered that he possessed facts, and not just rumors, about John. Now that those facts were revealed, however, the depression was returning.

"We must get John out . . . but how? How can I and three sons hope to break John and his family out of a walled compound that's manned with armed guards and under the control of a madman?"

Dunning looked puzzled. "Three sons? Where's the third?"

Bush looked up sharply. In the midst of this welter of information he'd actually forgotten that Sam was absent. "My eyes! What a fool I am! I should have never let Sam go off alone, not with all these rumors about us and a ransom and such. What was I thinking?"

"With all due respect, Pap, I've been wondering the same thing ever since you let him go."

"Who is Sam?" Dunning asked.

"One of my sons. He and Durham had some words today and Sam decided he'd take off alone to San Pablo. Had his eye on a saloon, probably. And like a fool, I let him go."

"Why'd you do that, Pap?" Cordell asked. "You didn't seem yourself today, especially after we met up with that fellow who was abusing his horse."

Bush made a face as if in pain. "Because I *wasn't* myself, Cordell. I wasn't thinking clearly. Seeing that young fellow with the horse threw me."

"Why?"

"Because of who he made me think of. I swear to you, Cordell, he was the absolute exact image of one of my worst old enemies. He looked exactly like Rafe Morgan in his younger days."

Cordell knew well the name of Rafe Morgan, for he knew the story of his aunt Marie's rescue from the Morgan brothers by Bushrod. "But you know it couldn't be him, Pap. If he even survived, Rafe Morgan would be your own age by now."

"I know . . . but the look was the same. It startled me half out of my mind to see him—like looking at a ghost from the past. I rode away from San Pablo half addled over it. And that's the best excuse I can give for being fool enough to let Sam go off alone at such a time and place."

Dunning spoke. "I've read the book about you, Mr. Underhill. This Rafe Morgan you speak of is, I suppose, the same Rafe Morgan named in the book as one of those who abused your sister so terribly?"

"Yes. The last time I saw him, he was staggering off across a burning warehouse in St. Louis with a knife wound in him. A wound I'd given him. I never knew whether he survived."

"Remarkable. Remarkable."

"What are you thinking of?"

"I'd have never dreamed they were one and the same. I assumed it was just a coincidence. Remarkable!"

"Explain yourself, sir."

"Mr. Underhill, there is a Rafe Morgan among Trippler's gunmen. One of the older ones, your age at the very least, and probably older. He leads Trippler's hired gunmen, answering directly to Trippler. When I heard his name spoken at the compound, I of course thought of the Rafe Morgan named in the book about you, but never considered it might actually be the same man."

"Good Lord . . . so Rafe Morgan *did* survive—and John's being held where Morgan is working!"

"But who was the fellow we saw?" Durham asked. "He was far too young to be Rafe Morgan."

"Rafe Morgan has sons," Dunning said. "Two sons, also among Trippler's little army, and the younger one, James, bears a strikingly close resemblance to his father. I can imagine that Rafe Morgan must have looked just like him in his younger days."

"That's who we saw, then," Bushrod said. "That explains the resemblance."

Cordell came to his feet. "Pap, we need to go fetch Sam right away. Think about it: Sam's the kind to brag about being an Underhill. If this Morgan is still in San Pablo, and hears who Sam is, and if the Morgans are the kind to bear a family grudge after so many years . . ."

No more needed to be said. Bushrod rose and fetched his coat, checked the loads of his pistols. His sons followed suit, and Dunning rose as well.

"Sir, if you wish to come with us, you're welcome, but you needn't feel compelled. This is family business, nothing you need feel obliged about."

"I've nothing better to do, Mr. Underhill. And, if you'll have me, I'd hoped to join your efforts in Texas in any case. Now is as good a time to begin as any."

Bushrod walked up to this most unexpected benefactor and

thrust out his hand. "Glad to have you along, Mr. Dunning."

They left the house, readied the horses with all haste, and began riding along the dark and windy road back toward San Pablo.

CHAPTER TWENTY-TWO

"There—see him?" Durham, straining his eyes in the darkness, pointed straight ahead and slightly to the right.

"Where? I don't see anything."

"Look, Cordell—he's there on the road. Kneeling down. *Somebody's* there, anyway."

"Now I see him," Bushrod said, and spurred his mount forward. "Sam! Sam, is that you?"

In the darkness a familiar figure rose, turned, staggered a moment, then came toward them. The Underhills, along with Dunning, rode in close and swung quickly out of their saddles.

Bushrod's eye brushed over the supine figure on the dirt road, then back to his son.

"Sam, are you all right?"

"I been shot."

"Good Lord! How bad?"

"Not bad. Just a nick through the fleshy part of my left arm, that's all." He moved the arm carefully, wincing. "A few inches over, though, and it would have gone through my heart."

Dunning was already walking over to examine the figure on the ground.

"Is that who shot you?" Cordell asked, nodding toward the body as he examined, mostly by feel, Sam's arm. Sam had removed his coat and torn the sleeve from his shirt, using it to wrap the wound. Cordell carefully unwrapped it, lit one of his father's improvised matches, and studied the blood-crusted hole.

"Yes. But I shot him back. I'm afraid I might have killed him."

"No," called back Dunning, kneeling over the body. "He's senseless, but alive."

"Who's that man?" Sam asked.

"A friend. You'll meet him later," Cordell said. "Does your arm hurt much?"

"Mostly numb right now."

"I think you're right that it ain't hurt bad." He began to rewrap the makeshift bandage around the arm. "We'll get you back to John's house and patch you up better there."

"Cordell, that fellow I shot—his name is Morgan. He's the son of Rafe Morgan."

"I see."

"You don't sound surprised."

"We've learned some things since we parted, brother. Like the fact that Rafe Morgan and two of his sons are among Gordon Trippler's hired gunmen. Too bad you had the misfortune to meet up with this one. What happened?"

Sam briefly recounted the events of the evening, culminating with a description of how Morgan had identified himself and fired on him, wounding him, knocking him flat, making him fire off his pistol toward the sky. What Morgan hadn't counted on was that Sam also had a second pistol, a small, pocket-variety weapon, that he managed to dig out and fire just as Morgan finished reloading, no doubt intending to deliver the death shot.

Bushrod crouched beside Dunning. He lit a match and studied the face of the young man on the ground. "That's him. The very duplicate of Rafe Morgan when he was a young man." He paused. "Makes me shudder to see that face."

"We've got to get this young man some attention," Dunning said.

"There's not likely to be a physician in so small a place as San Pablo."

"No. So we'll have to make do with me."

"You know much about treating wounds?"

"I've had some training."

"I knew an old colored woman once who could make up concoctions to heal or cure almost anything. Wish she was here now." Bush paused. "You know who took her life? The Morgan brothers."

"Small world we live in, eh?"

"He's got blood all about his head. If he's shot through the skull, what can be done for him?"

"I don't think it's as bad as it looks. See . . . mostly just a grazing wound. Knocked him cold, drew out some blood, but once he's cleaned up, he'll probably come around again and be fine except for having one very aching head for days to come."

"That's good. I wouldn't want Rafe Morgan learning that his own son was killed by an Underhill. If he's the same man he was, he'd be out for Underhill blood in recompense."

"If he's the same man he was, he probably doesn't need any further provocation to want Underhill blood. And that provides yet one more reason why your son and his family must be removed from that old mission. They may be in as much danger from Rafe Morgan as from Trippler himself. Not to mention the general danger to everyone inside that place should the citizenry rouse up a militia to take care of Trippler once and for all."

"Could that happen?"

"I think it *will* happen, eventually. I keep in contact with certain Texas Rangers, and hear from them that there's plenty ready to rise against Trippler right now. Let's hope that doesn't happen, though. Better to let Trippler run out of money, lose his hold over his men, and fall to pieces on his own."

"But if he's found support from Mexico, he might not run out of money."

"That's the big question, isn't it? One more complication in an already complicated situation. Now, give me a hand here, and we'll see if we can bandage this wound for the time being, and get this young rogue back to the house.''

"This is a dreadful turn of events, I'm afraid," Bush said.

"On the contrary, sir. It might be the best thing that's happened."

"I don't understand."

"We'll talk it over further once we're back at the house."

Sam seemed to be a different young man, Bush thought as he watched his usually cocky son sitting alone in the corner of the room, sipping slowly on a cup of water and looking more like the little boy he'd once been than he had in years. His encounter on the road had stripped something from him, dampened the spark that usually burned inside him. Bush wondered if the change was passing, or permanent. He'd long wanted Sam to grow up some, to lose some of his innate recklessness. But that didn't mean he wanted him to stop being Sam.

Bush had been watching his son while listening to Dunning expand upon the comment he'd made out on the road. Dunning, finishing now, leaned back in his chair and waited for Bush's response.

"So what you're saying, in short, is that before, we had no means of negotiating with Trippler. He held the hostages, we held nothing. Now we've got a hostage of our own."

"Yes."

"I'm not sure I can agree with you, Mr. Dunning. Having a son of Rafe Morgan in our custody might be useful in deterring Rafe Morgan from hurting John and his family, but I can't see how it would make a difference to Trippler, if he's the kind of man you say."

Dunning thought it over. "I do see your point, Mr. Underhill. Trippler isn't the kind to feel any personal concern for those under him. But Rafe Morgan is one of his most important men. Trippler has given him significant authority over his little army. And if Trippler wouldn't be concerned about young Morgan, Rafe Morgan would, and for the sake of keeping Rafe cooperative, Trippler might consider a negotiation."

"John's freedom in return for Rafe Morgan getting his son back?" Bush shrugged. "Maybe. But I doubt it. I wish we had a stronger hand to play." He paused thoughtfully. "Trippler never demanded a ransom, but maybe I should have offered one on my own. If he's in need of money, maybe he'd consider turning John over in exchange for some."

"I doubt it, Mr. Underhill. I know you're a man of some means, but I doubt any amount of wealth you have would compare in Trippler's mind to the value of having John Underhill serving as his spokesman. Trippler might consider trading John for someone of greater stature and influence, perhaps, but I doubt it would be wise to try to buy your son's freedom with money. Trippler would take the money, I'm certain, but I doubt he would actually release John."

Bushrod was frowning, thinking hard, and said nothing in reply.

Dunning rose and went back to the room where Durham guarded the still-unconscious Morgan. Bushrod listened to Dunning making muffled conversation with Durham. Rising, he went to where his baggage sat on the floor in a corner, and from it pulled out the crumpled copy of the Underhill almanac he'd received from the innkeeper Dedham back in Arkansas. Returning to his chair, he sat down and flipped through it, studying the pages by the faint flickering light of a lamp.

"I thought you hated that almanac, Pap," Cordell said. He was cleaning his pistol over near the fireplace.

"I do. Just thinking some things over, that's all."

Cordell laid down his pistol, rose, and went to Bushrod. "I can guess what you're thinking. Don't do it, Pap."

"How can you know what I'm thinking?" Bush said, looking up with a forced smile.

"Because I know you."

"You know what I was really thinking about? About how it's too bad we don't have that Eden box with us. Maybe that magic dirt would heal up Sam's wound right off. We could even give some to young Morgan."

Cordell grinned. "You know you don't believe in that old

box of dirt, Pap. That was just that old colored woman's crazy story.''

''Well, I got my doubts that anywhere on this earth today a single grain of honest-to-God dirt from Eden can be found, no matter what old Granny Mack claimed for that old box. But your mother believes in it.''

''You really think so?''

''Yep. You know she feeds me a bit of that dirt every year, just like Granny Mack said. Hides it in my cornbread so I won't know, but I can still tell. Even Lorry's cornbread ain't that gritty.''

Cordell chuckled. ''I didn't know she did that.''

''I suppose it's her way of trying to keep me alive and young and healthy. Granny Mack swore that eating some of that soil every year would give long life, keep a man youthful and vigorous.''

''Looks like it must be working. You don't look your age. Nor act it.''

''I've been blessed with good health, though I give no credit to boxes of magic dirt. I've lived a good and happy life, good things always outweighing the bad on balance. If I didn't live another day, I couldn't complain. What I want most now is for my children and grandchildren to have the same.''

''I don't like the whispers I'm hearing between the words you're saying, Pap.''

''Why, you speak downright poetical, Cordell. But I don't know what you're talking about.''

''Then I'll say it straight out: you're thinking of offering yourself to Trippler in exchange for John and his family. You're looking at that almanac and thinking about how you've discovered just how famous and admired a man you are. You're thinking that maybe Trippler would rather have Bushrod Underhill to offer up as his spokesman instead of John. Why, then he'd have Crockett and Underhill with him, the nation's two most admired men of the frontier. And then, when it all falls apart, it'll be you who goes down with Trippler, not John and his wife and his children.''

Bushrod looked away from Cordell, over to the fire, blinking fast, his eyes gone moist. "I just keep thinking of my grandchildren, Cordell. Locked up there in that fort, men with guns all around them, their father kept away. They have to be scared, Cordell. Little children shouldn't have to be scared that way. I remember when I was small, and Coldwater fell, and I watched the only man I'd known as a father being shot dead . . . I know what it is to be a child, and so frightened you're afraid to go to sleep come evening." He swiped quickly at his eyes, then looked up at Cordell. "But I ain't a child now. I'm a man, and I have duties to my own. If Trippler would take me in John's stead, and let him and his go free, I'd trade myself without another thought. Indeed I would." He nodded. "Indeed I might."

"Well, then, Trippler can take me, too."

Sam rose across the room. "And me, Pap."

Bush looked at his sons, and the tears came again. "You make me proud, boys. But 'boys' don't fit no more. You're men. Both of you. And Durham, too."

"Don't go offering yourself to Trippler just yet, Pap," Cordell said. "Maybe Mr. Dunning is right, and they'll be willing to deal for Morgan in there."

"Pap," Sam said, "it might be the wrong thing to do anyway. It might be like you going down and talking to that Brutus fellow, hoping to get me free, and winding up locked in beside me."

"I know. There's no perfect plan. Don't you worry. I'm not doing anything until I've thought it through. And tonight, all I have in mind is some sleep, and letting my head clear." Bush turned to Sam. "You going to be able to sleep with that arm hurting?"

"I believe I can. It's not so bad."

"Let's rest, then. Cordell, you can spell Durham and take over guarding Morgan in two or three hours. Then get me up to relieve you so you can sleep some more before dawn."

"I can help, too," Sam said.

"You sleep the night through, son. Let that wound get a good start on healing."

"When will we go take a look at Trippler's fort?" Cordell asked.

"Very soon. Maybe tomorrow."

The morning sun brought more than daylight. With the light came a sense of renewal, energy, mental clarity. Hope. Bushrod opened his eyes, sat up, yawned, and knew that somehow things were going to work. A solid night's rest, and a man woke up a new creature.

A solid night's rest . . .

Bush sprang up from his pallet. Why hadn't Cordell awakened him as planned? He rushed across the room, pushed open the door to the small adjacent bedroom where young Morgan had been placed.

Cordell sat in the corner on the floor, legs sprawled out, body limp, head tilted down on his chin.

The bed was empty. Morgan was gone.

"Cordell . . ."

Bush rushed to his son, knelt, grasped him by the shoulders and gave him a gentle shake. "Cordell!"

The eyes opened, puffy, heavy with sleep. "Pap? What's wrong?"

"Oh, son, I thought something had happened. I thought he'd killed you."

"Who?" Then Cordell's eyes shifted, he saw the empty bed, and knew. He rose. "Pap! He's . . ."

"He's gone. Must have come around in the night, slipped his ropes, and managed to sneak out that window."

"And me asleep . . . Pap, I'm sorry. I fell asleep. It's my fault."

Bush might have scolded, but it seemed pointless. Having Morgan as a hostage had never been part of the original plan . . . though if he were to admit it, Bush would have to say he hadn't had an original plan to begin with. He'd come to Texas not knowing what he'd find, much less how he'd deal with it.

Investigation showed that Morgan had gotten away hours before, probably shortly after Cordell had gone in to relieve

Durham. It was even possible, admitted Durham, that Morgan had come to and escaped during his watch, rather than Cordell's. He too had fallen asleep. And Cordell had been so groggy when he came in to take Durham's place that he hadn't even glanced at the bed to make sure Morgan was still there.

Dunning was more distressed by the escape than was Bush. "We've lost the only card we held," he said, scratching a night's growth of whiskers and glowering. "Now he'll go back to Trippler's fort, tell what happened. Rafe Morgan at the least will learn about this, maybe even Trippler himself."

"And so much the worse for John, either way," said Durham.

They explored the vicinity of the ranch in the hope that maybe Morgan hadn't made it far, considering his condition. But they found no Morgan, not even as many tracks as they would have expected. He'd apparently taken some pains to hide his trail. What they did find of it, however, was enough to tell them his destination. Dunning noted that the tracks led straight in the direction of Trippler's fort.

CHAPTER
TWENTY-THREE

"And there it is," Dunning said, gesturing toward the grayish-white stone enclosure on the clearing about a hundred yards back from the river. He, along with the Underhills, was crouched on a slight rise, hidden by grass and a line of scraggly trees. "Once a fine old mission, now the headquarters of the man who may be the greatest enemy Texas faces, barring Santa Anna himself."

"You really take Trippler seriously," Bush commented.

"I do, indeed. I know what the man is capable of."

Bush eyed the old enclosure closely. Its wall was not quite as high as he'd anticipated, maybe twice the height of an average man, but appeared to be very thick. Every dozen yards or so along its front it was abutted by brick support walls that connected with the main wall at a ninety-degree angle, tapering as they neared the top of the wall. Bush noted these closely, for they struck him as a potential means of entrance. A man could fairly easily climb the rough end of one of those abutting walls and reach a height sufficient to let him mount the top of the wall. If Bush had his guess, some of the interior buildings were built right against the outer wall, meaning one could easily reach their flat roofs off the top of the wall.

"There's the bell tower," Dunning pointed out. "And the flagpole atop it."

"With the flag of Texas, I notice," Cordell said.

"Yes. But don't let that fool you about Trippler's loyalties. He'd betray Texas in a moment." Dunning looked more closely. "Hmm. The Texas flag alone. Interesting. It means Trippler isn't in there."

"What do you mean?"

"There's another flag he flies, red and trimmed in yellow. It's his personal banner that indicates whether he's present in the fort, or absent."

"Why would he do that?"

"Arrogance, Mr. Underhill. The man is arrogance unbound."

Bushrod had brought a spyglass with him. He pulled it out and looked more closely at the enclosure. Though he could see little of the interior, several armed men patrolled back and forth inside the wall, heads and shoulders visible, which indicated they walked either on a raised rifleman's platform or the roofs of some of the interior structures abutting the wall. Smoke rose here and there in the enclosure from chimneys, outdoor ovens, or open fires.

Looking closely, Bushrod found he could see the roof and upper floor of one of the buildings in the center of the enclosure. It had a balcony extending all around. A big arched window on its side faced Bushrod, but was covered with interior shutters. Bushrod lowered the spyglass.

"Mr. Dunning, we met a man name of Jack Bean who'd done some work on wagons for Trippler. He'd seen John inside, up on a balcony in the building where he said Trippler lived. Is that big squarish structure in the middle Trippler's dwelling?"

"It is."

"Where do you think he'd be holding John's family?"

"I have no way to know. There are many buildings inside those walls. I've sketched out a rough map of the interior layout that I can show you when we're back at John's house."

"I don't see how anything less than a small army could get someone out of there," Cordell said.

"But the problem then would be what Trippler might do to his hostages while that small army was attacking," Bushrod said. "It seems to me that the best kind of army in such a situation might be one that's smaller than small."

"An infiltration by a rescue team?" Dunning asked.

"Yes, sir."

"It might work. But the odds would be poor. The best bet in my book is some sort of attempted negotiation. But we've lost our hostage."

"Any other suggestions, then?"

"The only suggestion I have is that we return to John's house and . . . what's this?"

Dunning pointed at the bell tower. On the pole above it, a red flag with a yellow stripe around the perimeter rose slowly. A moment later the bell moved, the clang reaching the ears of Bushrod and company a moment later.

"I'll be!" Dunning declared. "I believe we may have chanced upon the opportunity to see Trippler himself!"

The group crouched lower, scanning the landscape. At length Durham pointed. A line of riders was moving slowly across the countryside, somewhat down and to the right of where the Underhills and Dunning hid. Bushrod lifted the spyglass and examined the group. The spyglass was insufficient to pull their faces in closely enough to see them in any detail, but as Bushrod swept the glass slowly back along the line of riders, he felt a surging in his heart and the start of a warm tear in his eye as he saw the distant but clearly recognizable figure of John Underhill.

"Cordell," Bush said tightly. "There he is."

He handed over the spyglass. Cordell put it to his eye, adjusted it, and watched in silence, until Sam and Durham forced the glass away from him, eager for a look at their brother before the gray-walled enclosure swallowed him up.

Bush blinked back tears as he watched the distant line of men crawl toward the arched double gate at the main entrance. Dunning, understanding the emotions of the moment, kept quiet for a spell, until finally he said, "Mr. Underhill, I don't know if you noticed the man in front of John. That's Trippler."

"Let me have the glass, Sam," Bush asked. Focusing in,

he examined Trippler, and nodded. "Rather plain-looking fellow to think himself a Napoleon."

"He's a man with the remarkable ability to look as he needs to look in whatever situation he's in. He can appear to be a dirt farmer or a king as the occasion arises."

"You sound as if you've seen a lot of him."

Dunning paused, then said, "I'm basing that comment on what people tell me about the man."

"I see."

The bell in the high tower began to ring, its deep peals carrying richly across the wide sky to the ears of the watching men in the grass. Bushrod focused in on Trippler again, and saw the man seem to grow tall in his saddle, chest puffing out, an absolutely regal bearing overtaking him. Bushrod understood what Dunning had meant about Trippler's ability to change his bearing.

Bushrod swung the glass around to the now-open front gate, looking through to see what he could of the inside. Armed men were forming into rough columns on the broad dirt plaza inside—Trippler's ragged army coming into formation to meet the commander in chief.

The column passed inside and the doors swung closed so firmly that the dead thud of it reached Bushrod's ears a moment later. The bell ceased pealing, but the red and yellow banner continued flapping in the wind.

"So much for that," Dunning said. "At least you've now had the opportunity to see that John is alive and seemingly in good health, and to know the face of your enemy, too."

"Where do you think they've been? Mexico?"

"Perhaps."

Sam said, "Pap, I want to sneak in there. We can do it by night, and if we could find John and arm him, that would give us a fighting chance to get out again."

"What about John's wife? The children? We can't get into a shooting match with a whole blasted mercenary army."

"Then what are we going to do?"

Bushrod could find no answer.

"For now, I suggest we simply return and do some talking

and planning," Dunning said. "Perhaps there are options that simply haven't come to mind yet."

They returned to their horses. Using the lay of the land for cover to keep them out of sight of the fort, they rode back toward John Underhill's house, silent and somber, none of them feeling any better for having seen what they were up against.

They had just ridden out of a stand of scraggly trees and onto a trail that followed the stream that, some miles ahead, ran across the property of John Underhill, when they found themselves unexpectedly face-to-face with two ugly, flint-eyed armed men.

Sam, who had moved ahead and thus was the first to encounter the threatening-looking strangers, already had his pistol out and cocked before Dunning reached him and pushed his arm down. "For heaven's sake, young man, don't go shooting at Texas Rangers!"

"Rangers?" Sam lowered the pistol, thumbed down the lock, and looked sheepish. "I'm mighty sorry."

The bigger of the two Rangers, who had an exceptionally broad and floppy hat and a checked waistcoat beneath a heavy overcoat of thick wool, tugged at the end of his beard and said, "Apology accepted." His hand moved swiftly, and suddenly it was he who had a pistol leveled, which had appeared in his grip like a coin in the fingers of a conjurer. "Not that you'd have had any chance to do us harm." He grinned and put the pistol away much more slowly than he'd drawn it.

"You look a little pale, Sam," Durham side-mouthed to his brother.

The second Ranger looked at Dunning. "You been looking over Trippler's fort, Mr. Dunning?"

"Indeed. And you the same, I expect."

"Earlier on we were. But Trippler wasn't there, if the flag was an indication."

The bigger Ranger added, "But we heard the bell pealing fifteen minutes ago or so."

"Trippler's returned," Dunning said. "We watched him ride in with his armed guard."

"Damned treasonist has been meeting with the Mexes again, sure as hell," the big Ranger said.

"It appears these are friends of yours, Mr. Dunning," said Bushrod.

"Indeed they are. Meet Homer Gibbs"—he waved toward the bigger man—"and Lem Greenwood. And gentlemen, let me introduce to you Bushrod Underhill and his sons."

Homer Gibbs arched his brows. "*The* Bushrod Underhill?"

"Only one I know of," Bush said, sticking out his hand. He shook the callused paws of the Rangers, both men nodding and declaring their pleasure to meet the noted frontiersman. They gave nods and handshakes to the younger Underhills, as well.

"Mr. Gibbs and Mr. Greenwood have been working with me over the past months while we've been keeping our eyes on Trippler," Dunning said. "They've been ranging about this area for weeks now, watching the place, who comes and goes, and so on."

"There's been quite a lot of coming and going lately," Greenwood said in a voice and manner that suggested he was perhaps a little more cerebral than the bigger Gibbs. "Two, three days ago, there was a durn wagon rolled in there with a printing press and such on the back of it."

"A printing press?" Dunning frowned. "What would Trippler want with a printing press?"

Homer Gibbs said, "My guess would be he aims to print something," and it was hard to tell if he was speaking facetiously or thinking he was making a truly helpful comment.

"Have you seen anything else unusual?"

"Well, Trippler seems to be losing some of his men," Greenwood said. "We've seen maybe a dozen of them slipping off from the fort. Homer managed to speak to one without revealing he was a Ranger. Seems there's worry among the troops that the pay is about to dry up, and you know as well as me that the only thing keeping them mercenaries loyal to Trippler is the pay."

"Is worry about pay the only reason they're beginning to flee him?"

"Nope. Seems they're talking among themselves about the rising public sentiment against them. And believe it or not, there's more than a few who have a bit of Texian loyalty about them, and don't like these rumors that Trippler is conniving with the Mexes."

"Have you found any serious efforts under way among the common citizens to actually strike against Trippler?"

"It's starting. It won't take long now. There's some already beginning to form militia groups, figuring that an armed attack may be the only way to drive out Trippler and his mercenaries. But others hope that an official force will be sent to deal with Trippler in the end, or that maybe he'll just up and go away. This Crockett rumor has folks slower to act, too, and they're just confused about John Underhill and how he ties in with it all." He turned to Bushrod. "You have anything to share along that line, sir?"

"You know more than I do. If Trippler is really treasonous, my John would do nothing for him except what was forced under threat to his family."

"John Underhill's true and straight," Gibbs contributed. "I've never doubted him a minute. Old Trippler's just got John's thumbs in a vise, that's all. Folks with any sense know that."

"I hope there is no general uprising," Bushrod said. "Not until we can get John and his family out, anyway."

"The uprising won't hold off forever, especially not if things keep happening like they did over near the mouth of the Colorado the other day."

"What happened?" Dunning asked.

"You ain't heard? Why, some of Trippler's gunmen murdered two men and a woman and hauled some others off with them, either to make prisoners or maybe to murder them out in the chapparal where nobody would find them."

"What people were murdered? And why?"

"Ain't got no names. Some religious types, who'd come down from Kentucky all done up like Quakers. The why I can't tell you. Nobody we've talked to seems to know."

CHAPTER
TWENTY-FOUR

Durham Underhill sat stone-faced beside the hearth of his missing brother, staring into the flames. In the corner Sam cleaned his pistol, over and over, setting and resetting the flint, keeping his hands busy, wincing every now and then because his wound was hurting tonight. Cordell paced, a glowering bear of a man, shifting his eyes occasionally to his father, who had gone through a lengthy conference with Dunning, all to no avail. Despite all the talk they could find no good way to deal with the situation that faced them. Every kind of scenario had been considered and analyzed, and all had been discarded as unworkable or too dangerous to the captive Underhills. Now Bushrod and Dunning both sat in miserable, angry silence, frustrated at their lack of progress.

Durham rose and approached his father. "Pap, I want us to go find out what happened with them Purificationists."

"We know what happened," Bushrod replied snappily. "Some of Trippler's men killed some of them, and took the rest hostage."

"We can't just sit by. We know those people."

"Not really. They were just some folks we helped out when they needed it. Now there's nothing we can do. Them that are dead are dead, and if the others are inside those walls, then they're just as out of our reach as John and his family seem to be. And it's John and his family that we're obliged to worry about. Not those poor old Purificationists, who ain't even willing to put up a fight to protect themselves.''

"What if they murdered Chasida? You'd be willing to live with them killing a young lady?''

"Son, it ain't my situation, and it ain't your situation. That's what I'm trying to tell you. Our job is to rescue John and his bunch. If we can help somebody else, too, then fine. But it's John I'm worried about, not some near strangers whose business is their own.''

Durham spun and walked back to the fire. He sat down again, then muttered something beneath his breath and stalked out the door into the night, where they heard him pacing back and forth on the covered porch of John's house.

"What's his interest in these Purificationists?'' Dunning asked.

"He was smitten by a pretty young woman who was among them. Apparently more smitten than I realized.''

"I've been trying to understand why Trippler's men would have killed and kidnapped a simple bunch of religious fanatics out of Kentucky.''

"Because they aren't just a simple bunch of religious fanatics,'' Bushrod replied. "They came to Texas looking for Trippler's own brother, who you say he murdered. Maybe Trippler is nervous that they'll go poking around in a pile he thought was dried up and forgotten, and raise a new stink for him at a time he can't afford it.''

"Or maybe his men simply acted on their own,'' suggested Dunning.

"And took prisoners back to Trippler's fort? No. What they done, Trippler had probably told them to do.'' Bushrod yawned. "I'm tired. Believe I'll go on to sleep.''

Dunning rose. "Not me. I've got more energy than a tomcat. I think I'll head into San Pablo and bend my arm a little.''

"There was a time I'd have offered to go with you,'' Sam said from the corner as he swiped a cloth over the butt of his pistol, putting a shine to it. "But after what happened to me, I've got no love for that little hellhole.''

"You planning to get drunk, Mr. Dunning?'' Bushrod asked.

"Absolutely not. I'm planning to get inspired, that's all. And maybe dig up some more information. There's no placc like a tavern by night for a man to nose up facts." He put on his hat. " 'Evening. Don't wait up for me."

When Dunning was gone, Cordell said, "Pap, do you think he's who he says?"

"I don't know, son. Somehow I tend to trust him. But I'll tell you this: I think he knows Trippler better than he's letting on, and that his interest in this is more than professional. What do you think?"

"I think we're never going to find a way to get John out of that place alive. That's what I think."

Bushrod wished he hadn't asked.

Late in the night, as Bushrod, Sam, and Cordell slept inside, Durham sat bundled in his coat on the porch, smoking his pipe. He'd lain down hours earlier but hadn't slept a bit. Giving up, he'd risen and come out here so he could smoke without disturbing the others.

Dunning came riding in, and when Durham heard him singing low to himself, somewhat off key, he knew the man had drunk more than he'd said he would.

Dunning rode right past the porch without even noticing Durham, heading to the barn to stable his horse. When he came stumping clumsily back in, he noticed Durham and said, "Ah, young Mr. Underhill! A restless night, is it?"

"How'd things go in San Pablo?"

"Swimmingly, young man. Wonderfully. I was able to gain some more information."

"About John?"

"Not precisely. Actually, about those poor Quakers who fell victim to Trippler's men."

"Purificationists. Not Quakers. They just look like Quakers."

Dunning, so precise and clean-spoken most of the time, was quite slovenly and careless now that he had some liquor in him. "What the devil . . . all the same to me. Anyhow, it seems that these poor folks made the mistake of talking too freely around some of Trippler's men—guess which ones.''

"I have no way to know.''

"Rafe Morgan and one of his sons, that's who. And three or four others of Trippler's hired scoundrels. And when it was done, two men and a woman were dead, and another man and two young folks hauled away toward Trippler's fort.''

Durham stood. "Two young folks? Including a young woman?''

"Yes, indeed . . . oh, my. I just recalled your father telling me that this young woman had rather caught your eye.''

"Never mind that . . . she's alive? Was she hurt?''

"Not as I heard it . . . but I'm so sorry, Mr. Underhill. So sorry to have to tell you that she probably isn't well at all now, and maybe isn't even alive. So sorry . . .''

If Durham could have slapped Dunning back to sobriety, he'd have done it. He grew intense and stepped toward Dunning almost in a threatening way. "What do you mean, not alive?''

"There must have been more trouble on the way back to Trippler's, sorry to say. The next morning after the incident, they found the young man of this Quaker bunch—pardon me, this *Purificationist* bunch—staggering back into the settlement, wounded. And out on the plains, later, they found the body of the other man who had been taken. He was shot through the head.''

"The girl?''

"No sign of her, sorry to say. But most likely she's lying out there, too, her body just not yet found.''

"Where did this happen?''

"A little settlement called Cable Creek. Ten miles or so southeast of here. Not a town, just a few small farms and ranches not too far apart, and a trading post.''

"Kirk—the young man of the group—is he still alive?''

"I have no idea, young sir. No idea at all.'' Dunning belched and made a face, and Durham wondered how a man who seemed almost elegant normally could be so disgusting now. "I believe he *was* alive . . . they took him to the trading

post, I think they said. Yes. I think that's right.'' He stretched.
''Oh, I'm tired. So tired. And maybe a little drunk, too, if I
were to admit it. I'm sure you can't tell. I've always been
able to hold my liquor.'' He tipped his hat. ''Good night.
You'll be sleeping soon, too, I hope. Get your rest, young
man! Get your rest!''

''I'll be in shortly,'' Durham said.

He waited on the porch until he heard Dunning cease stir-
ring about inside the house, then slipped inside. Dunning
snored on his pallet, oblivious. The others were sleeping as
well. Durham moved, however, with the greatest of caution.
Bushrod Underhill was a light sleeper, his senses honed by
years of wilderness experience, his mind and body quick to
snap to alertness at the slightest out-of-place noise.

Durham readied himself as best he could under the circumstances, then sat down with a piece of paper and a quill pen
and ink bottle he found on John's writing desk. He scratched
out a note of explanation and apology, and read it through
several times, trying to picture how his father would react to
it. The picture wasn't pretty.

It didn't matter. From the moment he'd seen her he'd
known there was something there, something meant to be.
She was a stranger, to be sure, but this wasn't mere infatuation. She was meant for him; he felt it, just knew it. There
was destiny at work here; it was for her sake, not for his
brother John's, that he'd felt compelled to come with his father and brothers to Texas, even if he didn't know it at the
time. He'd leave it to them to deal with John's situation, and
help them as he could, when he could. But not before he knew
what had become of Chasida Gruenwald.

Durham rode away from the house slowly, until he was out
of any possible hearing range. Only then did he speed his
horse to a trot, putting as much distance behind him as he
could. Morning would come before long, and he wanted to
be far away when it did.

Bushrod read the note for the fifth time and slapped it down
on the desktop with disgust. ''Fool of a boy!'' he bellowed.

"What does he think he can do for her if she's dead? And if she's not dead, then she's inside Trippler's fort and just as out of reach as John!" Bush scratched his beard and muttered, turned on his heel and said, "You were right all along, Sam. I should have sent Durham straight back home when he followed us. I never should have brought him."

Over by the fire, Dunning held his head in his hands, quite hung over, and winced in pain at the sound of Bush's raised voice.

"I believe he loves the girl, Pap," Cordell said.

"Love? My eyes! How can he love a girl he doesn't even know? And how could he run out on his own kin in favor of a stranger who never even took a glance at him that I could see!"

Cordell's forceful reply rather shocked Bushrod. "Maybe Durham was tired of wasting his time sitting around here with all this hand-wringing and hopeless what-are-we-going-to-do-for-poor-John nonsense! Maybe he figured he might as well go off and help that girl, if he could, instead of doing nothing!"

Bushrod walked up to Cordell and stared him in the face. "What are you saying, son?"

"That we've talked and planned and studied that fort, and we're still no closer than we were to a plan to get John out of there. And as far as I can see, days might go by with nothing changing."

"So what do you recommend?"

"I don't know . . . something. Anything. Anything but setting here on our rumps and worrying."

" 'Anything,' you say. We should do 'anything' just so we can say we took action, never mind that 'anything' might get your brother killed, and his wife, and those innocent children."

"Pap, I'm just . . . tired. Tired of waiting."

"The waiting's over."

"What are you going to do?"

"What has to be done."

Cordell gazed at Bushrod a moment, then quietly said,

"You're going to do it, ain't you? What we talked about."

Bush also lowered his voice. Over by the fire, Dunning looked grateful. "It's the only hope we have."

"Pap, there's no assurance it would work. It just might be like you going down to get Sam out of that so-called jail. You might just become a prisoner yourself."

"Or I might just be able to get my son and his family out of there before all hell comes crashing in on them."

"Let me go with you, then."

"No. Because if it doesn't work, and Trippler ends up holding me as well as John, then it'll be up to you and Sam and Durham . . . maybe just you and Sam, if Durham doesn't get back . . . to find another way."

"But I don't know what other way there would be."

Bushrod's lips flicked for a moment into a little smile. "Then you understand the position I'm in right now, and why we haven't done 'anything' yet."

"I'm sorry I spoke like I did, Pap."

"Nothing to be sorry about. Just tell me that I'm doing the right thing. You opposed the idea before."

"I don't know if it's the right thing. But I do believe it's the only thing possible."

Despite his hangover, Dunning had told the others what he'd picked up during his drinking fest in San Pablo. As Cordell and Bushrod left the house to walk around toward the stable, Sam approached Dunning and crouched beside him.

"Please," Dunning said. "Whatever you're going to say to me, say it softly."

"I just want to be sure you told all you knew about Kirk."

"Kirk?"

"The young man with the Purificationists. His name is Kirk Gruenwald, and he's the best of the bunch. The only one willing to fight."

"Maybe that's why he was shot."

"The other men were all killed, too. And they didn't believe it right to lift a finger, even to defend themselves."

"Maybe they finally changed their minds." Dunning put his face in his hands and groaned painfully.

"Do you think Kirk is still alive?"

"I already told you, just like I told Durham last night. All I know is that I was told a 'young man' from the Purificationists was found wounded on the plains, and an older man was found dead. The girl wasn't found at all."

"I hope Durham finds her. I hope she's not hurt. And I hope Kirk is alive. He's got grit. He's the best of the bunch."

Dunning lay down. "Let me ask you a favor. If I ever get it in my mind to go drinking again, shoot me. Just pull your pistol out and shoot me."

CHAPTER
TWENTY-FIVE

He was dead

As many times as Chasida Gruenwald ran the indisputable
fact through her mind, it remained as hard to fathom as ever.
Her father was dead. She would speak to him no more, see
his face no more, touch his hand never again.

Chasida squeezed her eyes tightly shut, bit her lip, and tried
to stifle the jerking, painful spasms of grief that had wracked
her again and again since she'd been brought there. And just
what was this place, this big, walled stone enclosure full of
hardened, armed men who milled about beneath the shadow
of the stone bell tower and the high pole with its twin flags?
She didn't really know. Her father had described it, before
they killed him, as the place where the brother of Elder Pepperdine—Trippler, his real name had been—lived and ruled.
A wicked man, he said, so wicked that he'd killed his own
brother for the sake of money.

She was lying in a small, closed room with walls of plastered stone and no windows except a small high one barred
with wooden crossbars. Furniture was absent except for the
cot upon which she lay, a single three-legged stool, and a
small chest which concealed a chamber pot. Atop the chest
sat a cracked crockery basin for washing and a bucket of
drinking water.

In all her life Chasida had never been a prisoner, and it
was difficult to accept that she was one now. It was true that,

sometimes, the stifling life of the Purificationist sect back in Kentucky had seemed a kind of imprisonment. It didn't seem so now. She'd gladly give up ten years of her future if only she could go back to the Purificationist colony on the Rock-castle River, with her friends, her father, her brother . . .

Her brother. She wondered if Kirk was dead, too. She'd seen them shooting at him when he tried to run, and had seen him spasm as if struck. But Kirk was fast and strong, and he'd kept running. It made her proud. He'd outsmarted them, not letting them kill him easily as her father had. Go over yonder, they'd told Peter Gruenwald. Sit beneath that tree and we'll consider whether we should let you go or take you on to Trippler. He'd done what they said, and they'd shot him. And laughed to see him die.

She was glad Kirk had dared to run from them. She was proud of him. She prayed that he had survived, and that they'd somehow be together again when this was through.

She hated them. It was a sin to hate, but she hated them anyway. *They touched me. They murdered my father, shot at my brother, and they touched me. Terrible touches, terrible words . . . I hate them!*

She rolled over on her cot and stared at the crumbling ceiling above, trying to make sense of it all. She replayed everything in her mind from the beginning, back in Kentucky.

It had all started in ways that she hadn't been able to un-derstand in her younger days. The treachery and thefts of Elder Pepperdine had been known for several years, but no one had sought to track him down. She'd never quite under-stood that, even though her father was the one who'd made the decision to delay. "It is not God's time for us now to seek this fallen man," he'd declared to those who asked him if Pepperdine shouldn't be pursued. "When God's time comes, then we will pursue."

As Chasida had gotten older, she'd begun to see that her father had good personal reason not to pursue Pepperdine. In Pepperdine's absence he had become the acting elder of the colony, enjoying influence and power, even if the colony was

stripped of most of its resources. Good man as Peter Gruenwald was, he was yet a human being, and power and prestige
had pleased him. He'd been happy to let Pepperdine go, and
Chasida now suspected that "God's time" had little to do
with it.

Then word had come from a former Purificationist who had
yielded to worldly temptation and gone to Texas for land. He
wrote to his former fellow believers that a man who might
be Pepperdine was forming a colony on the Trinity River; if
a delegation from the Kentucky colony would come and in-
vestigate, perhaps there was hope of recovering at least some
of the wealth Pepperdine had stolen.

Given this information, the pressure upon Peter Gruenwald
to at last recognize "God's time" and launch a search for
Pepperdine had been overwhelming. He'd selected those who
would travel with him, including his own son and daughter
against the advice of others, and they'd set off downriver.

Then came the tragic accident with the steamboat, the beginning of their land journey across Arkansas and into Texas,
the meeting with the Underhills, the attack by those ruffians
and the Underhills' helpful response . . .

They'd gone on then and found the new religious colony,
and discovered that the man who might have been Pepperdine
was not Pepperdine at all, but merely a mild-mannered former
Methodist with an eye toward creation of a little religious
utopia in Texas. The long journey from Kentucky had seemed
a waste of time, until new information surfaced. Though the
man they'd initially suspected as being Pepperdine wasn't,
the real Pepperdine apparently had indeed been in Texas some
years earlier. Descriptions matched, as did all details but the
name, and the name didn't matter because they were sure that
he'd probably used a false name at least in Kentucky. The
man in question had been George Trippler, brother of a noted
early empresario. As they trailed George Trippler's years-old
track, it had led to that former empresario, William Gordon
Trippler.

She rose and went to the water bucket, taking a drink and
disliking the stagnant, alkaline taste of it. She paced about,

still mentally retracing the fateful steps that had led her there.

The more they had inquired about George Trippler and his brother, the stranger and more disturbing the story had become. They learned that George Trippler was dead, apparently killed by his own brother for the sake of his wealth—wealth that rightly had belonged to the people of the Purificationist colony.

It all might have ended at that point if not for Peter Gruenwald's driving need to prove himself after the humiliation they all had suffered in the attack of those drunks back in Arkansas. Though Gruenwald had officially yielded his leadership to Niles, he resumed it again, and urged that the quest be continued, redirected now toward William Gordon Trippler in the hope that the man still had some of the Purificationist wealth hidden away in his old mission headquarters. And so they had pursued, and somehow Trippler had learned of it, and sent out men to deal with the black-clad troublemakers . . .

And thus the end had come, and for Chasida, a new beginning. She was captive here, brought to this place by men who had murdered those she loved, leered at her, put their hands upon her, whispered terrible things to her about what would become of her once she was in William Trippler's hands.

Chasida wept again, and prayed, and wept some more.

She returned to the cot and slept, and was awakened by the rattling of her door. Sitting up, she saw a slender Mexican woman with sad deep brown eyes, bearing in a platter of food. The woman smiled at her and placed the platter on the end of her cot. Her words, in Spanish, went past Chasida, not understood, but her tone and the sympathetic light in her eyes provided the closest thing Chasida had known to comfort since this ordeal had begun.

But the woman left, barring the door, and Chasida was alone again.

She ate, though her stomach rebelled at the heavily spiced food. Alone . . . but not fully alone. She'd managed to pull her cot over beneath the high window and, by standing upon

it and stretching to full height, to look out onto the little
enclosed yard just beyond it. She'd seen two children there,
a boy and girl playing with one another, their faces similar
in appearance so that she knew they were siblings. And a
woman, a pretty but haggard, scared-looking woman with the
most beautiful eyes Chasida had ever seen.

She wondered if they were also prisoners, and why they
were there. And what would become of them . . . and herself.

Chasida finished the food and set the platter beside the
door. The room was growing dark, the sun setting outside.
She had no lamp or candle. Crawling back onto her cot, she
curled up beneath the single blanket she had been provided,
and slept.

When Durham Underhill had ridden away from the ranch,
he'd felt as wide awake and energetic as he would had he
enjoyed a full night's rest and half a pot of strong coffee. But
the feeling was illusory, the energy of tension, and by the
dark hour just before dawn, he was exhausted.

Sunrise found him encamped in a grove of trees, sleeping
hard. But he awakened well before noon and resumed his
journey.

By now his father knew he had gone, and probably hated
him for it. What he was doing would seem intolerable to
Bushrod Underhill, who believed in family above all else. But
how could he have done differently? From the moment Durham had seen Chasida Gruenwald, he'd been unable to put
her out of his mind. He had to know what had become of
her, and the only way to do that was to find Kirk.

He ate, fed his horse, and rode on, heading as best he could
navigate himself toward the little settlement on Cable Creek,
where Kirk had been, and with luck, still would be.

By late morning, Dunning was past the worst of his hangover,
and realizing that something was afoot. Bushrod and Cordell
had been in a world to themselves for hours, talking and
working and coming in and out of the house, always deep in
conversation.

"What's happening here?" Dunning asked Sam.

Sam knew—Cordell had told him—but his answer to Dunning was deliberately vague. "I suppose they're just talking over what to do."

"Do they have a plan?"

"Maybe you'd best ask them."

Dunning did ask, but Bushrod was as evasive as Sam had been, and Cordell had nothing to say, either. Dunning grew angry, which only caused his companions to grow more silent. He pulled away, sullen, eye on the door.

Bushrod, meanwhile, continued his preparations. Dunning rousted himself up a meal of bread and salted meat, then rose and declared that he'd be moving on for now. "I'm not achieving anything here, obviously."

"Neither am I," Bushrod said. "I'm thinking of heading out myself."

"Where to?"

"Just out."

Dunning approached him. "I'll speak directly, Mr. Underhill. If you're thinking of making some overture to Trippler, I have to advise you not to."

"An overture to Trippler? Why would I do that?"

"Because there seems nothing else to do."

Bushrod nodded. "And maybe that's the point."

Dunning squinted his eyes shut and rubbed his brow as if to wipe out what remained of his hangover, then looked earnestly at Bushrod. "Mr. Underhill, I understand your wish to do something, but giving yourself to Trippler is very unlikely to do anything to help your son."

"Maybe it won't. But doing nothing at all will certainly not help him. Tell me something, Mr. Dunning, do you have a family? A wife and children?"

Something dark was visible for a moment in Dunning's eyes. "There was a time," he said softly. "But no more."

"Then you understand why I have to try. And why there's only one way. You and I have sat together going over every possibility, and there's none that have any hope of success. Except for the one possibility that we didn't discuss."

"He's a dangerous man, Mr. Underhill. Erratic. Mad. You can't rely on him to react to anything you might do in a predictable way. I must advise you strongly not to go to Trippler. You cannot deal in a reasonable way with an inherently unreasonable man."

"You know Trippler better than you would have us believe, I think."

Dunning took a deep breath, and his answer wasn't really an answer. "Do what you must, Mr. Underhill. But be warned. And be very, very careful. And understand that I'll personally have no part in this. If you go to Trippler's fort, you go without my blessing and without my presence."

"I'll do what I must. I can only hope you understand why it has to be that way."

Dunning studied Bushrod's face, seemed to soften, smiled slowly, and put out his hand. "I do understand, sir, though I can't approve of it. In any case, it's been a pleasure to meet you, Mr. Underhill. And if you do let that fort swallow you up, I can only regret to tell you that I have no confidence at all that we'll be having the opportunity to meet again."

"Your cheerfulness and optimism," Bushrod said, with the smallest of grins, "thrills my soul like the music of a songbird."

CHAPTER
TWENTY-SIX

Bushrod rode alone beneath a darkening twilight sky, two sons behind him, side by side. No one spoke. The miles fell away slowly, yet when they finally reached the same spot from which they had observed Trippler's fort before, it felt to them all as if they had gotten there far too soon.

Bushrod dismounted and looked at his sons, one by one. Cordell was the first to climb down from his horse and go to his father, embracing him, patting his shoulder. Bushrod smiled, but a tear glinted in his eye.

Sam dismounted and embraced him as well. "Good luck, Pap."

"Say some prayers for me, boys. And for John and all his own."

"We will."

Bushrod pulled up to full height, sighed, and nodded. "Now's the time." He handed over his rifle to Cordell, and removed his pistol from its clip on his waist.

"You're taking no weapons?" Sam asked.

"I want Trippler to know that I'm coming to him in good faith, no threat."

"I don't like the thought of you going in there with no protection."

"Sam, the first thing they'd do is disarm me, anyway. I'd rather you have my arms than them."

"At least take my hide-out pistol, Pap. Maybe you can get that past them."

"No. They'll search me. It's best this way."

Sam turned away, staring silently across the broad, flat Texas landscape.

"You fellows wait here, and keep out of sight. If providence smiles, I'll be back with John and his family. Or maybe it will be just them alone, without me. Either way, I'll count it a success."

"He ain't going to do this, Pap," Cordell said. "He's going to take you hostage, too, and keep John all the same."

"It may be. But it's the only thing we can try, eh?"

"What if neither you nor John comes out?"

"Then it will be up to you fellows, and Mr. Dunning, to try to think of something else."

He embraced them both again, quickly and with struggling emotions, and turned. Drawing in another deep breath, he topped the low rise and began trudging, alone and unarmed, toward Trippler's fort.

The guards had been talking intently for several minutes, their voices low and deep with concern. Such conversations had become common the last several days among the increasingly worried mercenary guardians of William Gordon Trippler, for rumors were afloat, and they did not bode well for their future in this private little empire.

The taller of the two was the first to notice the man striding through the dusk toward the fort. He pointed him out to his partner. "Who the hell you think that might be?" he asked.

The other cupped his hands around his mouth. "You there! Halt and tell us your business!"

The walking man stopped, and called back, "I'm coming to see William Gordon Trippler."

"Who are you, and what's your business?"

"My name is Bushrod Underhill. I've come to talk to Mr. Trippler about my son John."

The guards glanced at one another, amazed.

"Are you armed?"

"No."

"Then come on, slowly. And wait beside the gate."

The man began striding again.

"What do you think *this* is all about?" one guard asked.

"Hell if I know," replied the other. "Whatever it is, I suspect old Trippler's going to be mighty interested."

The man's brown hair had been touched by gray years before, and was now almost overtaken by it. And the face was lined and weathered. Even so, Rafe Morgan was still a powerful-looking man, eyes as cold as they had been in younger days, when he and his brothers had spent their days embroiled in every kind of criminality across a territory ranging from the Kentucky wilderness to the country that was now Missouri, and all up and down the vast Mississippi River besides.

He walked down the wide hallway and grinned at a young Mexican woman who was lighting the wall-mounted lamps along its length. She looked fearfully at him and pulled away as he neared her. Laughing, he reached out and slapped her across the rump, making her squeal and twist away.

"Come on, honey, you need to loosen yourself up a mite. Learn to have fun."

She backed up against the wall until he was past.

Morgan turned left, down a shorter hallway. A heavy door of graying wood stood at the end of it, and beside it, a guard.

"Take yourself a rest, have a smoke or something," Morgan said. The guard nodded, hefted up his rifle, and walked off down the hall.

Morgan fumbled at a big ring of keys hanging just beneath the bottom of his waistcoat, and thrust a big rusted key into the door. He pushed it open.

Chasida Gruenwald, eyes big with fear, stood against the far wall, facing him.

"My, my, ain't you looking pretty this evening!" Morgan said. "I never saw a young woman who could make even a black frock look good. I believe Mr. Trippler's going to be pleased."

"Why have you come here?"

"To fetch you out for an evening of fun, girl! I only wish it was for myself. Trippler's a fortunate man, no doubt about it."

"I don't want to go."

"You don't want to get out of this little room? Mr. Trippler's waiting for you, deary, there in his big old chambers. Really nice, they are. Big old table, and they was setting it with some fine-looking food just now. You're going to be treated right, sweet thing. Now come on."

"No."

His smile did not fade. "You don't say no to Mr. Trippler. Out with you."

"I'll not go."

The smile vanished. "You will. You'll walk out of here, or I'll carry you. Which will it be?"

Chasida, fighting tears, hesitated, then pulled forward and walked slowly toward him. He smiled again, and reached for her. She pulled away.

"Very well, then. Maybe I don't touch you now, but my time will come. Mr. Trippler and me get on well. I bring him a gift, and he shares it with me sooner or later." Morgan winked. "I'm hoping for sooner."

Chasida rushed past him, as if to run away. But his big hand grabbed her arm and held her. He pulled the door closed and gave her a shove without letting go. "That way. And don't you try to run, for you'll not get away."

He all but pulled her down the hallway. "Yep," he said, "Mr. Trippler's been good to me. He's a powerful man, you know. Gets his way. There's a lot of talk that he's on his way down, but don't you believe it. He's made him some ties with Mexico, you see, that are going to fill his coffers full again before long. And who knows? If he likes you well enough, if you please him the right way, there may be some mighty good things in it for you down the road. Mr. Trippler does know how to share with them who are loyal to him."

"What does he want from me?"

Morgan laughed. "If you don't know that, honey, you're going to get an education tonight, oh yes."

"Who are you? Why did you murder my father and the others?"

"My name's Rafe Morgan. Sorry, by the way, about having to shoot your pap. He just didn't know when to keep his mouth shut. Mouthing off, accusing Mr. Trippler of killing his own brother . . . I just couldn't let that go. It's my job to keep trouble off of Mr. Trippler, and your pap was trouble."

"You shot him dead, in cold blood."

"Wasn't cold. There was steam rising from it, or didn't you see?" He laughed.

She hated him. "Let me go," she pleaded. "Let me go and I'll give you money."

"You ain't got no money, and you know it. And the only other thing you could give me I'll be getting anyway, later on."

Chasida thought she might be sick.

"Yep, there's a lot of good things that will come to me later on. Especially once Mr. Trippler gets his empire established. Lots of Mexican money will be flowing in. Lots of it, and I'll have my share. But the best part ain't going to be the money, fine as that will be. The best part is that Mr. Trippler's already promised to let me deal with Mr. John Underhill, once his usefulness expires. Me, I have quite a complaint with the Underhill clan. Goes way back, all the way back to John Underhill's damned sorry old pap. That bit of trash murdered my brothers, and tried to murder me. Then he comes along, years later, and has this book writ up that pictures me and my brothers as no more than river scum. Yes, ma'am, I owe them Underhills, and I'm going to enjoy taking my piece of them out of John Underhill's hide. Mr. Trippler's already promised it to me."

They left the building via an arching doorway. Chasida looked across the wide plaza, which was lit by numerous campfires and teemed with armed men milling around. Trippler's little army.

One group of them, she noticed, was hustling a man along,

much as she was being handled. The man lifted his head and she saw his face as he saw hers. She drew in a little gasp as she recognized him.

It was Bushrod Underhill. The very man who, with his sons, had been so helpful to her and the other Purificationists on their way into Texas.

The guards moved in around Bushrod and cut him off from her view. She twisted her head and watched them moving him across the plaza and into one of the buildings where the guards kept their quarters. It was obvious he was as much a prisoner as she, and she figured he was about to be subjected to the same kind of humiliating search that she had endured when first they brought her to this vile place.

Morgan hadn't noticed Underhill, for which she was glad. He was still rattling on, talking big talk about all the grand things to come his way once Trippler's "empire" was in place.

She grew angry all at once. "I don't know what Mr. Trippler is planning, but there will be no empire for him," she said. "Before you murdered my family, we spoke to many people outside this fort, and they hate Trippler. They're already arming themselves to come against him."

"It'll never happen," Morgan said. "Mark my words. Folks talk big, but talk is easy, and doing is hard."

"These people are Texians. They've already thrown off Mexico. If they can do that, they can deal with someone like Trippler."

"My, ain't you the smart one! But you'd best learn to mind your tongue, especially around Mr. Trippler. He don't take well to talk like that."

"I hate him."

"He'll teach you to like him quick enough. He'll teach you all kinds of things. And you'll be good to him, you hear? You'll cooperate. Because I brung you to this place specifically as a present for him, because he's good to them who are good to him. So you'll do what he wants, or you'll answer to me. You hear?" He gave her a hard shake. "There's his place, up there beyond that balcony. Got the lights burning bright, all ready for you. You just be a good girl for him . . . and a bad girl when he wants you to be.''

In a daze, Chasida went up the stairs. She felt the gaze of hardened men upon her from the plaza, heard their muted catcalls and whistles, picked up vile words drifting up her way. A hot coal lay inside her stomach.

A young guard approached Morgan. "Sir, I'd like to have a word with you.''

Morgan stopped, looking irritated. "What?''

"I'm worried, sir. There's a lot of talk about how every-thing's going to . . . I don't know, fall apart. How there's a lot of folks out there''—he waved toward the surrounding stone walls—''who are ready to attack this place.''

"Hell, them stories have been going around for weeks.''

"Yes, sir, but they say that now it's really beginning to happen. Because of the folks who were killed.'' The young man glanced at Chasida. "And because of that broadside that's gone out.''

"Ain't nobody going to attack this place.''

The young man grew a little more intense. "I hear they may, sir. I hear they *will*.''

"Then we'll stand them off and they'll run away tuck-tailed.''

"I don't believe it would go that way, Mr. Morgan. The men are saying that Mr. Trippler's out of money. There'll be no more pay for a long time. And nobody's willing to make an Alamo stand out of this place.''

"An Alamo stand? Hell! How many Texians do you think they could get to come against us? Not nearly enough!''

"There's a lot more Texians than there used to be, sir. And folks are mad because of the rumors that Mr. Trippler is aim-ing to help Mexico retake Texas.'' He paused. "And that ain't just folks on the outside. There's a lot of men right here who ain't willing to see such as that done.'' The young man swal-lowed nervously, as if fearing he had spoken too freely.

Morgan faced him. "Get out of here, if you're afraid. Walk out that gate and go. But if you do, know that the next time I lay eyes on you, I'll kill you.''

The young man, pallid now, turned and walked away. Chasida watched him, wondering if he really would leave. She didn't have the chance to find out, because Morgan shoved her on. They left the balcony and entered an arched hallway lighted by two torches. A heavy, barred door to the left was guarded by two armed men.

Morgan thumbed toward the door. "Know who's in there? Mr. John Underhill, that's who. The hero of San Jacinto, the man they talk up for a future in Texas politics . . . the son of the bastard who killed my brothers." Morgan laughed, surprising Chasida. "Know what old Texas-Forever John Underhill has gone and done? Signed his name to a big pile of broadsides Mr. Trippler had printed up. Put his name down, right along with Crockett's, urging the public to support William Gordon Trippler and his 'great plan for the future of Texas.' What do you think folks will think of that, huh? That'll sure still any talk of uprising, with them two names giving their backing to the Trippler empire!"

"Crockett is dead," Chasida said.

"Sometimes folks ain't as dead as people believe they are. Now turn on down this other hall. That door there is Mr. Trippler's."

Her heart pounding so hard that it hurt, Chasida moved on unfeeling legs toward the door. It opened suddenly, revealing a flash of lighted splendor behind it while the same Mexican woman who had brought her food earlier emerged, bearing an empty platter. The woman reacted with a look of fear when she saw Morgan, then turned a sad, sympathetic look on Chasida. The sort of look a kindhearted person might give to one being rolled on a tumbril toward a place of execution.

Chasida was overwhelmed with fear and a great sorrow. She pulled back against Morgan's painful grip. "I can't go in there."

"You *will* go in there."

"I hate you . . . I hate him . . . I hate this place! Let me go! You murdered my father! You shot my brother while he ran for his life!"

Morgan pulled her around to face him and thrust his face

close to hers. "You get control of yourself, you little trollop! You're going to be a pleasing little offering to Mr. Trippler tonight, and you'll pay a price you don't want to pay if you act up!"

"If you mean to kill me, then kill me!"

"No. Not you." He smiled, and his breath stunk. "You're way too pretty for that."

Morgan turned and hammered on the door. "Mr. Trippler? She's here."

CHAPTER TWENTY-SEVEN

When she saw him, Chasida had to close her eyes. She fought against the shudder that passed through her from head to toe, but could not restrain it. She opened her eyes again and looked into the hungry, broad, plain face of William Gordon Trippler.

One look verified what her father had learned of this man: he indeed had to be the brother of Elder Pepperdine. The gray eyes, the bushy white brows, the long fronds of dust-colored hair that fell on both sides of his bald-pated head, were almost identical to her own dim childhood memories of the treacherous founder of the Purificationist sect. But William Trippler was broader, shorter, and Chasida could sense a feeling of wickedness about him.

She couldn't avoid the piercing eyes, and when she met them, he smiled, and showed yellow teeth.

"Ah! Welcome!" he said. A long, wide tongue flicked out across his lips, like a snake sniffing the air. His eyes shifted to Morgan. "You were correct, Mr. Morgan. She indeed is a jewel."

Morgan smiled and nodded. "Hope you have a pleasant evening, sir."

Trippler reached out and took Chasida's arm, and pulled her inside.

The room was big, with an arched ceiling ornately decorated with tiles, the walls made colorful with tapestries hung upon them. Two tall candelabras, each holding a dozen thick white candles, poured flickering light across the room. They were supplemented by other candles that burned on the wide, polished table in the center of the room, and firelight that glimmered from two hearths. The floor was warmed by a thick, huge rug that extended beneath the table. Spread atop the table were platters of steaming food, bottles of wine, baskets heavy with bread. The many big windows were arched at the top in typical Spanish style, but their interior shutters were closed and barred.

"Do you like it, my dear?" he asked, closing the door behind her, still holding her arm. Without waiting for her to answer, he said, "Beautiful, isn't it? Very rich, very appropriate for the entertainment of such a fine young damsel as yourself." He chuckled. Though his speaking voice was rich, his chuckle was oddly high. "Tell me, for I've forgotten: what is your name?"

"Please, sir, I beg you in the name of Jesus Christ, in the name of God Almighty, in the name of all that's decent and holy, let me go!"

He squeezed her arm more tightly. "Yes, yes, you would use religious words. You come from a religious people, as I understand it. But I asked your name."

"My name is Chasida Gruenwald." Suddenly tears came. "My father was named Peter Gruenwald, but that man out there, Morgan, murdered him. And others, too. Morgan and one of his sons."

"They weren't murdered, dearest. They were simply moved out of the way. Such things happen when people make mistakes." His tone was that of a father explaining some hard concept to a small child. "And your father, good man though he may have been, was making accusations against me in public. He claimed that I killed a man! My own brother! Can you imagine such a thing?"

"Please, let me go."

He did not let her go. "Such a libel and slander! And when it's spoken against a man in such an important position as myself, and at such a crucial time in the history of our land, such words can cause irreparable damage. He and those with him simply had to be silenced. But believe me, I didn't intend for them to die. I would have gladly made them my guests here. Unfortunately, they chose to resist Mr. Morgan, and he simply had no choice. "

"Resist? They didn't resist! Only my brother did that. Mr. Morgan shot my father without cause and without mercy! If he told you they resisted him, he lied to you."

Trippler smiled and shook his head, dismissing her words. "We needn't talk of such unpleasant things. This is a night for joy!" He led her to the center of the room, then let go of her, but stayed close, as if fearing she might bolt for the door. Chasida did not, knowing it would be futile. Trippler looked her up and down. "You are indeed lovely. But that black frock does you no justice. Wouldn't you enjoy wearing a beautiful, bright dress, the kind the fine ladies of Texas and Mexico wear? Wouldn't you like that?"

He waved toward a tall dressing screen in a corner. "Go over there and look behind it. You'll see a lovely dress I've had brought in for you. I had to guess at the size, but I do believe it will fit you. Go and change into it. It's my gift to you."

Though Chasida had suffered many a doubt and dissatisfaction with the harsh strictures of her sect over the past few years, just now she felt a deep, heartfelt loyalty to them all. "I don't believe it's right to adorn myself in such a way."

Trippler threw back his wide head and laughed. "Oh, my dear, none of those things matter now! You're away from the community of fools! In this place, I make the rules. I decide what is proper." He paused and looked at her closely. "In this place, I am God."

"No. No, you are not. You are the devil!"

He didn't speak for a moment. His teeth ground beneath tight lips. His voice, when he did speak, was soft but threatening. "You will go now, and change into the dress you'll find behind that screen. Then you will come out, and we will sit down at that table and dine."

In the end there was no resisting. Feeling as if all that was good in her was left farther behind with each step, she trudged to the dressing screen, and behind it changed from her simple dark dress into a frilly red garment that made her feel foul and sinful. She thanked God for the shawl that accompanied the dress, and threw it across her shoulders and the low-cut bosom.

When she emerged, Trippler stared at her in a way that was itself a violation. But she didn't give in to tears, determined to endure this ordeal, somehow, without losing her pride.

"You are a vision, my dear girl. A vision of the grandest beauty . . . as lovely as an empress, you are."

He had her sit at one end of the long table. She feared he would sit close beside her, but instead he placed himself at the far end, facing her. Lifting a bell, he jingled it, and a moment later the door opened and the sad-eyed Mexican serving woman entered. She came to the table and dutifully began serving the food, every now and then casting her brown eyes Chasida's way, never lingering, but heavy with pity.

She knows what is in store for me, Chasida thought. *She pities me.* She looked up at the woman's face as she poured wine into her glass, and their eyes caught for a moment. Chasida felt a catch in her throat as she saw a tear come to the woman's eye, and her own eyes sent in return a silent plea: *Help me.*

When the food was served, Trippler dismissed the woman and fell to eating. Chasida picked slowly at her plate as Trippler ate with the enthusiasm of a starved shoat. When he'd sated the worst of his hunger, he began to talk as he ate.

She sat and listened to a man describe himself and his plans as a king might. Her depression grew the more she listened and the more she realized that this man, so deluded, so full of his own certitude of greatness, was surely not even sane. She stared at the ruby beauty of her glass of wine, still untouched, for Purificationists did not drink wine, and imagined herself far away, and safe, and this all a dream. But Trippler's voice droned on and on, spouting fantasies of grandeur, plans for empire and wealth and power.

At last he finished his food and his talk, and leaned back.

"Why, dearest, you've hardly touched your food. And is your wine not to your taste?"

"I don't drink wine."

"What? Another religious stricture? Bosh! Drink it, girl. I insist."

"It would be wrong for me to—"

"I *insist.*"

Fighting tears, biting back hatred, she lifted the glass and took a small sip.

"More."

She drank again, and at his insistence, again and again. He rose, came over, filled the glass once more, and made her drink it. Then another.

The wine was strong, and she began almost at once to feel its effects. He smiled as she drank, and the sated look that had come over his thick features after he had eaten was replaced again by that terrible look of hunger, and his tongue swiped his lips again and again.

"Come," he said at last, reaching down and pulling at her arm. "Come and be my empress tonight."

He pulled her up; she was dizzy. She tried to pull away but found her strength ebbing. She could not direct the movements of her hands correctly, and she tingled.

Maybe, she thought, *there was something more than wine in that glass.*

He pulled her toward him and she hung limply in his arms. He pulled her face up, lowered his lips toward hers . . .

Something rattled at the door.

Trippler jerked his head around, looking angrily in the direction of the door. He cursed softly and eased her into a nearby chair. Walking quietly to the door, he yanked it open.

Rafe Morgan almost fell as he pulled back, and gazed guiltily back at Trippler before he thought to slap a smile onto his face.

"Morgan! What the devil is this?"

"Sorry, Mr. Trippler. I thought you'd called for me."

"If I call for you, Mr. Morgan, you'll know it. And I don't believe you. I know what you were up to, with your ear pressed to that door. Hoping to at least hear what you couldn't watch, were you?''

Morgan said, ''I'm sorry, sir. I admit, I did have some curiosity to hear . . . I kind of like that, you see.''

Trippler moved closer to him, and spoke low, but Chasida was able to hear it. ''You'll have plenty of chances to enjoy this young woman, Mr. Morgan. But tonight is *my* night, and I want no audience, either watching or listening!''

''I'm sorry.'' Morgan tipped his hat and backed away. ''I'll be gone, then.''

Trippler closed the door and returned to Chasida. ''I'm quite sorry,'' he said. ''That was the rudest kind of interruption.'' He knelt and looked at her closely. ''Oh, you are beautiful. So fresh and innocent. Come here, my dearest. Give me a kiss . . .''

And he kissed her. She was numb, rendered helpless by the drugged wine, and could not even manage to turn her head away. She suffered through the terrible kiss, revolted but unable to protest.

The door rattled again. Trippler came to his feet, cursing, and stormed over. He yanked it open again. ''Morgan, damn you, I told you that—''

He stopped, for it was not Morgan at the door, but two other guards. Morgan was nowhere to be seen.

''Sorry to disturb you, sir, but there's someone who's come to the fort that we believe you'll want to see.''

''There's only one person I wish to see tonight, and she's with me already! Go away!''

''Sir, please . . . when you find out who it is, and why he's come, I believe you'll want to see him.''

''Who is it, then?''

''It's Bushrod Underhill, sir. And he's come to offer his service and influence to you in exchange for the freeing of his son and his family.''

CHAPTER
TWENTY-EIGHT

John Underhill had learned early in his captivity that the hall-way leading to William Trippler's door had the peculiar quality of conducting sound unusually well. Many an hour he had spent leaned against the barred door of the room that was his own prison, listening to snatches of muffled conversation that carried down that hall and through his door. At times the effort had been worthwhile; he'd heard mention of his family, things that told him they were still safe and unhurt. Trippler never allowed him to see them, so such assurances were always welcome.

He'd listened tonight, for three hours straight, and although he'd heard nothing about his wife and children, he'd learned about some matters of great interest. The guards' conversation revealed that they, and apparently most of their fellow mercenaries, were deeply worried about rumors of an imminent attack upon this old mission, as well as even stronger rumors that their next payday might bring no pay at all. Trippler was out of money, they whispered to one another, and they'd be hung and quartered before they'd put their lives on the line for a man who couldn't even pay them!

These words had given John Underhill hope, for anything that was bad for Trippler was probably good for him and his family. But he wasn't sure. Trippler wasn't a sane man, didn't react normally to events. What if a citizen militia did attack? Would Trippler order a mass execution of his hostages as some sort of final defiant gesture? Would the downfall of this fortification bring release and safety, or merely a hastening of death?

John Underhill had been mulling these things over for a long time now, but they were stricken from his mind by what he'd just heard a guard telling Trippler in his doorway.

My father is here . . . my father has come here, to help me!

John staggered away and plopped down onto his cot, suddenly weak. How had his father even learned what had happened to him? Someone must have contacted him in some way and let him know . . . Cantrell Smith, perhaps?

He couldn't believe it . . . Bushrod Underhill, ever faithful to his family, had come to offer himself in trade for his son!

John Underhill bowed his head and wept silently, biting his lip, suddenly overwhelmed with love for his father, whom he'd not seen for years.

But he did not weep only for love of his father. He'd been Trippler's hostage too long now to believe that his father's brave and self-sacrificing gesture would work. Trippler would never let him go, not even in exchange for the famous Bushrod Underhill. He was still too valuable to him, still exploitable. And he knew too much to be allowed to go free.

John stood, wiping his tears on his sleeve, and walked over to the little table in the corner. On it lay a copy of the document Trippler had had printed on a press he'd hauled into the mission some days before. John read it, and felt sickened. It was lies layered upon lies, declaration that Trippler was on the verge of a great announcement. He had a plan that would forge a new future for Texas, a future that would give security and wealth to every Texian, and provide a government not weakened by lack of funds as was the current independent republic. In flowery words that said much less than they appeared to, Trippler had laid out his brief manifesto, and forced John Underhill, at last, to do what he'd been resisting for months. To give in, and lend his name in support of a madman's lies.

John stared at his own signature at the bottom of the paper, then at the other scrawl beside it: "David Crockett." He crumpled it up into a ball and slammed it against the wall.

Pap, Pap, thank you for coming, thank you for trying, but it's too late now, he thought. *You shouldn't have come. I've been forced to give in to him, and I don't know what will become of me and mine . . . and—now that you're here—what will become of you.*

John wheeled and went to his cot. From beneath the packed mattress he pulled a foot-long piece of metal and looked it over. He'd found it in the corner of the room, stuck between two bricks, two days after he'd first been captured, and ever since he'd been working with it, scraping it against the wall at a place hidden by his bunk, sharpening it slowly to a point. He scooted the cot away and worked further at it now, intensely, with tears on his face, until finally the metal was sharpened to his satisfaction.

Stripping off his shirt, he tore a long strip of cloth from the lower hem, and wet it in his washbasin. He stretched it and sat down on the bunk and wrapped the wet fabric tightly around the unsharpened end of the makeshift knife, then tied it off. He held it up and looked at it. Not much of a weapon, but all he had.

And if anything should happen to his father, or to his wife and children, he vowed inwardly, he'd drive this knife through the heart of William Gordon Trippler. No matter what happened to him for it, he'd do it.

He'd keep this knife hidden in his boot from now on. They'd long since ceased to search him, sure by now he had no weapons. He had a feeling he'd need this knife soon.

Things were about to break loose in this place. He could feel it.

Five guards, Bushrod noted. Five guards, just for him. He wondered how a rather small-framed silver-haired man without a weapon on him could seem such a threat that five armed men had to guard him.

Maybe, he thought wryly, people take those legends in that blasted book and that fool almanac a lot more seriously than he'd imagined.

One of the guards walked up to the heavy door at the end of the hall and knocked on it. "Mr. Trippler? He's here."

The door swung open, and Bushrod studied the person of William Trippler up close for the first time. Not much to look at, he thought. But then, Napoleon hadn't been much to look at, either.

If Trippler was unimpressive to Bushrod, the reverse didn't seem so. Trippler examined Bushrod with undisguised fascination, scanning him up and down. Slowly a smile broke across his face. "Well! I'm honored to receive a visit from so famed a figure as yourself, Mr. Underhill! Though you came at a most inconvenient time, you are certainly welcome—a man worth changing an evening's plans for . . . and believe me, sir, I had planned quite a fine evening, indeed."

"I hope for the chance to talk to you in private, sir."

"Indeed you shall." Trippler glanced at a guard, who assured him quietly that Bushrod had been thoroughly searched. Trippler flashed an even brighter grin at Bushrod. "Come in, sir. Make yourself at home."

Bushrod stepped into the lushly decorated room and looked about at the tapestried walls, the table still laden with food. "You didn't have to go to such trouble for me, Mr. Trippler."

Trippler gave the wry comment a far bigger laugh than it deserved. "What you see here is the remnants of that special evening you managed to interrupt. Quite a beauty she was, too . . . but never mind that. A pleasure postponed is still a pleasure. Do sit down and tell me what gives me the honor of this visit."

Bushrod waited until the guards had closed the door and left himself and Trippler alone before he spoke. "I'll not sit, Mr. Trippler. I prefer to stand. And I'll give no other false cordialities, for that's not my way. I'd like the chance to speak plain to you, sir."

"Please do."

"I have no love for you, Mr. Trippler. You've kidnapped my son John, and his wife, and my very grandchildren, and you've got them hostage in this place."

"Where did you hear such a thing?"

"Pretty much any place in Texas you want to set your foot, you'll hear that very thing. Do you deny it?"

"I do have Mr. John Underhill and family as my guests, yes. But kidnapping? No, no. Why, John is here as my ally and supporter." He stepped to a nearby desk and brought out a copy of the same printed document John Underhill had minutes earlier thrown across his room down the hall. He handed it to Bushrod, who scanned through it and examined John's signature at the bottom.

"I'm not surprised he signed it, considering that he's concerned about what could happen to his wife and children if he didn't." Bush tossed the paper to the floor. "And it doesn't much matter, it don't appear to me. That paper don't say much. A lot of words that can be read a dozen different ways."

"What that paper says, sir, is that the real future of Texas doesn't lie in our present course, but in a new direction that I'm ready to lead."

"New way, or old way? As I hear it, you're ready to turn Texas back over to Mexico in exchange for wealth and power. And you kidnapped John for the sake of the credibility his name could give to such a mad scheme."

"I don't appreciate your use of the word 'mad,' Mr. Underhill."

"And I don't appreciate my son and his family being held under armed guard."

"I'll grant you this, Mr. Underhill. You do speak as plainly as you promised. Let's not play words with one another. Why have you come?"

"I've come to offer to take my son's place as your hostage . . . as your spokesman."

Trippler's eyes twinkled. "Now, that's a novel idea, I must say! And not at all a bad one. Your name is famous, Mr. Underhill. Almost as famous as that of Davy Crockett . . . whose signature, you may have noticed, was beside your son's on that paper you just dropped on my floor."

"That signature was a forgery. Davy Crockett is dead, and

if you've got somebody here claiming to be him, then he's a liar."

"You do seem to believe you know all things, Mr. Underhill. But never mind Crockett . . . even though you are wrong about his death. This proposition of yours intrigues me. Let me be sure I understand: I allow John Underhill and his family to go free, and in his place you remain here, and serve as an advocate for my cause?"

"That's right. Not that I know exactly what your cause is. I'm making this offer for *my* cause, which is to see that John and his brood are safe."

"You don't believe they're safe now?"

"Not for a moment. In fact, I don't believe anyone inside these walls is safe. There's a lot of anger at you out there, in case you don't know it. You can't have rumors of treason aired too long in a place that's spilled so much blood for its freedom, and not stir a lot of fury. And from what I hear of Texas, fury don't stay fury for long here. It turns into action."

"You're quite a speaker. You might make a fine spokesman at that."

"I'll do whatever you want me to do, say whatever you want me to say, if only you'll let John and his family go."

Trippler rubbed his chin, thinking. "I'm going to have to give some strong consideration to this, Mr. Underhill. Some very strong consideration. But it's going to take time. I don't rush to such decisions."

"And in the meantime, what happens to me?"

"Hmm? Oh, you'll be my guest, of course. We have a room waiting for you already. And you will be wanting to stay in it . . . there's a man who works for me here who is no great lover of the famous Underhill name. I'd seek to avoid him if I were you."

"That would be Rafe Morgan."

"Indeed. Isn't it a coincidence that you two should wind up within the same walls after all these years! I have to warn you, sir, that Mr. Morgan still holds quite a grudge against you. Calls you terrible things, such as the murderer of his brothers."

"The killing of his brothers was justice, not murder." Bush paused. "And at least it wasn't my own brother I killed."

Trippler's face twitched and for a moment went red, but he pulled himself back into control. "That's a comment I'll pretend was never said, sir." He called for the guards. "Now, Mr. Underhill, you'll be shown to your quarters. And I'm afraid you will be locked inside them. For your own safety, of course. To keep Mr. Morgan away from you. He's really quite hateful toward you. Not only does he resent what you did to his brothers years ago but he's also been saying something about one of his sons—who's among my little band of soldiers—being injured a night or two back by one of your own sons."

"The Morgan boy shot my son Sam. He shot back to defend himself. Both of them survived."

"Mr. Morgan isn't at all pleased about that little incident." The guards entered, and to them Trippler said, "Take our guest away. Put him in that extra guest room of ours, the one on down and to the right."

"Yes, sir."

"I want to see John," Bushrod said.

"Maybe that can be arranged. Later. For now, sir, you may enjoy the luxury of your own private quarters. I'll have some food sent in for you within the hour."

"You're more than kind."

They were just hustling Bushrod out the door when Trippler called for them to wait. "I almost forgot! Something you'll want to see." He went to the desk and came back with a copy of the Underhill almanac. "Quite an interesting publication, this one. More fame for the Underhill name!"

"Where'd you get it?"

"The printer we brought in to publish our little broadside apparently has been printing these as he travels across Texas, spreading them as he goes. More fame for your name, as I say, which of course makes you even more potentially valuable as my spokesman. I am indeed interested in your offer."

"You've got the man who printed that almanac here?"

"We allowed him to pass on through when we were finished with him. You've just barely missed him."

"Sorry to hear that. I'd hoped for the chance to shoot him."

They pushed Bushrod on out the door and down the hall. "Where's John being held?" Bushrod asked one of the guards.

"He's in yonder," the man said, pointing at a door they'd just passed.

"John!" Bushrod called. "John, it's your pap! Don't you worry, son! We're going to get you out of here!"

"Shut that up!" the guard demanded. "Mr. Trippler ain't going to like that!"

"The devil with Trippler. And it'll be the devil with you, too, if you don't get yourself shut of him soon. This place is in its last days. Mark my words."

The guards, Bushrod noted, did not dispute the point. And he thought, just maybe, that was a good thing. If the guards were worried and restless, maybe they'd desert this place. Maybe William Gordon Trippler would be turned into a cat without claws.

They were almost to the door of the "guest room" that was to house Bushrod when Rafe Morgan came around the corner. His eyes locked onto Bush at once, and Bush saw him at the same moment.

Underhill and Morgan, frozen in place, stared at one another for a long time. No words. Nothing but a cold, unblinking mutual stare . . . and the sweeping away of years, so that an old bitterness that had turned violent more than two decades before was suddenly alive and fresh and with them again, there in that hall.

The guards opened the door and pushed Bushrod inside, and locked him in.

The room was dark, but Bushrod had been allowed to keep his matches, which the guards who had searched him had found mystifying and unusable because they didn't know the trick of lighting them. Bushrod struck a match and searched the room for a lamp. Finding only a couple of candles instead, he lit one, then lay back on the narrow dirty cot that was the room's only item of furniture besides a little basin table, chair, and trunk.

He stared at the ceiling, and the single, high barred window near it, trying to shake off the strange, bitter feelings that the sight of Rafe Morgan had roused in him. He would have been no less shaken had he seen a demon. And it made him cold as winter inside to think that this man was roaming free in the place where Bushrod's own grandchildren were held helpless.

Bushrod rolled over, growing deeply depressed. He'd just tried the only ploy that had held any likelihood of success, and nothing had come of it yet, except getting himself locked up in a makeshift prison.

Trippler had declared himself interested in Bushrod's proposition, but Bushrod already knew his scheme had failed. Trippler had had only one Underhill to vouch for his cause before. All Bushrod had done was provide him two.

He closed his eyes and wondered what was going to happen now.

CHAPTER
TWENTY-NINE

Durham Underhill stared for a moment, too surprised to move, then slowly raised his hands.

"Easy there, sir. I didn't come here looking for trouble." But as he glanced past the man who held the rifle that was pointed toward the center of his belly, and scanned the band of a dozen or more armed men, Durham knew that he'd found trouble anyway, or maybe it had found him.

"Who are you, and why are you out riding this early?"

"My name's Durham Underhill, sir. I'm out because, to tell you the truth, I'm lost."

"Underhill, you say?" The man glanced at a companion. "You ain't of the Bushrod Underhill clan, are you?"

"Yes, sir. Bushrod Underhill is my father."

"I be!" The man lowered the rifle a little. "Come up a bit closer, young man. Let me take a look at your face."

"Can I lower my hands?"

"Yes, yes. Just come up here."

Durham rode closer to the gang of riders who had surprised him while he was pausing to drink at a spring. They'd ridden up over a low rise and leveled on him even before he'd been able to come all the way to his feet again. He let the man look him over, and was relieved to see the fellow begin to grin, and the rifle to lower the rest of the way.

"I be durned! He's the image of John hisself!"

"You talking about my brother John?"

"Yes, indeedy. John Underhill is a good friend of mine, young man, and I'm proud to have been at his side most of the way through the fight at San Jacinto."

Durham drew in a deep breath of relief. For a moment he'd thought he might just be shot down for no reason. But faces that before had worn scowls now were open and friendly all around him. Several of the men moved in close enough to shake his hand.

"Name's Sanders Rigsby—call me Sandy," the man who had quizzed him said. "We'd heard that Bushrod Underhill had come into Texas with some of his boys. Is your pap close by?"

"No," Durham said. "I left him back at John's ranch. I came out here . . . he sent me out here, I should say, to find out what happened to some folks we'd met coming into Texas. A group of religious folks out of Kentucky, called Purificationists—"

"Lordy, Lordy, son, I hope they weren't close friends of yours, for I got little good news to give you. They was massacred."

"I heard, though, that one young fellow survived, and that maybe a girl, his sister, might still be alive, too."

"The part about the young man is true enough. He's laid up to heal at my own house, not two miles from here."

"So I'm not as lost as I thought. I've been looking for the Cable Creek settlement."

"That's where I live. That spring you just drank out of runs right into Cable Creek not half a mile up from here."

"So Kirk is at your place! Can I see him?"

"Reckon you can. You being an Underhill, I'd say you can do anything you want among this group. We all know the Underhill family for what it is, and that's good folks."

Durham smiled, relieved all over again. It was good to be among men who held him in high regard. For the first time in his life Durham fully realized that the good name a man made for himself brought a natural good favor on his sons, as well.

"What about the girl?" he asked.

"Well, no one is sure," Rigsby replied. "It may be that she was shot dead, too, and her body just not found. But there are a couple who say she was seen being taken into Trippler's fort."

"So she may be alive, then!"

"Yes, but Lord only knows what might befall the poor girl in that terrible place, full of such wicked men."

Durham frowned. "John's in there, and his family, and now maybe Chasida, too."

"Nobody will be in there much longer, young man."

Durham only now considered the oddity of all these armed men moving, like a posse, across the plains. "Might I ask what all this is about?"

"What you're seeing, Mr. Underhill, is the beginnings of the end of William Trippler and his schemes."

"A militia?"

"A part of one. On our way to join thrice this many again at my ranch. And there are others who'll be joining us later, as we near Trippler's."

"There's going to be an attack?"

"Unless Trippler gives up without one, yes, there is."

"When?"

"Quite soon, young man. It's why we're gathering. Quite soon."

Durham rode with the militiamen to Rigsby's Cable Creek ranch, and was surprised at the number of men already gathered there. Arms bristled from the group like porcupine quills, and talk of vengeance against the treasonous Trippler was fierce and rampant.

Durham might have been stirred by it all under other circumstances. As it was, it worried him, and he decided to have a word with Rigsby about it. But not until he had visited with Kirk.

He was disturbed when he saw him. Kirk was pale, weak, looking almost corpselike lying on the narrow bed. His dark Purificationist clothing had been replaced by a linsey-woolsey nightshirt, and his hair was plastered back with sweat.

"Hey, there, friend. Want to smoke a pipeful?"

Kirk's eyes opened, with effort, at the sound of Durham's voice. "I'll be!" Kirk said in a whispery, weary, pain-filled voice. "It's a durned Underhill."

"That's right. I've come to see you. I heard what happened."

"Murderers," Kirk whispered. "Murderers, they were. Shot all of them, shot me . . ."

"But not Chasida. I hear they carried her off into Trippler's fort."

"I don't know. Maybe. I didn't see . . . they shot me while I was running."

"I'm glad you lived. Kirk, I'm going to get Chasida out of that fort."

"How?"

"I don't know. But I've got to. There's a militia forming up, planning to attack the place. But I can't let that happen, not yet. I have a brother in there, and his family. And now there's Chasida. I've got to get them out before any attack comes."

"A tall order . . . that one." Kirk was sounding more weary with every word. Durham hoped he never got shot; it looked like a terrible lot of suffering.

"I'm going to talk to the man who owns this house. Rigsby. It seems he has authority in this militia. Maybe I can convince him to hold off his attack until I've had a chance to . . . to do whatever I can come up with."

"I don't want Chasida hurt . . . she's all I got left. All I got." Kirk's bloodshot eyes moved from side to side, searching. "Where's Sam?"

"Sam ain't with me. He's with my father and Cordell, and a man named Dunning who's been keeping watch on Trippler for Sam Houston."

"Why'd you come, Durham? Didn't know you was so interested in me."

"I'll tell you the truth, Kirk. I came because of Chasida. I'd heard that she might have been shot, and I had to know. I just had to."

Even in his pain, Kirk managed a mischievous smile. "Believe you've got yourself all besotted . . . with my sister."

"You know, I believe I do."

"I want you to get her out of that fort . . . for me. Get her out safe . . . and then let this militia go in and destroy them. Every last damned one of them."

"You don't sound like a peace-loving Purificationist, Kirk."

"I ain't. Not for years, I ain't been."

"You rest, Kirk. I'm going to get your sister out of there."

"You promise me?"

"I promise."

Rigsby scratched his beard, frowning, looked into the earnest face of Durham Underhill, then turned away and paced in a small circle, still scratching at his whiskers. Durham, who had just made the most earnest plea he could for Rigsby to delay the planned milita action against Trippler's fort, held an impatient silence as Rigsby mulled it over.

"My, my," Rigsby said at last. "I find myself not sure what to do—or for that matter, what I *can* do. This uprising is widespread, and rolling along now like a boulder . . . and once a boulder starts to roll, it's often hard to stop it."

"All I ask, Mr. Rigsby, is that any attack on that fort be held off long enough for my father to see if he can't get John and his family out of there first. Just a little time."

"Does your father have a plan?"

Durham faced a crisis of honesty. When he'd left his kin and Dunning behind, there had been no plan. And what, if anything, his father and brothers might have done since he left, he had no way to know. But Durham sensed that an indecisive answer might not be enough to hold back an action by a growing militia of angry citizens. "My father does have a plan. He hasn't told me all the details, but I know he'll need a little more time to make it work. If the fort is attacked right away, it may ruin his chances."

"You must understand, son, that there's more at stake than the concerns of your family. We're talking about a man who seems ready to betray this entire republic to Mexico. A man who had several innocent, God-fearing folks murdered, and who murdered his own brother before that. We can't hold off forever on dealing with Trippler."

"But he *is* being dealt with, and that's why I'm urging you to hold off for now." Durham paused, debating how much to say, then went on. "And it's not just my father, or my family. There's an agent he's working with, hired by Sam Houston himself, assigned to find out what Trippler is doing, and to deal with him. And the Texas Rangers have been watching the fort, too. Please, Mr. Rigsby. Give all of them a little more time to work before you attack. For John's sake, if for nothing else. And the sake of his wife and children."

Durham, had he been fully open with Rigsby, would have spoken slightly differently. As concerned as he was about John and his family, what dominated his mind just now was Chasida Gruenwald. How he had come to care so deeply about a girl he'd barely met he couldn't have said. It didn't matter. He *did* care, and knew, just knew, that it was something far deeper than a momentary infatuation of the sort Sam had felt for that pretty Tauby girl. This was destiny at work, a young woman he was meant to be with, and she with him. He just *knew*.

Rigsby let out a long, slow breath. "Very well, young man. I'll do what I can to delay this. But as I said, the boulder is already rolling. It won't be long before that fort will be attacked, whatever I may say about it."

Durham stuck out his hand and shook Rigsby's. "I thank you, sir. And now, if I might arrange to obtain a fresh horse . . ."

"Going back in all haste, eh?"

"Yes, sir. I'll gladly pay for use of the horse. Mine is exhausted."

"It looks to me like you're exhausted, as well."

"I'm tired. But I couldn't rest if I had to."

"I understand. Tell me, son, is your father planning to enter Trippler's fort?"

"I believe he is."

"A dangerous move. Does he expect to overturn the place single-handedly?"

Durham could only grin. "Remember, he's Bushrod Underhill. A man who could throw a rope around the moon and climb up it, and who pulls the teeth out of Florida alligators and makes toothpicks of them. Or so says the almanac."

"Good luck to you, Durham. And especially to your father. Follow me. I've got a horse you're welcome to use as long as you need it, and there'll be no charge."

Durham paid one last visit to Kirk Gruenwald before he left. Kirk looked a little more full of life than before, though that wasn't saying much.

Durham kept his voice low. "I'll be going inside the fort, I suppose. I've managed to talk Mr. Rigsby into holding back any militia attack for the next little while—I'll be lucky to get two days out of it—and in the meantime, I'm going in there to get Chasida."

"I wish I could go with you."

"I wish you could, too, Kirk. But I don't think you'll be going anywhere for a good spell."

"What about your brother and his family?"

"I'll try to help them, too. But Pap and my brothers, and others, too, are going to be looking out for them. I believe it's my job, my fate if you want to put it that way, to try to help Chasida."

"Fate?"

"I knew when my father and brothers left Missouri for Texas that I was supposed to go along. Now I know why. It was because of Chasida."

"They left without you?"

"To begin with, yes. My mother didn't want me to go. But I sneaked away from her, lied to Pap that she'd said it was all right, and came anyway."

"Sounds like something I would have done." Kirk grinned, closed his eyes, and fell asleep even as Durham watched him.

Durham turned and left the dwelling, mounted his borrowed horse, and with weariness making every muscle feel sluggish and heavy, began the long ride toward Trippler's fort.

CHAPTER
THIRTY

Chasida Gruenwald lay back on her cot, eyes flooded with tears as she watched morning light pierce through the single high window of her room, and said her hundredth prayer of thanks that she had escaped, for now, the ugly, humiliating violation that Trippler had been about to inflict upon her when that wonderful, welcome knock had come on his door.

She had some trouble remembering every detail of what had happened the night before—the drugged wine still had her head feeling thick and fuzzy—but she did recall that the news the guards had brought Trippler about Bushrod Underhill had shifted the man's attentions away from her. She'd been removed from Trippler's chambers and hauled back to her own plain prison . . . but by comparison, this cold locked room seemed a wonderful place. At least *he* wasn't here, with his broad, homely face, his yellow teeth and stinking breath . . .

She tried to shove away the memory. And said her prayer of thanks for the hundred and first time.

Her mind turned to Bushrod Underhill, whose arrival had saved her. What a wonderful man he seemed! He'd helped with the rescue after the flatboat accident, shared food with her and the other Purificationists in his camp, fought those drunks who had harrassed them, then brought back the garments they had stolen. And now he'd arrived, seemingly miraculously, just in time to divert Trippler's attention and save her from a horrid fate.

Thank God for Bushrod Underhill. She knew little of him beyond the fact that he was a good man, a famous man according to her brother, and the father of some fine-looking sons. But she loved him. He seemed a guardian angel.

Chasida stood and walked back and forth in the small room, listening to the rustle of her dress. She hated the garment because Trippler had given it to her, but she had to admit it was pretty, and certainly wearing something besides the plain black frock she had known since girlhood was a novelty. She'd often wondered how it would be to dress like everyone else, and wear clothes that were pretty, simply because they were pretty.

But she wished she had her old dress back. Continuing to wear this one reminded her that the ordeal really wasn't over yet, merely interrupted. Trippler would come for her again, and this time there would be no interruption.

Chasida gasped as the door rattled. Her breath caught in her throat and her hand rose to her heart. Not now! Not already! She backed away toward the wall, knowing that when the door opened, he would be there, smiling and hungry . . .

The door swung wide, and revealed the sad-eyed Mexican woman who had brought her food. The woman had a bundle of cloth in her hand.

"Quickly!" she said. "There is little time . . . you must put this on."

She held the bundle of cloth forward. It unfolded partially, revealing itself as a plain dress, much like the one the Mexican woman herself wore.

"I don't understand."

"Please . . . the guard will not be asleep forever. I took some of the drugged wine you were given last night by *El Diablo,* and gave it to the guard. He drank much, much more of it than you did, but he could yet wake up. You must change quickly."

"You're helping me?"

"*Sí!* Yes! Can you not see?" She tossed the dress to Chasida. "I can't stand by and see *El Diablo* ruin you as he has ruined so many other innocents. As he ruined my own child Luisa . . . she is a harlot now, giving herself to the guards for money, and to strangers in San Pablo. She breaks my heart, and I fear for her soul."

Chasida stared at the dress in her hand, unable to believe what was happening, unable for the moment even to move.

"Now!" the Mexican woman snapped, closing the door behind her, leaving it open only a crack to allow herself to peer out unseen.

Chasida changed as fast as she could, though she trembled and was starting to feel light-headed. A rescue! She had prayed for just such a thing, but now that it was happening, she could hardly believe it.

"Where will you take me?" she asked.

"We will hide you within the mission for now, with the servant women," the woman replied. "Then we will find a way to get you out. There is going to be trouble and danger coming to this place very soon. Most of the guards are afraid, and ready to desert. There are people outside who are arming themselves, ready to be rid of *El Diablo* once and for all."

"Why do you call him *El Diablo?*"

The woman spat. "Because he is wicked . . . he is the devil! But we will save you from him. You will not be destroyed." The woman looked out the door. "Now come. And walk softly past the guard. He is a big man, and the medicine in the wine will not make him sleep for long. I'll take you to the servant quarters, and hide you. And later today, when I ride the wagon to the river to wash the laundry, you'll be hidden aboard."

Chasida wept. "Thank you . . . *gracias.*"

"No time for talk now! We must hurry before anyone else comes!".

Bushrod Underhill paced back and forth, back and forth, taking out his watch every few minutes to look at it. The room seemed smaller with each step. He wished the window wasn't so high, so that he could look out and maybe get his bearings, see where he was located in the compound and what was going on.

Maybe nothing was going on. Certainly nothing was happening with *him* just now. That was what frustrated and surprised him. He'd known he might be locked up, had half expected it, but he hadn't expected to be ignored. He looked at his watch again. Mid-afternoon, and still he'd had no word from Trippler.

Bushrod had vowed that he would be patient and cooperative so as to give Trippler no grounds for accusing him of anything. He'd even resisted the temptation to query the guards about his situation. But, hang it, he couldn't go on like this much longer. Was he to be ignored forever?

Bushrod couldn't wait. He went to his door and lifted his fist to rap on it and attract the guard, but just as he was about to give the first knock, he heard someone move on the other side of the door, and the sound of the bar scooting out of place. He backed up quickly and lay down on his cot, affecting a nonchalant attitude.

A young guard came through the door, carrying a basket that he set on the floor beside Bushrod's cot. Another young guard lingered in the doorway, rifle in hand. Bushrod's nose told him that beneath the cloth covering the basket was bread and meat. He was starved and would have dug in at once, but restrained himself as long as the guards were present.

"I was beginning to wonder if I was going to be fed," he said, deliberately yawning. "I was thinking maybe Mr. Trippler was leaving me to dine on whatever bugs and spiders I could catch in these fine quarters."

"You're eating better than most," the guard in the doorway said. "That there's fresh bread, and I ain't never seen any other prisoners given fresh bread."

"Prisoners? Mr. Trippler told me I was his guest. I'm hurt. Struck senseless. Feel like a man shot in the bowels with an utter disregard for his feelings."

"Are you really Bushrod Underhill?" the basket-bearer asked in a voice that revealed what a mere boy he really was.

"My family swears I am, and I've never known them to lie."

The fellow grinned. Just a simple young plainsman he seemed, not really a warrior at heart, probably in this solely for the money. Bushrod wondered how many others of Trippler's "army" were like him. "You're a famous man. I've met three famous men since I come to this place . . . John Underhill, Colonel Crockett, and now you. And I guess I've met four, if you count Mr. Trippler."

"Where is John kept?"

The guard at the door intervened. "Don't be answering his questions, Buel. We were to bring him his food, that's all."

"I ain't doing nothing wrong just for talking to him a little," the other replied. He turned to Bush. "He's kept in the room closest to Trippler's chambers. But his family is at a different place, away from him."

"Is he well? And them?"

"He's fine. His family is, too. But I think the woman worries a lot, and the children are afraid."

"I'd surely like to see them."

"Reckon that would be up to Mr. Trippler, sir."

"You said you'd seen Crockett here. I thought he was dead."

"No, sir. Mr. Trippler got him away from the Mexicans. He was hurt bad, but not dead."

"How do you know it's Crockett?"

"Well . . . it looks like all the pictures of him I've ever seen, and Mr. Trippler says it's Crockett. I reckon he would know."

"Why would Trippler have been able to get Crockett back from the Mexicans?"

"He talks to the Mexicans some. He's visited them quite a few times. Lately he's took John Underhill back and forth with him."

"That's what's going to be Trippler's downfall, this combobulating with the Mexicans. The people of Texas are beginning to hear of it, and they don't like it."

The guard in the door said, "Buel, that's enough talking. Come out of there and let's lock this door."

"Boys, let me give both of you some advice," Bushrod said. "I'd get away from this place as quick as I could. There's going to be trouble here before long, I feel sure."

"Buel, come on! Now!"

Buel, though, lingered. "I hear the same," he said quietly. "There's a lot of guards already planning to cut out real soon."

"Do tell! Are you one of them?"

"I don't know . . . I never been paid as good for anything as Mr. Trippler pays for this work, and there ain't been much to it."

"There'll be a lot to it if militias attack this place."

"I know. That's what all the guards are whispering among theirselves. And they're also saying that Trippler's about out of money, though a few declare he's going to be getting more money soon out of Mexico."

"Buel! That's enough talk. . . . come out of there. Trippler will have your backside for this. That man's a prisoner."

"You seem a fine fellow," Bushrod said solemnly. "Get out of this fort before it falls."

The young fellow stared at him, looking scared. The guard at the door entered, grabbed Buel by the shoulder, and pulled him away.

"One question, before you're gone," Bushrod said. "When will I see Trippler?"

The other guard answered this time. "You'll see him when he wants you to. He's been in his chamber all day. He does that sometimes after he sits up at night and drinks. And that's all I have to say to you. Come on, Buel. Out of here!"

William Gordon Trippler rubbed his head and groaned. The headache was still there, though lessening at last. He opened his eyes and looked around the dim room, blinking. Focusing on one of the big, closed shutters, he found he could bear the light that pierced through the cracks. Good. He was making progress.

Sometimes he wondered why he drank at all. The aftermath for him was always so miserable that it outweighed the pleasure of intoxication. The night before, though, he'd felt driven to drink. The arrival of Bushrod Underhill had been so unexpected and seemingly fortuitous that he'd wanted to celebrate. Unfortunately it had interrupted his seduction of that lovely young woman. But there would be other opportunities to be with her. As many as he wanted, until at last he tired of her and turned her over to Rafe Morgan.

Trippler stood and looked down at his rumpled clothing, the same clothing he'd worn to meet Chasida. It looked pretty rough now that he'd slept in it through the night and wallowed about in it half the day. He went to a big louvered wardrobe at the side of the room, opened it, and dug out a fresh suit of clothing. He washed at his basin, combed his hair, changed his clothing. By now his head had cleared almost fully. Looking in the mirror, he thought he looked quite fine. The way a man of power should look.

Trippler walked to the window and pulled back one of the shutters slightly. He seldom opened them fully, liking to keep himself visually separated from the world of the common folk outside his windows, and finding value in the sense of mystery that remaining hidden away gave him among his hirelings.

The afternoon light was bright and he squinted against it. As his eyes adjusted, he looked around the plaza, and slowly began to frown. Something was different today. Too much nervous tension evident in the way people moved and talked to one another in tight clumps. He saw several guards engaged in animated conversation, arms waving, an argument going on. As he watched, Rafe Morgan went to them and angrily broke them up, lecturing to one in particular, who argued back. Morgan lifted an arm and pointed at the front gate, shouting something into the man's face. The man shouted back, turned on his heel, and walked to the gate, exiting through the small door built into the structure of the bigger gate.

Trippler was displeased. It appeared to him that Morgan

had just allowed a guard to desert. Looking about, Trippler noticed that the number of "soldiers" seemed diminished overall. Where were they? What was going on?

His eye lifted to one of the rifle platforms where sentinels patrolled, just in time to see one of those sentinels glance about, then go over the wall. Trippler swore aloud. Another desertion, and right before his eyes!

Then he looked over the wall.

Off on the horizon, there was motion. A thin, dark line heading toward the fort. He stared at it, trying to make it out, failing.

Trippler closed the shutter and went to the big wardrobe. Opening it, he pulled out two small pistols and thrust them under his belt, then donned a bulky coat. He went to his door, opened it, and proceeded down the arched hallway. His own door was unguarded, as it usually was, because he disliked having people just on the other side of his doorway. He went past the door to John Underhill's prison room, nodding at the sentinels there. He descended a rear staircase, and continued on to the building that had once been the chapel of the mission. He entered and climbed the winding stairs that led up to the bell tower. Once in the tower, he looked hard at the same moving line he'd seen. A little closer it was. He gazed and made out the figures of distant riders. A small army, heading his way from the direction of San Pablo.

CHAPTER
THIRTY-ONE

Cordell filled his pipe slowly, watching Sam out of the corner of his eye. Sam paced back and forth, fidgeting, every now and then dropping to recline on the ground and attempt to relax, only to spring up again and pace some more. It had been that way since noon, and was growing worse.

"I don't like it," Sam said. "Pap or John or somebody should have been out by now, if things worked as he hoped."

"I believe you're right."

"I can guess what's happened. Trippler has locked Pap up, too. Now he's got him two Underhills held prisoner instead of just one. And everything is worse instead of better."

"I believe you're right about that, too."

"So what are we going to do? Set on our rumps here forever, waiting for those walls just to crumble down like the walls of Jericho?"

"That ain't my plan."

"Then what is?"

"I figure that if Pap or John or somebody ain't come out of there by tonight, then we go in."

Sam stopped, taking that in and digesting it. He seemed to like it. "Good. Good. I'm ready. But once we're in, what happens after that?"

"Frankly, Sam, I don't have the slightest idea. What will

probably happen is that we'll either get locked up, too, or get killed.''

Sam chewed on that one for a bit.

"Are you ready, if that should happen?" Cordell asked.

"I'm ready. I didn't come all the way to Texas just to sit idle.''

"I wish Durham was with us," Cordell said. "If he comes back and finds all of us gone, he'll not know what's happened.''

"Forget Durham. I wish Dunning had come along. At least he seems to have some knowledge about Trippler and his ways.''

"Seems to know him quite well, doesn't he? Better than a man who's done no more than talk to other people about a stranger.''

"What do you mean?"

"I think that Dunning knows Trippler better than he's saying. And I think there's more to his interest than just being hired by Houston. There's something personal in it. You can just smell it.''

"Cordell . . . look there." Sam was pointing toward the mission. Cordell looked.

"What? I don't see anything."

"Up, *beyond* the mission. See?"

Cordell lifted his eyes to the distant horizon and stared. He pulled out the spyglass and studied what he saw.

"I believe that uprising may have finally commenced," he said. "That's a gang of armed riders, Sam.''

"Oh, no . . . you think they'll attack the place?"

"I suspect that's what they have in mind."

"Oh, no. They'll strike the place, with Pap and John still inside, and Trippler will probably have his hostages killed!''

"Maybe they won't attack just yet. There's not enough of them yet. I'm betting that's just one little militia band, first one to arrive.''

"So they may wait for others before they do anything?"

"Maybe. I hope so, because we need more time. Sam, it's a sure thing now. Unless by some miracle John and Pap and all John's family get out of there first, you and me are going inside that old mission. Tonight.''

For a long time, Trippler huddled in a corner of the bell tower, cowering low, eyes flicking about, teeth dug into his knuckle.

Riders. Armed riders, gathering outside. And inside, his guards were unsettled, disloyal. And all his bargaining with Mexico, though promising, had so far reached no final resolution. Vague talk of money to come, of using this mission as a base for a new Mexican infiltration of Texas . . . but nothing definite yet.

Now, maybe, it was altogether too late. If the people of Texas were rising up against him now, there might never be an opportunity for any further bargaining. What could have sparked this unexpected new action? The killing of those religious fanatics? The publication of what Trippler had thought was a cleverly worded broadside that would buy him public favor and more time? He'd even included the signatures of John Underhill and Davy Crockett. Had the public ignored *them*?

He rose up and peered over the bell-tower wall again. The riders were closer now, but not advancing. They seemed to be setting up a camp, far out of range of the mission, but close enough that they could see any comings and goings. Trippler tried to count their number, but they were too far away for that. Still, he thought perhaps the band was smaller than he'd first perceived.

Maybe this wasn't what it appeared to be. No band that small would attempt to harass so strong a fortification. Perhaps the gathering was merely observatory, perhaps even unrelated to this fort.

Trippler steeled his nerves. Whatever was happening out there, he'd find out what it was, and deal with it. This was *his* empire, *his* future. He'd not let anyone toy with him!

He descended from the bell tower and reentered the building that housed his chambers. He was rounding a corner when two guards came walking his way. He didn't know the faces of all the gunmen who worked for him, but these he did. They were two of his best and most reliable men, often entrusted with important duties. They froze when they saw him.

"What are you two doing roaming about?" Trippler demanded. "Aren't you supposed to be at your posts?"

One looked at the other, then back at Trippler. "We would be, sir, if we still worked for you."

"Meaning?"

"Meaning that we're quitting you, sir. We're sacrificing whatever pay is still due us, and leaving."

"The hell you say! You get back to your posts, now! Where were you stationed, anyway?"

"Guarding the girl's room. And we'll not go back. Have you seen what's happening outside these walls? A militia is out there, and I'll wager you, sir, that it ain't going to be the only one. The people are rising against you, sir . . . and we're getting out while we can."

"Get back to your posts!"

The guards, over their surprise at encountering Trippler, grew more openly defiant. "No! You'll get nothing further from us, Mr. Trippler. Your men ain't behind you no more, sir. Some are already leaving, and others are doing whatever the hell they want. When we came to take over guard duty for Charlie Camp, we found him passed out drunk at his post. Nobody's listening to you anymore, Mr. Trippler. Nobody gives a damn about your rules, and nobody believes you're going to succeed in taking over Texas."

The other guard, silent until now, spoke. "And everybody says you're out of money, not even enough left to pay us next time it's due."

"I *am* still in charge of this fortification, I *do* still exercise authority, and furthermore, I've got wealth beyond anything your little minds could dream of," Trippler said, sticking out his chin. All he said was false, but he believed it as he spoke it. Self-delusion was a practiced habit for him.

The guards looked at one another again. One drew a pistol and leveled it on Trippler. "If you've got such wealth, sir, you can share some of it with us right now."

Trippler looked down his nose at them and smiled con-

temptuously. "So now you're down to robbing your own em-
ployer, are you?"

"Just give us money. Hell, you owe us pay for several days
anyhow."

"Fine. Very well." Trippler reached beneath his coat, drew
out one of the small pistols, and shot the pistol-wielding guard
through the forehead. The other gasped and jumped back,
reaching for his own pistol. Trippler tossed the first pistol
aside, drew the second from beneath his coat, and killed the
second guard with a ball through the heart while the man still
struggled to get his own weapon free.

Trippler looked at the corpses, listened to the sighing, settling noises they made, then stepped across them and to the
end of the corridor. Two men were running toward him,
drawn by the gunfire.

"Never mind the shots," he said. "I just killed two big
rats in the hallway, that's all."

The men nodded and turned away.

Trippler returned to the corpses. He needed to get rid of
them. In a place already filled with unrest, his mercenaries
would turn away from him even more quickly if they knew
he'd killed two of their number. There was no time now for
a permanent disposition of the bodies, but at least he could
find a temporary hiding place.

The girl's room. Yes. That was close, and would do nicely.
He'd let Chasida Gruenwald keep company with the deceased
for a bit; that would make her eager indeed to cooperate with
him, just to change her situation.

He dragged the bodies toward the door, working carefully
to minimize blood drainage onto the floor. Taking the key
from a peg on the wall, he opened the door.

Empty. Chasida was gone.

Trippler didn't know what to make of it. How could she
have escaped? Or who might have allowed her to?

The same guards he'd just killed, probably. Cursing, Trippler wheeled and left the room, stepping across the corpses
and running down the corridor.

He wouldn't let her get away from him. His men might

rebel, the people of Texas might raise militias to threaten him, but he would not be brushed aside by a mere girl! Especially not *this* girl. He'd never known a more beautiful young lady. Young enough to be his granddaughter, to be sure, but what a prize! What a wonderful toy to possess!

He'd not let her slip out of his grasp . . . and when he found out who had helped her, he'd see them pay dearly.

Trippler turned left and headed out to the balcony overlooking the plaza. Below was turmoil, people moving to and fro in a hurry, faces full of worry. Fewer sentinels on the rifle platforms and wall-side rooftops than there should be.

Trippler felt a burst of fear. It was really happening. Things were really beginning to fall apart.

A side gate, smaller than the main entrance but wide enough to accommodate a wagon, opened. Trippler watched as a wagon laden with heaped laundry rolled toward that gate. Laundry was being washed, now, with militias on the horizon and the life of Trippler's fort beginning to crumble?

He studied the wagon closely, leaning over the balcony rail. He sucked in his breath quickly.

The laundry heap had moved. A quick bump and shuffle, not caused by wind. He looked closer. A foot stuck out from under the heaped cloth for a moment, then pulled back under again.

Trippler ran down the stairs to the plaza. People looked at him, but not in the usual deferential manner. They looked at him now as they might a man just condemned to die. He didn't like it.

Trippler, a corpulent man, was unaccustomed to running. By the time he reached the wagon he was gasping for breath and the wagon was halfway out the gate.

"Wait! Stop! Now!" He could barely pant out the words.

The wagon driver, a Mexican man who was the second husband of the woman who usually served as Trippler's meal server and who also washed most of the laundry generated in the fort, turned with a frown, then looked frightened when he saw who had stopped him.

Trippler leaned on the end of the wagon, gasping for air for several moments before he could speak.

"Under these clothes . . . someone hidden . . ."

"I don't understand, Señor Trippler."

Trippler pulled down the tailgate and began sweeping clothing off the wagon onto the ground. In only a few moments Chasida was revealed. She sat up, face pale, and stared at Trippler.

His breathing had calmed down now. "So . . . unhappy with my hospitality, are you, dear girl? You hurt me, child. Why would you want to do such a foolish thing?"

"Please, sir, don't stop me. Please let me go free!"

"Not yet, not yet. We haven't yet gotten properly acquainted. Our little festivities were interrupted, or don't you recall?"

Chasida wished she could die. "Please don't take me back in."

"Señor," the wagon driver said, "I did not know she was there. I vow it to you!"

"Shut up!" Trippler snapped at him. He put out his hand to Chasida. "Come, girl. You and I have some talking to do."

"Why?" she asked. "Why do you care about me now? Don't you see that all of this is about to come crashing down? Haven't you seen the riders gathering outside? Don't you see that your own men are deserting you?"

He refused to talk to her. Grasping her hand, he yanked her off the wagon, and began hustling her back toward the building. She tried to break free, but he pressed a small pistol into her back. "Don't even try," he whispered.

She had no way to know the pistol had already been discharged in the murder of the two guards. She fought against him no more.

The driver climbed down and walked slowly around to the rear of the wagon, watching Trippler lead the girl away. He shook his head and began piling back onto the wagon the clothing Trippler had dumped.

His wife trudged slowly toward him. "It is too late for her now, I'm afraid."

"You tried, wife. You did your best. God will bless you for your tenderness. By the Virgin herself, God will surely bless you for it. And we can only pray that He will in His mercy bless this poor girl, as well."

CHAPTER THIRTY-TWO

Trippler shoved Chasida ahead of him into his room and closed the door behind him.

"Why did you try to get away?" he asked.

She went to the table and sat in a chair, turning her back toward him and curling down, wrapping her arms around her knees, saying nothing.

"What's wrong with you? Are you sick? Speak up!"

"Please let me go."

"You didn't answer my question. Why did you run?"

She raised her head and stared at him, incredulous. "Why did I run? You put me in a small room, like a prisoner! You brought me in here and treated me as if I were a . . . I don't even want to say it! How can you ask why I would run? I would rather die, *die,* than to be touched by you!"

He glared at her. "All I offered you, my dear young girl, was the opportunity to make a better life for yourself. A chance at real life, good life! That room, the locked door, that was only until you learned to trust me and love me. Didn't you understand that?"

She lowered her head again, withdrawing. He came closer.

"I just wanted to be your friend," he said softly. "I need a friend right now. Troubled times are descending on me. I may have to flee. But I could take you with me, and we could go into Mexico. I have friends there. Powerful and wealthy friends."

"I don't want to go with you! I could never be your friend! You're an old man, and a wicked man!" She burst to her feet, knocking the chair over and making Trippler step back in surprise. "I hate you! How could you think I could ever trust you . . . and *love* you? You're a madman!"

Trippler reddened and began blubbering.

Chasida, raised to believe in pacifism, taught it was wrong to turn to violence even to resist wickedness, threw these doctrines aside in one moment of fury. She drew back her hand and slapped Trippler across his wide face, as hard as she could. The spank of the blow echoed flatly in the room.

Silence followed. Trippler stared at her in disbelief, then balled up his fist and struck her on the side of the face. She jerked backward, her feet coming up from beneath her, her head driving down. The back of it slammed the edge of the table, very hard, and when she landed on the floor, she did not rise.

Cordell looked skyward. "Thank the Lord for them clouds. Moonlight is something we don't need tonight."

Sam was staring at the mission. "When should we go?"

"Just as soon as it's a little darker."

"I don't think there's any sentries on the wall."

"No, there's one, at least. See him? And there's another, near that far corner. But not nearly as many as before."

All afternoon they'd been watching people leaving the fort, usually on the run, some in groups, others alone. Bit by bit the realization had come that the human framework of the place was dissolving, and without doubt it had to do with the group of riders who had appeared on the horizon—a group that had grown steadily as the hours passed.

"Are you afraid, Sam?" Cordell asked.

The Sam Underhill of normal circumstances would have immediately made a scoffing denial. But this time, he said, "Yes. I am afraid."

"So am I. Sam . . . if something should happen to me in there, I want you to know I've been proud to be your brother, and to come to Texas with you."

"Me, too, Cordell. But don't you let anything happen to you in there."

"Tell you what . . . you look out for me, and I'll look out for you."

"It's a bargain."

They crouched together, waiting. Their horses were hidden beside a creek, in brush and trees, where they could find both forage and water. Their weapons, checked and double-checked, were in their hands and thrust into their belts.

Minutes dragged by slowly, building into an hour. The darkness was now full.

"Well, Sam, let's—"

Cordell stopped, and he and Sam ducked to the ground, turning at the same time, flattening themselves on their bellies.

A rider was coming up behind them, through the darkness. Sam and Cordell sighted down their long rifles, waiting . . .

The rider appeared, plodding slowly, pulling his horse to a stop. They could just make out his form against the night sky.

The rider spoke. "Cordell?"

Cordell and Sam lowered their rifles and rose as one. "Durham, you sound weary."

Durham Underhill dismounted and approached his brothers, hand out. They shook hands and patted shoulders. "I am weary. It's been a long spell since I slept."

"Where you been? Looking for that Purificationist girl?"

"Yes. But I didn't find her. Just Kirk."

"He's still alive?"

"Yes, but hurt bad. I think he'll recover, though. Where's Pap?"

Cordell nodded toward the fort. "In there."

"What?"

"We'll tell you all about it. But first you tell me about Chasida. Is she—"

"As best anyone knows, she's still alive." Durham pointed at Trippler's fort. "In the fort."

"Sounds like we've both got some stories to tell each other," Cordell said.

For the next half hour the brothers talked, Cordell filling in all the details of Bushrod's decision to try to trade himself for John. Durham in turn told all he'd found out about the fate of the Purificationists and about Chasida's apparent capture, and how he'd managed to buy a little extra time before the militia attacked.

"Maybe one militia is holding off, but there's others already gathering beyond the fort there," Cordell said. "If there's not a small war broke out come morning, I'll eat my boot. Durham, you look like you could fall over and sleep on a bed of hot coals. I don't know that you're in any shape to go into that fort. Why don't you stay here, keep your eye on the horses and so on, and let me and Sam do the inside work?"

"No. I didn't ride all this way just to do nothing. Chasida's in there. And Pap. And John and the others. I'm going in, too."

Cordell slapped his brother on the shoulder. "Somehow I knew you were going to say that."

Sam grinned. "It may surprise you to hear this coming from me, but . . . glad to have you along."

They made a final check, whispered secret, silent prayers, and waited until the moon was fully obscured by the heaviest of clouds. Rising, they moved out onto the plain that lay between them and the old mission, and ran with heads low toward the dark wall.

They were breathless by the time they reached the base of one of the several buttresses built up against the outside wall. They ducked into the shadows between the buttress and the wall and dropped to their haunches, listening, catching their breath.

Cordell looked up, twisting his head. A guard leaned over the wall, looking out across the dark plain, but not down. In a moment he pulled back again, out of sight.

"How are we going to do this?" Durham asked in a whisper.

"See how that arch support angles up?" Sam answered.

"We're going to climb it. The bricks stick out rough on the edge, so there's good footholds."

"What about the guards?"

"What about them? We'll just have to try not to be seen."

"Pardon me, but does anybody here happen to have anything resembling a plan?"

"Nope."

"Has it crossed anybody's mind that we're all probably going to get ourselves killed?"

"Yep."

Durham sighed. "Well . . . if that's the way it is, then I reckon we may as well get on with it."

They waited until, as best they could tell, there was no one close by on the wall above, then moved to the end of the buttress. Cordell went first, Sam holding his rifle. Cordell made the top of the wall without difficulty or apparent detection, and reached over to pull up all three rifles. Sam climbed next, so full of tense excitement that he didn't even feel the wound he'd received outside San Pablo. He was followed by Durham, who scaled the buttress in record time.

They'd come out not on a rifle platform, as they'd expected, but on the flat roof of one of a row of adjoining buildings constructed up against the wall. It was a stroke of good fortune, in a way, because the wide buildings made them less visible from below, but they worried about making noise and alerting anyone who might be in the building beneath them.

The flat roof was recessed slightly below the top level of the building wall, so that when they dropped on their bellies they were fully hidden from view behind the high rim of the wall. They snaked over to the edge, rose slowly, and peered out onto the plaza.

Fires burned here and there, casting an uneven, flickering light across the barren stretch of dirt and paving stone. There was about the place a general atmosphere of turmoil, no doubt caused by the now-invisible volunteer army out there in the blackness beyond the far fort wall. For a long time the three Underhills simply watched the scene, and listened to snatches of conversation that came to them. Most of it sounded fearful, and they heard much talk of abandoning the fort, and Trippler. But whether this was good they could not know; if Trippler was indeed a madman, as Dunning had said, he might simply turn on his prisoners as he saw his support and hopes falling away.

Durham touched Sam's arm. "Look!" he whispered, pointing.

Sam had already seen him. It was the same young Morgan who'd shot him, and he was angling toward a two-storied central building with a wide balcony around the second level. He was looking from side to side, as if searching for someone. He wore no hat, just a bandage wrapped around his skull, binding up the grazing bullet furrow that had left him unconscious for so many hours back in John Underhill's ranch house.

"Wonder what he's up to?" Sam asked.

"Looking for his daddy, I'll bet you," Cordell replied. They watched Morgan climb the stairs to the balcony and disappear into an arched hallway. The Underhills had turned their attention elsewhere when Morgan emerged again, shouting to others below and waving his arms wildly.

"What the devil?" Sam muttered.

Several men ran up the stairs to join Morgan, who led them back into the hallway. Perhaps two minutes later, they came out again, carrying bodies. Cordell brought out the spyglass and looked the situation over more closely. One of the men was obviously dead, but the other was moving slightly, and speaking. He watched as the wounded man, his body tight as a wire, whispered into the ear of one of the men who had carried him out. A moment later the tension left the man; his body relaxed and he lay back and Cordell knew he'd just watched a man die.

"Somebody's committed a couple of murders here," he said to his brothers. "God knows I hope them two weren't among Trippler's hostages."

"We've got to find Pap and John, fast," Sam said.

"And Chasida," added Durham.

"Her, too," Cordell said. "But we have to have some kind of plan. We're safe here for the moment. Let's talk this out a little. And then we'll move."

Dunning had to admire those Underhill boys. A daring bunch, and certainly willing to take risks for their loved ones. He actually got a lump in his throat thinking about it. His own family experience had been so very different. Despite the undeniable problems the Underhills faced just now, Dunning actually envied them.

He'd been watching the fort through a spyglass when he'd seen them go over the wall. It was sheer luck that he'd happened to have the glass trained at the right spot when they crossed the wall. Cordell first, then Sam, and Durham. As best he could tell, they'd dropped onto a rooftop inside the wall, but he'd lost his angle of view at that point and he couldn't know what had become of them since.

He stood, alone in the darkness and wind, and turned his head to the right, cocking his ear and listening to the distant noise of a fairly substantial encampment. Several bonfires blazed in clear view—defiant blazes, he was sure, designed for the eyes of William Gordon Trippler and his mercenaries. The growing militia was making no attempt to hide themselves. They *wanted* Trippler to know they were there, to know what was coming when dawn finally broke.

Dunning had considered riding over to the militia camp and trying to talk its leadership into delaying an attack, but had given up the idea. An entirely different militia band was gathering at a different spot, and soon, he figured, there would be others arriving, too. This was no regular military operation; there was no one central authority to which he could appeal for a delay until the Underhills had a chance to see what they might pull off on their own, inside those walls. It would be a waste of time now to try to avert the attack.

So there was only one thing Dunning could do. He'd scolded Bushrod for his plan to go inside the old mission. Now, here he was, ready to do the very same thing himself.

That buttress the younger Underhills had climbed had

looked like an easy enough route. He'd try the same approach himself, though on the opposite side of the compound. Folding his spyglass and dropping it into a pocket, he headed toward the fort at a slow trot.

CHAPTER
THIRTY-THREE

The door rattled so quickly that John Underhill barely had time to hide his homemade knife. Blast it all! He'd planned to be in a position to use it the next time a guard entered, but as it was, all he could do was sit on his cot, the knife behind him, and look up blankly at the young guard who came in.

"Get out," the guard said.

"What?"

"Get out! Go! I'm giving you your freedom!"

John had been too many weeks a prisoner for this to seem quite real. He stared quizzically at the fellow, still not moving.

"Damnation! Do you not speak American? I'm letting you out!"

John picked up the knife and managed to tuck it into the rear waist of his trousers. "Why?"

"Because this place is going to hell, that's why. Falling apart around our ears, with a militia ready to attack outside and half the guards already deserting. I'm getting ready to join them."

"But why let me go?"

"Because you're a Texas hero, sir. I never did like the notion of locking up a man who fought so brave at San Jacinto."

John went to the guard and pumped his hand. "Thank you. Thank you so much!"

"Hell, don't thank me. Thank Mr. Rafe Morgan. It was

him who made me mad enough to do this. I talked to him yesterday evening, told him all that was starting to be said among the guards, and he told me to run if I wanted, but that if I did, he'd kill me next time he saw me. The more I thunk on that, the madder I got. And I thought: I'm just going to go turn loose John Underhill when I get the chance, because I know nothing would make Rafe Morgan madder than losing John Underhill. And by the way, sir, let me give you warning: Rafe Morgan has had it in mind for a long time that he plans to kill you before it's done. He hates your family, he does. And he's been telling it all around the fort that Trippler has promised him he'll let him have you for whatever he wants to do, once your usefulness to him is played out.''

''I appreciate the warning. Morgan is a wicked man. Has been since he was young. My father killed his brothers years ago, and they deserved it. Speaking of my father, I want to find him. I believe he's locked up here somewhere, and he'll be in even more danger than me if—''

The young man made a strange, twisting shape with his mouth in tandem with the sound of a meaty thud. John stopped, wondering what had just happened, as the other slowly leaned toward him. John caught him and felt his body go limp.

A knife was sticking into the center of his back, rooted almost to the hilt.

''Well, well! I learned to throw a knife when I was no more than a boy, and I ain't lost the touch yet!''

John let go of the young guard's dead body and stood.

Rafe Morgan grinned at him from down the corridor. ''Good to meet you face-to-face at last, Mr. John Underhill. You know, you bear a right smart resemblance to your pap.''

''Why'd you kill this young man?''

''Hell, he's letting prisoners loose! He deserved it!'' Morgan's hand came up, bearing a pistol. ''Besides, it gets him out of the way so that I can finally begin settling an old score. The boy was right, you know—this place is falling apart. I admit I didn't look for it to happen, but it is. So I've got little time to take care of what's been waiting years to be took care of.'' He raised the pistol and pulled back the lock, squinting down the barrel at John's head. "First you. You'll die easy and fast, for I've got nothing against you personal. Then I'll go fetch out your pap. He won't die easy, and he won't die fast.''

The roar of the pistol echoed in the corridor, amplified to the level of a booming cannon. The flash of the shot was white and blinding, and right in the face of John Underhill.

Dunning jerked his head around, wondering who had fired that shot, and why. It seemed to have come from somewhere inside a building, but he wasn't sure just which building. There were so many passages and corridors in this mazelike compound that sounds carried in odd directions and were hard to trace.

He waited for a follow-up shot, but heard none. Hoping that the Underhill boys hadn't found themselves trouble already, he continued his crawl across rooftops, edging slowly down a row of buildings, keeping out of sight of anyone below. Thank God there was no sentry in the bell tower! A man up there could see almost every inch of the compound. He put it down to the luck of momentary circumstances that no guard was at that spot. It seemed that few of the guards were much concerned about attending to duty. They were far more interested in getting out before dawn. He wouldn't be surprised if—

Someone was before him. Someone had clambered up a wall and onto the same rooftop as he, and it had happened so fast that he couldn't even duck off to hide. The fellow, a middle-aged, rail-thin man, saw Dunning a moment later, and froze. A guard, Dunning supposed.

"Well? What do you intend to do now that you've caught me up here?" Dunning asked.

The man studied him, but said nothing. He cut to his left and to the wall, climbed over, and dropped. Dunning heard him hit the ground outside with a painful-sounding grunt, and wondered if he'd ruined an ankle in that fall. But a moment later the sound of his footfalls receding from the fort and into the darkness told Dunning that the man had made it. Another deserting guard, too intent on his own escape to care about strangers climbing across rooftops.

Dunning went to the edge of the roof at the same point the man had climbed up. A round roof-support log jutted out of the wall just below him. He lowered his rifle as far as he could and dropped it, then swung down on the jutting log, hung, and dropped to the ground. He was in a very dark alley between two buildings. One end of the alley butted up against the compound wall; the other opened into the windy, dimly lighted plaza.

Dunning crept to the open end and paused, looking out at the milling men, much diminished in number from what he'd seen the one prior time he'd managed to sneak into this fort, just to spy things out. Trippler's fort was a wounded place, bleeding away the mercenary soldiers who were its lifeblood.

Dunning wondered what William Trippler was thinking just now. He knew the terror and anger that must be filling his twisted mind, building like magma inside a volcano, heading for a sure eruption. What he couldn't know was in what direction Trippler's anger would be vented, or against whom.

He looked at the sprawling, multicorridored, two-story central building of the compound. Trippler's quarters, as well as the place, Dunning believed, where the hostages were held. He waited for an opportunity to dart across the clearing to that building without being seen, but the chance didn't come. Still too many men about. He couldn't move out of this alley without somebody spotting him.

He realized abruptly that it didn't matter. At the moment every man in Trippler's fort was looking out for himself, paying no heed to anyone else. Dunning could walk across to Trippler's quarters without anyone noticing, or if they did notice, not caring.

He marched out of the alley in a manner suggesting that he belonged in this place and had nothing to hide. And as he'd hoped, he received no attention at all. Fighting the impulse to speed up, he sauntered over to the central building and ducked into the shadows of a corridor entrance.

He found a staircase and climbed, reaching the second-level balcony that encircled the entire building. He studied the design of the second story. It was unusually high, the roof of that level being as high as a normal roof, plus half again.

Dunning edged along the wall and found a ladder, built against the wall. Access to the roof! Glancing about, he put hands and feet to it and climbed, dropping off onto a flat rooftop behind a high roof rim that was sufficient to hide him.

The roof, he found, wasn't perfectly flat. Walls of some of the interior rooms extended up through that roof, with separate, higher roofs of their own and windows cut through the walls for ventilation. The windows were crossed by entwined wooden bars.

Dunning went to the nearest window, which spilled dim light out across the roof. He knelt beside it and looked in.

A smile broke across his face. Luck was indeed with him.

In the room below, pacing back and forth, was Bushrod Underhill.

John Underhill stood, dripping with sweat, panting for breath, and stared at the still form of Rafe Morgan at his feet.

Good Lord . . . the man looked dead! Had he killed him?

It was difficult to mentally reconstruct what had just happened, for it had all come about so fast. Rafe Morgan had shot at him dead-on, and there seemed no good reason he should have missed, but miss he had. John had reacted out of instinct, lunging at Morgan, yanking the pistol away from him and smashing it against the wall so hard the lock bent and the flint flew free and was lost somewhere along the dark floor. Forgetting the homemade knife stuck into the back of his trousers, John had begun fighting in brutal, primitive fashion, grabbing Morgan by the head and hammering his skull again and again against the hard stone wall of the corridor. Then Morgan had gone limp with a groan . . . and now lay motionless at his feet.

John nudged the man with his toe, but he didn't move. Leaning against the wall, letting his strength come back slowly, John decided that if there was any man in the world who probably deserved to have the life beaten out of him against a stone wall, it was Rafe Morgan.

John hadn't had any ambition to be a killer tonight, but at least Morgan would now be no threat to Bushrod.

When his heart had slowed to a reasonable pace, John Underhill stepped across Rafe Morgan's body, down the corridor, and vanished into the darkness.

Rafe Morgan lay alone, motionless, for several minutes. A dog, wandering through the compound, entered the hall and went to him, licking at the bloody abrasions on his head, then moving on.

Rafe Morgan groaned softly, rolled over on his back, and opened his eyes.

"Mr. Underhill! Bushrod!"

Bushrod stopped in mid-pace, looking around in confusion, then up to the high window, where a ghostly, dim visage seemed to be looking down at him through the crossed wooden bars.

"Who's there?"

"It's Dunning! Thank God I've found you!"

"Dunning! How the devil did you get into this place?"

"I came over the wall . . . your sons are here, too, somewhere inside, but I haven't seen them since I came in myself. This place is falling apart like a dry cake! At least half of Trippler's men seem to have deserted, and the rest seem on the verge. There's militia gathering up outside the walls."

"Can you get me out of here?"

"These bars are wooden. I can break them away, or cut them. The window is small, but I think you can fit through it. I'll have to find something to drop to you to pull you up."

"We'll use my coat. You hold one sleeve, I'll hold the other. It ought to be long enough to reach."

"Very well. Let me work on these bars."

Dunning pulled and twisted on the wooden bars, but they held fast. "I'll have to cut them!"

"Hurry!"

Dunning pulled out a knife and began sawing at the bars.

Below, Bushrod paced again, stopping every few moments to look up and check Dunning's progress, then pacing some more.

CHAPTER THIRTY-FOUR

Chasida opened her eyes, but saw almost nothing she could make sense of . . . mostly just darkness, broken by lines of light in which dust danced. Her body ached, her head throbbed. She was in an odd, cramped posture, neck craned, the back of her head pressing painfully against something solid and vertical.

All was silent . . . no, not fully so. She heard a rhythmic shuffling, a masculine voice muttering. Something in the light pattern changed, then changed again, in tandem with the back-and-forth shuffling sound.

Chasida began to remember, slowly. A day of hiding in the quarters of that kind Mexican servant woman, an attempted escape in a wagon laden with dirty clothing and linens, a recapture at the last moment by Trippler. He'd dragged her to his chamber again; there had been angry words, and something had happened . . .

The ache in her head reminded her. He'd struck her and she'd fallen. Her last memory was of pain throbbing through her skull.

She moved, just a little, and found it difficult. But she was beginning to understand a little about her situation. She was inside something like a box, but too short for her to stretch out fully. And there were vents or louvers on one side; it was through these that the shafts of light came.

Chasida turned her head slowly to the right, and squinted, looking out through one of the vents.

Beyond she saw Trippler's chamber, and then Trippler himself, pacing back and forth endlessly, mumbling to himself like some sad resident of a hospital for the mad. She watched him, and realized where she was: he'd placed her inside the big wardrobe that sat against one wall of his room. Why would he have done that? She could only suppose that he must have thought he'd killed her when she fell.

Despite her pain and the fear that arose as she regained her grasp on reality, Chasida discovered something surprising: she wasn't panicky. Instead she was angry. He'd dumped her inside a wardrobe! Treated her like some piece of refuse to be laid aside for the moment and disposed of later.

She looked around her constricting little prison. Clothing hung above her, shirttails almost tickling her face. Beneath her was various clutter she could feel but not see. Cautiously she moved her hands about, feeling a shoe, a bit of string, a crumpled shirt that had fallen from above, a cravat, a bit of wood, like the handle of a knife.

Her hand closed around it. It *was* a knife! Not a big one, but a knife. A weapon.

Chasida picked it up and held it in one of the shafts of light. It was merely the kind of knife a kitchen maid might use to skin a potato or slice an apple. Its blade was rusted and dull, and why it had wound up on the floor of a wardrobe she couldn't guess. But she was grateful to have it. It was a tool she needed . . . one she would use, somehow, to get away from this place and the terrible man pacing out in the room beyond.

She shifted her head a little, very slowly, and winced. The spot where she'd struck her skull against that table hurt badly. She wondered if the skin had been broken. She fought back the pain. She would let nothing distract her now.

For several minutes she lay thinking, planning, praying, encouraging herself. She knew what she had to do, though it went against everything she had been taught.

She whispered a final prayer, then, deliberately, let out a soft, low moan.

Outside, Trippler's repetitive pacing stopped.

She moaned once more, a little louder.

His footsteps again. This time coming toward her.

"There!" Dunning said as the knife finally cut away the last of the wooden bars. He pulled it free and tossed it off onto the roof behind him. "Are you ready, Mr. Underhill?"

"Yes . . . but let's keep it quiet as we can. There's a guard outside my door."

"Are you sure? Most of the guards have deserted their posts."

Bushrod's whisper was hard for Dunning to hear. "Not this one. I can hear him."

"Very well. We'll be quiet. Can you toss your coat up to me?"

Bushrod did, and Dunning caught it on the first try. He gripped one sleeve in both hands, lowered the other back down to Bushrod, who took hold. "You got a good grip?" Bushrod whispered up.

"Yes . . . put your feet on the wall and walk your way up while I pull."

It worked better than Bushrod had anticipated. He held fast to the coat while Dunning pulled up. The wall was rough and his feet did not slip. Like a mountain climber he advanced up, slowly, toward the little window.

The sleeve tore loose with one great rip, and Bushrod plunged to the floor below, hitting hard.

"What's going on in there?" The guard's voice, through the door.

Bushrod sat up, but did not reply. Dunning looked on, aghast, wondering why Bushrod said nothing.

"Did you fall or something, Underhill?"

Still no answer, and then Dunning realized that Bushrod's breath had been knocked out of him. He was trying to speak, but had no wind in his lungs to give him voice.

"I'm coming in!"

Bushrod pulled in a sudden breath. "No . . . no, I'm fine," he said. "Just tripped over my own two feet and knocked the wind out of myself."

"You watch yourself, old man. Anything happens to you, it's my rump that takes a kicking."

Bushrod wondered why this guard still held his post with the little world of the fort spinning out of control all around. Either he was simply loyal and dedicated, or somehow word of what was happening simply hadn't gotten to him.

Dunning thrust his head through the window. "Got to find something stronger to get you out of there!" he whispered down. "Maybe a rope!"

"Hurry . . . and don't get yourself caught," Bushrod replied softly.

Dunning nodded, and was gone.

Rafe Morgan's dizziness was fading fast, and fury taking its place. He was mad at himself for missing that shot at John Underhill, and mad at John Underhill for doing such a job of nearly beating the life out of him. He realized how fortunate he was to have lost consciousness. If he hadn't gone limp and quit struggling, John Underhill would probably have continued to pound his skull against that wall until his brains ran out his ears.

He staggered along, leaning on the wall, until at last he reached a set of stairs. He descended them carefully, putting most of his weight on the rail, and reached the bottom. Blinking his eyes fast several times, trying to regain the rest of his equilibrium, he let go of the rail and walked out into the plaza.

"Pa!" The voice was that of Jimmy Morgan, one of his two sons here in Trippler's fort. He turned and saw Jimmy running toward him, still wearing that head bandage. "Pa, are you drunk?"

"Not drunk . . . just about got myself beat to death by damned John Underhill, that's all."

"But he's locked up, ain't he?"

"Not no more. He's loose, and I aim to find him, and his damned old pap, too. There's some old balances to be evened tonight, and if we don't do it fast, we'll lose our chance when this place is overrun. Where's your brother?''

''I ain't seen him the last little while. It's been loco around here, people sneaking away, going over the wall, stealing things. There's hardly a handful doing what they're supposed to do.''

''Hell with it. Let them run. Me, I've got other things to do. Like killing every Underhill I can, and protecting Trippler.''

''Why protect Trippler now? Why not let them wolves at the gate have him?''

''Because he could mean money for us. Mexican money. If we can get him out of here alive and safe into Mexico, there could be a reward. He's got friends there, Trippler does. Which is a good thing, I reckon, considering that he sure as hell ain't got nothing but enemies left in Texas.''

Dunning trotted across the roof toward another wall, another window. This one, he noticed, had no bars on it, just a pair of closed shutters. And it was bigger than Bushrod Underhill's window.

He reached it, and peered in as best he could through the vents of the shutters. The room was lighted, and he wanted to know who, if anyone, was in there before he began rattling shutters and drawing attention.

He tried many angles of view, but could see no movement, hear nothing to indicate human presence. He touched the shutters and found them unlatched; they swung inward with a faint creak. Light poured out onto the roof.

Dunning looked in cautiously. He stared down, and knew he had been wrong. The room *was* occupied, after all, though not by anyone who was likely to be a threat.

This window was lower than the one in Bushrod's room, so Dunning put his legs through, swung in, and dropped lightly to the floor. Straightening, he walked over to the single bed in the room and looked down at the face of the sleeping man who lay on it.

But the man wasn't sleeping. He opened his eyes slowly and looked up at Dunning.

"Hello, sir," Dunning said. "Sorry to disturb you, but I've come looking for a rope, if I can find one."

The man stared back at him, silent.

"Can you understand what I'm saying to you, sir?"

The man nodded.

"Can you speak?"

Another nod.

"But it's difficult . . . is that it?"

Again, a nod.

"Sir, my name is Dunning. Can you tell me who you are?"

The man's lips parted. His voice was raspy and tired, the voice of a man who had known pain for quite a while. Though he spoke softly, his words were clear: "My name is David Crockett."

Chasida blinked as the wardrobe door swung open, letting in the light of the many candles and several lamps that Trippler had burning about his chambers. Her eyes protested the light. She wondered why he'd lit so many.

He stared down at her. "I thought you were dead."

"No," she said. "I'm not dead . . . please help me out of here."

"Why should I help you, girl? You've made your feelings about me clear enough."

"I was wrong . . . I'm sorry. You're a good man and you've treated me well. I should not have been so ungenerous to you."

These words obviously took him by surprise. "What makes you talk that way? Why have your feelings changed?"

"I don't know. But I have. I've thought about it, and I know I was wrong."

He reached down and took her hand, pulling her up, helping her out of the wardrobe and onto her feet. She held the other hand behind her, out of his sight. She was stiff and unsteady, and when she touched the back of her head, found it crusted with drying blood.

"You took quite a blow when you fell," he said. "I thought it had killed you."

"Please," she said, "hold me. I'm afraid I'll faint."

He wrapped his arms around her. She laid her head on his shoulder and leaned her weight against him, slowly lifting her arms and embracing him. She felt him tense, then relax, and sensed rather than saw his smile.

"I do believe you've come to your senses at last, my dear," he said. "Perhaps that blow to the head cleared the mind of my little empress."

"I'm afraid," she said. "I need someone to take care of me."

"I'll protect you."

"There's a man, the one named Morgan, who has said terrible things to me."

"Don't be afraid of him. I can control Morgan."

"You'll protect me?"

"Of course I will."

"Hold me closer," she said.

He wrapped his arms more tightly around her. She nestled against him, and for a moment almost felt pity for him, knowing how utterly surprised he would be when she did what she had planned. It was enough to make her hesitate . . .

So she acted, quickly, while the will was still there. She felt his body spasm at the first stab. His arms tightened around her, almost crushing her. The second stab made them pull away. He screamed and staggered away from her so quickly that the knife was pulled from her hand. She saw it sticking into his back, between his shoulder blades, as he staggered across the room toward the table.

On that table, she saw, was a pistol. He leaned for it, reached after it . . .

She was too fast. Even with her bleary mind and throbbing head and unsteady feet, she was more than a match for corpulent William Trippler. She darted to the table and had the pistol in hand just before he reached it.

She held it in both hands, aimed at him, and backed away toward the door. He groaned, then began to weep, and reached behind himself, feeling for the knife. She got the door open just as he managed to pull the knife out. She was in the hall and closing the door again when he collapsed to his knees.

Chasida ran down the hall, turned left, and darted onto the balcony and down the stairs. On the plaza she continued running, not sure where to go, wanting only a place to hide until she could figure out what to do.

Bushrod heard a noise above and looked up. Dunning's face appeared at the window again.

"Did you find a rope?"

"No. But Mr. Crockett was willing to let me borrow his blanket. I tore it into strips and tied them together. It should be strong enough to hold you . . . I hope."

"Drop it down."

Things went much better this time. Bushrod climbed the wall again, Dunning pulling, working the blanket rope up a little at a time. Bushrod reached the edge of the window, reached one hand out, got a grip and held on. Dunning reached in and took his other arm, pulling him up.

For a moment Bushrod was ready to fall, but he refused to let go. With a grunt and heave, and with help from Dunning, he worked his elbows through the window, and after that it was easy.

He clambered out onto the rooftop, beside Dunning.

"Good bit of climbing there, Mr. Underhill," Dunning said.

"Good bit of pulling, Mr. Dunning," Bushrod replied. "Now, how about let's go find my boy John . . . wait—did you say Mr. *Crockett* gave you that blanket?"

"I did, indeed. But let's talk about that later. For now we've got much more important things to do."

CHAPTER THIRTY-FIVE

Jack Morgan, eldest son of Rafe, joined his father and brother in the middle of the plaza as the latter two strode toward the building in which both Jack and Bushrod Underhill had been imprisoned. Rafe, fighting dizziness, climbed the stairs and made his way to the door of Bushrod's room, and stopped in surprise to see it was still guarded.

"What the hell are you doing here?" he asked the guard.

"It's my post, sir. I'm supposed to be here."

"Don't you know what's happening? This whole fort is likely to be attacked come morning. Militia. The place is going to hell fast, a lot of folks deserting."

"I hadn't heard nothing of it, sir."

"Get on with you. I'm relieving you of duty. Clear out."

"Yes, sir, Mr. Morgan." The guard hoisted up his rifle and trotted off down the hall and descended the stairs.

Rafe Morgan put his mouth to the door. "Hello, Bushrod Underhill! Been a lot of years! An old friend here, eager to get reacquainted!"

No answer came. "I don't believe he's in there," Jack Morgan said.

"Hell, he's got to be in there! This room's been guarded straight on through."

Morgan opened the door and stepped in. The room was empty. He swore bitterly and looked around as if expecting to find Bushrod hiding when there was no possible place to hide.

"Look, Pa." Jack Morgan pointed up to the empty window.

Rafe Morgan gazed at it a moment, swore again, and stomped out of the room.

Rafe Morgan and his sons had just entered the main corridor when a voice called. Rafe wheeled and saw Trippler coming slowly down the adjacent corridor, leaning against the wall.

"Please, Mr. Morgan . . . please, you must help me!"

"What's happened to you, Mr. Trippler?"

"She, that girl . . . she stabbed me. Twice. In the back."

"What? The little Quaker-looking gal?"

"Yes . . . yes! Please look at my wounds, tell me how bad they are . . ."

Rafe went to Trippler and pulled off his coat and waistcoat, and pulled up his shirt in the back. There was blood, but not much of it, and the two knife punctures were already congealing closed again, no longer bleeding.

"How long was the blade?"

Trippler used finger and thumb to indicate the length.

"I don't think you have naught to worry about, Mr. Trippler. With a blade that short, and striking where she did, all that's happened is that you've had a bit of your flesh cut. Nothing to worry about."

Trippler seemed reassured. He stood a little straighter, moving his shoulders slowly, wincing but looking a little less panicked.

"Mr. Trippler, things seem to be going badly here tonight," Rafe said.

"Yes, yes . . . I know."

"Bunch of disloyal wretches, your hired soldiers. I'm sorry to tell you this, but half or more have already deserted."

"You must help me, Mr. Morgan. You must get me out of here safely. If you can, there will be great, great reward for you." He glanced at the younger Morgans. "And your sons, too."

"Where would we find this reward?"

"In Mexico. You must get me to Mexico!"

Though what Trippler was saying coincided with the plans Rafe Morgan had already discussed with his sons, he felt doubtful now that he was looking at the man. Trippler hardly seemed imperial just now, and any power he had wielded here clearly was gone. Would the Mexican government really pay a reward for this man's protection, simply because he'd been willing to connive with them to betray Texas?

Maybe not . . . but still, Morgan realized, there might be another reason to keep Trippler close by. If the Mexicans proved unwilling to pay for him, Texas even yet might. Rafe Morgan didn't care from what source reward came, as long as it came.

But it might not be easy to protect Trippler. From his son he'd learned of the two dead guards, shot to death in the hallway outside the room where the girl had been held. A discharged pistol on the floor had been identified as Trippler's, and anger was hot against him now.

"Mr. Trippler, tell me straight: did you shoot dead two of your own hired men tonight?"

Trippler's fat lips quivered. "No, no, I swear to you, I didn't. It was . . . that girl. She got away from me, got my pistols somehow, and she killed them!"

Morgan didn't believe it for a moment, but what the devil. Trippler was still worth going to some risk for, considering that he was bound to be of monetary value to someone when this was all done.

"Who'd have thought such a delicate little thing could be so fierce! Life does have its surprises, eh, sir? But don't you worry. We'll protect you, like you want. You just stick close beside us. But there's one condition."

"Name it, just name it."

"We don't leave this fort until I've found Bushrod Underhill, and settled an old, old debt, once and for all."

"Fine, fine. We'll go to his room now, and you can kill him on the spot."

"Done been. He ain't there."

"What?"

"But we'll find him." Rafe turned to his sons. "Go out, boys. Divide up and search, and when you find him, you bring him over to . . . there. The bell tower. Knock him cold if you have to, run a fishhook through his ear and pull him, do whatever you must to get him to the bell tower . . . but don't kill him. That's to be my pleasure, and mine alone." Rafe addressed Trippler again. "And now, sir, I suggest we find some way to disguise you. There's a right smart bit of hard feeling against you right now because of them dead guards. But you stick with me, I'll keep you safe. And when it's done, you'll reward me. Right?"

"Yes, Mr. Morgan," Trippler said. "I'll reward you richly, richly. Just don't let them kill me! I'm a great man, you see. I'm not supposed to die."

The stables stood against one side wall of the old mission, a long, low building with a seemingly endless series of stalls. Chasida was attracted to it because of its extreme darkness. It would make an excellent hiding place.

Remaining in the shadows, covering her head with a shawl she'd found near the well, hiding the pistol she carried in the folds of her dress, she moved toward the stables without being accosted. Behind the row of stalls she discovered a long common hall that allowed rear access to each stall. She entered this black tunnel and walked past several stalls. About half the stalls were empty. She chose one of these, clambered over, and dropped into the corner.

Closing her eyes, she did nothing but breathe for several minutes. At length she opened her eyes and looked around, and praised herself for making a good decision. Here she was fully hidden from view from the outside. Someone could walk right down the long run behind her, and not see her, either. And all she had to do was lift her head slightly to be able to see out across the plaza.

Chasida determined that she would remain there until morning. By then, perhaps something would have happened to allow her to safely escape. The idea of going over the wall by night terrified her. But here she felt safe.

She closed her eyes, and after a few minutes began to doze.

Her eyes snapped open again. *She was not alone.*

At first she did not move, just shifted her eyes from side to side, barely breathing at all. What accounted for this sense of another human presence? She could hear nothing, see nothing.

But her skin prickled, and she *knew*.

She heard a noise, in the long, corridor-like run outside the stall. Someone was moving slowly, stepping lightly. Was someone looking for her? Or, like her, seeking a place to hide?

She trembled, huddling up tight into the corner, hoping the darkness would hide her. Her nose began to tickle, making her want to sneeze, and her chest felt heavy, full of the dust of the stable, and she ached to cough. Every inch of her itched, but she dared not move or scratch. Her fingers rested on the smooth butt of the pistol.

Someone whispered. A male voice. Another replied, even more softly.

They were getting close now, almost directly behind her. Two of them . . . no, three.

Chasida squeezed her eyes closed and prayed as she'd never prayed before.

All was quiet, and she hoped they'd gone on by. But she jumped a little and almost gasped out loud when she heard someone fumbling with the latch of the rear entrance to the stall.

They were coming in!

The gate creaked open and Chasida came to her feet with a small, stifled yell, raising the pistol. The three men jumped back, and one lowered a rifle in her direction.

"No!" she pleaded. "Please . . . I was just hiding here, that's all! Go away or I'll shoot you!"

The rifle was lowered at once. "Chasida? Chasida Gruen-wald?"

The voice was familiar. "Who are you? How do you know me?"

The smallest of the three men stepped forward, hand extending toward her. "It's me, Chasida. Durham Underhill. And my brothers Cordell and Sam are here, too, right behind me."

Chasida lowered the pistol, so overcome with relief that she could barely stand.

Five minutes later, when they had exchanged enough information to allow Chasida to understand why the Underhills were here, and vice versa, Cordell said, "Finding Miss Gruenwald changes our situation some, fellows. Durham, given how much concern you've had for this young lady"— at this, Durham's face reddened, unseen, in the darkness—"I want you to remain here with her. Keep a watch across the clearing outside, and if you see John, or Pap, or any of John's family, go out and fetch them in here. This will be the place we'll rendezvous when everyone's gathered in, however and whenever it happens."

"What about me?" Sam asked. No more was he the defiant rebel. Cordell, the eldest and most sensible of the three, was the leader, and Sam did not question it.

"You'll go with me, and we'll divide and search in two different directions. Got your watch on you? Good. Give it an hour, then come back here, whether you've found them or not. Understand?"

Sam nodded.

"Good luck, Durham," Cordell said as he and Sam were about to leave. "Try to keep out of sight, but be ready to fight if you have to. A number of horses are left, and those men who are deserting may come to get their mounts. If you stay in this stall, though, you shouldn't be bothered. Now, wish me and Sam luck, and we'll see you back here in an hour at most."

John Underhill slipped around a corner and looked across the plaza. Though he was hidden in shadow, he felt exposed, naked. Funny thing what captivity can do to a man. Though he'd been Trippler's prisoner only a matter of a few months, he didn't feel like the independent, quick-thinking man he'd always been. Locked up, with decisions made for him, he'd lost some of the mental alacrity that had always stood him in good stead.

Right now he was deeply frustrated. He'd searched for his family and failed to find them. But his search had been far from constant. Time and again he'd been forced to duck into hiding while some stranger passed by. He realized that the order of this compound was dissolving, that loyalties weren't what they had been even a day before, but being John Underhill, the foremost prisoner of Trippler's fort now for months, he couldn't just assume that he'd be left alone if spotted and recognized. Every person here was potentially a betrayer and a threat.

In all the time he'd been at the fort, he'd never known exactly where his family was held. Trippler had always kept them apart. At one point early on, John had become convinced his family was dead, and after that Trippler had occasionally brought him notes written in his wife's hand and signed as well by the children, just to confirm they were still there . . . just to let John know what he had to lose if he didn't cooperate.

He stopped, unsure where to go. His mind was full of fears, one boiling up after another. What if someone had killed his family already? What if Trippler took them and held them hostage for his own protection? What if someone else had spirited them away?

He heard someone behind him, close. Reaching behind him, John pulled his homemade knife free from his trousers, and slipped back into a recessed doorway.

A dark figure stalked past, rifle out and cocked, a rifle John would like to have just now . . .

John lunged forward and wrapped an arm around the man's neck from behind, and raised the makeshift knife for a plunge into the fellow's heart. But something made him hesitate, and he peered around into the face of his would-be victim.

Immediately he released the man. ''Cordell?'' he said. ''Cordell, is it really you?''

''John . . . sweet Moses, John . . .'' Cordell rubbed his neck gingerly. ''Lord! You almost killed me!''

John Underhill dropped the knife, advanced to his bear of a brother, and wrapped his arms around his broad shoulders, embracing him powerfully, saying Cordell's name over and over again.

CHAPTER
THIRTY-SIX

Dunning slipped to the edge of the roof and looked down into an enclosed little courtyard below. "Mr. Underhill," he said softly, and gestured for Bushrod to join him.

Bushrod crept up beside him. The courtyard was empty, but a window opening onto it from the building on its other side was unshuttered, and through it Bushrod saw what had gotten Dunning's attention. Bushrod stared, silently, and when Dunning glanced over at him, tears ran down Bushrod's whiskered face.

"She's quite a pretty young woman," Dunning said, smiling. "She looks like she's held up quite well through what has surely been a very hard ordeal."

Bushrod nodded. "I'd say she has. Her name's Julia, by the way. Julia Ruth Claborn she was, before John married her. That was 1827, if I recollect . . . my, how the years do fly! Always a strong woman, but gentle, too. And a fine mother."

"Look . . . I see the children now."

They had just come to their mother, who was seated on the other side of the window. Bushrod's tears came a little faster at the sight of his grandchildren. He'd never have known them in other circumstances, for they had changed much.

"What's their names?" Dunning asked.

"The boy there is Henry. He'd be, let me see, seven or eight years old now. I ain't seen him since he was a newborn.

And the girl, she's about ten by now. Her name is Virginia, but they call her Jenny for short."

"Just the two children?"

"That's all. There was a middle child, but he was born small and frail . . . didn't live more than a couple of days."

"What was his name?"

A pause. "They called him Bushrod."

In silence the two men watched the strangely peaceful domestic scene through the window. Bush whispered a prayer of thanks that his daughter-in-law and grandchildren were still alive, still seemingly well.

"Families are a wonderful thing, are they not?" Dunning said.

"They are."

"I've wondered many times what it would be like to be part of a family such as yours, Mr. Underhill. The concern you show for one another, the way you work together toward the same ends, the way you tolerate each other's differences . . . that's how it should be. But that's not the way it is for so many of us."

"Mr. Dunning, I want to ask you a personal question, if I may."

"Go ahead."

"This is more to you than just a hired job, I think."

"Really?"

"Yes. Am I right? Do you have a personal interest in this, besides being the president's agent?"

Dunning seemed to be thinking. "Yes," he said. "There is indeed a personal interest. But please, sir, don't ask me what it is. It's not something I enjoy talking about."

"Then you'll hear no more about it from me."

"Mr. Underhill, I believe I'd like to meet your daughter-in-law and grandchildren. Would you introduce me?"

"With pleasure, Mr. Dunning."

They swung down off the roof into the enclosed courtyard. Together they walked to the window.

"Hate to scare them like this, but . . ." Bushrod rapped gently on the window.

Julia Underhill came up out of her chair and backed away, and the children let out a combined yell of surprise. Bushrod stuck his face close to the glass and smiled.

Julia stared at him as if he were a vision, a phantom, but her expression slowly changed. The children still held back, but she advanced slowly to the door that led into the courtyard, and opened it. "Papa?" she said, looking at him now face-to-face. "Papa Underhill?"

"It's me, Julia. I've come to get you out of here."

She broke into tears, ran to him, and threw her arms around his neck. For almost a minute she sobbed onto his shoulder. Dunning stayed off to the side, not wanting to intrude on their reunion.

The young ones stood together in the doorway, watching with wary expressions. She turned to them. "Come here, Jenny, Henry. Come here, and give your grandfather a hug!"

At that moment, the main door to the room rattled. The children turned, startled, then ran out into the courtyard with their mother and grandfather. Bushrod glanced at Dunning, who stepped around and into the room, dropping to his knee and raising his rifle, which he aimed at the locked but weakening door.

He was just opening his mouth to challenge whoever was at the door, when suddenly it burst open with great force, and into the room hurtled Cordell, and behind him, John Underhill.

Cordell had a pistol in hand, and when he saw Dunning with the upraised rifle, yelped and leveled it on the man. But recognition came soon enough to stop either of them from firing, and a moment later the place was exploding again with emotion, as Julia ran to the husband she'd not seen for months, and the children, wailing in a wild flurry of boiling feelings, followed after her, racing to their father with arms outstretched.

So intense was the moment that only Dunning noticed the gunshot that echoed flatly across the compound, muffled by the walls, but distinct. He frowned and went to the shattered door, looking out and wondering who had fired that shot, and

why it should trouble him so. The entire compound was moving more toward chaos every moment, and probably many
more shots would be fired before it ended . . . but still that
stray bit of gunfire worried him, though he couldn't have said
why.

As he listened, another shot was fired, then another almost
immediately after.

He only then realized that Cordell and John had come in
alone, and wondered what had become of Sam and Durham
Underhill.

As John and Cordell had been breaking down the door, Jack
Morgan was running to the dark, abandoned little woodhouse
that his brother had entered moments before. He put his back
to the wall, and with pistol gripped and cocked, looked cautiously around through the doorway, then stepped in.

His brother was there in the darkness, a smoking pistol in
hand, and the bandage around his head darkening with fresh
blood. He looked over as Jack entered. "Believe I managed
to tear my wound open again, somehow," he said.

"What the hell happened here? Why did you shoot?" Jack
squinted into the darkness and saw a figure lying on the floor.
"Damnation! Did you shoot him?"

"I did. Killed me an Underhill!"

"That's Bushrod Underhill? Hell, Jimmy, Pa said not to
kill him, just to bring him in!"

"It ain't Bushrod. Just one of his sons. I seen him poking
about, saw him come in here, and I followed. Got me a good
bead and brought him down."

Jack uncocked and put away his pistol. "Is he dead?"

"He's dead."

"He ain't . . . I just seen him move."

"You didn't. I swear, Jack, he's dead. I shot him clean
through the heart."

Sam Underhill rose up in the darkness. "Not through the
heart," he said. "*This* is how you shoot somebody through
the heart." And he fired.

Jack Morgan danced back as his brother bucked suddenly

and fell. Jimmy Morgan writhed, yelling, then lay still.

Sam Underhill, up on his knees, tossed his empty pistol to the floor and stared at the young man he'd just killed.

Jack Morgan, frozen for a moment, broke out of the stupor with a curse. He yanked his own pistol from the sash of the hunting shirt he wore and raised it.

Sam's hand moved swiftly, and another shot barked light and heat and the smell of flashing gunpowder in the darkness. Jack Morgan's pistol fell from his hand, and he lifted that hand to grip a pierced, bleeding throat. Sam had just shot him through the neck.

"Now you know what your brother learned the other night on a road outside San Pablo," Sam said to his dying victim. "Sam Underhill always carries a back-up pistol. Always."

Jack Morgan groaned, sank to his knees, and pitched over across the body of his brother.

Sam felt hot blood trickling down his stomach. The ball had entered his midsection, and he needed no doctor to tell him it was a bad wound. The thought came to him that he should go and find help, else there would be three dead young men in this room instead of just two, but when he came to his feet he found his legs too weak to hold him up. He managed only a couple of steps before falling, and once he fell, he lay there, feeling the blood passing out of him, pulse by pulse.

Durham hugged Chasida close and they both kept silent as death as a man three stalls down saddled and freed a horse. Durham raised his head and watched the fellow ride across the plaza to the wide front gate, which was now propped open wide enough to let horsemen pass.

"How many was that?" Chasida asked.

"I've lost count," Durham said. "A lot of men leaving here. I just wonder what's becoming of them once they get out. There's militia gathering all around this place. Trippler's downfall. That's what's going on here."

"He's a wicked man. I hate him."

"I didn't think Purificationists were supposed to hate."

"I don't think I'm a Purificationist anymore."

"I ain't surprised."

"Durham . . . what did your brother mean earlier, when he said you'd showed concern for me?"

"Well . . . I suppose he was talking about how I went looking for you at Cable Creek, after we heard about the massacre."

"You went looking?"

"Yes. Nobody knew for sure what had become of you, and I went to find out. But I didn't find you, of course. Just Kirk."

"You found Kirk?"

"Yes. Hurt but alive. He'll live, Chasida. I'm right sure of it."

"Thank God!" she said. "Thank God! Will you take me to him, when this is over?"

"I will. I promise."

Rafe Morgan examined his handiwork, and shrugged. "Well, you look as close to a farmer as you ever will, Mr. Trippler. Enough so we can sneak you out of here."

"Let's go! It's dark, and we can slip past the militia!"

"Patience, Mr. Trippler. Patience. I've still got Bushrod Underhill to find."

"Why haven't your sons returned? They've had abundant time to find him, if he's here to be found."

"Maybe he ain't. Maybe he's slipped away already. But we'll give it more time. It's many hours yet until dawn."

"Did you hear those shots earlier? They sounded close. Maybe your boys were involved in something."

"My boys know how to take care of themselves. They'll be back, and if Bushrod Underhill can be found, they'll have found him."

They were in the shadows beneath the balcony of the building where Trippler lived; the clothing Trippler had donned in disguise had been found in the servant quarters.

As they watched, two men rode out of the stable and toward the front gate. Trippler grew excited. "They're taking the horses! See? See? What about us? Won't we need horses?''

"You might have a good point there, sir. Tell you what— you stay here. I'll go to the stable and see if I can't get us some mounts.''

"Good, good. Because I don't want to walk out of here. A man in my position should ride.''

Rafe Morgan curled his lip. Trippler was a case, of that there was no question. Who else but he would be cowering in servant clothing, abandoned by his own men, surrounded by enemies who would gladly kill him and probably would, and yet still hold delusions of grandeur?

Rafe Morgan decided right then that if he couldn't get some reward for Trippler from somebody or another, he'd just haul the fool out into the badlands somewhere and blow his head off, just to remind him that ofttimes the true ruler in a developing land like this one wasn't man at all, but the gun.

"You hold fast right here, Mr. Trippler. If you see my boys heading for the bell tower, you go join them. Otherwise, wait and I'll be back real fast, with horses.''

Rafe Morgan was halfway to the stable when the crackle of many gunshots reached his ears. Distant shots, from outside the wall.

"Damn!'' he muttered, and detoured over to the nearest rifle platform. Climbing up the ladder, he looked over the wall.

Off on the plains, he saw bursts of light in the darkness, flashing like fireflies, but much brighter, and with the popping sound of exploding gunpowder following a moment later. Gunfire, all over, all around.

He sank to his haunches, understanding what it meant.

This changed things. A lot.

He climbed back down the ladder and continued on to the stable. Entering, he wished he had a torch or lantern to help him see. He found the long rear run that trailed behind the stable stalls and walked down it.

The horses were gone, all but a few sorry nags that would be of no use at all. He'd waited too long. Rafe cursed aloud.

And heard something, down in one of the stalls, that sounded human. Feminine, in fact. A whisper.

His mind worked fast. Maybe it didn't matter that there were no horses—horses certainly weren't helping those who had already fled and were now engaged in battle out there on the plains. Maybe what he needed was a hostage.

Rafe slipped out his pistol and began walking down the run, trying his best to make no noise. Inch by inch he moved along, not even sure he had heard anything, but hoping for a stroke of luck. He needed it just now.

Chasida, huddled next to Durham, leaned her face close to his ear and whispered, "I don't hear anything now. I think he's gone."

Durham nodded, and signaled for her to remain where she was.

He stood slowly, edging toward the rear of the stall, looking out over the gate—

The butt of Rafe Morgan's pistol struck him in the forehead with a loud crack, and he fell back, dropping his rifle, his back arching tensely for a moment, then relaxing.

Chasida screamed, rose, swung up her pistol, and fired.

Rafe Morgan swore and pulled back, then leaped over the gate and struck Chasida in the face. Because of her prior head injury in Trippler's chamber, the pain was intense, and for a few moments she passed out.

When she opened her eyes, she could make out little of the face looming over her, but she could tell that it was Rafe Morgan, and that he was smiling.

"Well, young miss, I never figured I'd find *you*! Sometimes bad situations lead to good things, huh? Now, get up. It's your lucky day—you're going to get out of this place." He lifted his head. "Hear that? That's gunfire. Outside. And what it means is that the folks who've left this place already ain't being allowed to pass unchallenged. The militia are stopping them. Which means I need a special advantage if I want to get Mr. Trippler out of here alive. That advantage, deary, is you."

Chasida tried to talk but could only manage a groan.

"Come on. Up from there. I didn't hit you that hard."

He forced her to her feet. The world spun around her. She tried to look at Durham and see how he was, but couldn't focus her eyes.

Morgan shoved her forward, out of the stable, and onto the plaza. They headed for the place he'd left Trippler, but Trippler wasn't there.

"Must have gone over to the bell tower," Morgan said. "That probably means my boys came back around with Bushrod Underhill. Come on. And step more lively! That's right!"

Just then armed riders came through the gate, maybe a dozen of them. Rafe saw them, but not clearly enough to know whether they were men who had earlier escaped the fort now being driven back inside by the resistance they'd met, or men from the militias now actually beginning to invade the place.

A quick hiding place was in order, he decided. He needed a few moments to ascertain just what was going on.

A shed stood nearby, apparently empty. "Over there!" he whispered sharply to Chasida, and gave her a shove that almost knocked her down. "Get inside!"

She obeyed, staggering through the door and sinking to the floor.

Rafe came in after, closed the door, and headed to the nearest window to look out. He didn't make it. His foot caught on something bulky and fleshy, and he tripped and fell, sprawling right across the corpses of his sons.

CHAPTER
THIRTY-SEVEN

Trippler stopped, panting, leaning over and putting his hands to his knees. The high, circling stairs weren't easy to climb when the climber was a portly man already terrified breathless by riders who'd burst through the front gate. Trippler looked out a small window on the side of the tower and saw even more riders coming in, and beyond the wall, a dark line of phantom soldiers advancing, firing.

A closer look revealed, to his relief, that those coming through the gate were not invading militiamen, but some of Trippler's own mercenaries, driven back to the fort after a failed attempt to escape. Someone closed the huge gate and barred it—but no one, he noticed, took to the rifle platforms. There would be no fight to defend this place. The men he'd paid to protect him were now concerned only with their own survival, and had reentered the fort merely to avoid capture or death outside.

Trippler resumed his climb, heading for the top of the bell tower. He'd run for the tower as the first riders came through the gate, instinctively drawn to that edifice as the highest, most remote refuge he could find within these walls. There, he hoped, they would not find him . . . though he knew that in the end, they surely would.

He rounded another turn of the stairs. The opening into the belfry was a dimly visible rectangle above him. The bell was huge and dark, swaying slightly in a rising wind.

Trippler reached the top of the stairs and cast himself onto the belfry floor, breathing hard, whimpering, and listening to the sound of gunfire outside.

His stab wounds hurt, and it felt like they were bleeding again. He wondered if he was going to die tonight, and was afraid.

Chasida watched Rafe Morgan weep over the bodies of his sons. It was a terrible sight, one that would have drawn her pity had this been any other man. She felt no pity now, only a sense that perhaps a mystical justice had been done. Now Rafe Morgan knew what she had felt when he and his sons had murdered her father and her companions, and gunned down her fleeing brother!

She edged back toward the door, realizing she might be able to flee while he was distracted . . .

But he saw her, swore, and lunged toward her, grabbing her ankle as she tried to bolt. She went down hard.

"Run from me, will you, girl? Run from me? Hell, no!"

"Let me go!" she screamed, trying to pull free.

"No . . . no . . . you're with me now, girl. You're my passage out of this place." He came closer, and struck her. She screamed.

"That's right . . . scream for me . . . show me how afraid you are of the big, mean man. It ain't going to stop me." He slapped her, and must have liked it, because he paused, then did it again.

Chasida cringed and tried to cover her already battered head with her arms as he struck her over and over . . .

Behind him, in the darkness, a figure loomed up. Chasida caught sight of it from the corner of her eye, and watched as it advanced, ghostlike, toward Rafe Morgan.

She saw something rise and fall. There was a loud, cracking noise, and Rafe Morgan grunted and slammed down onto his face.

Chasida rose, looking down at Morgan, then up at the man who'd just driven the butt of a rifle into the back of Morgan's head.

"Sam . . . is that you?"

"Chasida, I'm shot . . . I need help." He dropped the rifle.

"Shot?"

"Yes . . . I'm bleeding, hurting . . ."

"Let me help you . . ." She tried to reach him, but staggered to the side.

"You're hurt, too . . . he beat you." Sam's voice was frighteningly feeble.

"I'm not very hurt," she said, putting on a brave front. "He just slapped me a few times. Trippler knocked me senseless earlier, but I got away from him."

"Maybe if we help one another we can find my brothers . . ."

"Durham is still at the stable. Morgan hit him, hard."

"Cordell?"

"I don't know where he is."

"Help me, Chasida. Hold on to me and we'll go to the stable . . . see about Durham . . ."

She went to his side and put her arm around him. He leaned on her and she on him, and together they moved toward the stable.

Around them horses and men ran about in confusion and outside the fort rifles cracked. The air stank of burnt gunpowder. No one paid any heed to the bloody, wounded, shuffling pair who moved slowly across a seemingly unending plaza.

They were almost to the stable when Durham came out, rubbing his head gingerly, a look of pain on his face. It changed to deep concern when he saw them. He ran to them as Sam finally gave out and sank to the ground.

"Help me move him, Chasida," Durham said. Together they moved his brother to the relative safety of the stable.

"He's been shot," Chasida said. "I don't know how it happened, but I saw two dead men in the shed with him . . . Rafe Morgan's sons, I think."

"He's in bad shape," Durham said. "I've got to find my father."

"I'll stay with him, Durham. You go."

Durham wasn't a bold young man, usually. But he leaned

over and kissed Chasida on the cheek. "Be careful . . . and don't let my brother die." He came to his feet and ran out of the stable.

On the opposite side of the compound's central building and the bell-towered chapel building nearby, Bushrod and Dunning led John Underhill and family, unseen by Durham, across an open space toward one of the servants' quarters, a secure-looking place where the children would be safe until the madness ended.

"In here," Bushrod said, pushing open a door. "Go inside, lock yourselves in. I'm going to find Durham and Cordell and Sam."

"I'll go with you, Pap."

"No, John. Stay with your family. You've been apart long enough. Don't let them out of your sight. Mr. Dunning, if you would, sir, I'd appreciate it if you stayed with them, as well, seeing that . . . Mr. Dunning?"

Bushrod looked around, but Dunning was gone. "John, did you see where he went?"

"No."

"I did, Grandpap," little Henry Underhill said. "He went up there."

"Where?"

"Up into that tower. He looked up at the top, then ran over to that door, where the stairs start."

"Good boy, Henry. John, get them inside."

"Where are you going, Pap?"

"Dunning must have seen something up there. I'm going to find out what. Take care of them, John. And take care of yourself." He gave John a quick, fatherly embrace, and loped back across the clearing toward the tower.

Inside the tower, Bushrod felt cut off from the chaotic world inside the compound walls. He turned his full attention upward, wondering what Dunning had seen, and what he himself would find, at the top.

Unlike stocky Trippler, Bushrod had no difficulty climbing

the stairs. Passing years had left no mark upon him except silvering his hair and deepening the crags of his face. He wasn't even winded when he reached the top of the stairs.

But what he found did take his breath away. There was Dunning, rifle upraised, and on the other end of it, standing in a hunched, cowering posture, trembling hands upraised, was William Gordon Trippler.

"I'll be!" Bushrod said. "You've surely caught the prize rabbit, Mr. Dunning!"

Dunning didn't look at Bushrod when he spoke. His voice was different, intense, snapping, as if he were angry at Bushrod. "Go away!" he said. "I stood aside to let you have your little family reunion in peace. Now you go away and let William and me have ours."

"No, don't leave me here with him!" Trippler pleaded. "He'll kill me! He's mad . . . he'd kill his own brother!"

"Brother?"

"Go away, Bushrod!" Dunning barked again.

"It's true!" Trippler said. "He's my brother, my own flesh and blood . . . but he'll kill me, if you let him!"

"Dunning, is this true?"

"And what if it is?"

"So Dunning isn't your name at all!"

"It's my name . . . my Christian name. My surname, which I ceased to use years ago out of pure shame, is Trippler. And yes, that murderous, foul *thing* you see quaking before you is indeed my own brother."

"Don't let him kill me!" Trippler pleaded.

"And why shouldn't I?" Dunning shouted. "Did the bond of shared brotherly blood keep you from killing George? Not for a moment!"

"Please, please . . ."

"Listen to him whine, Mr. Underhill. Listen to a man who murdered his own brother—*my* own brother!—beg for his life! Did George beg, too, William? Or did you even give him a chance?"

"I had to do it, Dunning! You must understand . . . I was almost out of money, and George had all that cash, those valuables . . . I needed them more than he did!''

"That cash and those valuables rightly belonged to a band of religious colonists in Kentucky!''

"But they gave them up willingly! George told me all about it! They gave them to him!''

"No they didn't. They gave them to the *colony*, not to George. He stole that wealth from them, William. In a way, I guess he was no better than you! You a murderer, him a thief.'' Dunning glanced at Bushrod. "Do you know what it's like to grow up in a family that shames you so much you put aside the family name? Can you suppose what it is to know that one of your brothers is a religious fraud and thief, and the other a deluded little Napoleon and murderer?''

"Dunning, tell me straight: did Houston really hire you?''

"He did. You saw the credentials.''

"Did he know that you were William Trippler's own brother?''

"He did not. There was no need for it.''

"Dunning, don't shoot him. This isn't the right way. Take him prisoner, turn him over to Houston, and let justice be served as it should.''

"This *is* justice! The justice of one brother avenging another!''

"Avenging him by killing the only brother you have left? Are you going to become guilty of the same crime you're avenging?''

"A murderer kills, and so does an executioner, but the former is murder while the latter is not.''

"You're not an executioner. You're a hired agent of the Texas government, and what you're about to do goes far beyond your rights and duties.''

"It's a brother's right. A brother's duty.''

"No, Dunning, no. Please. Step back . . . let me go to him and bind his hands behind him. We'll take him to Houston together.''

Outside and below, rifles fired, men shouted. The front gate of the compound burst open and the militiamen entered the compound at last.

"It's almost over, Dunning. Let's do this the right way."

Dunning blinked rapidly, three times, then stepped back one pace, another. His jaw trembled, and he slowly lowered the rifle, just a little.

Bushrod stepped toward William Trippler, but the man surprised him. With a scream like that of a diving hawk, William Trippler charged straight at his brother, moving so fast that Dunning had no time to react. Trippler shoved Dunning hard against the chest. Dunning's rump went back against the edge of the belfry wall and his shoulders tilted back into empty space. He teetered, dropped his rifle behind him to the ground far below. Trippler shoved him again.

"No!" Bushrod yelled. But it was too late.

Dunning had already fallen.

William Trippler leaned over the edge of the belfry wall, looked down, and laughed. A moment later he was on his rump, knocked there by Bushrod. Bushrod leaned over the wall and was surprised to see that Dunning hadn't fallen to the ground. He was clinging to a small stone lip that encircled the belfry about two feet down.

Bushrod leaned out over the edge, reaching down. "Grab hold of my hand!"

"I can't . . . I'll pull you over!"

Bushrod wrapped his other arm around a pillar and braced his body as best he could against the stone belfry wall. "No . . . I can hold on!"

Dunning's hands were slipping. He had no choice. With a yell of exertion he pulled himself up, just a little, and shot his left hand up to grasp Bushrod's right one. Bush held him firm.

"Good, good . . . now your other hand, too . . ."

Dunning let go of the wall and wrapped his other hand around Bush's wrist. Bush grimaced, feeling his arm was about to be pulled off, but yelled encouragement to Dunning to hang on.

Suddenly a sharp pain tore through his other arm, wrapped around the belfry pillar. He looked back. Trippler was pounding at his hand and arm with both his fists, balled together into one. Bushrod tried to kick at him backward, but it was too awkward and he missed him.

Trippler laughed and shoved Bushrod between the shoulder blades. Despite his best effort to stay upright, Bush jolted out, almost falling, Dunning's swinging weight threatening to pull both of them down.

Trippler began beating him about the back and shoulders, occasionally giving another blow to the arm braced at the pillar. Bushrod leaned farther and farther over, almost falling, Dunning still hanging on to his right arm, trying to pin his feet against the wall but failing.

"Can't . . . hold . . . you . . ."

Bushrod saw Dunning's eyes fill with tears, but it struck him that the man's look was not one of terror, but fierce anger. Dunning roared in fury, let go of Bushrod's wrist with his right hand, and reached beneath his coat while swinging in space by only one hand. He brought out a small pistol.

Roaring one more time, he bent his legs, pushed the soles of his boots against the wall, then straightened, swinging himself out from the wall for a moment. Bushrod screamed at the pain this inflicted on his stretched arm, but realized at once what Dunning was doing.

Bushrod lowered his head as Dunning fired. The pistol roared loud in Bushrod's ears. Suddenly, for some reason, the great bell behind him began to clang, dully.

Then Dunning let go, and Bushrod knew he did so on purpose. To hang on any longer would have pulled Bushrod over the side, and Dunning chose to take the fall alone. Bushrod watched him plunge to the ground, and slam against it hard. He closed his eyes.

Then the weight of the world was on his shoulders. Or so it felt. But what it really was, he realized, was the body of William Gordon Trippler, who'd taken Dunning's bullet right in the face, slammed back against the bell, then pitched forward again, across Bushrod's body and then down.

It was too much to take. Bushrod lost his grip and his balance, and plunged over the wall after Trippler.

*   *   *

He never knew how he managed to grasp the little lip of stone, the same one that had initially saved the life of Dunning. Bushrod clung there, hurting, weak, feeling his fingers straining and abrading. He wouldn't be able to hold on long.

A face leaned out above him. John was there, reaching down to him . . .

"Take hold, Pap!"

Bushrod tried, failed, then tried again. His hand closed around John's. Then, as Dunning had done, he slapped his other hand into place around John's wrist.

"Climb, Pap. Put your feet on the stone and climb."

Bushrod tried, but his boots slipped. With the toe of his left boot he worked his right boot off his foot, letting it drop. Now he was able to hook his toes into a crevice in the wall, and push up. John pulled. Bush found another toehold, and came up another foot, until finally he was able to get his toes onto the little ledge that he'd held on to before.

From there on it was easy. He came up over the belfry wall and collapsed onto the tower floor, breathing very hard and feeling faint.

John knelt beside him, leaned over, and laid his arm across Bushrod's back.

"I love you, Pap."

"I love you, too, son."

Dunning was still alive, astonishingly, but it was obvious that in minutes he would be as dead as his brother, whose bloated body lay ruptured and gruesome beside him, the eyes wide open and staring, a clean bullet hole right in the center of his face. Bushrod was a man with a strong stomach, but it was hard to look at what remained of William Gordon Trippler.

Dunning looked up at Bush. "Never expected . . . to go this way."

"Rest, Dunning. Don't try to talk."

"No reason . . . not to. No hope for me now. William is dead?"

"He's dead. His body is lying right over nearby you. No.

Don't try to turn your head. I think your neck is broken.''

"And so it ends for . . . the Trippler family.''

"It appears so.''

"But for the Underhills . . . a new beginning.''

"Yes. Thanks to you. We couldn't have done this without your help.''

Dunning managed a smile. "I thought . . . Bushrod Underhill could . . . do anything . . . rope the lightning . . . drink down the ocean . . .''

"That's only in the almanacs.''

But Dunning didn't hear those words. As quietly and quickly as the flashing of a firefly, the spirit had gone out of him, and he was no more.

Bushrod rose, sighing, swallowing hard. He walked out alone into the center of the compound, which was now relatively quiet. All Trippler's former mercenaries had been rounded up and were in the custody of the militiamen who now held the fort. All was strangely peaceful. Bushrod looked to his left and saw four militiamen bearing a bed out of a doorway. On it was a weak-looking, dark-haired man who looked familiar. Bushrod realized that he looked like a man he'd seen in portraits: David Crockett. Idly he wondered if it really might be he.

Bushrod looked up at the belfry. The colorful flag of William Gordon Trippler was being removed by a militiaman. The man ripped the banner free and tossed it down. Bush watched it flutter to the earth.

He walked over, picked it up, and carried it over to where Dunning lay. He stretched the cloth over the body, then turned and walked away, eager to see how Sam was faring. A doctor newly arrived in Texas had been among the militiamen, and he'd gone to work on Sam as quickly as he'd come in, removing the bullet from him.

Bushrod prayed for Sam to live. He couldn't bear to lose him.

Besides, he'd promised Lorry that he'd bring her children home safe, and a man who could rope the lightning, drink the ocean dry, and win the hearts of all America and Texas, too, had to keep his promises.

CHAPTER
THIRTY-EIGHT

Lorry Underhill stood beside her husband and looked out across the snowy Missouri landscape. There were tears in her eyes, but Bushrod knew they were the right kind of tears, and didn't begrudge her them.

"We could have lost any of them at any time . . . so easily," she said. He'd just told her the full story of the great adventure in Texas. She'd been a rapt audience.

"We could have, but we didn't. Cordell came through pretty much without a scratch, and John as well. Durham took a pounding, and Sam very nearly died. But he didn't. Julia and the children, all well. And all eager to see you."

"And I'm eager to see them. And Sam and Durham."

Neither Sam nor Durham had made the return journey to Missouri. Sam, with his wound, had been in no condition to travel, and Durham had stayed—ostensibly—to be close to his brother and help him through his recovery. But everyone knew the real reason was to be near Chasida. She was busy helping her own brother recover from his wounds, so her duties and Durham's paralleled. That struck Bush as appropriate, considering that she and Durham were already making plans for the wedding.

He wondered if Sam was jealous of Durham—his little brother, getting married before he did, and to a girl of remarkable beauty. No, Bush decided, Sam wasn't jealous. The old Sam would have been, but Sam had grown up a lot through his ordeals. Not much boyishness left in him now. He, like Durham, was a man now.

"What about the man Trippler claimed was Crockett?" Lorry asked.

"A sad story, really. He was just a poor old volunteer soldier who got hurt at San Jacinto. Lost the very memory of who he was, and wandered for days after the fight until, somehow, Trippler got hold of him. According to what some of Trippler's mercenaries said, he noticed the fellow bore a strong resemblance to Colonel Crockett and decided that, by gum, Colonel Crockett he'd be. And apparently that's where he got the notion of giving his plan credibility by attaching the names of Davy Crockett and John Underhill to it. It was shortly after that he sent his men in to kidnap John and his family."

"What's become of this 'Crockett' now?"

"His son was among the militiamen who invaded the fort. The fellow's real name was Chester Broyles. His son took him back home with him to let him heal, and with any luck, get his memory back. Trippler had convinced the poor fellow that he was really Davy Crockett."

Lorry leaned her head onto Bush's shoulder and was silent for a minute before speaking again. "I'm glad I didn't know Rafe Morgan was to be involved in all this. I'd not have been able to bear it, knowing you were having to face him again."

"It was an unwelcome surprise to encounter him, I grant you."

"Do you think he's dead?"

"Somehow I doubt it. Sam and Chasida left him unconscious in a shed inside the fort, lying right beside the corpses of his sons. But when the militiamen went to look for him, he was gone." Bush chuckled. "It's almost like it was the first time. I came out of that fight with the Morgans not knowing—until I reached Texas—whether Rafe was alive or dead. Now I still don't know."

"Whichever way, at least he's gone."

"Yes. For now."

Lorry didn't like the implications buried in that latter

phrase, and diverted the conversation onto new ground. "Let me see that paper again."

Bushrod pulled a parchment document from beneath his coat and handed it to her. She opened it and studied it closely. "Is that really Houston's signature?"

"It is. Signed and sealed on a grant giving me more land than you can see across in two days, all for my part in ending the 'threat to the future of Texas' embodied in the late, very ungreat William Gordon Trippler."

"What will we do with so much land, Bushrod?"

"Live on it. Raise cattle on it. Farm it. Hunt it. Give homes to our children on it. And to Marie and her husband. Enjoy it. Treasure it."

"Going to Texas! I never would have thought I'd agree to such a thing."

"Well, if you wanted to see John and Sam and Durham anymore, you pretty much had no choice but to agree. You'll never get them to come back here, not with all that land there." He hugged her. "You'll love Texas, Lorry. It's a new place. A grand place. The kind of place a man can settle and spend his last years."

She laughed. "Bushrod, your last years are still too far away to see, and you'll be restless to move on out of Texas within five years. Don't try to deny it."

He laughed and kissed her. The snow began to fall harder.

"Come on, wife," Bushrod said. "Let's get back to the house. I'm cold."